CONTENTS

USA TODAY Bestselling Author

LINDA TURNER

The Lady in Red

KYLIE BRANT

Dangerous Deception

HARLEQUIN®

TORONTO • NEW YORK • LONDON
AMSTERDAM • PARIS • SYDNEY • HAMBURG
STOCKHOLM • ATHENS • TOKYO • MILAN • MADRID
PRAGUE • WARSAW • BUDAPEST • AUCKLAND

Recycling programs
for this product may
not exist in your area.

ISBN-13: 978-0-373-68818-0

THE LADY IN RED & DANGEROUS DECEPTION

Copyright © 2011 by Harlequin Books S.A.

The publisher acknowledges the copyright holders of the individual works as follows:

THE LADY IN RED
Copyright © 1997 by Linda Turner

DANGEROUS DECEPTION
Copyright © 2004 by Kimberly Bahnsen

Praise for *USA TODAY* bestselling author Linda Turner

"Ms. Turner is in super fine form in an exciting duel of hearts no reader should miss."
—*RT Book Reviews* on *The Lady in Red*

"With *A Ranching Man*, Turner has maintained her usual high standards... This author's writing ability makes her books memorable."
—*The Romance Reader.com*

"This outing has an engaging plot, and it's terrific fun watching two people who've vowed never to fall in love again fight it every step of the way."
—*RT Book Reviews* on *His Wanted Woman*

Praise for bestselling author Kylie Brant

"In *Dangerous Deception*, Kylie Brant skillfully blends interesting elements of mystery, romance and sexual tension with a strong emotional twist."
—*RT Book Reviews*

"[An] elegant and suspenseful story that was mighty difficult to put down!"
—*The Best Reviews.com* on *Entrapment*

"Filled with nonstop action and a couple with sizzle that zings right off the page."
—*RT Book Reviews* on *Terms of Engagement*

LINDA TURNER began reading romances in high school and began writing them one night when she had nothing else to read. She's been writing ever since. Single and living in Texas, she travels every chance she gets, scouting locales for her books.

KYLIE BRANT is a bestselling, award-winning author of twenty-five novels for the Silhouette Romantic Suspense line. When she's not dreaming up stories of romance and suspense, she works as a teacher for learning-disabled elementary students.

Kylie invites readers to check out her website at www.kyliebrant.com for news, backlist and information about upcoming releases. She can be contacted by email at kyliebrant@hotmail.com.

THE LADY IN RED

USA TODAY Bestselling Author

Linda Turner

Chapter 1

"What do you mean you don't want me to cover sports?" Blake Nickels demanded in surprise. "I'm a sports reporter, Tom. And a damn good one, too."

"And at one time you were a hell of a news reporter, too," Tom Edwards reminded him as he searched his desk drawers for a stick of gum. He was in the process of giving up smoking after twenty years, and he scowled when he could find nothing but a eucalyptus cough drop to fight his craving. "In fact," he continued as he popped the foul tasting candy into his mouth, "the way I remember it, you won several national awards."

"That was before," he growled.

He didn't have to explain before what—they both knew. Once Blake had been one of the hottest crime reporters in New York City. Then an informant had given him some information that had ended up costing the snitch his life. Devastated, he'd packed up his toys and gotten out of the game, moving from the notoriety he'd earned in New York to the obscurity of covering sports in a town in New Mexico that was no bigger than a pimple on the map. That had been eight years ago. As far as Tom knew, Blake hadn't gone within a hundred miles of a police scanner since.

Which made what he had to ask him all the more difficult. Wishing he had a cigarette, Tom pushed himself to his feet to restlessly prowl the confines of his office. "Lynn Phillips took maternity leave four months early this morning on the advice of her doctor," he said grimly. "If she doesn't get complete bed rest, she could lose the baby."

On the job for only two days, Blake racked his brain for a face to put with the name. "Phillips. The crime beat, right? Oh, no, you don't!"

"Now, Blake, don't go flying off the handle. Just give me a chance to explain—"

"You crafty son of a bitch, there's nothing to explain. I can read you like a book. I know you, remember?"

They'd been best friends since grade school—there wasn't anything that one didn't know about the other, including how the other's mind worked. "You called me up offering my own column on the sports page just to get me over here, didn't you?" Blake demanded, jumping to his feet to glare at Tom. "It was all just a trick."

"You were thinking about leaving Lordsburg anyway. You said so yourself. Ever since Trina ran off with that truck driver and married him when you weren't looking—"

"Leave Trina the hell out of this," he growled. "The woman's name is no longer in my vocabulary."

"Fine," Tom agreed. "Then what about Pop? With your parents going off to France for a year, you know you were worried sick about him being here in San Antonio all by himself. By accepting my job offer, you killed two birds with one stone—you got away from *that woman* in Lordsburg and you could come home to watch over your grandfather until your parents get back. Instead of yelling at me, you ought to be thanking me, you old goat. I did you a favor."

"Favor?" Blake choked. If he hadn't been so irritated, he would have laughed. Leave it to Tom to twist things so he looked like a choirboy. "You call manipulating me to get me on the payroll, then assigning me to the crime beat a *favor?* If you'd mentioned what you were planning at the beginning, I never would have left New Mexico."

"I wasn't planning anything. I wasn't," he insisted when Blake merely lifted a dark brow at him. "Oh, I knew Lynn was pregnant, of course, and that she'd be leaving eventually, but I expected to have another four months to fill the position if I couldn't talk you into it. Dammit, Blake, take it, will you? At least for a little while until I can hire somebody else? You're the only one I've got on staff who can give Sabrina Jones some competition."

Blake might not have known Lynn Phillips and most of the rest of the *Times* staff, but he'd only been in town one day when he'd read Sabrina Jones's bylined story on the front page of the San Antonio *Daily Record,* the other major paper in town. She was good, dammit. Good enough to be writing for any major newspaper in the country, which was, no doubt, why Tom was worried. The *Times* and *Daily Record* were in a knock-down-drag-out, no-holds-barred subscription war right now, and the *Times* was going to get its butt kicked without someone who could give the Jones woman a run for her money.

"I'm out of practice," he hedged. "It's been eight years since I've done that beat."

"I don't care if it's been a hundred. You're the best damn reporter I've ever known. That includes sports, crime—hell, even the obits. The second you catch the scent of a story, you'll be off and running, just like old times. It'll be great."

His expression shuttered, Blake couldn't share his enthusiasm. He wanted to tell him that he didn't care how many murders and sex crimes he covered, it would never be like old times again, but he was afraid Tom was right. He'd really enjoyed covering sports, but nothing had ever challenged him like crime. It was like an addiction that had called to something in his blood—he'd thrived on it. And in the process, he'd lost his objectivity and become obsessed with getting the story. Nothing else had mattered. And because of that single-mindedness, a man had lost his life.

A man who had trusted him, Blake remembered grimly. A man who had seen something he shouldn't have and who should have gone to the police for protection. Blake had sworn not to reveal his identity and he'd stuck by that, but it hadn't done any good. The day after the story hit the paper, the informant had turned up dead, supposedly killed from asphyxiation due to running his car in a closed garage. The police had ruled it a suicide and let it go. Blake had known better. The prominent businessman the informant had exposed as the brains behind an extensive money-laundering and drug-smuggling operation had obviously gotten to him and shut him up for good.

Almost a decade had passed since then, but just thinking about it brought it all back like it was yesterday. He couldn't go through that again. He couldn't put someone at risk just because of a damn story. It wasn't worth it.

So what are you going to do, Nickels? You quit the job

in Lordsburg. Remember? You can go back, of course. But what about Pop?

His grandfather, eighty-three and forgetful at times, had no business living alone. Blake could try to convince him to go to New Mexico with him, but the old man could be as stubborn as a mule when he wanted to be. And if he wouldn't go to Paris for a year with Blake's parents, he sure wasn't going to leave his home and everything familiar in San Antonio for Lordsburg.

Stuck between a rock and a hard place, Blake had no choice but to accept the inevitable. "All right." He sighed. "I'll take over for Lynn. For *now*," he stressed when his friend grinned broadly. "So don't go getting any ideas that this is permanent. As soon as you can hire someone to replace Lynn, I'm going back to sports. I mean it, Tom. I see that gleam in your eye—I know what you're up to. You're hoping that once I get a taste of hard news again, you won't be able to pry me away from it with a crowbar, but that's not going to happen. I'm a sports writer, dammit."

Not sure if he was trying to convince him or himself, Tom only grinned. Blake might think he could walk away from investigative reporting twice in a lifetime, but Tom knew better. One good story. That's all it would take for Blake to be hooked.

The woman was young—mid-twenties—pretty, and dead.

Arriving at the murder scene only seconds after the cops themselves, Sabrina got her first look at the victim at the same time that the two officers did. Her eyes wide open, a look of horror etched in her pale, stone-cold face, the dead woman lay just inside the open front door of her house and appeared to have been there all night. Dressed in a lacy white nightgown and negligee stained with her own blood, she'd been shot in the heart, probably seconds after she'd opened the door.

"Jesus," Andy Thompson, the younger of the two cops and a rookie, muttered. "She looks like she was waiting for a lover."

"If that's who popped her, then she was a lousy judge of men," his partner, Victor Rodriguez, said flatly. "I'll call the ME and Detective Kelly. This one's got his name written all over it."

He turned and only just then became aware of Sabrina's presence. An old friend, he scowled disapprovingly. "What the heck do you think you're doing in here, Sabrina? This is a crime scene."

Not the least bit intimidated, she flashed her dimples at him. "No kidding? Then I guess that's why I'm here. C'mon, Vic, gimme a break. Let me look around. I'll be out of here before Kelly arrives, I swear."

"That's what you said the last time, and I got a royal chewing out for it." Blocking her path, he refused to let her peer around his broad shoulders and shooed her outside instead. "You know the rules, Sabrina. You want the particulars, you wait till the detective gets here. He'll tell you everything he thinks you need to know."

"You're all heart, Rodriguez," she grumbled as he escorted her well out into the yard, then blockaded the crime scene with yellow police tape to keep her and the curious out. "Kelly won't tell me squat until he's good and ready, and you know it."

"Wah, wah!" he said, grinning as he mimicked a baby's cry. "Quit your crying, Jones. You'll get your story. You always do."

"That's because I'm good at what I do," she called after

him as he turned and disappeared back inside. And because she didn't stand around and wait for someone to hand her a story on a platter.

Her hands on her hips, she surveyed the neighborhood. Quiet and moderately affluent, with neatly trimmed yards and houses that would easily sell for a hundred grand or more, it wasn't the type of place where you expected a shooting, let alone a murder. From the small, unobtrusive signs in the front yards, it was obvious that most of the homes had security systems, including the victim's. Yet a woman had been killed—shot, no less—and no one had noticed anything unusual during the night.

Wondering how that could have happened, she headed for the house next door. When Kelly got there, he wouldn't like it that she'd snooped around before his men had a chance to question possible witnesses. But then again, she thought, mischief flashing in her brown eyes, it wouldn't be the first time she'd skirted the rules to get a story. Kelly had to be used to it by now.

Her chances of finding anyone at home at eleven o'clock in the morning on a weekday were slim to none, so she wasn't surprised when no one answered at the first four doors she knocked on. On the fifth, she got lucky.

The man who opened the door to the house directly across the street from the victim's was thin and balding, with a face full of wrinkles and piercing blue eyes that were as sharp as a hawk's. Peering over the top of his bifocals at her, he scowled in annoyance. "If you're selling something door-to-door, lady, you didn't pick a very good day for it. There's been a murder across the street, and any second now this whole block's going to be crawling with police."

"I know, sir. I'm a reporter. Sabrina Jones, with the

Daily Record. I was wondering if I might ask you a few questions?"

"I didn't see jack squat," he retorted. "Just her body lying in the doorway when I came outside to get my paper this morning. I take the *Times*."

Sabrina bit back a smile. Readers, as loyal as fans to their favorite pro team, always seemed to be under the mistaken impression that they couldn't talk to her if they didn't read the *Record*. "It's a good paper," she said easily, her brown eyes twinkling. "But so is the *Daily Record*. Did you know the victim?"

His gaze drifting back to the still figure now draped in a yellow plastic sheet, he nodded somberly. "Her name was Tanya Bishop. She was a sweet girl. And smart. A legal secretary. From what I heard, she made good money, but she didn't blow it. She socked it away and bought that house, and she wasn't even thirty yet."

His loyalty to the *Times* forgotten in his need to talk about the victim, he reminisced about her at length while Sabrina jotted down notes and an image of Tanya Bishop formed in her mind. A young professional woman who was responsible and hardworking, she wasn't the type to make enemies. She didn't drink or smoke or party till all hours of the night. And she was dead…just like Charlene McClintock.

Barely two weeks ago, Charlene had also been found dead. Like Tanya, she'd been young, pretty and professional. Everyone who had known her had loved her. Yet someone had shot her in the heart…just like Tanya Bishop. The similarities between the two murders was not lost on her.

"Were you home all night, Mr.—?"

"Dexter," he replied automatically. "Monroe Dexter. Yeah, I was home. And let me tell you, nobody sleeps lighter than I do. A shift in the wind will wake me up, but I didn't hear anything last night." Emotion suddenly clogging his throat, he swallowed. "What I want to know is how the hell somebody could kill that poor girl without making a sound."

Sabrina was wondering the same thing. After thanking Mr. Dexter for his help, she questioned the two other neighbors that were home, but apparently no one had heard anything during the night, not even a dog barking, or noticed any visitors at the Bishop house. Which was damn odd, Sabrina thought, on a street where the homeowners had formed a neighborhood watch to watch over each other.

Questions buzzing like bees in her brain, she headed back to the crime scene to see if the police had found any more answers than she had. As she crossed Tanya Bishop's front yard, she saw that Detective Kelly and the medical examiner had arrived and were in deep conversation as they examined the body. Anxious to catch what they were saying, she hurried forward and never saw the man who deliberately stepped in front of her until she plowed into him.

"Oh! I'm sorry. I didn't see you—"

"I didn't mean to knock you out of your shoes, ma'am, but you don't want to go in there. It's a pretty gory scene—"

They both spoke at once, each rushing to apologize as they broke apart. Feeling like she'd just run full tilt into a brick wall, Sabrina laughed shakily, intending to take all the blame for not watching where she was going. But the second her eyes lifted to the man in front of her, her mind just seemed to go blank and she couldn't do anything but stare.

He towered over her own five-foot-four frame by a good

eight inches and wore a black cowboy hat that only added to his impressive height. In spite of that, he didn't appear to be the type of man who would draw a second glance in passing. His face was too ordinary, too lived-in, like the boy next door who grew up into just an average Joe. But looks, she decided, studying him, were deceptive when it came to this man. His mouth seemed to quirk with perpetual good humor, but his angular jaw looked as unyielding as granite, and deep in the depths of his green eyes was a sharpness that missed little. It was, to say the least, an interesting combination.

Intrigued, Sabrina reminded herself she was there to investigate the city's latest murder, not to drool over a tall, dark stranger who seemed to think she was a little woman who'd faint at the sight of blood. Amused, she said dryly, "I've already been in there, and you're right, it is gory. Now if you'll excuse me, I need to talk to Detective Kelly."

Before she could step around him, however, he moved, lightning-quick, to block her path again. Her patience quickly reaching its limit, Sabrina stopped just short of plowing into his broad chest again and frowned up at him in growing irritation. "Look, I don't know who you think you are, but I've got work to do and you're in my way. Do you mind?"

"Not at all," he said easily. But he didn't move. His mouth twitching with the promise of a smile, he stared down at her searchingly. "What do you mean, you've already been in there? Are you a cop?"

"No, I'm not. I'm a reporter. Sabrina Jones, with the *Daily Record*. Now, if you'll excuse me…"

Stunned, Blake stared down at her in disbelief. *This* was Sabrina Jones? The pride of the *Daily Record*? The ruthless, go-for-the-throat investigative reporter who would do anything short of murder for a story? The way Tom had talked about her, Blake had pictured her as some type of Amazon with more guts than a Marine and a hide like leather. A pushy broad with a reputation for being as tenacious as a bulldog, she should have been tough, brash, and hard as nails.

But the woman who stood before him was anything but hard. In fact, dressed in a gauzy summer dress that draped her slender figure in a cloud of pale pink and fell to just below her knees, her black hair a mass of curls that tumbled artlessly down her back, she looked as soft as cotton candy. A very delectable, feminine piece of cotton candy, he thought with a frown as his gaze slid over her with an ease that had his jaw clenching on an oath. She was short, her bones delicate, the curves revealed by the gently clinging material of her dress enticing. And she was wearing sandals.

His eyes lingering on her toes, he found himself fighting a smile. This was his competition? This dainty woman who looked like she'd swoon at the sight of blood? Oh, she was a good writer, he admitted to himself. He'd read her stuff. She had a way with words. But so did he. And the day that he couldn't write circles around this slip of femininity was the day he'd pack up his computer and find something else to do for a living.

His green eyes starting to twinkle, he deliberately stepped in front of her again, blocking her way. "So you're Sabrina Jones," he drawled. "I've got to admit, you're not what I expected."

Brought up short, her nose just inches from his broad chest, Sabrina glared at him in growing exasperation. "Look, cowboy, I don't know who or what you are, but I've got work to do, and you're in my way."

"Get used to it," he said, grinning as he watched temper simmer in her brown eyes. "I plan to be in your way a lot more before all is said and done."

Her gaze narrowing dangerously, she arched a brow at him. "And how do you plan to do that, Mr....?"

"Nickels," he supplied, holding out his hand as he grinned down at her. "Blake Nickels. With the *Times*. Lynn Phillips had to take maternity leave early. I'm her replacement."

Sudden understanding dawning, Sabrina eyed his hand warily, amusement flirting with the edges of her mouth. The man had more than his share of cockiness. And charm. But if he thought he could best her in a war of words, he was sadly mistaken. Placing her hand in his for a perfunctory shake, she purred, "I can't say I've ever read any of your work, Mr. Nickels. Should I be quaking in my shoes?"

"If you know what's good for you."

She laughed; she couldn't help it. He certainly didn't lack confidence. But then again, neither did she. "Sorry," she said with a chuckle, "but I don't scare that easily."

"Maybe you should. I'm good, Ms. Jones. Real good."

"And modest, too," she tossed back, grinning.

Undaunted, he only shrugged, devilment dancing in his eyes. "No brag, just fact. Check me out, sweetheart. You might be impressed."

"Maybe on a slow day when I've got nothing better to do," she agreed sassily. Her gaze moving past him to the crime scene, she watched the ambulance crew that had arrived with the ME load Tanya Bishop's body onto a stretcher and knew that the police were just about finished with their investigation of the crime scene. "Right now, I've got work to do. See you around, cowboy."

She darted around him before he could stop her and quickly ducked under the police tape strung between the trees in the front yard. Swearing, Blake started after her just as a tall, redheaded man in a rumpled suit stepped out of the house and caught sight of Sabrina bearing down on him. "Why did I know you'd be here, Jones?" he groaned. "Every time I turn around, there you are. Are you following me?"

"I got here before you did," she reminded him with a cheeky grin. "So what's going on, Sam? From where I'm standing, this looks an awful lot like the McClintock murder."

His brows snapping together in a fierce glare, he gave her a hard look that had Back Off written all over it. "You start a rumor like that, Jones, and I'm going to hold you personally responsible. There's nothing to indicate that the two murders are in any way connected."

Frowning, stuck in the position of playing catch-up and not liking it one little bit, Blake stepped forward. "Blake Nickels, with the *Times*," he told the other man. "What's this about another murder, detective? I'm new in town and this is the first I've heard about it."

Sam Kelly introduced himself, then explained, "Charlene McClintock, one of the city's up-and-coming attorneys, was killed two weeks ago, but there's no connection—"

"Was there any sign of forced entry or signs of a struggle?" Sabrina cut in.

"No, but—"

"Does anything appear to be missing?"

"Not that we can tell at this time," he said patiently, "but we won't know for sure until we can find a friend or neighbor to go through the place. You're beating a dead horse here, Jones. Drop it."

Sabrina, well used to holding her own with Kelly, had no intention of doing any such thing. "I got it from one of the neighbors that Tanya Bishop was a legal secretary, Sam. That means two women, young and pretty and both involved in the legal profession, have been shot to death within a two-week period, apparently by someone they knew. Are you really going to stand there and tell me that they're unrelated incidents? C'mon, Sam, get real!"

"I'm not telling you anything more than I already have until the lab results come back and we have time to look into both murders further," he said curtly. "Until then, I suggest you stick to the facts and not jump to any unwarranted conclusions. Now if you'll excuse me, I've got to question the neighbors, then get back to the station." With a nod to both of them, he stepped past the two reporters.

Staring after him, Blake swore under his breath. So much for his first day on the job. He'd stood there flat-footed and listened to Sabrina ask questions he hadn't even known to ask, and there hadn't been a damn thing he could do about it. It wouldn't, he promised himself, happen again.

And the sooner Sabrina Jones knew that, the better. Glancing down at her, he found her watching him with brown eyes that were just a little too smug for his liking. Oh, she was something, he thought, fighting a reluctant grin. She thought she had him right where she wanted him, a distant second to her first place in a race in which she had the head start. She was all but crowing and she hadn't even reached the finish line yet. The darn woman didn't realize that he had her right where he wanted her.

"I wouldn't start celebrating just yet if I were you," he

warned dryly. "Just because I was unprepared this time doesn't mean I will be again."

Not the least bit worried, she only cocked her head at him and teased playfully, "What's the matter, Nickels? You don't like coming in second to a woman? Get used to it, cowboy. I'm just hitting my stride."

That was the wrong thing to say to a man who thrived on a challenge. "Oh, really?" he drawled. "Well, just for the record, sweetheart, the fact that you're a woman has nothing to do with anything. I don't care if you're purple—I don't like eating your dust. Next time I'll be ready for you."

It was an out-and-out warning, one that only a foolish woman would have ignored. And Sabrina was nobody's fool. Blake Nickels might have been a little out of his depth this time, but as she watched him stalk off to his car, she had a feeling that he was going to be a force to be reckoned with. His eyes had held a sharp intelligence, and then there was that jaw of his—as hard and immovable as concrete, it had had determination written all over it. Not that she was worried, she quickly assured herself as she turned to her own car. This was her town, her beat. Blake Nickels was the new kid on the block. She knew her own abilities and could handle anything the man could dish out.

She deliberately pushed him from her thoughts, but hours later, when she was back at her desk at the *Daily Record* working on her story about the city's latest murder, it wasn't poor Tanya Bishop's lifeless body that stirred to life in her mind's eye—it was the memory of Blake Nickels' smile. Wicked, teasing, dangerous. No man had a right to look so good just by curling up the edge of his mouth, she decided, trying to work up a good case of irritation. A frown furrowing her brow, she tried to force her attention back to what was sure to be a front-page story, but just thinking about Blake and that grin of his made her lips twitch.

And that worried her. Blake Nickels was full of charm and devilment, and she wouldn't, couldn't, like him. She didn't care if he was the next best thing to sliced bread, he was the opposition, the competition, a male chauvinist who didn't like standing around with his hands in his pockets while she asked all the questions. Given the chance, he'd snitch a story right out from under her nose if she relaxed her guard for so much as a second.

If that wasn't reason enough to avoid him like the plague, the fact that she found herself thinking about him when she had a hot story to write was. She wasn't looking for a man to distract her, or do anything else with her. The women in her family didn't handle relationships well. Between the two of them, her mother and grandmother had been married eight times, and Sabrina had decided at an early age that she wasn't going to follow in their footsteps. Then, three years ago, she'd met Jeff Harper.

She winced at the memory. All her fine resolves had gone up in smoke the first time he'd kissed her. In spite of the fact that they'd had absolutely nothing in common, she'd fallen for him like a ton of bricks. When he'd asked her to marry him, she'd convinced herself that *she* wasn't like her mother or grandmother—*she* could make a relationship work. She'd then spent the next two years trying to do just that, and they'd both been miserable. When they'd inevitably agreed to divorce last summer, it had been a relief.

In spite of that, she didn't regret her marriage. She'd

learned the hard way that she, too, like the rest of the women in her family, had a defective gene when it came to commitment. Unlike her mother and grandmother, however, she didn't have to go through one divorce after another to learn her lesson. Once was enough. She wasn't cut out to be anything but single, and that was just fine with her. As long as she remembered that—and she didn't plan to forget it—she and Blake Nickels would get along just fine.

Caught up in trying to find a possible link between Tanya Bishop and Charlene McClintock's murders, as well as cover the more interesting stories that came across her police scanner, she was actually able to forget that the *Times* even had a new reporter. Then, just as she was about to grab something for lunch the next day, news of a bank robbery in progress had her rushing over to the southside location. It was just the kind of breaking story she loved, and normally, she was the first reporter on the scene. Not this time, though. Blake Nickels was already there, standing in the bank parking lot interviewing a witness, and the rat was obviously watching for her. The second she pulled into the lot, he looked up and waved.

Grinning broadly, he pushed his cowboy hat to the back of his head. "Hey, Jones, what took you so long?" he teased. "You having a slow day, or what?"

Heat flushed her cheeks, the grin that tugged at her mouth impossible to hide. "Put a sock in it, Nickels," she tossed back, trying and failing to maintain a frown. "I know this might come as something of a surprise to you, but some of us actually cover more than one crime a day."

"No kidding? So where were you when I was covering that assault on a nun at Main Plaza this morning?"

"Interviewing a string of restaurant owners who were conned by a homeless lady on the northside. So what have you got to say about that?"

His eyes dancing, he shrugged. "How about I'll show you my notes if you show me yours?"

She wanted the story on the nun, but Fitz, her boss, would have her hide if she so much as shared the time of day with a *Times* reporter. "Not on your life, cowboy," she replied, and turned away to snag a policeman who'd just walked out of the bank.

Turning down Blake's offer, she quickly discovered to her chagrin, proved to be a mistake. Oh, the police were willing to give her the details of the heist and a brief description of the robber, who had escaped with fifty thousand dollars and was last seen racing west on Loop 410 in a white van. But there was only one witness—the teller—and after she'd given the police a statement, the only reporter she'd agree to talk to was Blake.

Unable to believe she'd heard her correctly, Sabrina said, "What do you mean you won't give your story to anyone but Blake Nickels? You talked to the police."

"Oh, I had to tell them," the pretty blonde said airily. "But Blake asked for an exclusive, and I said okay." All innocence, she smiled sweetly. "So you see, I can't go back on my word. It just wouldn't be ethical, now would it?"

Indignant, Sabrina just barely bit back a scathing retort. If the bubblehead of a teller wanted to talk ethics, she never would have let Blake talk her into an exclusive in the first place. And for a darn bank robbery, of all things! She'd never heard of anything so ridiculous in her life. She only wished she'd thought of it.

Frustrated, steam all but coming out of her ears, she forced a smile. "I appreciate your ethics, Ms. Walker, but your boss might not be too pleased when he hears that you're only talking to one reporter. The bank just lost a substantial amount of money that probably won't be recovered—unless word gets out about the robbery and a possible reward." Reaching into her purse, she pulled out a business card and handed it to her. "Think about it. If you change your mind before my deadline, give me a call."

The woman took her card, but Sabrina knew better than to hold out hope that she would use it. You only had to see her staring after Blake like he was the greatest thing since Elvis to know that she was thoroughly smitten. And for some reason she couldn't explain, that irritated Sabrina to no end.

As her gaze followed the teller's to where Blake stood fifty yards away, finishing an interview with one of the first officers on the scene, she told herself he wasn't going to get away with it. He could sweet-talk every woman he saw for all she cared—some people would stoop to any level to get a story—but he wasn't going to stop her from doing her job! Not if she had anything to say about it. Her jaw set, she started toward him.

Thanking the investigating officer, Roger Martinez, for his help, Blake was jotting down notes in the small notebook he never went anywhere without when he looked up to see Sabrina bearing down on him like a ruffled hen with her tail feathers in a twist. So, he thought as a slow grin skimmed his mouth, she'd found out about the exclusive. Now the fur was really going to fly.

"Hey, Jones," he greeted her as she drew near. "You look a little out of sorts. Something wrong?"

Color flying high in her cheeks, she gave him a withering look. "You're damn right something's wrong! You're a yellow-bellied, toad-eating weasel. How dare you!"

Grinning, he chuckled. "Honey, when you get to know me better, you'll find out that I'll dare just about anything. I take it you've been talking to Jennifer Walker."

"If you want to call it that. She wouldn't tell me a darn thing, and you know it. Because *she* promised *you* an exclusive."

Enjoying himself, Blake grinned. "And all I had to do was ask." Leaning closer, his eyes dancing with mischief, he confided, "I think she likes me."

For a moment, he could have sworn he heard her grinding her teeth. "Then the woman has no taste," she snapped in a low voice that didn't carry any further than his ears. "You ought to be ashamed of yourself."

"Why? Because I thought of it before you did? C'mon, Sabrina, admit it. The only reason you're in a snit is because I outfoxed you."

"Don't be ridiculous," she fibbed. "This story is a matter of police record, and I'll get it with or without that blond bimbo teller's cooperation—"

Making no effort to hide his amusement, he cocked a teasing brow at her. "Blond bimbo? Do I detect a little jealousy here? Why, Jones, I didn't know you cared."

Sabrina's lips twitched. Lord, he was outrageous! She'd always liked a man with a quick wit, and if she didn't watch herself with him, she was going to find herself charmed into liking him. And that could be nothing but a disaster.

Somehow managing to look down her nose at him in

spite of the fact that he towered over her, she studied him consideringly. "Don't let it go to your head, cowboy. The only thing I care about is the story, and you're throwing up roadblocks. Now, I wonder why that is? You running scared, Nickels, or what?"

"Of you?" He chuckled. "I don't think so. I read your story in this morning's paper, sweetheart." Not batting an eye, he quoted word-for-word from her front-page story on the Bishop murder in the morning edition of the *Daily Record*. "'Tanya Bishop was dressed to meet a lover. A lover who may have killed her.'" Clicking his tongue at her in teasing disapproval, he grinned. "Naughty, naughty, Jones. Of course she was dressed for bed—she was killed during the middle of the night—but that doesn't mean she was expecting a lover. And what's this *may* business? The last I heard, a good reporter stuck to the facts and nothing but the facts, not supposition."

Her cheeks flushed at the gentle criticism. Darn the man, she should have caught that. And when she hadn't, her editor should have! But she'd have eaten worms before admitting it. Instead, she purred silkily, "Why, Nickels, I'm flattered you went to the trouble to memorize my work. Are you one of our new subscribers? You should have told me and I might have been able to get you a discount."

"To the *Record*?" He snorted, amused. "I don't think so. I like my news hard and gritty, and I'll bet your readers do, too. In fact, I'll bet you dinner at the restaurant of your choice that before the month is out, my paper, not yours, is winning the subscription war."

"Watch it, Nickels. I have expensive taste."

"So it's a bet?"

Hesitating, Sabrina reminded herself that he was a man

who didn't always play by the rules. And there were some very expensive restaurants in town. If she lost, she'd feel the blow not only in her pride, but in her pocketbook. But she'd never been one to play it safe, and there were some things a woman with daring just couldn't walk away from. And Blake Nickels, she reluctantly admitted, was one of them.

Grinning, she held out her hand and silently prayed she didn't live to regret her impulsiveness. "You're on, Nickels. If I were you, I'd start saving my pennies. This is going to cost you."

Chapter 2

She was running late. Her alarm clock hadn't gone off, and she'd unconsciously taken advantage of it, waking a mere ten minutes before she was due at work. Horrified, Sabrina jumped out of bed and threw on some clothes, but even moving at the speed of sound, it was well after she should have punched in at the paper when she slammed out of her house and dashed to her car. Mumbling reminders to get herself a new clock, she raced down the street, tires squealing, and headed for the freeway three blocks away.

She'd barely shot onto the entrance ramp when she had to hit the brakes. A four-car pileup a half a mile ahead blocked all three lanes, slowing traffic to a virtual crawl. She'd be lucky if she made it in to the paper by noon.

Fitz was not going to be pleased.

Sabrina winced and rubbed at her temples, where a dull pounding started to hammer relentlessly. It was not, she decided, going to be a good morning. As far as bosses went,

Fitz was a real gem when it came to letting her run with a story, but he was a real stickler when it came to reporting in in the morning. If you were going to be late, you'd better have a darn good excuse.

Staring up ahead at the whirling lights of at least three patrol cars and two ambulances, Sabrina saw a uniformed officer slap handcuffs on one of the drivers and started to smile. This wasn't evidently one of your average rush-hour fender benders. Things were starting to look up. Fitz wouldn't be nearly as inclined to give her one of his patented speeches about punctuality if she came in with a story. Sending up a silent prayer of thanks for gifts from God, she eased over onto the shoulder of the freeway and raced down it toward the accident scene.

It wasn't noon when she rushed into the *Daily Record,* but it was pretty darn close to it. Glancing at the clock in the lobby, Sabrina winced. Fitz was going to have a hissy. It wouldn't, she thought with an impish grin, be the first one that she'd caused. She seemed to have a talent for it where he was concerned.

"Well, well, well," a familiar, gruff voice drawled sarcastically as she stepped off the elevator and turned to come face-to-face with her boss. "If it isn't our star reporter. And she's actually putting in an appearance at work. Glad you could join us, Ms. Jones. I hope it wasn't too much of an imposition."

Well used to the cutting edge of the old man's tongue, she ignored his sarcasm and gave him a cheeky grin. "Not at all, boss. I'm sorry I'm late, but I knew you wouldn't want me to leave the scene of a story—"

"What story?"

"A four-car pileup on the Loop. It seems that a red van was weaving back and forth between the lanes before it plowed into a car full of college kids from Austin on their way to the coast. The van driver was drunk as a skunk—and you'll never guess who it was."

"Who?" he growled. "And this better be good, Jones. I've been trying to track you down all morning."

"I know it, boss, but I was stuck on the freeway with no way to call you. And it was the mayor's son, Jason Grimes! He'd been out carousing all night in daddy's car."

"What? Why the hell didn't you say so?"

Knowing she was forgiven, Sabrina laughed. "I would have given a hundred bucks to have had a camera. Nobody was hurt, but those kids from Austin were fighting mad when it looked like the cops were going to let Jason off the hook. He's an obnoxious little brat at the best of times, but when he's drunk, he's an arrogant son of a gun. He made the mistake of telling one of the kids from Austin that his daddy would see that he didn't even get a ticket for reckless driving, let alone arrested for a DWI, and the kid took a swing at him. He's not quite as pretty as he used to be."

Fitz's sharp gray eyes started to twinkle. "Now ain't that a shame? And he was such a good-looking boy. Write it up, Jones. Then nose around down at the police station and see if you can find out what the policy has been in the past toward young Jason's drunk driving. If he's gotten special privileges, I want to know about it."

He started to turn away, only to remember her tardiness. Glancing over his shoulder, he warned, "And don't be late again, Jones. Next time, you might not be lucky enough to have a story fall in your lap the way this one did."

"No, sir. I mean yes, sir, it won't happen again." Saluting smartly, she dared to wink at him. "I'll get right on it."

He scowled like an old Scrooge, but Sabrina caught the twitch of his lips before he headed for his office. Chuckling to herself, she turned toward her own desk, her thoughts already jumping ahead to the opening line of her story.

Distracted, she didn't see the note lying right in the middle of her desk until she sat down and started to turn toward her computer monitor. Then she saw it—a single sheet of white, unlined paper folded in half with her name handwritten on the front. Perched precariously on top of some notes from yesterday's bank robbery, it could have been left there by anyone—her co-workers left notes for her all the time. But those were handwritten on little yellow stickies, not typed ones on what looked like fairly expensive textured paper.

Wondering who it was from, she reached for it and had a sudden image of Blake teasing her yesterday about her coverage of the Bishop murder. It would, she thought, unable to hold back a smile, be just like him to take it upon himself to critique another of her stories. Only this time, he'd put it in writing and obviously bribed someone in the lobby to deliver it to her desk, since there was no envelope. She could just imagine what it said.

But when she leaned back in her chair and flipped the note open, her eyes dancing with expectancy, she saw in a single, all-encompassing glance that it wasn't from Blake. Then the typed words registered and a cold chill crept like a winter fog through her bloodstream, chilling her to the bone.

Sabrina,
Tanya Bishop thought she could compete in a man's world, and she was wrong. I tried to tell her differently. Women are the nurturers, the homemakers, the babymakers. They should be home, raising the next generation and saving the world, not having power

lunches and taking jobs away from men who can do the work ten times better. It's not right. I told Tanya that, but she wouldn't listen. She laughed at my warning that she was in danger of upsetting the natural order of things. I didn't want to kill her, but what else could I do? She didn't know her place, so she had to be eliminated. She gave me no other choice.

I know how your mind operates, Sabrina. You think I'm some kind of nut case looking for publicity for a murder I didn't commit. But I really did kill her. We were friends. I hoped we could be more, but she couldn't be what I wanted her to be. *Who* I wanted her to be. So I decided to end it and called to tell her I needed to see her. She was dressed in a white gown and negligee and opened the door to me the second I rang the bell. That's when I shot her. She fell right where she stood in the doorway, and I can't feel bad about it. Other professional women might want to take heed while they still can.

Stunned, her heart starting to pound in her ears, Sabrina stared at the cold, unfeeling words and told herself this was a hoax—one of her fellow reporters was probably watching her right now, grinning like an idiot as he waited for her reaction. But even as she cast a quick look around the city room, she knew deep in her gut that this was no practical joke. The note had a ring of truth to it, a sick logic, that sent goose bumps racing over her skin.

Pale, her fingers not quite steady, she dropped the note as if it were a lit firecracker and reached for her phone, quickly pushing the button for the receptionist's desk in the lobby. "Valerie," she said as soon as the other woman came on the line, "this is Sabrina. Did anyone hand-deliver a note for me late yesterday afternoon or this morning?"

"If they did, this is the first I've heard of it," Valerie replied cheerfully. "Lydia Davidson in classifieds got flowers from her latest heartthrob, but other than that, things have been pretty quiet. Why?"

"No reason," Sabrina said quickly. "I was just wondering. If anyone does come in asking for me, let me know, okay? Thanks."

She hung up, frowning, refusing to even consider the possibility that Tanya Bishop's killer had hand-delivered a note to her. *If* the thing was even legit, she amended silently. Whoever wrote it must have gotten one of the other staff members to drop it off at her desk. It was the only explanation.

But when she asked around, she got nothing but negative answers. No one had passed a message on to her. No one had seen any strangers or visitors loitering around her desk. For all practical purposes, the note had simply appeared there and no one had a clue how.

Not easily scared, Sabrina told herself she wasn't worried. She could take care of herself—she always had. And if there was a threat in the note, it wasn't meant for her. How could it be? She didn't even know the killer. Whoever he was, he obviously wanted his fifteen minutes of fame, just like everybody else. She could give him that. But first she had to talk to Sam Kelly. Picking up her phone, she punched in the number for the police department.

"C'mon, Kelly, I know you've got the coroner's report—I called the ME's office and asked," Blake said with a grin as he lounged in the chair across the desk from the detective.

"What's the big secret? Everyone knows Tanya Bishop was shot in the heart. All I want is the time of death."

"You'll get it just like everyone else at the press conference this afternoon at three," Sam said firmly. "That gives you plenty of time to make the morning edition."

In years past, Blake had worked with detectives who hoarded information like misers stockpiling gold, giving it out in beggarly bits and pieces like they were doing the world a favor. Sam Kelly didn't strike him that way. He didn't play games or do anything that might have been considered unethical. He was a strictly by-the-book man, and Blake had to admire that. In a world where whole police departments were as crooked as a dog's hind leg, it was nice to know there were men like Sam Kelly still hanging in there, doing things the right way, fighting the good fight. But it made getting information out of him damn difficult.

"The morning edition's not the problem," he said ruefully, opting for the truth. "It's Sabrina Jones."

His craggy face cracking in a smile, Sam leaned back in his chair and surveyed him knowingly. "So Sabrina's giving you fits already, is she? Somebody should have warned you."

"Somebody did—I just didn't believe him. She's quick, damn quick. And if you tell her I said that, I'll flat out deny it. The woman's already too cocky as it is."

Sam laughed, agreeing. "She never has lacked for confidence. Some men have a hard time handling that. I heard you two have a bet going on—"

Before he could say more, the phone on his desk rang, and with a murmured apology to Blake, he reached over and answered it. Recognizing Sabrina's husky voice, he started to smile. "Well, speak of the devil. I was just talking about you, Sabrina. What's up?"

Snapping to attention at the mention of Sabrina's name, Blake watched Sam's expression turn from teasing to grim in the blink of an eye. All business, the detective reached for a pen and started jotting down notes. "No, don't touch it any more than you already have," he said quickly. "We'll need to test it for fingerprints, then send it to the lab to see what they can make of it. I'll be right over."

Impatient, the one-sided conversation giving him few clues to what was going on, Blake started throwing questions at the other man the second he hung up. "Don't touch what? Is Sabrina in some kind of danger? What are you sending to the lab? Dammit, Sam, what's going on?"

For a moment, he thought the other man wasn't going to tell him anything, but then Sam sighed and said, "I guess there's no reason to keep it a secret—you're going to find out soon enough anyway. Sabrina got to work late today—just a few minutes ago, in fact—and found a note someone had left on her desk. It appears to be from Tanya Bishop's killer."

"What?!"

"*Appears* is the operative word here," he stressed. "At this point, we can't be sure it's from the real killer, but Sabrina's not taking it lightly. In fact, she sounded pretty shaken."

"Well, I would think she damn well would be. Why would the bastard send her a note?"

"The man's a murderer, Blake. He's already killed once, possibly twice, if he offed Charlene McClintock. Who knows what's going on in his head? And he didn't *send* it. Sabrina thinks he hand-delivered it."

"Son of a bitch! You mean he just walked right into the *Daily Record*?"

"That's the way it looks. I'm heading over there right now to check it out. I'll see you later at the press conference."

"The hell you will," Blake said, rising to his feet. "I'm going with you."

Sitting at her desk, her gaze trained unseeingly on her computer monitor, Sabrina tried to focus on her story about the mayor's son and his drunken joyride, but her concentration was shot. She couldn't write a logical sentence to save her life. All she could think about was the series of veiled threats in the note, threats that could have been meant for every professional woman in the city. Including herself.

When the thought had first occurred to her, fear, uncontrollable and unwanted, had surged in her before she could stop it. And she hadn't liked it one little bit. She didn't like being afraid, especially where she worked. This was her desk, her paper, and no murdering wacko was going to waltz in there and scare the bejabbers out of her just because he had a problem with women in power positions!

Giving up any attempt to work, she sat back and glared at the note, a thousand angry questions spinning in her head. Had the writer really killed Tanya? And why had he sent his note to her? Obviously he wanted his message to get out to professional women who were, in his words, "tampering with the world order," but that didn't mean that she was the only reporter who could relay his message for him. Any television station or newspaper in the country would have done the same thing once the note was declared valid by the police. So why her? From the way he sounded, he didn't even like career women, and she'd never claimed to be anything else. What did he want with her, anyway?

Frowning, she was still trying to figure that out when Sam Kelly walked into the city room. And right behind him was Blake Nickels, strolling in as if he was taking a walk in a park!

Stunned, Sabrina couldn't believe her eyes. "What's he doing here?" she asked Sam by way of a greeting.

"Now don't go getting all bent out of shape, Sabrina," he soothed. "He was at the station when you called, sitting right across from me at my desk. What was I supposed to do? Lock him up so he couldn't follow me?"

"It's a thought," she replied, shooting Blake a narrow-eyed look that didn't faze his teasing grin one iota. "You've got a lot of nerve coming here, cowboy. What do you want?"

"A story." Plopping down on a corner of her desk, he tilted his cowboy hat to the back of his head and crossed his arms across his chest as if he planned to stay awhile. "The last I heard, you were it."

Despite the fact that she was still unsettled about the note, she couldn't help but appreciate the vagaries of Fate. Biting back a smile, she asked, "Have you ever heard that old saying 'what goes around, comes around,' Nickels? Well, it looks like it's your turn to get what's coming to you. Yesterday, you had an exclusive. Today, I do. Isn't life funny?"

"Oh, yeah. It's a regular riot," he drawled.

Captivated by the flash of her quick grin, he wondered if she had any idea how tempting she looked, her gaze level with his for once since he was sitting, satisfaction dancing in those expressive brown eyes of hers. A man could be forgiven for kissing a woman under such circumstances, and the sudden need to do just that stunned the hell out of him. Where the devil had that come from?

You've been too long without a woman, his common sense muttered in his ear. *That's the only explanation. Sure, she's a pretty little thing, but she'd just as soon have you for breakfast as look at you. She's the competition. Remember?*

Brought up short by the reminder—and annoyed at the need for it—he scowled and glanced down at her desk. "So where's the note? At least let me take a quick peek at it before you toss me out of here."

Lightning-quick, she grabbed his hand and tried to tug him to his feet. "Not on your life. You've seen and heard all you're going to, so get. I'm sure Sam has a lot of questions, and I have no intention of answering them in front of you."

"Spoilsport."

Her efforts to move him about as effective as a gnat's, she dropped his hand and squared off in front of him like Sugar Ray Leonard. "Don't make me get tough with you."

"At last she's going to get physical!" he teased, his eyes laughing at her. "Yes, Virginia, there is a Santa Claus."

"Blake—"

When she used that tone, he knew she meant business. "Okay, okay. You win." Though he was left with no choice but to back off, he had no intention of going far. Not until he had some answers. Reluctantly, he pushed himself to his feet. "Enjoy your victory, Jones. The next one may be a long time coming."

Shooting one last, searching look at her desk, he turned away and gave every appearance of leaving as he headed for the exit. But just before he reached it, he glanced back over his shoulder and found Sabrina in a serious discussion with the detective, who was carefully examining a sheet of paper on her desk. That was all the opening Blake needed.

Stopping at the water fountain in the hall to talk to a pretty young copy girl who looked like she was hardly old enough to be out of high school, he shot her his most charming smile, pushed his cowboy hat up off his forehead, and prayed she hadn't heard of him as he introduced himself. "Hi, I'm Blake Nickels. I came with Detective Kelly—"

Her blue eyes bright with shy interest, she said huskily, "I saw you when you came in. Are you a detective, too?"

"Not quite," he hedged, and told himself it wasn't a lie. He hadn't actually misrepresented himself, which would have been unethical—he'd just let her jump to her own conclusions because he had no other choice. If he identified himself as a reporter with the *Times,* she and everyone else in the building would send him packing as fast as Sabrina had. Pulling out his notebook, he said, "I was hoping you could answer some questions for me."

"About the note Sabrina got?"

"You know about it?"

"Oh, sure. The news went through the building like wildfire. The killer just walked in and left the note on her desk."

In the process of reaching for the pen in his shirt pocket, Blake glanced up at her in surprise. "Someone saw him?"

She hesitated, then had the grace to blush. "Well, no, not exactly. But how else could it have gotten there if he didn't deliver it in person? All the employees have been questioned, and no one knows a thing about it."

She had a point, one that Blake didn't like one little

bit. Tanya Bishop's killer was no stumbling novice. The man—he'd heard of no evidence that pointed to the sex of the murderer, but his gut was telling him it had to be a man—had been smart and cunning enough to surprise her, then kill her without leaving a single clue. Just the thought of him walking into the *Daily Record* and finding Sabrina's desk without anyone being the wiser turned Blake's blood cold. If the bastard could track her down so easily at work, what was to stop him from following her home?

His expression darkening at the thought, he said tersely, "That must have been a hell of a note, if he was willing to take that kind of risk to deliver it. Any idea what was in it? I haven't seen it yet."

The girl nodded, indignation sparkling in her blue eyes. "It was a bunch of garbage about women not knowing their place and taking jobs away from men. Supposedly, that's why Tanya Bishop was killed. She was warned to stay home where she belonged and she laughed in the jerk's face."

His pen flying over the pages of his notebook in his own brand of shorthand, Blake took down every word and could already see the headlines. But the elation he should have felt at outsmarting Sabrina in her own backyard just wasn't there. Not when she had drawn the attention of a murderer. He tried to tell himself that he would have been disturbed by the thought of any colleague receiving what sounded like a threatening note—it was nothing personal. But this felt distinctly, disturbingly, personal.

"Did I say something wrong? You look awful mad all of a sudden."

Glancing up from his notes, he found the copy girl staring at him with a puzzled frown. "No," he said quietly, forcing a crooked smile that didn't come as easily as it usually did. "You didn't say anything wrong. My mind just wandered for a second. Is that the gist of the note?"

She nodded. "Pretty much. Except that it was a warning to other professional women that the same thing could happen to them if they're not careful."

To Blake, that sounded more like a threat than a warning, one directed right at Sabrina. And if she didn't have the sense to recognize that, she wasn't as smart as he thought she was. Thanking the copy girl for her help, he returned to the city room to find Sabrina pounding out a story on her computer while Detective Kelly questioned the other *Record* staff members.

Crossing the room in four long strides, Blake came up behind her and boldly began to read the opening paragraph on her monitor. "That'd better not be what I think it is, Jones."

Startled, she whirled in her chair, her hand flying to her throat. "Damn you, Nickels! You scared the stuffing out of me! What are you doing here? I thought I told you to leave."

He grinned, but there was little humor in his eyes when he said, "Nobody scares me off a story that easy, honey, especially a shrimp like you." Dropping with lazy grace into the chair positioned across from her desk, he nodded to her computer monitor, where the opening lines of her story were still clearly visible. "You're not really going to print the contents of that note, are you?"

"Not print it?" she choked, swivelling the monitor so he could no longer see the screen. "Are you out of your mind? Of course I'm going to print it!"

"Don't you think that's a mistake? What if it's bogus? You'll come off looking like a fool."

"I'd rather risk that than not let the professional women

of this city know that there's a psychopath out there with a vendetta against them. This man, whoever he is, doesn't live in a vacuum, Blake. Somebody out there knows him, and when they read his note in the paper, they just might come forward. Anyway, the note's not bogus. If you don't believe me, ask Sam."

Dammit, he didn't have to ask Sam. He'd heard enough from the copy girl to know that she was right. And that's what worried him. "Then that's just one more reason not to print it," he said stubbornly. "If the killer really wrote it, he didn't send it to you because he wanted to be friends or give you the scoop of the century. It was a threat to you and every other career woman out there, and you'll only encourage him if you print it."

"Don't be ridiculous," she scoffed. "You're just ticked because I've got the inside track on the best story to hit this town in years. You know you're going to lose our bet and it's driving you up the wall." Daring to smile at him, she goaded sweetly, "Better save your pennies, cowboy. You're going to need them, and then some."

Frustrated, his hands curling into fists to keep from reaching across her desk to shake the stuffing out of her, Blake couldn't for the life of him understand why he was so burned. He didn't want to see her or anyone else get hurt, but the lady meant nothing to him. Oh, he liked her well enough, but he'd always been a sap for smart, independent women. He liked bran, too, but he knew better than to overindulge. And Sabrina Jones was definitely an indulgence he wanted no part of, especially after Trina had made a fool out of him. He was concerned, just as he would be for any other woman who was standing on the edge of disaster and didn't know it.

Still, she could obviously take care of herself. She

might look as soft as a powder puff, but underneath that cloud of silky black curls and the soft blouses and skirts that emphasized her femininity was a woman who had a reputation for being tough when it came to her work. If she wasn't worried about developing a tenuous relationship with the killer, why should he be?

Because two other career women had no doubt once thought they could take care of themselves, too. And now they were dead.

"This has nothing to do with the damn bet," he said curtly, pushing to his feet. "I was just concerned for your safety, but I guess that's not my problem, is it?" Not waiting for an answer, he headed for the door.

He walked away from Sabrina because she hadn't given much choice, but there was no way in hell he was walking away from the story, he decided as he pulled out of the *Record*'s parking lot a few minutes later. There was a reason the killer had sent it to Sabrina, and he meant to find out what it was—with or without her cooperation.

And there was no better place to start his investigation than with the lady herself. When she found out about it, she was going to be madder than a wet hen. Grinning at the thought, he stopped at a convenience store and borrowed a phone book to look up her address. Seconds later, he was headed for the near north side.

She lived off St. Mary's Street in an older neighborhood that had once been quite nice but had declined as the city grew. Most of the homes were wood-framed, with wide porches, many of them sagging and sad-looking. More often than not, graffiti marked fences and walls, a by-product of the gangs that had taken over the area and claimed it as their own. It went without saying that crime was high.

There were pockets of hope, though, Blake noted. A cluster of homes here and there, even a whole block where homeowners were trying to reclaim their neighborhood. Here, the homes were painted and restored, the yards mowed. And it was here that Sabrina lived.

Parking at the curb in front of her house, Blake found himself smiling at the sight of it. Somehow, out of all the houses on the street, he would have known without asking that this one was Sabrina's. The winding walk that led from the curb to her front porch was bracketed with flower beds that were bursting with wildflowers, and on the porch itself were bright pots of geraniums and begonias that were as thick as thieves. Every yard on the street seemed to have flower beds, but while the others were neatly trimmed and organized, Sabrina's were wild and free and bold with color. Just like the woman herself, he thought with a frown. And it was that boldness that was going to get her into trouble if she wasn't careful.

But that wasn't why he was there, he reminded himself grimly. The killer had made Sabrina a part of his story when he'd delivered that note to her. Until the murderer was identified and caught, Sabrina was the only living tie to the man that anyone was aware of, and Blake meant to find out why. What it was about her that attracted the killer's attention?

Studying the homes of her neighbors, he decided to check the one on the left, where there were two cars in the driveway. The old lady who answered the door was round and jolly, with a double chin and inquisitive blue eyes that twinkled behind the lenses of her glasses. Lifting a delicately arched brow at him, she said, "Yes? May I help you?"

"I certainly hope so, ma'am." Introducing himself, he

pulled his wallet out of his back pocket and showed her his credentials. "I'm Blake Nickels, with the *Times*. I wonder if I could ask you a few questions about your neighbor, Sabrina Jones?"

Alarmed, her easy smile faltered. "Why? Has something happened to her?"

"No, she's fine," Blake quickly assured her. "In fact, I just left her a few minutes ago at the *Daily Record*." Knowing there was no way he was going to find anything out about Sabrina without her friends' cooperation, he quickly told the older woman about the note. "The police are aware of the situation and are checking out the note in the hopes that it will lead them to Tanya Bishop's murderer, but I'm more inclined to check out Sabrina. The killer didn't just pick her name out of a hat. He chose her for a reason. I was hoping you or one of the other neighbors might be able to tell me why by giving me some information about her background."

For a moment, Blake thought she was going to turn him down flat. Not committing herself one way or the other, she studied him through the screen door, then nodded as if coming to a silent decision and pushed open the door. "I'm Martha Anderson. Come on in. If Sabrina's in trouble, I want to help."

Blake only meant to ask her a few questions, but the old lady was obviously lonely and hungry for visitors. After settling him at her kitchen table, she fixed them each a glass of iced tea, then settled into the chair across from him, eager to talk.

"Sabrina's such a wonderful girl," she confided. "And everybody around here is just crazy about her. It's such a shame about her husband—"

"Husband?" Blake echoed, sitting up straighter. "I didn't know she was married."

"She's not…now," Martha replied. "How that girl could be so smart and make such a huge mistake, God only knows. Anyone with eyes could see that Jeff Harper was about as wrong for her as a bad case of the flu, but she was infatuated and just threw caution to the wind. She's like that, you know," she added, leaning closer as if she was confiding a secret. "Impulsive. Lord, that girl's impulsive! I swear she doesn't have a self-protective bone in her body, but you won't find a better friend or neighbor in this city. When I broke my hip last year, she was over here just about every evening to cook supper for me. And then when Louis— Louis Vanderbilt, he lives on the other side of Sabrina—had to have his dog put to sleep last summer, Sabrina went out and bought him another one. I cried myself, just seeing how moved he was."

"What about this Jeff Harper character?" Blake asked with a frown. "Where's he? And how does he feel about her dating again?"

"Well, that's just it, dear," the old lady replied. "She doesn't date. Ever. As far as I've been able to tell, she hasn't been out a single time since she and Jeff split. Not that he would care. He's already remarried and got a baby on the way. As far as I know, Sabrina hasn't seen him in over a year."

Intrigued, Blake found that hard to believe. Whether he wanted to admit it or not, Sabrina Jones was a beautiful woman with a sassy personality that any man with blood in his veins would find hard to resist. She had a job that took her all over the city and gave her plenty of opportunities to meet people. So what was wrong with the men in San Antonio? Were they blind, or what?

"So she doesn't date and there's no men in her life," he said thoughtfully. That ruled out the possibility of the killer being someone she'd been involved with romantically. "What about enemies?"

"Enemies?" Martha laughed, her blue eyes fairly sparkling behind the lenses of her glasses. "You obviously don't know Sabrina very well or you wouldn't even ask that. She can be as nosy as an old woman when she's after a story, but she's just doing her job. Nobody holds it against her."

Obviously extremely fond of Sabrina, she drew a tantalizing picture of her that Blake found thoroughly captivating. But she didn't tell him anything that even hinted at why Tanya Bishop's killer had turned his sights on Sabrina. Thanking the old lady for her help, he went looking for more answers from the other neighbors.

Since most of Sabrina's neighbors were retired, he didn't have any trouble finding someone to talk to. Unfortunately, he didn't get the information he was hoping for. All of them knew and liked Sabrina and had their own stories to tell about her, but none could think of a single reason why a killer would send her a threatening note. Except for Louis Vanderbilt.

A quiet, unassuming man who was out walking the now-grown Labrador that Sabrina had given him as a puppy, he paled when he stopped to talk to Blake and was told about the note. "Sabrina did a special series last year about sexual discrimination in the workplace," he said quietly. "It was excellent. In fact, I think she won several awards for it. But one of the editors at her own paper quit over allegations that she stirred up, and from what I heard from Sabrina, he vowed to get even. But that was months ago. Sabrina probably forgot all about him. Do you think he could be the one who sent her the note?"

Blake didn't know, but it was definitely worth checking out and mentioning to the police. Feeling like he was finally getting somewhere, he quickly jotted down notes. "What was the man's name? Do you have any idea what happened to him after he quit the *Record*?"

A thin, balding man with wire-rimmed glasses and the kind of ageless face that didn't show the passage of time, Louis murmured to the Lab, who was impatient to resume his walk, and tried to remember. "It seems like it was Saunders or Sanders or something like that. Carl, I think. Yeah, that was it. Carl Sanders."

Shaking his head, he whistled softly as the facts came rushing back to him. "He was a nasty sort. If I'm remembering correctly, he was arrested for punching his wife about a week after he lost his job. She later dropped the charges and he sort of faded from sight after that. Which isn't surprising considering the fact that all the TV stations in town picked up the story," he added. "After all the negative publicity, he'd have been lucky to get a job as a dogcatcher, which was no more than he deserved."

"Did he ever contact Sabrina? Ever show up here at her home and harass her or send her any kind of threatening letters?"

Shocked, the older man said, "Oh, no! Not that I know of. Sabrina never mentioned any kind of letters, and I know for a fact that he never came around here. This is a very close-knit neighborhood, Mr. Nickels. We're all friends and watch out for each other. Sabrina and only a handful of others work—the rest of us are retired—so there's always someone home on the block. If Carl Sanders or anyone else had tried to get to Sabrina, you can bet one of us would have seen him.

"Of course," he added with a rueful smile, "we can't do much to protect her when she's out on the streets. She does tend to take chances."

Blake snorted at that, his lips twitching into a grin. "She's a regular daredevil, Mr. Vanderbilt." Holding out his hand, he said, "Thanks for the information. You've been a big help. If you remember anything else that might be important, would you give me a call at the *Times*? I'd really appreciate it."

A twinkle glinting in his eye, the older man hesitated, then nodded as he returned the handshake. "Sabrina won't like me helping the competition, but if it'll help keep her safe, I'll be glad to do it." The Lab tugged on her leash again, and with a murmur of apology, the man continued his walk.

Staring after him, Blake grinned. Whether he knew it or not, Louis Vanderbilt hadn't just helped the competition. He'd given him enough information that would—if it proved reliable after further research—blow Sabrina and the *Daily Record* right out of the water. It was, he decided, picturing the huge steak he was going to let her buy him next month, his lucky day.

Chapter 3

An hour later, Blake hung up the phone at his desk at the *Times* with a muttered curse. Louis Vanderbilt's story had checked out—to a point. Carl Sanders *had* lost his job at the *Daily Record* after Sabrina did a series of stories on sexual harassment. And in the single, bitter exclusive interview he'd given the *Times* after his abrupt resignation, he had placed all the blame on Sabrina. There was no question that the man was a chauvinist of the worst kind and that he had the mind-set and motive to at least be considered a suspect. The only problem was that less than a month after he quit the *Record,* he had apparently moved to Billings, Montana. A check with information and a short call to a C. Sanders there had verified that he was still there and wanted nothing to do with anyone from San Antonio.

Considering that, and the fact that he couldn't stroll into his old workplace without being recognized, the odds were slim that he'd threatened Sabrina, let alone killed Tanya

Bishop or Charlene McClintock. So he was back to square one, Blake thought in disgust.

"Problems?"

Looking up from his musings to find Tom grinning at him, he growled, "No, thanks. I've got enough of my own. One, in fact, that you're probably not going to like."

"Let's hear it and I'll let you know," his friend and boss said as pulled up a chair. "Lay it on me."

"Tanya Bishop's killer sent a threatening note to Sabrina Jones." He filled him in on his conversation with the copy girl at the *Record* and his canvasing of Sabrina's neighbors. "This Carl Sanders character sounded like just the type of lowlife who would do something like this, but with him out of the picture, there aren't any other suspects. So the only story I've got is a note I haven't actually seen. I know its general contents, but not any specifics I can quote. And even if I did, I don't like the idea of encouraging the jerk."

Tom frowned. "If you're suggesting we don't print the story at all, I can't go along with that. Two women have died in two weeks, Blake. The whole city's abuzz about it, and just this morning, I heard on the radio that a record number of women are buying guns to protect themselves. Any developments in the case have to be reported—even if it concerns a reporter for the competition."

"But the killer wants recognition," Blake argued. "Why else would he have sent the note to Sabrina? If we give him that recognition, not only do we chance turning this into a media circus, but we'll be giving him what he wants. He could get a real taste for this type of thing."

"And kill more?" Tom asked shrewdly. "I doubt it. He didn't need any encouragement for the first two. I can't see why he would now."

"But—"

"This isn't anything like the situation in New York eight years ago, Blake," he cut in quietly. "You don't have information that's going to get someone killed. If anything, letting everyone know what kind of threats this jerk is making could save lives. Exposure and the knowledge that most of the city is on the lookout for him may be the only things that keep him in check."

Put that way, Blake had to agree. Still, he didn't like the idea of publicizing the jerk's sudden interest in Sabrina. Who was he? What did he want with her? And why was he—Blake—so concerned about her safety when she could obviously take care of herself? She wasn't his problem. Why did he have such a hard time remembering that?

It was nearly dark when Blake finally left the paper and made his way home. When he'd first moved to town two weeks ago, he'd planned to move in with his grandfather so he could keep an eye on him, but the old man had let him know that first day that he didn't need a baby-sitter, despite what Blake's mother thought. Amused, Blake hadn't pushed the issue. Pop had always been an independent cuss, and arguing with him only made him dig in his heels. So Blake had assured him that he'd moved to San Antonio for a job, not to watch over him, and backed off.

He'd had, however, no intention of leaving the old man to his own devices. Finding himself an apartment several blocks away from the house his grandfather had lived in for over sixty years, Blake had planned to come up with an excuse to check on him every day. So far, that hadn't been necessary. If his grandfather didn't call him around supper time every day, he was invariably waiting for him when he got home. After the first few days of finding him waiting on the landing outside his second-story apartment, Blake had given him a key.

Now, as he climbed the stairs, he caught the scent of chicken frying and had to grin. The rest of the world might be cutting back on cholesterol, but Pop didn't have much use for what he considered a conspiracy dreamed up by a bunch of quack scientists who wanted to control the world. A cook in the navy, he'd been eating bacon and eggs and fried foods all his life, and at eighty-three, he was still going strong. Why the devil would he want to change his diet at this late date?

Letting himself in, Blake followed his nose to the apartment's small kitchen just in time to see the old man slip a pan of homemade biscuits into the oven. Propping a shoulder against the doorjamb, he teased, "You'd make some old woman a great husband, Pop. Want me to place a personal ad for you?"

The old man only snorted, his grin a mirror image of Blake's. "What makes you think I could only get an old one? In case you didn't know it, I'm a damn fine catch. I've got all of my own teeth—"

"And most of your hair," Blake added, chuckling.

"You're damn right," his grandfather agreed, playfully patting the cloud of wavy white hair that was his only vanity. "And you're going to look just like me. If I were you, I'd be thanking my lucky stars you got your looks from the Finnigans, boy. Your daddy's bald head shines in the moonlight."

"Only when he polishes it," Blake retorted, repeating one of his father's favorite jokes about his lack of hair. Pushing away from the doorjamb, he strode over to the stove and started lifting lids. "You making gravy, Pop? I can't remember the last time I had your gravy."

With pretended fierceness, the older man swatted at him, shoving him away from his cooking. "Get out of there before I forget you're my favorite grandson."

"I'm your only grandson." Blake laughed, snatching a green bean before he stepped back. "When do we eat?"

"When you set the table. I can smell those biscuits, son. Get moving."

His stomach grumbling, Blake didn't have to be told twice. Grabbing plates and silverware, he quickly set the table, then moved to help his grandfather dish up the food. Five minutes later, they sat down to a feast that would have fed a small army.

Filling his plate, the old man, as usual, asked about work. "So how'd it go today? You run into that Jones woman today?"

The question was smoothly, casually added, almost as an afterthought, but Blake wasn't the least bit fooled by his grandfather's attempt at subtlety. He'd made the mistake of telling the old man about Sabrina that day he'd met her at the scene of Tanya Bishop's murder, and ever since then, Pop had been convinced that Blake was interested in her. A day didn't go by that he didn't ask about her.

Shooting him a hard look, he warned, "There's nothing going on between Sabrina and me, Pop, so don't start getting any ideas."

As innocent as a choirboy, he arched a craggy brow. "Did I say there was? All I asked was if you ran into her today. If you read more into that, then it seems to me that you're awfully sensitive where that girl's concerned."

"I'm not sensitive," he began defensively, then caught the gleam in the old coot's eye. "You old rascal, I know what game you're playing and it's not going to work," he warned, grinning. "Just because Sabrina and I run into each other covering the same stories—"

"So you did see her!"

"Yes, but—"

"I knew it!" he cackled gleefully. "You just can't stay away from her. So tell me about her. Is she pretty? How old is she? I know she's got spunk—you can tell it from her writing. I always did like a girl with spunk."

Amused in spite of himself, Blake said patiently, "Yes, she's pretty, but that's got nothing to do with anything. She got a threatening letter from Tanya Bishop's killer, and I went over to the *Daily Record* to cover the story. That's all there was to it."

The old man snorted, unconvinced. "You went over there to make sure she was okay and you know it. That's good. A man should protect the woman he cares about—even if she can take care of herself. So why haven't you asked her out?" he demanded, pointing a chicken leg at him. "A girl like that won't stay single for long."

"I don't know about that," he said dryly. "According to one of her neighbors, her ex-husband burned her bad and she doesn't even date. Anyway, even if I was interested— which I'm not saying I am—I can't ask her out. She works for the competition."

"So? What's that got to do with anything? Your grandmother's family didn't even talk to mine, but Sadie was the prettiest thing I'd ever seen. And she had just as much spunk as your Sabrina. I'm telling you, boy, you'd better snap her up while you can. Women like her don't come along every day of the week. Believe me, I know. Why do you think I never married again after your grandma died? A good woman is hard to find."

Giving up in defeat, Blake laughed. "Okay, okay! I'll think about it."

Pleased, the old man passed the platter of chicken to him and grinned. "If you're going to get mixed up with a woman like that, you're going to need to keep up your strength. Here. Eat."

Tired, a nagging headache throbbing at her temples, Sabrina pulled into her driveway at twenty minutes to seven and sighed in relief. Finally! It had been a long, disturbing day, and all she wanted to do was collapse into bed, pull the covers over her head, and forget the world. Tomorrow would be soon enough to worry about the two women who had been murdered and the note personally delivered to her from their killer.

But as she cut the engine and stepped from her car, she found herself wondering if the killer who had dared to track her down at work had made it his business to find out where she lived. A first-grader could have done it—she was in the book, under S. Jones. There were three others, but that wouldn't present much of a problem for a man who had committed two murders without leaving behind a single clue that could be used by the police to identify him. All he would have to do was scout out the others or follow her home from work.

A cold chill slithering down her spine in spite of the fact that the heat of the day had yet to ease much, she whirled, her heart thumping, and searched the street in both directions. But the neighborhood was blessedly normal, and there wasn't a stranger in sight. Louis was washing his car next door, and across the street, the Garzas' oldest son, Chris, was mowing the lawn. Other than that, the street was quiet and deserted.

"You're being paranoid, Sabrina," she chided herself as she waved to Louis and Chris, then turned back to unlock the front door. "And that's just what the killer wants. Why else do you think he sent you that damn note? He's trying to scare you and you're letting him. What's the matter with you? You're not the type to jump at your own shadow. Straighten up, for God's sake! No one's been here, so quit looking over your shoulder and get inside. You're perfectly safe."

Her chin up, she hurried inside and did something she rarely did except at night when she went to bed—she shot the dead bolt into place. The click it made was loud in the silence, and she couldn't help but smile sheepishly at her own foolishness. "You're losing it, Jones," she chided herself, and turned toward the kitchen to see about supper.

She'd barely taken two steps when there was a sudden knock at the door. Startled, she jumped, then cursed herself for being so skittish.

It was probably just Chris wanting to know if he could mow her lawn, she decided. He was saving for a car and did chores for her and everyone else in the neighborhood whenever he got a chance.

But when she opened the front door, it was Mrs. Anderson who stood there smiling gaily, a plate of just-baked brownies in her hand. "Hi, sweetie. I saw you drive up and thought I'd bring you some dessert for after supper." Not the kind to stand on ceremony, she didn't wait to be invited in, but simply swept inside and headed straight for the kitchen. "I won't stay long—you look a little tired. Did you have a rough day?"

If she hadn't been so drained, Sabrina might have laughed. "Don't ask." She caught the scent of warm chocolate then and lifted her nose to the air. "Mmm. That smells heavenly. How did you know I needed a chocolate fix, Mrs. A.?" she asked as she followed her down the entrance hall to the kitchen at the back of the house. "I didn't even know it myself."

"That isn't surprising, considering the day you've had," the older woman said as she set the brownies down on the table and waved her into a seat. "Sit down and dig in, honey, while I get you a glass of milk. My mama always said nothing tasted better than something sweet from the oven after a bad day. What do the police say about that nasty note you got? I hope they're doing something about it. Just imagine, a cold-blooded killer waltzing into that paper and leaving you something like that! All I can say is, if I was in charge, I'd string him up by his thumbs the second I got my hands on him."

In the process of bringing a nice thick square of brownie to her mouth, Sabrina stopped halfway. "You know about the note?" she asked in surprise.

Her faded blue eyes dancing, Martha Anderson sank down in the chair across from her and leaned close to confide, "That nice Mr. Nickels came by asking about you earlier and told me the whole story. I tell you, I was shocked, dear!"

"Blake was here? Asking about me?"

"Oh, yes. And he was very concerned." Helping herself to one of her own brownies, she took a healthy bite and frowned. "I think these need a little more sugar. My sister gave me the recipe, and this is the first time I've made them. What do you think? Should they be a little sweeter?"

Struggling for patience, Sabrina assured her they were delicious just the way they were. "But what about Blake? Just what kind of questions was he asking?"

"Oh, the usual thing," she said airily. "I think he thought the killer might be someone you know, so he wanted to know about your background, if you had any enemies or former boyfriends who might have a grudge against you, that sort of thing. I laughed, of course. I just can't imagine you having any enemies. Why, you even managed to stay friends with Jeff after you two split, and how many people can say that?"

"You told him about Jeff?"

She nodded and rattled happily on. "It just came up when I mentioned that you didn't date much. Then Mr. Nickels just naturally assumed that there must be some bad blood between the two of you, so I had to set him straight."

Suddenly realizing for the first time that she might have let her tongue get away with her, she frowned worriedly. "You're not mad because I told him about the divorce, are you? I really didn't mean to tell tales out of turn, but he was so nice. And he seemed genuinely concerned that you were in danger. I just wanted to help. If something happened to you because I kept a vital piece of information to myself, I'd never forgive myself."

Knowing the way Mrs. A dearly loved to gossip, Sabrina knew that was never going to happen, but she only smiled and patted her hand. "Nothing's going to happen to me," she assured her. "And no, I'm not mad." At least not at her. But Blake Nickels was another matter. Temper starting to simmer in her eyes, she said, "You did the right thing, Martha. I'm just surprised that Blake felt the need to question you and the rest of the neighbors. I saw him this afternoon at the paper, and he never said a word about his plans to check me out."

"Well, you work for opposing newspapers," she pointed

out with a mischievous grin. "Maybe he wanted to outscoop you on your own turf."

"He wouldn't dare," Sabrina began, only to hear his teasing words ring in her ears as clearly as if he were standing beside her.

Honey, when you get to know me better, you'll find out that I'll dare just about anything.

"Oh, I'd like to see him try," she seethed. "That note was delivered to me, not him, so that makes it my story. He's not going to come in through the back door and snatch it right out from under me. Just wait till I see him again—he's going to get an earful."

Martha laughed gaily at that and rose to her feet. "Just don't be too hard on him, sweetie. He's such a nice-looking young man. And he wasn't wearing a ring," she added with twinkling eyes. "Who knows what might develop if you give him a chance?"

A snowball had a better chance in hell, Sabrina thought with a snort, but there was no use telling Martha that. A hopeless romantic, she had been trying to find Sabrina a man ever since she and Jeff had split. In spite of Sabrina's insistence that she wasn't looking for a man, Martha refused to believe that she was perfectly happy going through life alone.

"The only thing that's going to develop between me and Blake Nickels is an all-out war if he doesn't quit trying to muscle in on my turf," she replied as the older woman turned to leave. "But thanks for the brownies—they were just what I needed."

Wandering back to the kitchen after she'd shown Martha out, Sabrina couldn't shake the image of Blake canvasing her neighborhood, questioning the neighbors about each other and her friends. And the more she thought about it, the more indignant she got. Talk about nerve! The man had it in spades. Who the heck did he think he was, anyway? She wasn't the story here—the note and whoever wrote it were, and if Blake didn't realize that, maybe it was high time she told him.

Steaming, she walked over to the kitchen wall phone, snatched it up, and punched in the number for information. Seconds later, she had his phone number and address. Scowling down at them, she started to call him, only to hang up before she completed the call. No, she thought, her brown eyes narrowing dangerously. Some things were better said in person. Not giving herself time to question the wisdom of her actions, she grabbed her purse and car keys and headed for the door.

Blake and his grandfather were in the middle of watching a baseball game and arguing over which was the better team when the doorbell rang. Seconds later, someone pounded angrily on the front door. The old man arched a brow and said dryly, "Somebody sounds madder than a hornet. You expecting company?"

"Nope. Not that I know of." Pushing to his feet, Blake strode over to the apartment's front door and peeked through the peephole. At the sight of Sabrina standing there, glaring up at him as if she could see him through the door, he started to grin. Evidently, she'd found out that he'd been asking around about her, and she was more than a little ticked about it. He could practically see the steam pouring from her ears.

Pulling open the door, he made no attempt to hide his grin. "Well, well," he drawled. "If it isn't Ms. Jones. And to what do I owe the honor of this visit?"

Giving him a look that should have turned him to stone

where he stood, she didn't wait for an invitation to come inside, but simply stepped around him and whirled to let him have it with both barrels. "All I can say for you, Nickels, is you've got a hell of a nerve. How dare you badger my neighbors and friends about me and pretend to be concerned about my safety when all you were really after was a damn story! Of all the low-down, underhanded, despicable—"

"You tell him, missy," an unfamiliar gravelly voice said encouragingly from behind her. "He ought to be ashamed of himself, and if he wasn't too big to take a switch to, I'd do it for you."

Startled, Sabrina jerked around to find an old man seated in a rocker in front of the television and obviously enjoying her tirade. Mortified, she blushed all the way to her toes. Driving over there, all she'd been able to think about was what she was going to say to Blake when she saw him, and like an idiot, she hadn't even stopped to make sure they were alone.

Wishing she had a hole to climb into, she said stiffly, "I'm sorry. I didn't see you sitting there."

"That's all right." He chuckled, rising to his feet. "It's been a while since I've heard a woman give a man a piece of her mind. I enjoyed it." Offering his hand, he stared down at her with sparkling green eyes that reminded her of Blake's. "I'm Damon Finnigan, Blake's grandfather. Most people call me Pop. You must be Sabrina Jones. I've read your stuff. It's good."

Surprised, Sabrina blinked. "You read the *Daily Record*?"

"He likes to keep up with my competition," Blake confided as he shut the front door and strolled over to join them. "He's one of your biggest cheerleaders."

"You're damn right," the old man agreed, giving Sabrina a playful wink. "If I was just a little bit younger, I'd give this young rascal here a run for his money."

"Pop—"

"A run for his money?" Sabrina echoed in confusion, frowning. "What—"

"Pop likes to tease," Blake said, shooting the old man a hard look that should have shut him up. It didn't.

Unrepentant, his grin daring, his grandfather only laughed. "It's one of my better talents, but I know a pretty woman when I see one. And so does Blake. He told me you were pretty, and he was right."

Swallowing a groan, Blake wanted to strangle him, but Pop had had his say and was obviously content to leave while he was ahead. "Well, I guess I'd better get out of here and let you two talk," he said cheerfully, heading for the door. "I need to get home anyway. I don't like to drive after dark."

"It was nice meeting you, Mr. Finnigan," Sabrina called after him.

"You, too, missy. And it's Pop. Mr. Finnigan's that old man that used to be my granddad."

With a promise to call Blake later, he shut the door on his way out, leaving behind a silence that all but hummed. Her temper now under control, Sabrina let the silence stretch a full minute before she said coolly, "I like your grandfather. He's sweet. Too bad you don't take after him more."

A dimple in his cheek flashing, Blake chuckled. "Actually, I've been told I'm just like him. I guess you'll have to get to know us both better, though, before you see the similarities."

"Fat chance, Nickels," she retorted. "In case you

haven't figured it out yet, I didn't come here to be sociable. Especially with a rat like you."

Instead of insulting him, her hostility only seemed to amuse him. "No kidding? Now why doesn't that surprise me?"

"You are the most aggravating—"

"Guilty as charged."

"Sneaky—"

"I know," he agreed cheerfully. "It's deplorable, isn't it? But my mother swears that once you get used to it, it's one of my more endearing qualities."

Her lips pressed tightly together, Sabrina swore she wasn't going to laugh. Damn the man, how was she supposed to tell him off when he agreed with everything she said? Stiffening her spine, she said through her teeth, "If that's an invitation, thanks but no thanks. I'd just as soon cozy up to a snake. Any man who would go behind my back and grill my neighbors about me and the men in my life is a—"

"Damn good reporter," he finished for her easily. "Of course, I could have come to you for that information, but somehow I don't think you would have told me that you spend your Saturday nights in bed with a good book."

"You're darn right I wouldn't have! Because it's none of your business. And who said that about me, anyway?" she demanded huffily. "I have lots of friends and go somewhere almost every weekend."

"We're not talking about friends here, sweetheart, but boyfriends. You know…men? Those good-looking, superior creatures who take a woman out, wine her and dine her, and sometimes want something more than a peck on the cheek in return? If you had any contact in the past with the pushy sort and offended him, he just might be the kind to hold a grudge and go after you and all the other women who gave him the cold shoulder over the years."

"That's ridiculous! *I* am not the story here."

"Aren't you?" he asked quietly. "Think about it. If any other woman but you had gotten the letter, you would be asking the same questions of her neighbors that I asked of yours. There's got to be a personal link. If all the killer wanted was a forum to express his view, he could have sent the note to the editor for the letters column. But he didn't. As far as we know, he hand-delivered it to you personally. There's got to be a reason for that."

He had a point, one that made her more than a little nervous and irritated her at one and the same time. Tamping down the uneasiness that stirred in her stomach, she turned away to pace restlessly. "This is all just conjecture. It has to be. Don't you think I would know if someone I knew was capable of murder?"

"Maybe. Maybe not," he said with a shrug. "Psychopaths are damn clever."

"But I don't know any psychopaths."

"Not that you know of, anyway."

"Dammit, Blake, stop that! I know what you're doing, and it's not going to work."

"Oh, really? And what am I doing?"

"You're trying to distract me from the real issue here, which is *you* poking *your* nose into my life. It's got to stop."

His eyes searching hers, Blake couldn't believe she was serious, but there was no doubting her sincerity. She actually expected him to walk away from what could be the story of the decade because she asked him to. Roguish humor tugging up the corners of his mouth, he said, "Sorry, sweetheart. No can do."

"What do you mean...*no can do?* Of course you can! If you really want to find the murderer, go talk to the friends and family of those poor dead girls. That's where the story is."

"Bull. *You're* the story, Sabrina. We both know it—you just don't want to admit it because it scares you to death."

"That's not true! I've never been afraid of anything in my life."

"Well, you'd better be," he growled, stepping toward her. "Because a little healthy fear keeps people like you and me alive. Whether you want to admit it or not, someone out there means you harm. Until I find out why the killer sent you that note and who he is, everything about you is my business."

"The hell it is!"

"And if you don't like it, that's just too damn bad. Get used to it. I'm a hell of a good investigative reporter, so if you've got a secret, I'll warn you right now that I mean to find out what it is. By the time I get through with checking you out, honey, there won't be a panhandler on the street you've given a dollar to that I won't know about."

She swore at him then, highly imaginative curses that didn't include a single curse word but put him in his place, nonetheless. Against his will, he couldn't help but notice that she was something to see when she had her dander up. Temper blazed in her dark eyes, and twin flags of color burned in her cheeks. Dressed in a red dress that would have looked like a sack on another woman but somehow seemed to emphasize her every curve, she looked soft and feminine and full of fire. And he couldn't remember the last time he had wanted a woman so badly.

The thought caught him off guard, killing the grin that curled his lips. This wasn't the time to even think about getting romantic with a woman. Especially this woman, he told himself firmly. She wasn't in the mood. Hell, she was practically spitting daggers at him and would probably scratch his eyes out if he so much as touched her.

But even as he ordered himself to back away from her, he was eliminating the distance between them, as drawn to her as a moth to the scorching heat of a candle. And something of his intent must have gotten through to her because she faltered suddenly, her eyes wide, as he reached for her. "What are you doing?"

"Giving in to temptation," he said with a devilish grin, and hauled her into his arms. Before she could do anything but stiffen and gasp in outrage, his mouth was hot and hungry on hers.

He'd only meant to catch her by surprise and steal a kiss that would shut her up, but the second his lips touched hers, there was a spark of heat, a flash of desire that caught fire like a gasoline spill, and in the next instant, he felt like he was going up in flames. Burning for more than just a taste of her, he could have no more stepped away from her than he could have cut off his right arm. Her name a prayer, a curse, on his lips, he dragged her closer and gave in to the need that had the blood roaring in his ears.

Stunned, her head spinning and her knees threatening to buckle at any second, Sabrina clutched at him like a drowning woman going under for the last time. Trying to hang on to her common sense, she told herself that they had been headed for this from the second they met. Every time their eyes met, the attraction was there like a tiger hiding in the shadows, waiting to spring. She could handle it. She could handle *him*. Or so she'd tried to tell herself.

But now, caught tight against him, every nerve ending she had throbbing from his closeness, she felt as giddy as a young girl being kissed, *really kissed,* for the first time. All her senses were attuned to him...his hardness, the feel of his heart slamming against hers, the underlying tenderness of his kiss, the rush of his hands over her. And with every slow, intoxicating rub of his tongue against hers, the craving that he stirred in her grew stronger, hotter. Her lungs straining, something deep inside her just seeming to melt, she crowded closer, aching for more.

How long they stood there, lost in each other's arms, she couldn't have said. Magic engulfed them, holding the world at bay, and she was entranced. But it couldn't last. His breathing as hard as hers, he wrenched his mouth from hers, glazed eyes sharpened, and suddenly they were both staring at each other in disbelief as reality returned with a painful jolt.

Dear God, what was she doing? This was Blake Nickels, her adversary, the man who could irritate her faster than anyone else she'd ever known, and she'd kissed him like an old maid who'd been given one shot at Prince Charming.

Stunned, her cheeks on fire, she never remembered moving, but suddenly half the distance of the room was between them and it wasn't nearly enough. She had a horrible feeling that putting the entire state of Texas between them wouldn't have been enough. She could still taste him, still feel him against her, still draw in the spicy male scent of him with every breath she took.

And that frightened her more than a dozen notes from a killer. "I don't know what you think you were doing, but if you ever do that again, you're liable to lose a lip, not to mention a finger or two."

As shaken as she, Blake knew he should have taken the warning to heart and gotten the hell out of there while he still could. But the lady had just thrown down a gauntlet that no man with any blood in his veins could walk away from.

His green eyes alight with wicked laughter, he took a step toward her. "I don't know about you, sweetheart, but that sounds like a dare to me."

"Dammit, Blake, you stay away from me!"

"Make me," he said softly, and reached for her.

Ready for him, she made a break for the front door, but she never made it. On the television, the baseball game was interrupted by a special report, and they both instinctively turned to catch it.

"We interrupt scheduled programming for this breaking news story," the local ABC anchorman announced somberly. "There has been another murder of a young professional woman. The police are still investigating the scene in the four-hundred block of San Pedro, but preliminary reports indicate that the murder appears to be similar to that of Tanya Bishop and Charlene McClintock. We hope to have more details at ten. At this time, we return to regularly scheduled programming."

Stunned, Blake and Sabrina stared at each other. A split second later, they were running for the door.

Chapter 4

Her name was Elizabeth Reagan. She was a twenty-eight-year-old loan officer for one of the city's oldest and most successful banks. She made good money, had a lot of friends, and had a reputation for giving the shirt off her back to anyone in need. And she was dead, killed by a single bullet to the heart in her own living room while "Chicago Hope" played on the TV.

Standing on the edge of the crowd that had gathered in the front yard to watch from a distance as the police investigated the crime scene, Blake questioned shaken neighbors and crying friends, but just as with the other two murders, no one had seen or heard anything. All the neighbors had apparently been home at the time, in their homes on a summer evening with their windows and doors shut and the air-conditioning on, totally oblivious to what was going on at Elizabeth's house. Apparently, someone had walked in and shot her and not even a dog had barked a warning. She might have lain there for hours, staring glassy-eyed at her living-room ceiling, if the elderly woman across the street, a Mrs. Novack, hadn't let her cat out and noticed Elizabeth's front door standing wide open, all the lights on in the house, and her car missing from her driveway. She'd immediately called the police. It was a young rookie who'd been on the job barely a week who had made the grisly discovery and called for backup and Detective Kelly.

Frustrated, unable to believe that three murders could take place in three weeks, apparently by the same killer, without anyone seeing anything, Blake slowly made his way through the crowd, asking the same questions over and over again. Did Ms. Reagan have any known enemies? Any old boyfriends who might hold a grudge? Any acquaintances that she'd recently argued with? And always the answer was the same. No. No. No. She was a sweet girl. Everybody loved her. Her killer couldn't have possibly known her. It all had to be a tragic mistake—she must have surprised a burglar, who killed her and took her car.

Kelly and the rest of the investigative team was still inside, but there was no sign of a break-in or forced entry, and nothing but the car seemed to be missing. Blake had barely finished questioning Mrs. Novack about whether or not the vehicle had been there at all that evening when a pale and drawn teenager pushed his way through the crowd and announced to the police that he was Elizabeth's brother. He'd borrowed her car for a date after she got home from work and was, apparently, the last person who'd seen her alive. He, like everyone else, didn't have a clue as to who could have killed her.

Frowning, Blake searched the crowd of neighbors for Sabrina and finally found her talking to a young mother who was standing in the shadows under a magnolia tree, a curly-haired toddler clutched protectively in her arms. Throwing questions at her, Sabrina obviously wasn't having any better luck than he was. The woman just kept shaking her head and wiping at the tears that trailed down her ashen cheeks. As he watched, Sabrina touched her arm in sympathy, but when she turned away, her jaw was clenched with frustration. He knew just exactly how she felt.

Reading over the few facts he'd been able to gather, he swore. There just wasn't much to go on. And what little he had been able to find out, he didn't like the sound of. It went without saying that the victim was a young, single professional woman. She was also, according to the neighbors, petite and slender, with a cloud of black, curly hair that cascaded down her back. From her physical appearance alone, he could have been describing Sabrina.

His expression grim, he tried to tell himself that he was letting his imagination get the better of him. Just because the killer had left her one damn note didn't mean he'd started picking victims who looked like her. It was just a coincidence. But Blake was a man who didn't believe in coincidence…especially when it came to murder.

His gut knotting at the thought, he was just wondering if Kelly had made the connection when the man himself appeared at the entrance to the cordoned-off house and spoke to the uniformed officer standing guard there. A few seconds later, the man ducked under the yellow crime tape that blocked the doorway and slipped into the crowd. When he returned, he had Sabrina with him.

Pale and shaken, Sabrina stood in the dead woman's kitchen and stared in disbelief at the note found by the evidence team on the kitchen table. It was already stored in an evidence bag, but through the clear plastic, she could see that the handwriting was the same as that on the note she'd found on her desk at the *Daily Record* earlier in the day. And like that one, it was addressed to her.

"I can't believe this is happening," she told Sam. "It has to be some kind of sick joke. Who would do this?"

"I was hoping you could tell me that," Kelly said. "I don't have to tell you that all kinds of weirdos come out of the woodwork on a case like this—you've covered the police beat long enough to know that some people get a real kick out of the thought of being connected to something like this. We could be dealing with that here, but I don't think so."

"You don't? Then who—"

"This particular weirdo knows you, Sabrina."

"No!" Denial instantly springing to her lips, she took a quick step back. "Don't start with me, Sam. You sound just like Blake—"

She started to say more, but there was a commotion at the front door, and they both turned to see Blake trying to talk his way past the junior officer stationed there. With a nod to the rookie, Sam allowed him access, then said curtly, "Since you were in on this earlier, you might as well hear the latest. I'm going to have to make a statement to the press later, anyway." Holding up the bagged note, he showed him Sabrina's name on the front. "We found this on the kitchen table. I was just telling Sabrina that there's a good likelihood that the killer is someone she knows. Apparently, you agree."

Blake nodded, his eyes on Sabrina. "She doesn't want to believe it. What's in it?"

"Basically, it's pretty much a replay of the other one,"

Kelly replied. "The perp wanted to make sure that Sabrina got the message this time. *'Learn your place,'*" he quoted. "He doesn't want to see her end up like Elizabeth and all the others."

"So why doesn't he just leave me alone?" she demanded. "That'll solve that problem easily enough."

"Because you're the one he's been trying to kill from the very beginning," Blake said flatly. "Dammit, haven't you noticed?"

Confused, she frowned. "That's ridiculous. He hasn't come anywhere near *me*. Except to leave the notes, of course, and I wasn't anywhere in the vicinity when he did that."

"But every time he kills, he's striking out at you. Look at the victims. If you put their descriptions and yours in a box and picked one out, they would all be the same. A young, single, professional woman who lives alone and has a slender build and dark, curly hair."

Kelly, looking more dour than Sabrina had ever seen him, nodded in agreement. "This guy, whoever the hell he is, is too methodical and careful to do anything by chance, Sabrina. He chose his victims for a reason, and considering these damn notes, I've got to agree with Blake. The killer seems to be obsessed with you and is working up the courage to come after you."

Apprehension clawing at her, she shook her head, immediately rejecting the idea even as it struck a chord deep inside her. "None of this makes any sense. Why me?"

Blake shrugged. "Who knows? You're in the public eye. You're a fighter. You live off the St. Mary's strip and look great in red. There's no telling what's going on in this guy's head. But he knows where you work and there's a good possibility he knows where you live since he's getting closer to your front door with every killing. The McClintock woman lived ten miles away from you, Tanya Bishop only four. And this one's practically right around the corner."

It was, in fact, a little over a mile and a half from her place to Elizabeth Reagan's, but that was still too close for comfort. "That could just be coincidence," she began desperately.

Blake swore in frustration, wanting to shake her. "C'mon, Sabrina, you don't believe that anymore than I do! This crackpot's after you and he's going to get you if you don't do something to protect yourself. Dammit, Kelly, talk to her before she gets herself killed!"

Raising a brow at the sudden tension crackling between the two reporters, the detective watched them glare at each other and forced back a smile. "I hate to sound like a parrot, but he is right, Sabrina," he told her. "For your own protection, you might consider letting someone else cover the murders until we can catch the jerk. Preferably a man."

"And let that murdering slimeball dictate to me how I can live my life?" she gasped. "Never in a million years! Would you expect a man to do that?"

"You wouldn't be in this fix if you were a man," Blake answered for him. "But that's okay. You go ahead and risk your pretty little neck just to prove a point to a madman. When we plant you six feet under, we'll have it carved on your tombstone that you went to your grave a martyr for women's rights."

"I'm not proving a point—I'm just doing my job." Exasperated, she turned to Sam. "Is there anything else we need to discuss? If not, I need to get to the paper and get this written up so it'll make the morning edition."

He hesitated, obviously wanting to add his two cents to Blake's comments, but he only sighed and gave in in defeat. "No, go on. But I want to see you down at the station first thing in the morning with the names of everyone you ever knew who might have a grudge against you. I don't care if it was some jerk in college who didn't like working with you on the school paper—I want his name. Got it?"

She nodded. "I'll come up with a list tonight." Not sparing Blake a glance, she turned on her heel, stepped outside and headed for her car.

Blake almost let her get away with it. Then he remembered a kiss that just over an hour ago had rocked him back on his heels. The lady might think she could take care of herself, but he'd held her in his arms and knew just how delicate and vulnerable she was. He didn't even want to think about what a bullet shot at point-blank range from the gun of a crazy could do to her. His jaw hard with resolve, he started after her.

He caught up with her just past the outer fringes of the grim-faced, silent crowd that still stood on the perimeter of the front yard. "Wait just a damn minute, Jones," he growled as the shadows of the night swallowed them whole. "I've got a bone to pick with you."

She didn't even slow her pace. "I've already said all I have to say to you, Nickels. Don't even think about getting in my way."

With two quick strides, he was not only in her way, he was blocking it. "You're either crazy as a loon or you've got a death wish—I haven't decided which," he muttered. "Stand still, will you?"

"I'm in a hurry, Blake. Unlike you, I seem to be the only one around here concerned with a deadline."

"Oh, I'm aware of it, all right. It's just that some things are a little bit more important than making the morning edition."

"Like what?"

"Your life."

"We've been all over this, Nickels," she said, letting her breath out in a huff. "There's nothing left to say."

"Maybe not," he agreed, surprising her, "but I'm going to say it anyway. For what it's worth, Jones, I used to be like you, obsessed with a story—"

"I'm not obsessed!"

"Then a snitch got killed because of something he told me," he continued as if she hadn't spoken. "It was my fault."

Stunned, she gasped, her eyes wide with instant sympathy. "Blake, no! You shouldn't blame yourself. You're not responsible."

"I lost my objectivity," he said simply, making no excuses for himself. "I was so determined to get the story that I didn't even realize I was putting that kid in danger. I don't want you to do the same thing."

"But this is different."

"Is it?" he asked sardonically. "Think about it."

"It isn't just the story," she said earnestly. "It's the principle of the thing. You wouldn't let a murdering piece of trash scare you off a story and I can't either. Because if I do, the word'll be all over the street that all you have to do is threaten Sabrina Jones when she gets too close to a story and she'll fold like a deck of cards. I might as well go back to obits because they're the only stories I'll be able to dig up."

He winced at the play on words, but he didn't smile. Not about this. "You won't dig up any stories with a bullet in your heart, either. Have you thought about that?"

"That's a chance I'll have to take."

"Dammit, Sabrina, you take chances at the horse races, not with your life. I don't like the idea of you traipsing all over the city with a killer on your tail."

"I don't like it, either," she said. "But it's not going to stop me from doing what I have to do." Suddenly suspicious, she studied him through narrowed eyes. "You're not getting all bent out of shape over this because of that kiss, are you? It was just a kiss, Blake. Nothing else. It didn't give you any rights where I'm concerned, so don't start getting any ideas."

Normally, Blake would have agreed with her and thanked God that she was being so levelheaded over what he'd intended as nothing more than an impulsive kiss. But somewhere between his intentions and the execution of the kiss itself, things had gotten out of hand. Her response had nearly blown the top of his head off, and her casual dismissal of that irritated him to no end. If she hadn't wanted him to get any ideas, she damn sure shouldn't have kissed him the way she had!

"That wasn't *just* a kiss and you damn well know it," he said huskily, his green eyes dark with temper. "You forgot what planet you were on, and so did I."

"I did not!"

"Little liar," he retorted softly, taking a step toward her. "Shall I prove it to you?"

He would have done it, right then and there, but she never gave him the chance. Lightning-quick, she shied out of reach. "Oh, no, you don't! You stay away from me, Blake Nickels!" she warned, throwing up a hand to hold him at bay as she walked backwards away from him. "Do you hear me? You just keep your distance, and we'll both get along fine. I've got a job to do, and so do you, and we're not going to complicate the situation by getting involved. So just stay away from me."

She reached her car then, and darted around it like the devil himself was after her. Letting her go, Blake watched her climb inside and drive away and didn't know whether to laugh or curse. Didn't she know that he'd tried staying away from her from the very beginning? He wasn't looking for the entanglement of a relationship any more than she apparently was. Fate, however, seemed to have other ideas.

The note left at Sabrina's desk was splashed across the front page of the *Daily Record* the next day, and the phones at the police station were swamped with calls from people who were sure they knew who the murderer was. Two days after that, the report on the note found at the scene of Elizabeth Reagan's murder came back from the lab and confirmed what everyone had already suspected—it was exactly like the one found at the *Record*. Written on paper that could have been bought at any one of a hundred or more office-supply stores in the city, it was wiped clean of fingerprints and any clues that might have led to the identity of its author.

With no murder weapon, no witnesses, and none of the phone calls to the police panning out, Blake did what he did best—he went looking for leads. And he started with the victims. Figuring there had to be some kind of connection between the three women, he checked out their hobbies, any clubs or associations they belonged to, even their churches. And everywhere he turned, he reached a dead end. Frustrated, he was left with no choice but to hit the streets and start making friends with snitches and other lowlifes that were in a position to know what was going down in the city.

He didn't like it. Even though he knew that the chances that the past would repeat itself were slim to none, he wanted nothing to do with informants. That, unfortunately, was a luxury he didn't have—not if he wanted to keep up with Sabrina.

The lady really was incredible. And as much as he hated to admit it, she kept him on his toes and pushed him to do his best work. She covered the city like a blanket, digging up stories on everything from a drug ring and money-laundering scheme on the west side to embezzlement at city hall. He couldn't go anywhere without running into her or hearing that she'd already been there and gone. He found himself looking for her everywhere he went and reading his own work with a critical eye, comparing it to hers. Their styles were different—who could say whose was better? His was grittier, yet hers was just as compelling. With a simplicity that he couldn't help but admire, she pulled the reader into a story and didn't let him go until he reached the end.

If she hadn't worked for the competition, Blake would have subscribed to the *Daily Record* just to read her stuff. As it was, he couldn't do that without helping her win their bet, and that was something he was determined not to do. So he had to be content with picking up the *Record* in coffee shops whenever he could and sneaking a peak at her work so he could tease her about it when he saw her.

And he did see her, in spite of her best efforts to avoid him. In the week after Elizabeth Reagan died, they ran into each other often, but Sabrina was as wary as a kitten

with a thorn in its paw. If she saw him first, she cut a wide
swath around him and left just as soon as she could. If he
surprised her and approached her before she knew he was
anywhere within a ten-mile area, she kept the conversation
strictly professional and just dared him to bring up the
subject of a certain kiss. He didn't. But the knowledge was
there between them every time their eyes met.

Grinning at the memory, Blake dragged his attention
back to the grumblings of the snitch who'd insisted on
meeting him at an out-of-the-way bar on the east side. The
place was a dive and smelled like it. Blake wouldn't have
touched a drink there if his life had depended on it, but the
bar's other occupants weren't nearly as particular.

Watching Jimmy, his snitch, pour rotgut down his throat,
Blake wondered how the man had any lining left in his
stomach. "Okay, spill your guts, man. What's the word on
the street?"

"Nothing," Jimmy claimed, wiping his mouth with
the back of his hand. "Honest. Whoever's knocking off
those broads is doing it with a clean piece. I've talked to
everybody I know and no one sold a hot shooter to the nut
case. He already had it or he bought it legit."

Blake swore. He'd figured as much, but with a serial
killer on the loose, you couldn't take anything for granted.
Jimmy had connections in most of the hellholes in the city.
If someone out there had sold a stolen gun to the killer,
he would have heard about it. "That's what I was afraid
of, but thanks for asking around. If you hear anything—I
mean anything—let me know. And get yourself something
to eat. You're skinnier than a fence post."

Taking the bill Blake slid him, he grinned, exposing
crooked yellow teeth, and snatched at the money as if he

was afraid it was going to disappear any second. "Sure thing, man. Later."

He was gone, slipping away and into the shadows of the bar between one instant and the next. Shaking his head over the man's ability to fade into the woodwork, Blake did a disappearing act of his own and headed outside to his car.

His thoughts still on the gun, he was heading back to the paper when the crackling report on his police scanner finally penetrated his concentration. Someone had called in a mugging at an ATM machine. Normally, he wouldn't have bothered to cover such a minor crime, but it wasn't the crime itself that interested him—it was the location. It was just a couple of miles from where Sabrina lived.

Later, he would have sworn he never made a conscious decision to check it out, but he turned right instead of left at the next intersection and found himself heading for the near northside. It only took him minutes to get there, but the police were already there, blocking the parking lot where the ATM was located, leaving him no choice but to find a spot around the corner to park. Not surprisingly, Sabrina's red Honda was already there.

The minute his gaze landed on the sporty little car, he knew he was in trouble. Because it wasn't, as it should have been, the story that had brought him to that part of town. It was the possibility of seeing Sabrina Jones.

In the process of interviewing the victim, Thelma Walters, an elderly neighbor who was surprised by the mugger when she stopped at the ATM to get money for groceries, Sabrina glanced up and felt her heart constrict at the sight of Blake slowly walking toward her. The smile that usually flirted with his mouth was noticeably absent, and in his eyes was something—a heat, a dark intensity—that was aimed right at her. Her mouth suddenly dry, she couldn't remember what she was going to ask next.

"Is something wrong, sweetie?" Mrs. Walters asked suddenly, reaching out to feel her forehead. "You're awfully flushed all of a sudden. Are you feeling all right? Maybe you've been out in the sun too long."

Her blush deepening, Sabrina blinked her friend back into focus. "Sorry," she said, forcing a laugh. "I guess I just drifted off. It must be this heat. It is awfully hot today." Fanning herself, she struggled to concentrate. "Now, about the mugger. I understand you caught him all by yourself after he took off running with your purse. The police said you threw a rock and hit him in the head?"

Pleased with herself, Thelma Walters laughed gaily. "It was more like a pebble than a rock, but yes, I beaned him one in the noggin. He glanced over his shoulder to see what had hit him and ran right into a security officer from the apartments across the street who heard my cries for help." Grinning, she confided, "I used to be a softball pitcher in high school, but it's been fifty years since I threw a ball. I guess I've still got it, huh?"

"You can be on my team any day of the week," Sabrina said, chuckling. "You did get your money back, didn't you?"

"Every penny," the older woman said proudly. "The next time that young man decides to go after a senior citizen, he'd better think twice about it. We're not all old fogies sitting around waiting to die."

Her lips twitching, Sabrina promised to include that little tidbit of information in the story. "Well, that's a wrap, Thelma. Thanks. You want me to call someone to come and get you? I know you weren't hurt, but finding yourself face-to-face with a mugger would shake up just about anyone. Maybe you shouldn't drive."

Her eyes crinkling, the older woman held out her hand to show her she was steady as a rock. "I'm fine, sweetie," she confided, "but if you don't mind, I'm going to see if I can talk one of those good-looking policemen to take me home. I noticed the blonde wasn't wearing a wedding ring, and my niece, Jenny, is looking for a good man."

"Well, then, hey, don't let me get in your way." Sabrina laughed as she stepped back and motioned for her to preceed her. "Go get him, girl."

She was still grinning when Blake strolled over and joined her. Her heart, remembering a kiss she had tried her damndest to forget, knocked out an irregular rhythm in greeting. Annoyed with herself, she lifted a brow at him and gave him a smile guaranteed to set his teeth on edge. "You having a slow day or what, cowboy? These types of stories are usually beneath a superstar like you."

His eyes glinting in appreciation of the dig, he shoved his hands in his pants pockets and rocked back on his heels. "That's funny. I was just about to say the same thing about you, sweetheart. And the last I heard, you were the only superstar around here. When I first came here, all anyone ever talked about was the great Sabrina Jones. For a while there, you really had me shaking in my shoes."

She might have been pleased if he hadn't begun the admission with a qualifying phrase. "For a while," she repeated, her smile tightening ever so slightly. "But not now?"

Delighted that she'd asked, he grinned. "Do I look like I'm worried?"

No, he didn't, she had to admit, irked. In fact, she'd never seen a man who appeared less worried. Loose-limbed and relaxed in jeans and a polo shirt, his dark hair windswept by the afternoon breeze, he looked as if he didn't have a care in the world. If he was concerned about losing their bet at the end of the month, he certainly didn't show it.

Perversely irritated, she said, "For your information, Nickels, I happen to know the victim. She called me right after she called the police. Now that we know why I'm here, what's *your* excuse?"

Opting for the truth, knowing she wouldn't believe him, he teased, "I figured you'd be here, since it was so close to where you live, and I couldn't pass up the chance to see you again. We haven't talked much the last week. Did you miss me?"

"Like a dog misses a flea," she tossed back, not batting an eye. "Why don't you do us both a favor and go back to sports? This town's not big enough for the two of us to both cover crime."

"Then we've got a problem," he said with a chuckle, "because I'm not going anywhere. Anyway, I kind of like running into you just about everywhere I go." Her words suddenly registering, his grin broadened. "Why, Jones, you had me checked out! I'm touched."

She laughed, she couldn't help it, and cursed her slip of the tongue. Damn the man, did he have to be so charming? Lifting her chin, she said, "Don't go jumping to conclusions. Of course I checked you out. I'm a reporter. That's what I do for a living."

She might as well have saved her breath. "Yeah, yeah," he teased. "That's what they all say. Why don't you just admit it, honey? You're crazy about me."

"Me and half the female population of S.A.," she retorted, going along with him. "I bet you can't go anywhere without beating the women off with a stick."

His green eyes dancing, he shrugged modestly. "It's rough, Jones, but I somehow manage to make time for all of them. Shall I pencil you in for Saturday night? It's the only night I've got free this week."

"And I'm busy. Darn! Isn't that the pits?"

"Yeah," Blake drawled, enjoying himself. "I can see you're real broke up about it."

"Oh, I am," she claimed with mock seriousness that was ruined by the smile that tugged insistently at her lips. "I just don't know how I'll get through the rest of the day."

"Oh, I'm sure you'll manage. You can always bury yourself in your work."

"True," she agreed. "And speaking of work, I guess I'd better get back to it." Reaching up, impish mischief sparkling in her eyes, she dared to pat him on the cheek. "See you around, Nickels."

Letting her go, Blake grinned. Little witch. It would serve her right if he snatched her up and laid a kiss on that beautiful mouth of hers. But the next time he kissed the lady—and there would be a next time; he had no doubts about it—he wanted her all to himself, preferably in a dark, secluded place where he could take his time with her. Then they'd see just who was crazy about whom. But for now, there was work to do.

It didn't take him long to get Thelma Walters's side of the story—thoroughly enjoying the attention, she was only too eager to talk about the mugging. Her attacker, however, was a little more tight-lipped; the arresting officer had to supply the thug's name and the information that he had a long record.

Armed with that, Blake had all he needed. And so, apparently, did Sabrina. He saw her heading for her car, which was parked around the corner near his, and fell into step beside her. "Now that we're through with that," he said easily as they rounded the corner, "why don't we grab something to eat? I know this great little Chinese place right down the street."

"Sorry, Nickels. I can't. I—"

Whatever she was going to say next seemed to stick in her throat. Puzzled, Blake frowned down at her. "You okay, Jones? You're looking a little strange around the gills."

Strangling on a laugh, she said, "I'm sorry. I know I shouldn't laugh. It's really *not* funny—"

"What?"

Unable to manage another word, she only shook her head and pointed down the street. His eyes following the direction of her finger, Blake didn't see anything at first to explain her amusement. Then his gaze landed on his pickup.

Someone had set it up on blocks and stolen the two rear tires.

"Dammit to hell!"

Sabrina tried, she really did, to summon up some sympathy, but she was fighting a losing battle. Muffled laughter bubbling up inside her like a spring, she bent over at the waist and buried her face in her hands, whooping for all she was worth. "I'm sorry," she choked, giggling as she wiped at the tears that streamed from her eyes. "Really, I am! But if you could just see your face…"

He scowled at her, and that set her off again. "Stop it, Blake. You're killing me!"

"I ought to kill you," he retorted, his lips twitching in spite of his best efforts to appear stern. "What kind of neighborhood is this, anyway? Those were brand-new tires!"

"Well, I should hope so." She laughed. "What's the point

of stealing old ones? Dammit, Blake, don't you know better than to drive a new truck into this part of town?"

"Apparently not," he said dryly. "I guess I'll have to get an old clunker like yours."

Smirking, she retorted, "At least I don't get my tires stolen in the middle of the day. C'mon, I'll give you a ride to my place and you can call a wrecker from there. It looks like you're going to need one."

She'd only meant to offer a helping hand to make up for laughing, but the minute Blake followed her inside her house, she knew she'd made a mistake in bringing him there. The small two-bedroom home her grandmother had given her when she'd married husband number five was her personal space, a retreat from work and crime and the senseless violence she made a living from in the streets. As she watched Blake look around the living room with interest, she knew she would see him there long after he left.

Panic hit her then, right in the heart, shaking her. Lord, what was wrong with her? He had kissed her one stinking time—*one time*—and she hadn't been able to get him out of her head since. She had to stop this, dammit! She wasn't the type to moon over a man, especially one like Blake Nickels, and she wasn't going to start now. Still, she couldn't help noticing how right he looked in her house.

You're losing it, Sabrina. Really losing it. Shaking her head over her own fanciful thoughts, she motioned to the old-fashioned, Forties-style rotary on the small table at the far end of the couch. "The phone's right there. It'll probably take a tow truck a while to get here. Would you like some iced tea while you're waiting?"

"Oh, don't go to any bother," Blake began, but he might

as well have saved his breath. She was already gone, heading for the kitchen as if the hounds of hell were after her. Staring after her, his lips twitched into a smile. He'd never seen her nervous before, but she was showing definite signs of it now. And he had to ask himself why. If he'd been the conceited type, he might have wondered if it had something to do with him.

Grinning at the thought, he strode over to the phone and called information for the number to the garage down the street from his apartment. Placing the call, it took him only minutes to explain the situation and request a tow truck.

Sabrina was still in the kitchen when he hung up, and he couldn't resist the urge to look around. Reasoning that he wasn't going to go through her drawers or anything, he found himself wandering over to the photographs that covered nearly all of one wall. Most of them were wedding pictures taken over the course of what looked like half a century, if the style of dress of the wedding guests was anything to go by.

"They're something else, aren't they?" Sabrina said as she returned to the living room with a glass of iced tea in each hand. Strolling over to him, she handed him his glass and nodded at the picture of a beaming older couple he was studying. Standing on the deck of a ship before a judge, they were dressed in full scuba gear, complete with masks. "That's Grandma and Grandpa Bill," she said, smiling fondly. "Number four."

"Number four?" Blake repeated, lifting a brow in inquiry. "Number four what?"

"Husband number four," she explained. "Grandma likes to get around."

His brow climbed higher at that. "Your grandmother's been married *four* times?"

"No, actually it was five at last count. Well, six, if you count Grandpa Mason," she amended. "She married him twice."

Amazed, Blake turned back to the wedding pictures and frowned, unconsciously counting them. "But there's more than six wedding pictures here."

"Oh, not all of those are Grandma." She laughed. "The rest are Mama. She favors Grandma a great deal, don't you think? In fact, Grandpa Harry said the two of them looked so much alike that they could have passed for twins if they'd been closer in age. It's a shame he and Grandma didn't stay together. I really liked him. But he had this daughter who couldn't stand Grandma, so that was the end of that."

"He divorced her?"

She nodded. "Six months after they married. Grandma was heartbroken until Chester came along."

"Then why is his picture still with the rest? I would have thought she'd have tossed it out."

"Oh, Grandma doesn't hold grudges. Once your picture goes up on the wall, you're up there for life."

Blake almost laughed. She had to be kidding. But there was no question that the wedding pictures were legit. Frowning, he said, "Just for the record, how many times have your mother and grandmother been married?"

Sabrina didn't even have to count. "Eight and holding—if you don't count Grandpa Mason twice. Of, course, things could change at any time. Mom's in Alaska with Hank right now, and Grandma's touring the country with Grandpa George, and I haven't heard from any of them in a while. If there's a shift in the wind, who knows what can happen?"

It wasn't something to brag about, but Sabrina had

learned a long time ago not to apologize for it, either. Her mother and grandmother were what they were, and there was nothing she could do to change that. At this late date, she wouldn't even try, but there were times, like now, when she could use their atrocious number of divorces to make a point.

"The women in my family are very good at saying 'I do,'" she said quietly. "They're just lousy at commitment, and it's not even something they can help. It's a defective gene, and the only cure for it is not to get married."

Her tone was light, amused, almost facetious, but as she watched Blake frown, she knew he'd gotten the message. If he was looking for a relationship, he could look somewhere else. She wasn't interested.

Chapter 5

She should have been pleased that she'd made her point and he didn't give her an argument about it. But long after Blake left with the tow-truck driver who stopped by to give him a ride to the garage where he would take his pickup, Sabrina stood in her front yard, frowning as she stared down the street after him. She felt sure he wouldn't try to kiss her again. Why didn't that bring the relief she'd expected it to?

"Somebody having trouble?" Louis asked as he passed by on the sidewalk with his Lab, Lady. "I thought I saw a tow truck stop here."

Jerking out of her musings, Sabrina summoned a smile. "Oh, hi, Louis. Yeah, there was a wrecker here. Mrs. Walters was mugged at the ATM on McCullough when a mugger tried to rob her. While Blake and I were covering the story, somebody stole the back tires off his pickup."

"In broad daylight?" Louis exclaimed. "And no one saw anything?"

"Well, I don't know about that," Sabrina said dryly. "A mockingbird can't land on the back fence without old lady Charleston seeing it two blocks over, so I thought I'd ask around and see what I could find out. If you happen to see two slightly used Michelins lying around while you're walking Lady, let me know, will you?"

"I'll keep my eyes open," he promised. "But if I were you, I'd check first with that Gomez kid down on the corner. From what I've seen, he's a little thug. The police have already questioned him a number of times about several robberies in the area. Stealing tires sounds like something that'd be right up his alley."

Sabrina nodded. She'd been thinking the same thing herself. "You might be right. I think I'll check him out right now."

"Be careful," he warned as Lady grew impatient and started to tug him farther down the street. "With someone like that, you never can be sure of what he's capable of."

That might have been true of someone else, but Sabrina had known Joe Gomez since he'd been in grade school. Despite the fact that he was a gang member with a reputation for stealing just for the heck of it, he had a twisted code of ethics when it came to robbing his own neighbors. He just didn't do it. But that didn't mean he wouldn't know who did.

Heading up the street, she approached the Gomez house cautiously, more out of respect for Killer, the Rottweiler that was usually chained to the tree in the front yard, than because of any fear of Joe. The dog, however, was nowhere in sight. Relieved, she strode boldly up onto the front porch and knocked on the weathered siding next to the wrought-iron grillwork that covered the front door.

Deep in the bowels of the old wood-frame house, she heard Killer's fierce growl and a terse command to knock it off. Then Joe was opening the door and looking at her as if he'd just found his favorite centerfold on his threshold. Seventeen and full of himself, he propped a shoulder against the doorjamb and looked her up and down with wicked, dancing eyes. "If you've come to borrow a cup of sugar, I'm the only sweet thing in the house." Grinning, he held his arms wide. "Take me. I'm yours."

Sabrina laughed and shook her head at him. It was an old joke between them, his flirting with her, and she never took him seriously. She liked his sense of humor and enjoyed jawing with him, but even if he hadn't been ten years her junior, she wouldn't have been interested in Joe. The teenage girls that followed him around like puppies might be impressed with his flagrant macho antics, but Sabrina didn't find them the least attractive and would have never stood for them from any man, young or old.

"Sorry, Joe, but I'm on a diet. No sweets allowed."

"Well, hell, honey, don't let that stop you. Cheat."

"I don't think so," she said, grinning. "Anyway, that's not why I'm here."

Just that quickly, his smile vanished. "Oh, boy, here it comes," he groaned. "The third degree about that mugging over on McCullough." Glancing over his shoulder to make sure his grandmother had heard nothing of the conversation, he quickly stepped outside and shut the door behind him. "You think I had something to do with it, don't you? Just because I knew old lady Walters stopped there every Monday to get money for her bratty grandson doesn't mean I told anyone about it."

Amused, Sabrina lifted a brow at him. "You sound just the teensiest bit defensive, Joe. Did I accuse you of anything?"

"No, but—"

"*Should* I be accusing you of anything?"

"No!"

"Then what's the problem? The mugger was caught. I just wanted to talk to you about some tires."

"Tires?" he echoed, frowning. "Now what would I know about tires?"

Another reporter might have been fooled by the scowl and innocent tone he adopted in the blink of an eye, but Sabrina had known him too long to be taken in by such a display. Grinning in appreciation of the act, though, she said lightly, "Oh, nothing. I just thought you might put the word out for me that two Michelins taken off a certain black, 4X4 Chevy pickup belonged to a friend of mine."

"No kidding? You talking about that tall dude that was down here earlier in the day? Somebody stole his tires?"

"Apparently so. And I'd really appreciate it if they were returned."

Slipping his hands into the back pockets of his tattered jeans, he rocked back and forth on his heels, considering the matter with a twinkle in his eye. "I don't know anyone who's into that kind of thing, you understand," he finally confided, "but I can see how tempting two new tires would be to someone running around on retreads. Life's tough, you know."

Sabrina just barely managed to hold back a smile. "And two new tires don't come rolling by every day. You think if I offered a reward it might convince whoever took them to give them up?"

At first, she thought he was going to jump at that, but

after careful thought, he shook his head. "Nope, that'd only encourage whoever did this to try it again. Just sit tight. I'll drop a hint in a few ears."

That was all Sabrina could ask for. Beaming, she said, "Thanks, Joe. I knew I could count on you."

"Yeah, yeah," he snorted. "I'm a regular prince."

"That's what all the young girls around here say," she said with a laugh as she took the porch steps. "'Bye, Joe. Behave yourself."

He wouldn't—the kid just didn't seem to have it in him—but he would do as he promised. And that was all Sabrina could ask for.

When she came home from work late the following afternoon, the tires were sitting on her front porch with a big red bow on them. And suddenly a day that hadn't been all that good got better. Pulling into her driveway, Sabrina laughed. Glancing down to the corner, she thought she saw a movement in an upstairs window at Joe's grandmother's house. It was Joe, of course, but she knew he wouldn't come out for her thanks, or even admit that he was the one responsible for getting the tires back—that would clash with his bad-boy image. But without his help, those tires would be on the back of somebody's low-rider, and they both knew it. Waving gaily, she saw the curtain swish again and grinned.

Five minutes later, she was headed for Blake's place with the tires loaded in the trunk of her Honda. She'd leave them by his front door, she decided, and let him wonder how they had gotten there. It would drive him nuts. Her eyes starting to sparkle at the thought, she turned into his apartment complex and found a parking spot within a few feet of the stairs to his second-floor apartment. Seconds later, she was rolling the first tire up the steps.

As quiet as a mouse, she propped it against the doorjamb, then went back to her car for the second. She would have sworn she didn't make a sound, but just as she leaned the second tire against the first one, the door was suddenly jerked open and both tires fell across the threshold with a soft thud. Caught red-handed, she glanced up, a quick explanation already forming on her tongue, only to find herself face-to-face with Blake's grandfather.

"Oh! Mr. Finnigan! You startled me. I didn't think anyone was here."

"Pop," he automatically corrected her. "I thought you were Blake." His green eyes, so like his grandson's, lit with mischief as his gaze slid from her to the tires and back again. "You know, in my day, I had a few women surprise me with a cake or two, but I don't believe one ever showed up on my doorstep with a load of tires. Have you got a car hidden somewhere to go with those?"

Sabrina laughed. "No, but Blake does. These are his— the ones stolen off his truck yesterday. They sort of showed up on my doorstep."

"Just like that?" he asked, arching a brow at her. "Why do I have a feeling you're leaving something out?"

"Well, I did sort of feel responsible since it happened in my neighborhood," she admitted. "So I put the word out that Blake was a friend and I'd like them back. But I'd prefer that he didn't know that," she added quickly.

"Didn't know what? That you consider him a friend or that you're the one who got his tires back for him?"

He was, Sabrina thought, fighting a blush, altogether too sharp for her peace of mind. "Let's just say this is our little secret," she suggested with a smile. "I wouldn't want

Blake to feel beholden or anything. Especially since we're both usually fighting for the same stories. He might feel like he has to step back and let me have an exclusive, and that's not what I want."

"You want to beat him fair and square at his own game." It wasn't a question, but a statement from a man who obviously read her like a book. Grinning, he pulled the door wider. "I like your style, missy. Since Blake's not going to be able to thank you for the tires, the least I can do is offer you a drink after you carted those dirty things up the stairs in this heat. Come on in."

"Oh, that's not necessary," she began.

"Then humor an old man," he said with a shrug, blatantly playing on her sympathies. "I don't get a chance to talk to a pretty girl very often. Blake doesn't bring too many home, and when he does, they're not interested in jawing with an old geezer like me."

The pitiful look might have worked on somebody else, but Sabrina wasn't buying it. "Nice try, Finnigan, but somehow you don't strike me as a lonely old man who roams around an empty house talking to himself all day. You've lived here all your life, haven't you? You probably know more people than God."

Laughter deepening the wrinkles lining his weathered face, he nodded. "Probably. But most of them are on the downhill side of seventy, and all they want to talk about is aches and pains and where they've got their money invested. I bet you can tell some stories that are a sight more interesting than that. So, you coming in or not?"

She should have said "Thanks, but no thanks," then come up with a quick excuse to get out of there. She already knew all she wanted to know about Blake Nickels—he kissed like something out of one of her dreams—and the less she saw of him and his family, the better. But she really did like his grandfather, and what harm could a few minutes do?

"Well, it is hot, and I would like to wash my hands," she said, finding more excuses than she needed to ignore her common sense. "But I can't stay long."

Thirty minutes later, she was still there. Sitting at Blake's kitchen table and on her second glass of iced tea, she couldn't remember the last time she'd enjoyed herself more. Pop Finnigan had a real gift for storytelling, and more than once, she laughed so hard, she cried. He told her outlandish tales about his stint in the navy as a cook and his travels around the world, stories, she was sure, that he'd carefully edited for her delicate ears. She could have told him that there wasn't much she hadn't heard covering crime in some of the city's worst neighborhoods, but she appreciated his old-fashioned courtliness. He was a wonderful old man and Blake was lucky to have him for a grandfather.

He was also sneaky as a fox. Without Sabrina quite realizing how it happened, he cunningly shifted the focus of the conversation to Blake. One minute he was telling her about shore leave in Italy, and the next, he was confiding that as a child, Blake had traveled all over the world with his parents, who were career diplomats.

"That kid had a ball," he said with a grin. "He could speak French and German fluently by the time he was eight and knew Rome like the back of his hand when he was fourteen. Karen—that's my daughter—really thought he would go into politics." Laughing softly at the thought, he shook his head. "She'd better thank her lucky stars he didn't. Blake always did have a nose for secrets. With all the intrigue in international politics, he would have asked questions he had no business asking and ended up starting a war or something by now. The kid's a born reporter."

"I'll give him his due," Sabrina said, eyeing him knowingly. "He does seem to know what he's doing."

"You're darn right he does," the old man agreed promptly. "He always knew what he wanted and went after it. Of course, his mother still thinks this writing stuff is an act of rebellion on his part, but you won't find a better man anywhere. When Karen and Richard got assigned to France for a year, she had this crazy notion that I was too old to live alone. I told her I was just fine, thank you very much, but you know how daughters are. She worried, so Blake quit his job in New Mexico and moved here to watch over me. I told him I didn't need a baby-sitter, but he still checks in with me every day. I know what he's doing, of course, but I don't say anything because I don't want Karen to worry."

Fighting a smile, Sabrina nodded solemnly. "Of course. I'm sure your daughter sleeps a lot easier at night knowing Blake is here to watch over you."

"Sure she does. She'd sleep a lot better, though, if he'd settle down with a wife and a couple of kids. A man his age needs a good woman in his life, don't you think?"

A blatant matchmaker, he winked at her, just daring her to disagree with him, and it was all Sabrina could do not to laugh.

Lord, he was outrageous—and as bold as his grandson! She didn't have the heart to tell him that he was talking to the wrong woman. "Mr. Finnigan—"

"Pop," he corrected her, flashing his dimples at her.

"Pop," she repeated with a smile. "Blake's marital status is really none of my business—"

"It could be."

"Stop that!" Sabrina laughed. "If Blake wanted a wife and children, I'm sure he'd have them. You said yourself that he always knew what he wanted and went after it. Anyway, that has nothing to do with me. I just came over to deliver his tires. And now that I've done that, I really do need to get out of here."

He tried to talk her into staying a little longer, but she was adamant. Thanking him for the tea and the entertaining conversation, she headed for the door. But she'd waited too long. The sound of a key in the lock stopped her in her tracks. A split second later, Blake pushed open the door with his shoulder and stepped into the apartment carrying the two tires she'd left on his doorstep.

Surprised, he lifted a brow at the sight of her as a slow smile stretched across his face. "Well, look who's here. And you came bearing gifts. At least I assume I have you to thank for these," he said, dropping the Michelins on the floor next to the door. "And I didn't think you cared, Jones. That just goes to show you how wrong a man can be about a woman."

"Don't let it go to your head, cowboy," Sabrina returned sweetly. "I just didn't want you to have an excuse when I won our bet."

Pop, watching them with a broad grin, stepped into the conversation at that. "Bet? What bet?"

"We have a little wager over who can bring in the most new subscribers by the end of the month," Blake informed him without ever taking his eyes off Sabrina. "Right now, I'd say it's a dead heat."

"In your dreams," Sabrina snorted. "I just checked the numbers this morning, and I've got nothing to worry about where you're concerned, Nickels. I'm so far ahead of you, you'll never catch up."

Not the last bit concerned, he only grinned. "I'm a patient man, sweetheart. And the month's not over with yet. With a little luck, you just might have to eat those words, not to mention buy me the thickest steak in town."

"Speaking of which," his grandfather cut in smoothly, "I think I smell my roast cooking. How about staying for dinner, Sabrina? There's plenty."

"Oh, no," she began. "I couldn't."

"What's the matter?" Blake teased. "Scared of breaking bread with the competition?"

"No, of course not!"

"Maybe she has another date," his grandfather supplied.

"No—"

"Then there's no reason why you can't stay," Blake said easily. "After all, feeding you is the least I can do after you got my tires back for me."

Put that way, there was no way she could gracefully refuse, and he knew it. "All right, all right," she said, laughing. "I'll stay. I just feel guilty about showing up here at suppertime without an invitation. I should have waited until later."

"That's okay," Blake assured her, his smile crooked. "If it'll make you feel any better, we'll make you work for it. You can do the dishes."

The meal that followed was one that Sabrina knew she would remember until her dying day. The food was delicious, but it was the company that was superb. Unlike most men she knew, who were reluctant to show their emotions, Blake made no attempt to hide his affection for his grandfather. And the old man was just as affectionate with Blake. They teased and cut up and traded stories about each other until Sabrina could hardly eat for laughing. Long after the meal was finished and the roast was just a memory, they sat at the table talking and reminiscing about old times, fascinating Sabrina. Enthralled, she could have sat there for hours and just listened to them talk.

Which was, in fact, what she did. No one was more surprised than she when she glanced at her watch and saw how late it was. "Oh, my God, it's going on ten o'clock! And I still haven't done the dishes yet."

"You don't have to do that," Pop said when she jumped up and started collecting the dirty plates. "Blake was just teasing."

"Oh, but it's the least I can do," she argued. "I can't remember the last time I had such a wonderful meal. It was delicious, Pop."

Pleased, he grinned. "I'm glad you liked it. You'll have to come again. Won't she, Blake?"

Blake, recognizing the mischievous glint in his grandfather's eyes, shot him a quelling look behind Sabrina's back, and said easily, "Sure. Maybe next time, you can make that stuffed-pig dish you learned to make in Fiji."

"I don't know," the old man said. "That sort of smokes up the house. And I wouldn't want to go to all that trouble when you never know when you're going to be called out on a story. Maybe you should just take her out instead."

"Oh, no, that's not necessary—"

"Pop—"

Ignoring Sabrina's automatic refusal and his grandson's warning tone, the old man said innocently, "Weren't you looking for someone to go with you to the awards ceremony at the National Newspaper Convention next weekend?

Sabrina's probably going, too, so why don't you go together? It seems kind of dumb to go in two cars."

Under ordinary circumstances, Blake would have agreed. If he and Sabrina had just been rivals, he wouldn't have hesitated to suggest the same thing. Just because they worked for competitive papers didn't mean they couldn't be friends. But there was nothing friendly about that kiss they'd shared or the way the memory of it made him ache in the middle of the night. He was having a damn difficult time getting her out of his head, and taking her out, even to an awards ceremony, would only make the situation worse.

But before he could think of an acceptable reason to sidestep his grandfather's suggestion, Sabrina came up with one for him. "Thanks for the offer, Pop, but I wasn't even planning on going. I don't get much out of those kind of things, and even if I did go, I'd sit with the *Daily Record* staff. Arriving with Blake could be…awkward."

As far as excuses went, it was a good one, and Blake knew he should have been thanking his lucky stars for it. But she'd come up with it damn quick. And what the hell did she mean…arriving with him could be *awkward?* He was no Cary Grant, but he wasn't some homeless guy off the street, either. He knew a lot of women who would jump at the chance to go out with him!

Perversely irritated, his ego bruised, he should have let it go. But a man had his pride, dammit, and she'd just stepped all over his. "Why don't you tell him the real reason you don't want to go with me?" he challenged her. "This has nothing to do with work or your boss and co-workers seeing you with me. You're chicken."

It was the wrong thing to say to a woman who prided herself on being gutsy. Gasping as if he'd slapped her, she carefully set the dirty plates she'd collected back on the table, drew herself up to her full five foot four inches, and planted her hands on her hips. "Let me get this straight, Nickels. You think I'm afraid? Of *you?*"

His grandfather's presence forgotten, he nodded. "You got it, sweetheart. You can't take the heat."

"I can take anything you can dish out."

"Then prove it. Go to the awards banquet with me."

"I told you—I can't sit with you!"

"That's okay. I'll pick you up and take you home. Is seven o'clock okay?"

He knew the exact moment she realized she'd walked into a trap. Her brown eyes widened slightly with panic, then in the next instant, snapped with fire. If she could have gotten her hands around his throat, she probably would have squeezed the life out of him, but she apparently had more self-control than that. Her nostrils flaring as she drew in a calming breath, she nodded curtly. "Seven will be fine."

For the span of ten seconds, Blake savored the victory and started to grin. Then it hit him. Sabrina wasn't the only one who'd walked into a trap. He'd sworn the last thing he was going to do was ask her out, then he'd turned around and done just that. And it was all his grandfather's fault! Turning to glare at the old man, he found him watching the two of them with glee dancing in his eyes. If Blake hadn't been so disgusted with himself, he might have laughed. Lord, he was going to have to watch Pop. If he wasn't careful, he'd have him married with children before he even knew what hit him!

She had to be out of her mind.

Standing in front of the mirror on the back of her

bedroom door, Sabrina stared at her image and, for the fifth time in as many minutes, gave serious thought to calling Blake and claiming that she was too sick to go anywhere. It wouldn't be a lie. Her stomach was in a turmoil, her nerves jumpy, and she was definitely sick in the head. She had to be. Why else would she be standing here decked out in a new dress wondering if Blake would find her pretty?

Dear God, what was she doing?

Turning away from the sight of herself in a red silk dress that showed more skin than she'd ever showed in her life, she nervously paced the length of her bedroom. This was crazy. *She* was crazy! She didn't even know how she had gotten talked into this madness. She didn't like these kinds of shindigs, even if she was up for one of the most prestigious awards in the business. And she didn't go out with men who made her heart skip in her chest. It just wasn't smart when she had no intention of getting emotionally involved.

Turning back toward the mirror, she caught sight of herself again and winced. What had ever possessed her to wear red? It made her look...hot. Lord, she had to change!

But before she could even think about going through her closet for something more subdued, the doorbell rang and time ran out. Her heart jumping into her throat, she froze, every instinct she possessed urging her to run.

Why don't you tell him the real reason you don't want to go with me? You're chicken.

She stiffened, heat spilling into her cheeks. What was she doing? she wondered, disgusted with herself. She wasn't afraid of Blake Nickels or the feelings he stirred in her. After all, it wasn't as if they were even going out on a real date. For most of the evening, they would be seated at separate tables and she wouldn't even have to look at him if she didn't want to. So what was she getting into such a stew for? He was basically giving her a ride, nothing more. She could handle that—and him—with one hand tied behind her back.

Or so she thought until she opened the front door and caught sight of Blake Nickels in a tux.

No man had a right to look so mouth-wateringly good in formal wear. Or so comfortable. He should have been pulling at his collar or at the very least grimacing at the fit of the rented tux, but instead, he looked like he'd just stepped off the cover of *GQ*. Relaxed, one hand casually buried in the pocket of his black slacks, he grinned down at her with that familiar devilish sparkle in his green eyes and had no idea what he did to her heart rate. Stunned, Sabrina knew she was staring, but she couldn't take her eyes off him. How could she have ever thought this man was just an average Joe?

His grin suddenly tilting boyishly, he glanced down at himself and patted his bow tie. "What? Have I got this thing on crooked, or what?"

"No, I…" Unable to stop herself, she reached up and straightened his tie. When her eyes lifted to his, something passed between them, something hot and intimate and private. A wise woman would have stepped back then and run for cover, but she couldn't seem to make herself move. Her pulse was skipping, her legs less than steady. And he hadn't even touched her.

Her breath lodging in her throat, she struggled for a light tone, but her voice was revealingly husky when she said, "You know, Nickels, you clean up real good when you put your mind to it."

He should have come back at her with a smart remark

that would have eased the tension sizzling in the air between them, but his brain was in a fog and had been ever since she opened the door to him. He'd expected her to be dressed up—formal wear was required for the banquet— but nothing could have prepared him for the sight of her in that dress. There was nothing the least bit risqué about it, but it made him think of satin sheets and candlelight and touching her everywhere.

She'd put her hair up, confining her usually wild curls in a sophisticated, provocative style so that only a few wisps tumbled down to sweep the nape of her bare neck. Lord, how he envied those curls! His fingers curling into fists to keep from reaching for them, he dragged his eyes away from her hair and immediately regretted it. Her skin was like the silk of her dress, soft and smooth. The rich fabric hugged her breasts and waist, revealing every curve before flaring out to a full, flirty skirt that fell to just below her knees. A man could spend hours just wondering what she had on underneath it.

His mouth suddenly as dry as west Texas, he said hoarsely, "Thanks. You don't look half bad yourself. Ready to go?"

She nodded. "Just let me get my purse and lock up."

He waited for her on the porch, then escorted her to where he'd parked his pickup at the curb. When he opened the passenger door for her, Sabrina stopped in surprise, her eyes impish as they lifted to his. "Why, Blake, I didn't know you had it in you."

"There's a lot about me you don't know," he retorted, flashing a wicked smile at her. "You ain't seen nothing yet, sweetheart."

They were both grinning when he closed the door and walked around to the front of the truck to climb behind the wheel. But the second he slid in beside her and started the motor, their smiles faded. In the close confines of the pickup cab, they weren't touching, but they might as well have been. Scents, tantalizing and sexy, mingled and teased, and every time one of them moved, the other felt it deep inside. It was only five miles to the convention center, but it seemed like a hundred.

Breathless, her palms damp and every nerve ending attuned to Blake's nearness, Sabrina should have been relieved when they finally reached the banquet hall. The place was already packed, crowded with reporters and newspaper publishers from all over the country. And somewhere in the mass of humanity, her boss and the rest of the *Daily Record* staff were waiting for her to join them. But instead of hurrying off when it was time for them to part, she found herself reluctant to leave Blake.

"Well," he said as she hesitated at the entrance, "I guess this is it. I'll meet you here after this shindig's over." Suddenly noticing her silence, he frowned down at her. "Hey, you okay?"

Forcing a smile, she moved closer to him as the crush of people coming through the doorway jostled them. "I just don't care for this sort of thing. In fact, I wouldn't be here now if you hadn't dared me."

"Don't blame me." He chuckled. "It's not my fault you rose to the bait like a trout after a fly. Anyway, what are you worried about? I know the guys you're up against for the best crime story, and they can't hold a candle to you."

Surprised, she smiled. "My, my, Nickels, that sounds an awful lot like a compliment. Are you sure *you're* feeling all right? You must be coming down with something."

He grinned in appreciation and caught her hand before she could feel his forehead for a temperature. "Don't let it go to your head. You'll win. *This* year. Next year's a different matter. Then you'll be competing against me, and I'll warn you right now, I like to win." Giving her hand a squeeze, he dropped it and urged gruffly, "Go on and find your table before your boss sees you standing here holding my hand. I'll see you back here in a couple of hours."

Sabrina could have pointed out that *he* was the one who'd been holding *her* hand, but honesty forced her to admit that she'd started it by trying to touch him first. And she wanted to do it again. Color stealing into her cheeks, she stepped away from him while she still could. "Okay, okay. But we're going to talk about this later, Nickels. You're not the only one who likes to win."

She found the *Daily Record* staff at a large table near the stage at the far end of the room and wasn't surprised when her attire drew a few friendly wolf whistles. Most of the crew had never seen her in anything more sensuous than a business suit, and she took their ribbing in her stride. Then the master of ceremonies, a well-known television news journalist, stepped up onto the stage, and the awards ceremony began.

He was an entertaining speaker, but the awards were what everyone was waiting for, so he quickly got to them. Reporters from all over the country were nominated for everything from the best entertainment column to best obit, with each category divided into subcategories based on the size of the newspaper. With nominations restricted to work done over the course of the past year, Blake was up for sports coverage he'd done for the *Hidalgo County Gazette* in Lordsburg, New Mexico, while Sabrina competed with other police-beat reporters from larger papers.

She hadn't lied when she'd told him she didn't care for awards. It was the tracking down of stories and the writing itself she enjoyed, not the accolades of her peers, but when Blake's category came up and he was announced as the winner, she was thrilled for him. Sitting back in her seat, she found herself smiling as he strolled up to the microphone with an easy grace she couldn't help but admire. Relaxed and at ease, he joked with the crowd, then eloquently thanked the association for the honor.

Then it was her turn. Just as Blake had predicted, she was the winner. Unlike her *date,* she didn't shine at public speaking, so she kept her thanks short and sweet and got off the stage as quickly as she could. Back at her table, Fitz and the other reporters from the *Record* gave her high-fives and hugs, then it was time to party.

She should have stayed right where she was and celebrated with her friends until it was time to leave—but the only person she wanted to celebrate with was Blake. Later, she knew that was going to worry her, but for now, all she could think of was finding him in the crowd.

With the ceremony itself over, people were milling about, renewing old friendships, congratulating winners and commiserating with losers, and it seemed like everywhere she turned, someone wanted to talk to her. Struggling to hang on to her patience, she finally reached the *Times* table, but he was nowhere in sight.

Seeing her frustration, Vivian Berger, a crusty old gossip columnist who made a healthy living out of knowing who was seeing whom around town, grinned at her knowingly. "Well, hello, Ms. Jones. You looking for Blake?"

Sabrina didn't ask her how she knew—the woman had eyes in the back of her head and had probably seen them come in together. Cursing the color that spilled into her cheeks, she said casually, "As a matter of fact, I was. I thought I'd congratulate him on his win."

"Then you're going to have to get in line," the old lady said with a cackle, gesturing behind her. "He's right over there."

Turning, Sabrina expected to see him accepting the backslaps and handshakes of the other sports writers he'd beat out for the award. Instead, she found him in the arms of another woman.

Chapter 6

She wasn't the possessive type. She never had been. When it came to men, she didn't get jealous or catty; it just wasn't in her. She'd caught Jeff talking to attractive women dozen of times during their short-lived marriage, and she'd never even lifted a brow—not because she hadn't cared, she'd assured herself at the time, but because she'd trusted him. But the man hugging the pretty redhead across the room wasn't Jeff. It was Blake, and for some reason she didn't want to examine too closely, that made all the difference. Something that felt an awful lot like jealousy slammed into her, knotting her gut and heating her blood, stunning her. This wasn't even a date; she was hardly entitled to an explanation, she reminded herself. But that didn't stop her from taking a step toward them anyway.

Before she reached them, however, someone in the crowd stepped around her, jostling her and bringing her back to earth with a thud. Mortified, she stopped in her tracks. What in the world was she doing? She had no claim to Blake and didn't want one. He was a free agent and could hug a dozen women for all she cared—it was nothing to her.

Then why are your eyes green right now, Sabrina? a mocking voice whispered in her head. *You'd like to scratch that woman's eyes out and you know it.*

God, she had to get out of there!

But before she could turn away, Blake looked over the woman's shoulder and saw her. He grinned broadly, murmured something to his companion, then he was hurrying toward Sabrina. "There you are! I was just going to come look for you." Surprising her, he swept her into a bear hug. "Congratulations, Jones. I knew you could do it."

He was so exuberant, she couldn't help but smile. With his arms tight around her, squeezing her close, all she could think of was how good it felt to be held by him again. Then she caught the faint scent of perfume that clung to his tux jacket—perfume that belonged to the redhead he'd hugged just seconds ago. Unable to stop herself, she stiffened.

"Congratulations to you, too." Suddenly needing to get out of there, to think, she quickly drew back. "The party looks like it's going to drag on awhile and you probably have a lot of friends you want to talk to—"

"Yeah, I do," he cut in, grinning down at her. "The whole gang's here from New Mexico, and I didn't even know they were coming. C'mon, I want you to meet them." Not giving her a chance to object, he grabbed her hand and dragged her through the crowd after him.

And before Sabrina was quite ready for it, she found herself face-to-face with the redhead. Up close and personal, she was just as beautiful as Sabrina had feared. Dressed in a pale mint-green sheath of a dress that showed off her petite figure to perfection, she was positively glowing. And she didn't seem to mind in the least that Blake had left her to return with another woman. Her smile friendly, her big blue eyes alight with expectation, she waited patiently for him to make the introductions.

"Sabrina, this is Sydney O'Keefe Cassidy. We used to work together at the *Gazette* in Lordsburg," Blake confided with a grin.

"Actually, he used to pester the *H* out of me," Sydney corrected, her blue eyes dancing as she shook hands with Sabrina.

"I was just keeping you in line until Dillon came along," Blake retorted, and nodded to the tall, lean man who stood behind Sydney, towering protectively over her. "The big guy there is Dillon Cassidy, Sydney's husband," he told Sabrina. "God only knows why, but he's crazy about her."

A slow smile stretched across Dillon's square-cut, good-looking face. "I think it's the red hair—"

Huffing, Sydney said, "It's not red—"

"It's strawberry blond," her husband and Blake said together, laughing. "Anyway, it's nice to meet you, Sabrina," Dillon said, smiling down at her. "I don't know what plans you two have for the rest of the evening, but we were talking about getting out of here and partying on the River Walk. I hope you'll come with us."

"Hey, that's a great idea," Blake said, grinning. "Let's go."

Sabrina hesitated, wanting to go, but knowing she didn't dare. Not after the jealousy that had sunk its claws into her. And over a married woman, too—a friend who was obviously very much in love with her husband. How, dear

God, had this happened? When had she begun to think of Blake as hers? She had to be out of her mind!

Hanging back, she immediately drew a frown from Blake. "You go ahead," she told him huskily. "I'm sure the three of you have a lot to catch up on, and I've got to be at work early in the morning. I'll just call a cab—"

"Don't be ridiculous!" Blake said. "I'll get you home before midnight. I promise." The matter settled, he linked his fingers with hers and pulled her outside after him.

It was a beautiful night. The heat of the day had passed, and a lover's moon lit up a clear sky filled with stars. Not surprisingly, the River Walk was packed with summer tourists and locals who were drawn to the music and lights and the cooling breeze that rippled over the slow-moving water of the San Antonio River as it wound its way through downtown.

Walking hand in hand with Blake, Sabrina felt as if she'd stepped into a dream and any second now, she was going to wake up. She hadn't even planned to go out with him, yet here she was on what was virtually a double date with him and the Cassidys. And in spite of the voice murmuring in her ear that she was going to regret this, she was having too much fun to even think about calling it a night.

Any reservations she had about Sydney had died the second her husband stepped forward to claim her, and it hadn't taken Sabrina long to realize that she and the other woman had a great deal in common. Sydney, too, was an investigative reporter who, according to her husband and Blake, didn't know the meaning of the word fear. She had once worked in Chicago, covering the crime beat, as Sabrina did in San Antonio, and had some fascinating tales to tell. Chatting like old friends, they could have talked for hours if the men hadn't interfered.

"No shoptalk," Dillon said as they finally got a table at the Hard Rock Cafe, which was packed to the rafters. "This isn't a night for blood and guts."

"Dillon's right," Blake agreed. "We came here to party. C'mon, Jones, I want to dance."

And with no more warning than that, he pulled her out onto the dance floor. Chagrined, Sabrina stood flat-footed in front of him and felt like a duck out of water as the crowd gyrated around them to the heavy beat of the ten-year-old hit blaring on the speakers. There were a lot of things she could do well, but dancing wasn't one of them. She loved music, but she just couldn't loosen up enough to move in time with it.

But Lord, she hated to admit it. Especially to someone who appeared to dance as well as Blake. His body already starting to languidly move in time to the beat, he looked as if he didn't have a bone in his body. Just watching him made her mouth go dry. Embarrassed color stinging her cheeks, she reached up to slip a hand behind his neck and pull his head down so he could hear her over the throb of the music. "There's something you should know about me, Nickels."

Casually draping his arms around her, he smiled down into her eyes. "What's that, Jones?"

"I've got two left feet."

His gaze, sparkling with amusement, dropped to her feet. "No, you don't. You've got a lefty and a righty just like everybody else."

She grinned, she couldn't help it, and struggled to give him a stern look. It wasn't easy when his mouth was only scant inches away from hers and he was so close that she could almost feel his body swaying against hers. "Blake, I'm trying to be serious."

"Don't," he growled low in his throat as his arms tightened around her to pull her more fully against him. "You can be serious tomorrow. Tonight, let's just... dance."

"But I can't!"

"Sweetheart, nobody who moves like you do has two left feet. Trust me. You're doing fine."

She wasn't—they both knew it—but when his voice turned all rough and deep and seemed to reach out and physically stroke her, warming the dark, secret recesses of her being, she found it impossible to care that she was a step behind everyone else on the dance floor. She was in his arms, her cheek pressed against his chest, with his heart knocking out its own erotic rhythm in her ear, and nothing else mattered. Like Cinderella, she was at the ball with a make-believe prince and it would all come crashing to a close at the stroke of twelve. For now, at least, she intended to enjoy herself.

Midnight, however, came and went and she never noticed the passage of time. They left the Hard Rock and checked out Planet Hollywood, then stopped in at a little jazz place where the music was as low as the lights. When they weren't dancing, the four of them were talking and laughing and trading stories about everything from high school to first dates to their most embarrassing moments. By the time they called it a night, it was going on three in the morning.

She'd talked all evening without once having to search her brain for a topic of conversation, but the second she and Blake were alone in his pickup and headed for her house, silence slipped into the truck with them. For the life of her, she couldn't think of a single thing to say to break it. Downtown was left behind, the odometer clicked off the miles, and the quiet, accompanied by a growing tension, thickened.

Desperate, she broke it just as Blake turned down her street. "I liked your friends. They were fun."

His smile flashed in the darkness. "They liked you, too. Dillon doesn't open up like that for everyone, you know. When he and Sydney first met, he was pretty much a loner, and wanted to stay that way. She's brought him out of it, but I've never heard him tell stories about his days in the DEA like he did tonight."

Breaking to a stop in front of her house, he cut the engine and turned to her. She'd left the porch light on, but it hardly touched the shadows filling the truck. "He must have really been taken with you," he said huskily. "I can't say I blame him. Did I tell you what a knockout you are in that dress?"

He didn't move so much as an eyelash, but Sabrina could feel his touch as surely as if he'd reached out and trailed his fingers across her bare neck. Between one breath and the next, her heart was hammering and the temperature in the cab seemed to have risen ten degrees.

Blindly, she fumbled for the release to her seat belt. "Not in so many words, but I sort of got the general idea, thanks," she said in a voice she hardly recognized as her own. "I'd better go. It's late."

"Wait! I'll walk you to the door."

She opened her mouth to tell him that wasn't necessary, but she was too late. He was out of the pickup like a shot and walking around to open her door for her before she could tell him that was the last thing she wanted. Left with no choice, she stepped out and joined him on the sidewalk.

The walk to her front porch had never taken so long. With the neighborhood quiet, asleep, they could have been the only two people in the world. Her pulse skipping every other beat, Sabrina half expected him to take her hand, but he seemed content to shorten his strides to match hers and walk along beside her without touching her. Then they reached the porch.

"Thank you for a wonderful—"

"I had a great—"

They both spoke at the same time as they turned to face each other. Normally, Sabrina would have laughed, but in the glare of the porch light, there was nothing comical about the heat in his eyes. It stole her breath and weakened her knees and set off alarm bells in her head. He was going to kiss her. She knew it as surely as she knew her own name, and if she had a single ounce of self-preservation, she'd get inside while she still wanted to.

But she just stood there, her heart knocking against her ribs so loudly that he had to hear it, and waited. In the quiet of the night, it seemed like an eternity, but something of her need must have shown in her eyes because in the next instant, he was reaching for her and she, God help her, was stepping into his arms. "Blake..."

All she said was his name. Just that. She didn't use his first name often, and had no idea what it did to him when she called to him in quite that way. He considered himself a civilized man who could easily control his passions, but she'd been driving him crazy for hours. They'd laughed and talked and casually touched and all he'd been able to think of was this moment, when he'd take her home and finally have her all to himself. He'd been so sure that he would sweep her up into his arms and ravage that beautiful mouth of hers the first chance that he got, but the hunger he heard in the simple calling of his name—and the trepidation she couldn't quite conceal—echoed the confusing mix of emotions churning in his own gut. God, he wanted her, even when she scared the hell out of him. He should back off and give his head time to clear, but he couldn't, not when she was this close.

Silently cursing himself, aching for her in a way he had for no other woman, he found himself murmuring reassurances as he gathered her closer. "It's okay, honey. It's just a kiss."

But the second his mouth settled on hers, nothing was quite that simple. Not with Sabrina. Not since that first kiss that had tied him in knots and left him wanting for days now. Did she know how soft her mouth was? How hot? How giving? He could have spent days just learning the taste and texture of her, and still it wouldn't have been enough. Not when she was flush against him like a heat rash, her arms climbing around his neck, her tongue sweetly welcoming his in the liquid heat of her mouth. If he never kissed her again, a month from now, a year, he would still be able to taste her.

That thought alone should have brought him to his senses, but at that moment, every sense he had was occupied with the woman in his arms. His blood rushing through his veins, need like a fist in his gut, he wanted her. In his bed. Under him. Her arms and legs and body surrounding him, taking him in, holding him like she would never let him go. Uncaring that they were standing under her porch light in full view of anyone who cared to look, he slanted his mouth across hers to take the kiss deeper.

Her head spinning, Sabrina clung to him as if he was the

only solid thing in a world that had suddenly turned topsy-turvy. All her life, she'd promised herself she would never lead with her heart the way her mother and grandmother had. She just wouldn't let herself be that weak. But Blake was a man who could shatter convictions she would have sworn were carved in stone. If she hadn't known that before, she knew it now, when he kissed her as if she was something infinitely precious that he needed more than he needed his next breath. That alone should have had her fighting her way out of his arms, but his hands seduced, even while his mouth wooed her, and her mind blurred. As if from a distance, she heard the whisper of silk as he blindly caressed her, then his fingers were closing over her breast, his thumb searching out her nipple. Lightning, sweet and warm, streaked through her, and with a soft moan, she melted against him.

For long, breathless moments, she held on tight as their kisses turned hot and wild and desperate. She couldn't think and didn't want to. Then his hands slid to her hips and pulled her against him, trapping his arousal between them. Urgency firing her blood, she whimpered.

At that moment, she would have given just about anything to be the type of woman who could enjoy the moment for the pure sake of pleasure and not ruin it by thinking too much. But she couldn't. She just couldn't.

She never remembered moving, but suddenly she was pushing out of his arms. "No! I can't do this!"

Stunned, Blake instinctively tried to pull her back into his arms. "Sweetheart, wait—"

"It's late," she said huskily, gliding out of reach as she fumbled for her keys. "You should be going."

The only place he wanted to go was inside with her, but when he ducked his head to get a look at her face, he knew that wasn't going to happen. She was pale except for the wild color that fluctuated in her cheeks, and her eyes were dark with what looked an awful lot like panic as she tried to avoid his gaze. His desire-fogged brain abruptly clearing, he frowned. "In a minute. First I think we should talk about what just happened here."

"There's nothing to talk about," she said curtly, turning away. "You kissed me. I kissed you back. End of story."

End of story?! She'd just knocked him loop-legged in front of God and any of her neighbors who cared to look at that hour of the night, and she thought that was the end of the story? The hell it was!

Wanting to strangle her, he followed her across the porch to her front door. "If you really think that, then maybe I should kiss you again because that sure didn't feel like it was the end of the story to me, honey. In fact, it damn well felt like the beginning. Dammit, Sabrina, will you at least look at me?" he fumed.

She didn't even bother to answer him. Her back to him and ramrod straight, she just stood there, staring at something in front of her. Frowning, he stepped around her and swore when he saw that she was as white as a sheet. "What is it? What's wrong? What are you looking at?"

"The door," she whispered, her gaze focused on the latch. "It's unlocked."

His eyes following hers, Blake saw that not only was it unlocked, but it was slightly ajar, pulled to, but not quite closed. "Are you sure you locked it when we left? We were both distracted. Maybe you just thought you pulled it shut."

Shaking her head, she hugged herself, suddenly chilled. "No, I know I locked it. This isn't the kind of neighborhood where you can leave your doors unlocked. I always check it twice just to be sure."

"Then someone's been here." His face grim, Blake moved between her and the door. "And for all we know, they could still be in there. Stay out here while I check it out."

It was the wrong thing to say to a woman who made her living covering crime. "Not on your life, Nickels," she said quietly. "In case you've forgotten, this is my house. If someone's still in there, they're damn well going to have to answer to me!"

Ignoring his muttered curses, she was right behind him as he stepped into the entrance hall and soundlessly switched on the light. Tension scraping against his nerve endings like a jagged piece of glass, Blake cocked his head and listened for sounds of an intruder, but nothing moved. The old house, in fact, seemed to be holding its breath and didn't even creak. Whoever had been there was, in all probability, long gone.

Still, he had no intention of bumbling through the house like an idiot in search of trouble. His pace slow and measured, his eyes watchful as he moved from room to room with Sabrina just a half step behind him, he flipped on lights and patiently waited for her to inspect the contents of each room and take a quick inventory. Nothing had been moved, let alone stolen.

By the time they reached the kitchen, Sabrina was beginning to wonder if maybe she *had* forgotten to lock the door. Considering how nervous she'd been about going out with Blake, it was a logical explanation. She'd taken one look at Blake in his tux, and evidently everything else had gone right out of her head, including locking the door. Granted, she'd never done such a thing before, but that made more sense than a thief breaking into the house and leaving without taking anything.

An invisible weight lifting from her shoulders, she almost laughed at her own foolishness. Then her gaze drifted to the kitchen table and a piece of paper that hadn't been there when she'd left. A piece of paper that was folded in half with her name scrawled on the outside.

She froze, her blood chilling in her veins at the sight of that familiar jagged handwriting. She'd only seen it twice before, but she would have recognized it in the depths of hell. "Blake…there's a note…."

He followed her gaze to the table and swore, reaching it in two strides. Touching only one corner, he flicked the unlined piece of paper open and quickly, silently, scanned the typed message inside. When he finally looked up, his face was set in harsh lines. "I think you'd better call the police."

Her heart in her throat, she stepped closer. "What does it say?"

"It doesn't matter," he retorted grimly, moving to block her path. "Call Kelly."

Ignoring him, Sabrina tried to move around him, but he anticipated her and once again stepped in front of her. Scared and hating it, she knew what he was doing and couldn't even be angry with him. "You can't protect me from this, Blake," she said gravely. "Whoever wrote that damn thing was in my house! He knows where I work, where I live, where I go and when. Do you have any idea how that makes me feel, knowing he's out there somewhere, watching my every move? He's a sicko, a murderer, and I've got a right to know what kind of threats he's making, especially when they're made in my house."

Hesitating, he stood his ground. "It's just trash. Not worth worrying about."

"I deal with garbage every day on the streets," she retorted. "I can handle it. Just because I'm wearing silk tonight doesn't mean I'm soft."

He didn't like it, but she saw something flare in his eyes and knew she had won. "All right," he said with a sigh. "Read the damn thing if you insist. I'm calling Kelly." Striding across the room, he picked up the phone.

For all of ten seconds, Sabrina almost reconsidered. But if she could be intimidated by a simple note, how could she ever look herself in the mirror again? She was a reporter, and if the innocent-looking paper on the table really was from the murderer, which it certainly appeared to be, then it was news. And she didn't cower behind anyone when it came to covering a story.

Squaring her shoulders, she approached the table as if it was a nesting ground for rattlers and cautiously lifted the same corner of the note Blake had, careful not to put any more of her prints on the paper than she had to. The pounding of her heart loud in her ears, she braced herself and began to read.

You slut! I thought you were different, that you cared, but you're just like all the rest. You got your story and your headlines—headlines I gave you!—but it was him you went out with. And it should have been me, damn you! It should have been me you dressed up for in that pretty red dress, but you couldn't see anyone but him. Did you sleep with him when you got home? Just thinking about the two of you together made me sick to my stomach. I won't allow it! Do you understand? You're mine! That's why I killed

her, the girl in the red dress like yours. Now you have
another story to write, and you don't have to think
of anyone but me. Just me. I'll kill them all if I have
to to make you happy.

Horrified, Sabrina dropped the note, snatching her hand
back as if she'd been burned. "No!" she said hoarsely.
"It isn't true! He couldn't have killed someone else just
because I went out. That's crazy!"

Finished with his call, Blake hung up and said, "Of
course he's crazy! Why do you think I didn't want you to
read the damn thing? He's a sicko who doesn't know reality
from a hole in the ground. For all we know, he could be
making the whole thing up."

"But what if it's true?" she whispered, stricken. "What
if he really did go out and kill a girl in a red dress because
he was angry with me? You read the note. Some poor girl
could have died tonight because I went out with you."

"Bull!" he growled. Placing his hands on her shoulders,
he swore at the guilt he saw already darkening her eyes
and gave her a shake. "Don't you dare blame yourself for
this, Jones! You didn't do anything wrong. If the bastard
really did kill again tonight, he did it because he wanted
to, not because of anything you did. Dammit, Sabrina, he's
a loony tune! This isn't your fault."

Deep down inside, she knew that, but that didn't make
her feel any better. The killer had been there tonight, not
only in her home, but watching her from the shadows
somewhere like a panther waiting to spring. He could have
been anywhere…hiding in the bushes in some neighbor's
yard, mingling with the crowd on the River Walk, following
her all night and growing angrier by the second as he'd

watched her laugh and dance with Blake and his friends. And she hadn't even known it.

Damn him, who was he? And what did he want from her?

"It might not technically be my fault, but I can't help but feel that I should know who this jerk is."

"What about the list you came up with for Kelly?" he asked as she kicked off her high heels and began to pace in her stocking feet.

She laughed, but there was little humor to the sound. "Believe it or not, the list wasn't that big. And somehow I can't see the guy I turned down for the senior prom in high school doing something like this ten years later. It's got to be somebody else, but who? He's leaving clues all over the place, just daring me to figure out who he is. Why can't I put it all together and come up with a name?"

"Because he's just playing with you the way a cat does with a mouse, Jones," he said flatly. "He hasn't given you that much information, just enough to tease you and drive you crazy. If you let yourself, you'll spend hours just thinking about him, and that's what he wants…your total attention. Don't let him win that kind of head game with you."

Sam Kelly arrived then with two uniformed officers. While the officers searched the house for signs of a break-in that would explain how the killer got into the house, Sam read the note, his expression stony, then silently slid it into an evidence bag. "Since you're both dressed fit to kill, you obviously went out tonight," he said as he dropped the bag on the table with a grimace of distaste and pulled out a chair. "Tell me about it. When you left, where you went, when you got back. Everything."

Unable to sit, Sabrina roamed around the kitchen, her

words jerky as she began to recount the events of the evening. "It didn't start out as a date. Since Blake and I were both going to the awards banquet for the National Newspaper Association, we decided to go together. Blake picked me up—"

"What time?" Sam asked sharply.

"Seven," Blake said, answering for her. "It was still light out. A man down the street was mowing his lawn, and a couple of ladies two houses up were gossiping over the fence between their yards. There was a jogger passing the house just as I drove up, but I didn't get a look at his face. He was about six foot, a hundred and seventy pounds, with blond hair."

Jotting down notes, Sam nodded. "I'll check it out. Go on."

Amazed that Blake had noticed such things when all she'd been able to see was him, Sabrina told the detective about their arrival at the convention center, where they'd parted company until after the awards ceremony. "The banquet hall was full," she added. "But everyone seemed to belong there. If someone was watching either one of us, I didn't see them."

"From there we went to the River Walk," Blake told him, picking up the story. He gave him a list of every night spot they hit, including the Hard Rock Cafe and Planet Hollywood. "We were with friends until about three," he concluded. "Then I brought Sabrina home. She didn't notice the front door was unlatched until she started to unlock it."

His expression shuttered, Sam scribbled notes, then made them both go over the details again, questioning them sharply about who might have seen them leave together, then followed them. Unfortunately, Blake wasn't familiar enough with Sabrina's neighbors to know if there'd been any strange cars parked within view of the house, and Sabrina hadn't paid attention. If anyone had followed them—and someone obviously had—they'd been damn discreet about it.

They appeared to be back at square one again, with no clues but the note itself, when one of the uniformed officers stepped into the kitchen and informed Sam quietly, "There seems to be no sign of a break-in. All the screens and windows are securely latched, and neither the front or back doors were jimmied."

"What are you saying?" Sabrina asked sharply. "That whoever left the note had a key? That's impossible!"

Sam shrugged. "Maybe. Maybe not. Have you had your car worked on recently or loaned it to anyone who might have had the opportunity to have a copy of your house keys made?"

"No. Nothing. I haven't even had the oil changed, though God knows it needs it."

"What about a spare key to the front door?" Blake asked. "Do you keep one hidden somewhere in case you lose your keys?"

"Well, yes, but nobody would be able to find it without knowing where it was."

That was all Sam needed to hear. "Show me," he said, and pushed to his feet.

Obediently, Sabrina lead the way to the front porch. "It's here," she said. "Behind the mailbox. The box is loose, but you can't tell from just looking at it. So I put a small magnet on the back of the box and just stuck the key to it."

She started to show him, but the detective quickly stopped her, grabbing her hand before she could touch the small metal box that was attached to the wall right next to the front door. "Don't touch it," he said curtly. "I want to dust it for prints first."

Stepping around her, he examined the black mailbox in the light of the front porch light, then dusted the entire area for prints. "Most of these are probably yours and the mailman's," he said when the task was complete, "but we can't take any chances. Now, where's the key?"

It was just where Sabrina had said it would be, held in place by a small magnet that was about the size and thickness of a dime. Relieved, she let out the breath she hadn't even known she was holding and smiled shakily. "See, I told you no one could find it."

Sam wasn't so sure. "Not necessarily. Whoever left the note for you could have put the key back to make you think he didn't know where it was or he could have already had himself one made at another time. Either way, we can't assume that your locks are secure. You need to get a locksmith over here in the morning to change them for you."

"Then see about having a security system installed," Blake added, his face carved with harsh lines in the glare of the porch light. "In fact, you should have already done that. Dammit, Sabrina, this neighborhood isn't safe! Especially for a woman living alone."

Put on the defensive, she frowned. "Crime happens everywhere. You know that. And at least here, I know my neighbors, which probably wouldn't be the case if I moved into some newer, fancier subdivision where people don't even talk to each other." Wound up, she would have said more, but she suddenly spied the circle of neighbors that had collected in her front yard, drawn there by the flashing lights of the patrol cars. "See?" she told Blake triumphantly. "Everybody cares about each other here. I'm perfectly safe."

"Sabrina? Is there a problem?" Martha Anderson called worriedly. Her iron-gray hair in rollers and a hot-pink cotton robe wrapped around her rounded figure, she hugged herself and stepped closer to the porch. "When I saw the police lights, I came running as soon as I could. What's wrong?"

"It's nothing," Sabrina assured her. "Just a break-in. Nothing was taken."

"A break-in! Oh, my!"

"Did any of you see anyone lurking around Ms. Jones's house this evening between seven and three-thirty?" Sam asked the group as he moved to join them.

"No, but I did hear a dog barking around eleven-thirty," Martha said. "I thought it was Louis's, but I didn't get up to check. When he quieted down after only a few minutes, I just thought he was after a cat or something."

"It was a jogger," Louis said quietly, pushing up his wire-rimmed glasses from where they'd slid down his thin nose. "I had just turned out the lights to go to bed when Lady starting throwing a fit. I thought it was a cat, too—she really hates them—but when I looked out the front window, all I saw was a jogger trotting down the street."

Blake lifted a dark brow at that. "At eleven-thirty at night? Do you usually have people running through the neighborhood at that hour of the night?"

Suddenly chilled, Sabrina felt goose bumps ripple down her bare arms. "No, of course not. Can you describe the man, Louis? And which way was he running? Toward my house or away from it?"

"Away," he said reluctantly. "And I'm sorry to say I didn't have my glasses on, so I didn't get a very good look at him in the dark. He was tall, with sort of a lanky build and dark hair. Sort of like Jeff."

"Jeff?" Blake repeated sharply. "Jeff Harper, her ex-husband?"

"I'm sure it wasn't him, dear," Martha told Sabrina when Louis nodded reluctantly. "I know you two had your differences, but I can't see him breaking into your house. Not after all this time."

Sabrina didn't think so either, but when she saw Blake and the detective exchange speculative looks, she had no choice but to come to Jeff's defense. "Louis didn't say it *was* Jeff, just that the jogger was built like him. There must be hundreds of men in San Antonio who fit the same description. And it was dark, and Louis didn't have his glasses on. It could have been anyone."

"She's right about that," the older man agreed. "I'm the first to admit that I'm blind as a bat without my glasses. Anything more than three feet away tends to be rather blurry. I guess that doesn't do you much good, does it?"

"I wouldn't go so far as to say that," Sam Kelly said with a smile as he closed his notebook. "You've given us a general description of the man and the approximate time of the break-in. If you or any of the rest of you think of anything else, I'd appreciate it if you'd call me at the station."

They all promised to do just that, then reluctantly returned to their homes. Sam conferred with the two uniformed officers, then sent them on their way. When he turned back to Sabrina, his face was set in somber lines. "Considering the circumstances, I think you'd better find some place else to stay for a while. At this point, we have to conclude that that note is from the same person who killed Charlene McClintock and the others, and if he's to be believed, he killed again tonight. We can't be sure until a body's found, but one thing is for sure—he's furious with you. For your own safety, you need to get away from here for a while."

Blake couldn't have agreed more. "She can stay at my place until the bastard's caught. No one will bother her there."

"Oh, no! I couldn't!"

Sabrina's response was automatic and held more than a trace of panic. Watching the color come and go in her pale cheeks, Blake could understand her reservations. He didn't have to read her mind to know that her thoughts, like his, were on the kisses they'd shared on that very porch less than an hour ago. He wanted her. More than he should, considering the painful lessons Trina had taught him. And Sabrina, in spite of her claims to the contrary, wasn't exactly indifferent to him. Together, the two of them could set a forest ablaze, they were that hot. Living with her, even for a day or two, and keeping his hands to himself, would be impossible.

"Yes, you can," he said, throwing caution to the wind. "I'll stay with my grandfather, and you'll have the whole place to yourself. No one will know you're there but me and Sam and Pop. You'll be perfectly safe as long as you make sure no one follows you there after work every evening."

Safe. Just thinking about it made her want to jump at the chance to get away, but she'd never been one to run from a threat before, and she couldn't start now. "I appreciate the offer, Blake, but you haven't talked to your grandfather. He told me himself how independent he was. He may not want you to move in with him."

He laughed at that, his grin rueful. "Are you kidding?

He'd do just about anything for you, even put up with me for a couple of weeks."

"But it could take longer than that," she argued. "And I don't like the idea of letting this monster, whoever he is, drive me out of my own house."

"What's more important?" he tossed back. "Your life or your pride?"

Put that way, she had no argument. Left with little choice, she gave in. "All right, you win. Give me a minute to pack some clothes, then we can leave."

Chapter 7

It was nearly four-thirty when Blake unlocked the door to his apartment and waited for Sabrina to precede him inside. Tired, her nerves frayed from an evening that had had more emotional highs and lows than a roller coaster, she stepped over the threshold and could have sworn she heard her heart pounding in the dark, intimate silence that engulfed the place. Moving past her, his shoulder just barely brushing hers, Blake switched on a light, but it didn't help ease the sudden tension. Standing just inside the door, she stopped, her mouth dust-dry. This was a mistake. A terrible mistake.

What was she doing here? she wondered, hugging herself. It wasn't as if she were destitute or friendless. She could have gone to a hotel. And any one of her co-workers would have been happy to put her up for as long as necessary.

She stopped short at the thought. She couldn't drag her

friends into this mess, any more than she could afford to go to a hotel for an extended stay. And with the police not even close to making an arrest in the case, it could be weeks, months, before it might be safe for her to go home again. She couldn't impose on even the best of friends for that long.

So she was stuck, left with no choice but to be beholden to Blake. And there didn't seem to be a darn thing she could do about it, either. She'd tried to explain to him before they'd left her place that she couldn't, in good conscience, put him out of his apartment indefinitely, but the stubborn man had flatly refused to listen. He'd hustled her into her car, warned her that he was going to take a circuitous route to make sure they weren't being followed, and like a lamb to the slaughter, she'd followed him.

She shouldn't do this. She couldn't! She was already having trouble handling the emotions he stirred in her. How was she going to put the man out of her head when she would be living among his things—sleeping in his bed, for heaven's sake!—for God only knew how long? She had to be out of her mind.

But if Blake noticed her sudden trepidation or was the least bit shaken at the thought of her living among his things, he gave no sign of it. Striding toward the short hall that opened off the far end of the living room, he opened one of the two doors there and set her suitcase inside. "The bedroom's through here, and the bathroom's right across the hall," he told her. "There's a laundry room off the kitchen, and clean sheets and towels in the linen closet in the bathroom. Feel free to use whatever you need."

She shouldn't, she was already taking advantage of him—but she hadn't thought to bring her own sheets and towels. Nodding, she whispered, in no mood to argue with him tonight, "Thank you."

"Well, then, I guess I'd better pack some things, then get out of here if either one of us is going to get any sleep tonight. Another couple of hours, and it'll be time to get up."

Sabrina could have told him she didn't expect to sleep much anyway, but he'd already disappeared into the bedroom. When he returned to the living room a few minutes later, all he carried was a single duffel bag. "This'll do me for now," he told her as he headed for the front door. "I'll drop by in a couple of days for the rest."

Her throat tight, she forced a smile that wasn't nearly as breezy as she would have liked as she followed him across the living room. "It's your apartment. Drop by whenever you like."

Stopping just short of the front door, Blake barely stifled a groan at the suggestion. No, he thought as he stared down at her, he wouldn't be dropping by, not without a damn good reason. Not if he had a brain in his head, which at this point was doubtful. She looked damn good there. The only place she would look better was in his bed.

Images hit him then, hot and intimate and seductive. His teeth grinding on a curse, he told himself to get the hell out of there while he still could. His blood pressure was already through the roof, his fingers itching to reach for her and haul her close. But even as his head ordered his feet to move, he came up with reasons to linger.

"Are you sure you're not going to be scared here?" he asked in a voice that was as rough as sandpaper. "I know we weren't followed, but it is a strange place and you don't know any of the neighbors."

Her face lifted to his, her eyes meeting his in the shadows

near the door, she murmured, "I'll be fine, Nickels. Really. You don't have to worry about me."

She might as well have asked him not to breathe. Like it or not, he was worried, and he didn't like leaving her. He hadn't realized how much until just now. "If you have any problems, you can reach me at Pop's. The number's in the directory by the phone in the bedroom."

She nodded, her voice as hushed as his. "I don't think that's going to be necessary, but thanks."

Seconds passed, long moments of silence that seemed to hum and throb with expectation. Fumbling for his keys, he held them out to her. "The silver one is for the dead bolt, the other one for the main lock. Make sure you use them both."

Her gaze never leaving his, she reached for them and, in the process, brushed her fingers against his. It was an innocent touch, over in the blink of an eye, but he felt the warmth of it all the way to the soles of his feet. And she was just as stirred by it as he. He watched her eyes darken, heard her nearly silent gasp as her breath caught in her lungs, and keeping his hands to himself was almost more than he could stand. With no conscious decision on his part, he started to reach for her, only to let his arm fall back to his side. He couldn't. She was a guest in his home, there because he'd promised her she'd be safe and have the place all to herself. If he kissed her now as he longed to, as his body cried out for him to, he'd never be able to walk away from her.

Cursing himself for being a man of scruples, he had to content himself with cupping her cheek in his hand and rubbing his thumb with painstaking slowness across her bottom lip. "Lock the door behind me," he said thickly. When she nodded, dazed, he gave in to temptation and brushed his thumb across her sweet mouth one more time. A split second later, he was gone, quietly shutting the door after him.

For what seemed like an eternity, Sabrina just stood there, the thunder of her racing heart roaring in her ears. She never remembered reaching for the dead bolt, but suddenly her hand was on the latch, shooting it home. From the other side of the door, she heard Blake whisper a husky good-night, then the fading sound of his footsteps as he walked away.

She *almost* called him back. Her hand was on the dead bolt, the words already trembling on her tongue, when she realized what she was doing. Muttering a curse, she snatched her hand back as if she'd been burned. Dear God, dear God, dear God! What was she doing?

"Sabrina Jones, stop this!" she said out loud to the empty apartment as she whirled away from the door. "You're not here to drool over the man, so just get him out of your head right here and now."

It was sound advice, but she soon found that it was almost impossible to follow. Too wired to even think about going to bed, she wandered around the apartment and saw Blake everywhere she turned. The refrigerator was filled with hot dogs and Twinkies and enough cholesterol to choke a horse. With no effort whatsoever, she could picture him drinking directly from a half-gallon carton of whole milk, then flashing a grin at her as he wiped his mouth with the back of his hand. And then there was the bathroom. His shampoo was there…and his cologne. She didn't open it, but she didn't have to. She only had to close her eyes and he was holding her again, kissing her again, the clean, spicy, sexy scent of him surrounding her as surely as his arms.

"Don't start, Sabrina," she muttered, heading for the bedroom. "Don't you dare start."

She should have gone to bed, but she unpacked her suitcase instead, which meant she had to go through Blake's dresser and closet to find space for her things. Touching his clothes was like touching him. Shaken, she felt like she was peering into his soul. There were some things, she decided, that a woman had no business knowing about a man she'd claimed she wanted nothing to do with. Like the way he arranged his sock and underwear drawer.

Lord, she needed to get out of there. But there was no place to go except to bed. She told herself she was tired— she would be more in control of her thoughts tomorrow. But when she pulled on a sleeveless cotton gown a few minutes later, turned out the lights, and crawled into Blake's queen-size bed, she knew she wasn't going to get any sleep in the remaining few hours that were left of the night. Not when his scent clung to the sheets, making it impossible to think of anything but him.

Her heart thumping crazily, she couldn't stop herself from clutching at his pillow, muttering curses all the while. Tomorrow, she promised herself, she was going to wash every sheet and towel in the place with her own laundry detergent. Maybe then she'd be able to at least bathe and sleep without her senses clamoring for a man who wasn't there.

How long she lay there like that, she couldn't have said. The deep, dark silence of predawn enveloped her, surrounding her like a blanket, weighing her down. Exhaustion pulling at her, she should have slept, but her mind was too busy, her pulse too erratic. Restless, she couldn't even seem to lie still. She was all over the bed, searching for a comfortable spot that just wasn't there.

Finally giving up in defeat, she rolled over with a disgusted sigh and stared up at the darkened ceiling. Maybe she should just forget the whole thing and get up.

When the phone on the bedside table suddenly rang, shattering the silence, she nearly jumped out of her skin. Instinctively, she reached for it without turning on a light, her heart slamming against her ribs. It was nearly five o'clock. Who could possibly be calling Blake at that hour of the morning? "Hullo?"

"Did I wake you?"

Blake's deep, rough voice rumbled softly in her ear, as clear as if he was there in the bed beside her. With a will of its own, her heart slowly turned over and picked up speed. Just that quickly, she was smiling and couldn't for the life of her say why. "Do you make a habit of calling women at five o'clock in the morning, Nickels?" she teased softly.

"Only ones who are sleeping in my bed when I'm not there," he countered smoothly, chuckling. "You are in my bed, aren't you?"

She should have said no, that she'd decided to just stay up the rest of what was left of the night, but the truth popped out in the most provocative way. "Yes, cowboy, I'm in your bed," she murmured huskily. "I've been hugging your pillow for the last fifteen minutes trying to get to sleep."

He groaned and admitted thickly, "I don't think I needed to know that part, Jones. Now *I* won't be able to sleep."

She laughed, not the least bit repentant. "Don't expect any sympathy from me. You're the one who insisted on giving up your bed for me."

"Only because I was worried about you. Are you okay?"

"I'm fine. Really," she assured him. "Anyway, if you

want to worry about someone, you'd better worry about yourself. Once word gets out on the street that you've got a knight-in-shining-armor complex, you're going to have damsels in distress from all over the city beating a path to your door. If I were you, I'd get out of town while I still could."

His chuckle vibrated in her ear, warming her inside and out. "I'll have you know I don't pull out the armor for just anyone. Only a particularly feisty female reporter I have a bet with."

"A bet you're going to lose," she reminded him sweetly.

"Time will tell. Speaking of time," he said gruffly, "I guess I should get off of here and let you try to get some sleep. You know where I am if you need me, Jones."

She should have made some lighthearted, breezy comment, but his raspy words seemed to reach right through the phone line to squeeze her heart. Her smile faltered, and emotions, thick and warm, clogged her throat. "I know," she whispered. "Good night, Blake."

His soft good-night echoing in her ear, she hung up and hugged their conversation to her breast as fiercely as she did his pillow. It was a long, long time before she finally fell asleep.

The morning sun was bright and cheerful, and if he'd had a shotgun, Blake would have shot it out of the sky. Slamming his eyes shut against the glare, he cursed long and low, damning his throbbing head, the too-small twin bed in his grandfather's guest room, the hot, sensuous dreams of Sabrina that had haunted the few hours of sleep he'd finally been able to snatch from what was left of the night.

In spite of his best efforts, a reluctant smile propped up one corner of his mouth as he thought of their whispered phone conversation while most of the rest of the world slept. It was, he realized, a good thing that they'd been almost two miles apart, or he would have had a damn difficult time keeping his hands off of her. God, what was he going to do about her?

She was tying him in knots, taking over his thoughts, his dreams, haunting him. And that didn't even begin to touch the emotions that gripped him every time he thought of the note that had been left for her on her kitchen table. Just the thought of some sleazeball following her, watching her every move, wanting her, enraged him. She was in danger, more than she seemed to realize, and every instinct he had urged him to lock her up somewhere safe, out of harm's way, until the bastard was in custody.

Slinging an arm over his eyes to blot out the sun, he rolled to his back and tried to laugh at the thought of anyone trying to protect Sabrina Jones when she didn't want to be protected. She'd take his head off if he even suggested such a thing. The lady was a fighter, with more guts than any woman he knew. He didn't doubt for a minute that in most circumstances, she could take care of herself, but that gave him little comfort. There was nothing ordinary about her current situation. She had a serial killer on her tail, and that wasn't something she or any other woman should have to deal with alone.

And *that* was something he could do something about. Rolling over onto his side, he reached for the phone. A few seconds later, he grinned as a familiar voice drawled, "Alamo City Investigations. This is Adam Martin. May I help you?"

"Well, that depends. How much is it going to cost me?"

"Blake?" his friend said, shocked. "Is that you? Son of a gun! I tried calling you last week in Lordsburg, but your number had been disconnected. Where the hell are you?"

"Some P.I. you are," Blake teased, his green eyes twinkling. "I'm right here in town. I've been working at the *Times* ever since the beginning of August."

"Hey, man, I've been working my tail off. Who's got time to read the paper?" An old college friend, Adam gave him a hard time about not calling sooner, then proceeded to catch up on the latest news. "So what's going on?" he asked finally. "And don't tell me you need a P.I. I told you before if you ever wanted to give up reporting, I'd hire you in a second. I've got employees with ten years' experience who can't hold a candle to you when it comes to investigating. Say the word, and you've got a job."

Blake's smile faded. "Actually, I do need your services," he said seriously. "I want you to watch Sabrina Jones for me."

"Sabrina Jones, the reporter for the *Daily Record*?" he asked in surprise. "Why? Is she stealing your stories or what?"

"I can hold my own with the lady when it comes to reporting. This is something else. I guess you've heard about the serial killer going around town killing professional women?"

"Of course. Every woman I know is as jumpy as a scalded cat, and I can't say I blame them. What's that got to do with Sabrina Jones?"

"The killer's become fixated on her. The bastard's sending her notes, threatening her. Last night, she came home to find one on her kitchen table. The police think he has a key."

"Damn! And she doesn't have a clue who he is?"

"No. Detective Kelly and I finally convinced her that she needed to stay someplace else until the son of a bitch is caught, so she's taking over my place until it's safe for her to go home. I'm staying at Pop's."

"So she's still alone at night and roaming all over the city during the day," Adam concluded. "If the jerk really wants to get her, she's an easy target, Blake."

"I know. That's where you come in. I want you to watch her night and day and not let her out of your sight."

"And the lady's agreeable to this?"

"Are you kidding?" Blake laughed. "She'd be all over my case in a heartbeat if she suspected that I was even talking to you about her, let alone hiring you. So you're going to have to be damn discreet. She's no dummy."

"Hey, discreet's my middle name," Adam joked. "Give me all the particulars, and I'll put someone on her right away. And don't worry. She'll never suspect a thing."

Relieved, Blake gave him a detailed description of Sabrina, his address, and the license-plate number of her red Honda. When he hung up a few minutes later, a worry that he hadn't allowed himself to acknowledge lifted from his shoulders. She'd be furious if she ever found out he'd put a tail on her, but for the first time in what felt like days, he knew she was safe. Maybe now he could get her out of his head and sleep at night.

Her head sluggish from what amounted to a little over an hour of sleep, her eyes bloodshot, and her stomach rolling at the mere thought of food, Sabrina reported to work on time, but God only knew how. She didn't remember dressing, or for that matter, actually driving to work. And things only went downhill from there. On a day when she would have liked nothing better than to trade places with someone on the obit desk, Fitz sent her all over town, chasing one breaking story after another. By three in the afternoon, all she wanted to do was drag herself back to Blake's apartment, crawl into bed, and not move for another twenty-four hours.

"Jones, get over to Comanche Courts," Fitz yelled across the city room at her. "There's been a drive-by shooting. Go see what you can get on it."

She groaned, but she went, hanging on to the thought that in another couple of hours, she could call it a day. Just two more hours. Surely she could get through that.

Comanche Courts was a housing project on the near east side of downtown, mere blocks from the River Walk and Alamo and the hundreds of thousands of tourists who visited the city every year. Since it was so well-known to her, Sabrina could have driven there with her eyes closed. A hotbed of poverty and crime, the courts had, over the years, been the site of more drug busts, murders and shootings than Sabrina could hope to remember. And she'd covered almost all of them.

It was not a place where you dropped your guard, but Sabrina had never been scared there. As usual, the police were present in intimidating force, the lights on top of their patrol cars silently whirling as they questioned possible witnesses. No one had been hurt—this time—but too many times before, she'd arrived to find an innocent victim lying in his own blood while his family screamed and wailed, helpless to save him.

Making her way through the crowd, Sabrina started questioning people, but if anyone had seen anything, they weren't willing to talk about it. Then she found herself next to a young girl who couldn't have been older than twelve. An innocent with dimples, she looked like a baby—until you got a look at her eyes. Dark and knowing and *old,* they had obviously seen things that no twelve-year-old should have even dreamed about, let alone witnessed firsthand.

"It was the Demons," she said in a voice so low that Sabrina had to bend her head to hear her. "They were after Joshua Cruz because they think he joined a rival gang."

At the mention of one of the most dangerous gangs in the city, Sabrina arched a brow. "I thought the Demons stuck to the west side."

"Not anymore. They declared war on the Devils."

"So this is the start of a gang war?" Sabrina asked in surprise, jotting down notes. "Is the Cruz boy a member of the Devils?"

Hugging herself, goose bumps rippling across her skin in spite of the heat of the afternoon, the younger girl shook her head, tears of frustration gathering in her dark eyes. "No, but they don't care. Franco Hernandez is a bully and a killer. He doesn't care who he hurts as long as it makes him look tough."

Studying her, Sabrina asked quietly, "Are you saying you saw the shooting? Was Franco the shooter?"

For a minute, she could almost see the word *yes* hovering on the girl's tongue. Then fear crept into her eyes and she clammed up. "I'm sorry. I can't say any more." And before Sabrina could even ask her her name, she disappeared into the crowd.

"Damn!" Muttering curses under her breath, Sabrina knew her one shot at getting anyone to talk to her had probably just slipped through her fingers. The people in the courts had their own brand of justice that had nothing to do with the legal system, and that, unfortunately, led to more shootings, more deaths, a catch-22 without end.

Still, she couldn't give up. Not when there was a chance that someone among the fifty or so people milling around might give her a little more information. And she still needed to question the officers investigating the shooting.

All her concentration focused on pulling information from witnesses who wanted nothing to do with her, it was a long time before Sabrina felt the touch of someone's eyes on her. Frowning, she turned, half-expecting to find Blake watching her with a mocking grin, but he was nowhere in sight. And no one else seemed to be paying the least attention to her. In fact, no one even made eye contact with her.

"You're losing it, Jones," she muttered to herself. "That's what happens when you only get an hour of sleep. Chill out."

She tried, but when she turned back to the rookie officer she'd just started to question, the fine hairs at the back of her neck rose in warning. Suddenly chilled, her heart lurching in her breast, she fought the need to glance over her shoulder.

"Something wrong, ma'am? If you don't mind me saying so, you look a little green around the gills."

Sabrina winced at that *ma'am*. She must look more haggard than she realized, she thought with a groan. She couldn't be five years older than the fresh-faced officer, and he was treating her like his grandmother.

Forcing a smile, she said, "Actually, I'm fine, just a little paranoid at the moment. You're going to think I'm crazy, but could you do me a favor?"

"Sure, if I can. What is it?"

"Just casually look behind me at the crowd. Do you see anyone watching us?"

Rubbing the back of his neck, he glanced around with a nonchalance that would have done an Academy Award winner proud, then shrugged, his smile crooked, as he turned his attention back to Sabrina. "People always stare when the police show up, but I don't see any suspicious characters if that's what you mean. Why? Has someone been bothering you?"

"Not bothering me exactly. Just…watching me." Unable to explain the disquiet that had her pulse jumping in her veins, she laughed shakily. "Just forget I said anything. I didn't get much sleep last night—I guess it's catching up with me. If you hear anything else about the shooter, I'd appreciate it if you'd give me a call."

She gave him her card, then drove back to the paper, double-checking her rearview mirror every couple of blocks. The traffic shifted and flowed normally enough around her, giving her no reason to think that she was being followed, but her gut was churning, the back of her head itching in awareness, and nothing she could say would reason her growing uneasiness away. Her fingers curling tightly around the steering wheel, she hit the gas, zipped around the car in front of her, and made a sharp right turn at the next corner without bothering to use a signal. Horns honked and someone threw an obscene gesture at her, but she didn't care. The *Daily Record*'s fenced-in parking lot was a half a block away, the security guard clearly within sight. Sending up a silent prayer of thanks, she raced into the lot like the devil himself was after her.

It wasn't until she braked to a stop and cut the engine, however, that she realized she was shaking like a leaf. Laying her head back weakly against the headrest, she let her breath out in a rush. "This isn't like you, Jones," she lectured herself in a voice that wasn't nearly as firm as she would have liked. "You don't jump at every shadow like a 'fraidy-cat. Those notes must really be getting to you. Maybe you really should think about taking a long vacation and letting someone else deal with this for a while."

It sounded good, but she knew she wasn't going anywhere. Whoever had left those notes for her could threaten her as much as he wanted, stand in the dark and stare at her, try to follow her if he thought he could keep up with her, but it wasn't going to do him any good. She was scared—only a fool wouldn't be—but there was no way she was letting a sniveling coward of a murderer scare her off the story of a lifetime.

The matter settled, she strode into the city room of the *Daily Record* with her chin at a confident angle. If her knees still had a tendency to knock and her heartbeat wasn't as slow and steady as she would have liked, no one knew that but her.

"Hey, Jones," Fitz called out the minute she stepped into the city room. "Did ya get the skinny on that drive-by?"

She nodded, holding up her notebook. "Got it right here, boss. Give me a few minutes to transcribe my notes, and I'll have it to you by five."

"Atta girl! Now if I can just light a fire under the rest of the bums around here, we just might be able to put out a paper tomorrow."

Sinking down into the chair at her desk, Sabrina grinned at the old man's familiar litany. He'd been with the paper for nearly forty years, and as far as she knew, he'd never yet missed a morning edition. But he still worried like an old woman, pacing and grumbling and fretting until the paper was put to bed every night. That kind of stress might have eaten away the lining of someone else's stomach years ago, but Fitz seemed to thrive on it. It was, she knew, what made him so good at his job.

The city room was, as usual, mayhem, with her co-workers coming and going and putting the last finishing touches on stories for tomorrow's edition. Flipping open her notebook to her notes, Sabrina hardly noticed. With the ease of years of practice, she blocked out everything but her thoughts and started to pound out the story on her computer keyboard.

Concentrating, she couldn't have said when she first became aware of the fact that someone had stalked into the city room and crossed directly to her desk, where he stopped and glared down at her, waiting for her to notice him. Her gaze trained on her computer monitor, she caught sight of movement from the corner of her eye and figured it was one of the copyboys. "Just a minute," she said absently. "I'll be right with you."

Frowning, she closed her eyes, searching for the ending to her article, and suddenly there it was. Her fingers flew over the keys. Saving it, she smiled in satisfaction. "There! Now, what can I do—"

Her eyes widened, the words dying on her tongue as she looked up into her ex-husband's furious face. "Jeff!" Straightening in shock, she blurted out, "What are you doing here?"

"Looking for you," he said through his teeth. "I want to talk to you."

Taken aback by his hostile tone, Sabrina blinked in surprise. Jeff was a man who prided himself on his self-control. He didn't get angry—he just got very very quiet, and his gray eyes took on a coldness that chilled you to the bone. But something had his shorts in a twist. From the looks of the hot, red flush staining his cheeks and throat, he was more interested in yelling at her than talking, but she wisely kept that thought to herself. One wrong word just might push him over the edge and she had no intention of doing that while they were the object of at least a dozen curious pairs of eyes.

Rising to her feet, she forced a smile. "Why don't we talk outside? Would you like a Coke or something from the break room?"

"No."

So much for good manners. "Okay. Let's go."

Her curiosity killing her, she led him through the maze of corridors to the rear door that opened onto the parking lot, where they wouldn't be disturbed. Before it had even closed behind them, she was demanding some answers. "Okay, Jeff, let's have it. What's going on?"

"What's going on?" he echoed, outraged. "Don't you dare stand there and pretend to be Miss Innocent! You know damn well what's going on. You told the police that I was threatening you!"

"What?"

"You heard me," he growled. "A Detective Kelly showed up at the office this morning asking questions about my whereabouts last night." A pained expression crossed his thin face just at the memory of it. "I don't have to tell you what Mr. Druthers thought of that. I spent two hours in his office trying to explain myself, and I don't even know what this is about. If this costs me a partnership…"

The phrase was an old familiar one that left Sabrina cold. A partnership. It was all he'd ever thought of when they were married, all he'd ever wanted. A lawyer with one of the oldest, most prestigious firms in the city, Jeff would have sold his own mother to get in the firm if he thought

Mr. Druthers and the other partners wouldn't have severely disapproved.

"I'm sorry you were inconvenienced," she said coolly.

His eyes glacial, he sniffed, "'Inconvenienced' doesn't begin to describe what you did to me."

"*I* didn't do anything. Louis was the one who mentioned your name to the police, but only because someone had broken into my house and he saw someone in the neighborhood who favored you."

She tried to tell him that she had become the unwitting target of a serial killer, but as usual, he wasn't interested in anyone but himself. He didn't even hear her.

"Wasn't it convenient that you had an ex-husband to blame?" he said snidely. "So what can I expect next, Sabrina? The police showing up at my house? Searching it? Just because you've gotten mixed up with a sick character who'll do anything to get his name in the paper? I don't think so. I won't have it. Do you hear me? Whatever your problems are, you keep me out of them."

For a man who never broke a sweat if he didn't have to, he stormed off with an amazing amount of energy. Watching him disappear around the corner, Sabrina could only shake her head. She'd actually been married to that pompous ass for two years. What had she ever seen in him?

Her temples starting to throb, she headed back inside and told herself to forget him. She could not, however, forget what had brought him back into her life. The killer. For all she knew, he could be watching the parking-lot exit, waiting for her to leave. He would follow her, of course, all the way to Blake's if she wasn't careful.

Sick, her nerves jumpy at the thought of playing cat and mouse with a man she couldn't name or put a face to, she considered the idea of working late. But what good would it do? She would have to leave eventually. It would be better to do that now than after dark when she couldn't see who might be watching her, tailing her, from a distance.

Still, that didn't make driving out of the secured parking lot any easier. Her heart in her throat, she turned left instead of right, away from Blake's apartment, then spent the next half hour trying to make her way unobtrusively back to it. It was nerve-racking business. By the time she finally pulled into the apartment complex and pulled the door down on Blake's private garage, hiding her car from prying eyes, she was shaking.

Deep down inside, she found herself hoping that Blake would be waiting for her in the apartment. She hadn't seen him all day, not even when she'd gone to Comanche Courts to cover the drive-by, and as much as she hated to admit it, she'd missed him. She wanted to see that crooked grin of his, that spark of devilment in his eyes, and, just for a minute, walk into his arms and feel them close around her. Later, she would deny it, but for now she just needed to be held.

But when she unlocked both locks and pushed open the door, she knew before she ever stepped over the threshold that he wasn't there. The apartment was too quiet, the air too stale. She'd turned off the air-conditioning when she'd left that morning, and the place was like an oven. Disappointed, she shut the door and shot the dead bolt home and tried to find comfort in the sound of it clicking into place.

Instead, all she felt was lonely, and that horrified her. Flipping on the air conditioner, she told herself to knock it off. Just that afternoon, she'd had an excellent reminder of why she didn't need a man in her life. She was just like her mother and grandmother when it came to the male of the species—she was a lousy judge of character. If she didn't want to be married a zillion times like they had been, then she was going to have to resign herself to living alone. That didn't mean she couldn't be attracted to Blake or enjoy his kisses. She had the same needs as any other woman. She just had to be on guard and make sure her romantic heart didn't trick her into thinking there was anything more between them than physical attraction.

Satisfied that she'd finally resolved that issue, she headed for the bathroom and a cool shower in the hopes that it would wash her nagging headache down the drain. It didn't. She knew it was just a combination of exhaustion and tension, but she found it impossible to relax. For her own safety, she was virtually a prisoner here until the following morning, and the walls were already beginning to close in on her.

Outside, the sudden yapping of what sounded like a terrier broke the quiet. Figuring it belonged to one of Blake's neighbors, who was no doubt walking the dog after it had been locked up in the apartment all day, she strolled over to the window and looked out. The dog was nowhere in sight, and at first glance, the street outside the apartment seemed to be deserted except for tenants on their way home from work. Then she saw the man blending into the shadows beneath an Arizona ash tree across the street.

He was just standing there, during the hottest part of the day, watching her.

Chapter 8

"You ought to go check on that girl and make sure she's okay."

Hardly tasting the meat loaf his grandfather had made for supper, Blake only grunted. Pop had been hounding him about Sabrina from the moment he stepped in the front door from work, blatantly playing matchmaker, and had no idea how close to success he was. Over the course of the day, he'd had to force himself to stay away from her, to let someone else cover stories where he knew he might run into her. Knowing Adam or one of his men was watching over her had eased his mind considerably, but not enough. He wanted to see her with his own two eyes, touch her, pull her into his arms and assure himself that she really was okay.

Which was why he was staying the hell away from her.

His jaw set, he pushed the food around on his plate, his

appetite nonexistent. It was that late-night phone call that had done him in, he decided, and knew he had no one to blame but himself. He'd lain on that torture device that was disguised as a bed in Pop's guest room and listened to her murmur in his ear, his body hard and aching and hurting. Given the chance, he'd have done it again in a heartbeat.

And that was what had him worried. She'd gotten under his skin, into his head, and was in danger of worming her way into his heart, and he couldn't just stand by and let it happen. He'd learned the hard way that you never really knew a woman, no matter how good a friend or lover you thought she was, and that wasn't a lesson he had to learn twice.

So he was staying well away from Sabrina Jones. He'd done what he could to make her safe; that was all he could do. From here on out, she was on her own. If he couldn't sleep for thinking about her, well, that was just too damn bad.

"I just don't understand you," his grandfather complained. "In my day, when a lady was in trouble, a man didn't leave her to fend for herself. Have you even talked to her today? How do you know she's not lying dead in a ditch somewhere?"

"She's fine, Pop."

"You don't know that. What if that bastard who's leaving her all those notes found out she was staying at your place? He could have surprised her like he surprised those other women."

Knowing how his grandfather would jump to all the wrong conclusions, he hadn't meant to tell him about his arrangement with Adam, but if he didn't, he'd hound him until he finally gave in and gave Sabrina a call. "That's not going to happen, Pop—"

Scowling at him, he growled, "And just how the heck do you know that? She's a gutsy girl—"

"Too gutsy for her own good sometimes," Blake agreed. "Which is why I called Adam Martin today."

His mouth already open to argue, his grandfather snapped it shut as his green eyes started to twinkle. "You put a P.I. on her? Oh, boy, are you going to be in hot water when she finds out!"

"Hopefully, she'll never know," Blake said just as the phone rang. Glancing at his grandfather, he lifted a brow. "You want me to get that?"

"Yeah, it's probably your mother. She calls just about every day at this time to remind me to take my blood-pressure medicine. You'd think I was a senile old man or something," he grumbled.

"You?" Blake laughed as he rose from the table. "You'll be as sharp as a tack when you're a hundred, and you know it." Snatching up the phone, he said, "Finnigan residence."

"Blake, is that you?"

Recognizing Sam Kelly's voice, he stiffened. "Yeah, Sam, it's me. What's up?"

"I thought you'd want to know that Sabrina just placed a 911 call from your place. Evidently she spied someone watching her from across the street. I'm heading over there right now."

Blake's heart stopped in midbeat. "I'll meet you there." Hanging up, he hurriedly told his grandfather what was going on, then headed for the door. "I don't know when I'll be back."

He drove like a madman, breaking every posted speed limit without a thought, just daring a cop to try and stop him. But if there were any black-and-whites in the vicinity, he didn't see them. Within three minutes of rushing out of his grandfather's house, he braked to a rough stop in front of his apartment.

In spite of the fact that he'd made the short drive in record time, Sam Kelly was already there. His unmarked car was parked at the curb across the street, the portable red light he'd slapped on the roof whirling. He was standing in the shade of an Arizona ash talking to a man who was dressed like a jogger in T-shirt, shorts and running shoes. One look at him and Blake knew the fat was in the fire. It was Adam Martin.

"Well, damn!" Muttering curses, he got out of his pickup and crossed the street, a sheepish grin curling the corners of his mouth as he approached the two men. "I guess I don't have to introduce you two. Dammit, Adam, you weren't supposed to let Sabrina see you!"

"I know," he said with a grimace. "I blew it. But I wasn't expecting her to be staring out the window. I was just going to sit under the tree and pretend I was catching my breath, but she caught me looking. The next thing I knew, the police were driving up. I'm sorry, Blake. I guess you're going to have to tell her now, huh?"

"If he doesn't, I will," Sam said, shooting Blake a reproving look. "You should have told her the minute you put somebody on her tail."

"I didn't think it would be necessary. Anyway, she never would have agreed to it." Glancing up to the apartment's living-room window, he wasn't surprised to see Sabrina standing there, a worried frown furrowing her brow. "Who's on the next shift, Adam?"

"Mitch Hawkins, then Don Sanchez," he said, then gave him a description of both men. "I take it you're not going to pull them?"

"Hell, no. She's not going to like it—in fact, I can pretty much guarantee she's going to read me the riot act—but that's just too damn bad. She'll be safe, and that's all that matters. Well, I'd better get this over with."

Amused, Sam drawled, "If she tosses you out the window, at least there'll be a witness to call for an ambulance. Keep up the good work, Adam."

Blake's mouth twitched, but he wasn't smiling when he crossed the street and took the stairs to his second-floor apartment. If all she did was toss him out the window, he'd be damn lucky.

Standing at the window, watching the three men laugh, Sabrina frowned as Blake crossed the street toward the apartment complex. When she'd seen Sam drive up, she'd expected him to immediately arrest the man across the street posing as a jogger, not chat with him like this was old home week. Couldn't he see the man was definitely stalking her? What in the world was going on?

Troubled, she was seriously considering going down there to find out for herself when there was a knock at the door. She didn't have to check through the peephole to know that it was Blake. Crossing to the door, she snatched it open. "Thank God you're here! I was just going down there," she said as she pulled him inside. "Who is that man? I couldn't believe it when I looked out the window and saw him watching me. Why isn't Sam arresting him?"

"It's all right. It's not what you think—"

Turning back toward the window, she hardly heard him. "I've had this feeling all day that someone was following me. It was like an itch at the back of my neck. I thought I was going crazy, then suddenly, there he was. He never tried to get into the apartment, but he scared me to death."

"I'm sorry about that. I should have told you—"

Frustrated, she cried, "What does he want? He just stands there...." His words suddenly registering, she whirled back to face him. "What do you mean, you should have told me? Told me what?"

He hesitated, and when he did, a flush started at his throat and slowly worked its way up to his face. Sabrina didn't like the suspicions suddenly stirring in her head. Her eyes narrowing dangerously, she stepped toward him. "What have you done, Nickels? What do you know about that man down there?"

There was no help for it—he had to tell her. "He's a friend," he began reluctantly.

"A friend!"

"His name's Adam Martin. We went to college together."

"College," she repeated, sounding like a broken record. "You went to college with a stalker?"

Here it came. Bracing himself, he said bluntly, "He's not a stalker. He's a P.I. I hired him to watch you."

"You *what?!*"

"I hired him—"

She waved him off, not needing to hear the words again.

Stunned, outrage and confusion warring in her eyes, she just stared at him. "Why? Why would you do such a thing? Who gave you the right?"

"No one, but—"

"You're damn right no one did!" Working herself up into a fine temper, she started to pace, muttering half to herself. "God, I can't believe you did this! Jeff, yes—he didn't think I had the sense to get off the tracks when a train was coming. But I do the same work you do, go to the same sleazy places in this town that you do. I've never been hurt, never been shot at, never even been scared. But you think I need a bodyguard."

Blake told himself to keep a tight rein on his own temper. She was entitled to her anger. He just had to let it blow itself out. But damn, he didn't like being compared to her jerk of an ex-husband in any way, shape or form. "You never had a serial killer after you before, either," he pointed out tersely.

"Whether I have or haven't isn't the point. *You had no right!*"

"I don't see it that way," he said flatly. "Three women are dead. Three women who were probably just as independent as you are. Right or wrong, I wasn't going to stand around flat-footed while you became the fourth, so I did something about it."

Her hands on her hips, she glared at him. "Without so much as a by your leave."

It wasn't a question, but an accusation, and he didn't flinch from it. "You're damn right. It was easier that way. You would have just given me a hard time about it when there was nothing left to discuss. I hired the tail and I'm the only one who can fire him."

Too late, Blake realized he probably should have found a more diplomatic way to put that. It was nothing less than the truth, but he didn't have to rub her nose in it. She started to sputter, her brown eyes sparking fire. He should have been backpedaling, trying to soothe her ruffled feathers, but instead, he found himself perversely struck by the humor of the situation. Grinning, he said, "Go ahead and blow a gasket, but if you're going to get mad, get mad at the right person. This is all your fault."

That stopped her in her tracks. "*My* fault? How the heck

do you figure that? You were the one who took it upon yourself to hire that man," she snapped, motioning in the general direction of the street. "I didn't do anything."

"Except bring out the caveman in me."

The admission came out of nowhere to steal her breath. Caught off-guard, her heart lurching in her breast, Sabrina blinked, sure she must have heard him wrong. "I beg your pardon?"

Wry humor glinted in his eyes. "You heard me. I've never considered myself a chauvinist, but there's something about you that just seems to bring out the caveman in me. Logically, I know you can take care of yourself, but this doesn't have a whole hell of a lot to do with logic."

"Blake—"

"I know, it's crazy, but there it is. So if it'll make you feel any better, I didn't hire Adam for you—I hired him for me. So I don't have to worry about you when I'm not around."

Not sure what he was admitting to, Sabrina couldn't seem to drag her gaze away from his. He was still smiling, but there was something in his eyes, an emotion that drizzled through her like honey, warming her to her soul and alarming her at one and the same time. With no effort whatsoever, he was slowly, bit by bit, carving a place for himself in her life, in her heart. She'd only known him for a matter of weeks, yet she was already living in his apartment, sleeping in his bed. Granted, he wasn't in there with her, but for how long? How long before she lost her head, then her heart?

Dismayed, she shook her head. "No," she whispered hoarsely. "I appreciate your concern, but you aren't responsible for my welfare. If you're getting ideas about me just because I'm staying here, you can forget it right now. I can find somewhere else to stay."

She started to brush past him, but he grabbed her, hauling her in front of him. "Oh, no you don't," he grated. "You're not going anywhere until we get this settled."

"There's nothing to settle!" she insisted, tugging at her arm. "Let me go, Blake. I've got to get out of here."

That should have gained her her release. Instead, he drew her inexorably closer. "I don't think so," he murmured. "You can't walk away from this any more than I can. Not this time."

Her spine ramrod straight, she didn't bother to tug at her arm again. "Did I ever tell you that I've never cared much for Neanderthals?" she purred. "You might remember that."

He *almost* laughed. Lord, she was something! He watched her try to stare him down and couldn't for the life of him look away. Or let her go. Not when he had her this close and he was aching to kiss her again. She was probably going to be furious with him, but he'd just have to risk it. Murmuring her name, he leaned down and took her mouth with his.

Half braced for a struggle, he felt her stiffen, felt every muscle go perfectly still as her breath seemed to catch in her lungs. Her palms were flat against his chest, wedged there to push him away—with the slightest pressure, she could have won her release. Because as much as he wanted her, he would have never forced her. But instead of shoving him away, her fingers curled into the material of his shirt. It was just a faint movement, a caress that she probably wasn't even aware of. But it told him far more about what was going on in her body than she knew.

She couldn't fight the attraction between them any more than he could.

A wise man would have stopped there, content with the small victory. But the emotions raging within him had nothing to do with contentment, and there was no way in hell he could stop now. His mouth gentling, softening, cajoling, he planted tiny, nibbling kisses at the corners of her mouth, the curve of her cheek, the sweet, sensitive hollow at the base of her throat. "God, I want you, Jones," he breathed huskily into her ear. "Can't you feel how much? Tell me I'm not the only one going crazy here."

"No," she whispered, but even as she denied it, her mouth lifted to his.

"Yes," he insisted in a rough growl. Swooping down, he pressed her lips open with his, seducing her with his tongue in a series of long, slow, drugging kisses that were guaranteed to drive her quietly out of her mind. He was the one, however, who felt his control slipping. His breathing ragged, he tore his mouth from hers, but he didn't let her go. He simply couldn't. His arms tightening around her, he held her close, his eyes locked with hers. "Tell me, honey."

Dizzy, the thunder of her heart loud in her ears, she couldn't for the life of her look into those forest-green eyes of his and deny what he did to her. Not when her pulse was all over the chart and her knees had long since lost the ability to support her.

Her arms tightening around his neck, she muttered, "Damn you, Nickels, I don't know how you keep doing this to me. I can't think when you kiss me like that."

She didn't know another man she would have trusted enough to make that admission to. One more kiss, and he could have turned her to putty in his arms, but he didn't take advantage. A half smile curling one corner of his mouth, he lifted a hand to her cheek and admitted thickly, "I seem to be having that problem myself. What do you think we should do about it?"

Her senses beginning to cloud, she leaned into his hand. "Talk about it later," she murmured, pulling his mouth down to hers. "I can't think right now."

Later would be too late. She didn't give her heart lightly, and instinctively she knew that Blake could hurt her in ways Jeff never had. But they had, by fits and starts, been racing toward and fighting this moment from that first day when he'd stepped in her path and tried to protect her from something she didn't need protection from. She couldn't deny it any longer. Couldn't fight it any more. She wanted him. Here. Now. In every way a woman could want a man. Just once, she promised herself dreamily as she gave herself up to his kisses. She would have him just this once and get him out of her system. Maybe then she could sleep at night without reaching for him in her dreams.

But if she thought they were just going to have sex, she soon discovered how wrong she was. Nothing that they stirred in each other was that simple, that uncomplicated. His hands moved slowly over her, charting every dip and curve with a touch she somehow knew as well as the beat of her own heart, and intimacy was there between them, strong and sweet and sure. The world was just outside the apartment, waiting to intrude, but all she heard was the sigh of his breath, the thunder of his heart, the whisper of their clothes as they strained against each other, wanting more as need coiled tight between them.

"Blake—"

His name was all she could manage, the only thought in her head. How long had she been waiting for this, for him? He scared and thrilled her and shook her with the way he seemed to know her better than she knew herself. He nuzzled her ear and smiled softly when her breathing changed. And there were her breasts. She never said a word, never indicated by so much as a gasp how sensitive her breasts were to the play of his fingers even through the cotton of her shirt and bra, but he knew. Gently, tenderly, he trailed a finger around the crest of her nipple, circling, circling with infinite slowness, until all her attention was focused just there.

Shuddering, throbbing deep inside, she held her breath, waiting. Then, just when she thought she couldn't stand the torture any longer, he brushed against the tight bead he had created with a touch that was as soft as the brush of an angel's wing and heat streaked like an arrow straight to the core of her. Moaning, she turned into his hand, her breast filling his palm. Nothing had ever felt so good.

Holding her, caressing her, Blake told himself he'd been waiting too long for this moment to rush it. But, God, she made it difficult! She was so sweet, so responsive, that it was all he could do not to strip her clothes from her, drag her down to the living-room floor and take her like the caveman she so easily turned him into.

Tearing his mouth from hers, struggling for the control that was suddenly as elusive as a snowflake on a hot summer day, he forced himself to release her breast, but only so he could lock his arms around her and mold every soft, beautiful inch of her to him. But that, too, was agonizing. Snuggling close, her arms trapped between them, she plucked at the buttons of his shirt, undoing them one by one. Then she was touching him, running her hands under his shirt, stroking him like a cat and kissing him wherever she could reach, and in ten seconds flat, he was hotter than a two-dollar pistol.

Even then, he might have found the strength to stop. But when he burrowed his fingers in her dark, wild hair and turned her face up to his to ask her if she had any idea what she was doing to him, her brown eyes were nearly black with passion and lit from within by a fire that burned just for him. Staring down at her, he felt something shift in the region of his heart, something he couldn't control, something that swamped him with emotion and stole the breath from his lungs. His control going up in flames, he swept her up in his arms and carried her to his bed.

The last rays of the setting sun were streaming through the blinds at the window, striping the sheets with bars of golden light, but all he saw when he laid her on the bed and came down next to her was Sabrina. Her lips slightly swollen from his kisses, her cheeks flushed, her hair spread out across his pillow, she looked like something out of a fantasy, the answer to a lonely man's dreams.

He hadn't realized just how lonely he had been for her until then.

Urgency filling him, tearing at him, he fought out of his shirt and jeans. Before they even hit the floor, he was reaching for the buttons to her blouse. He couldn't remember the last time he'd fumbled with any kind of fastenings on a woman's clothing, but suddenly his fingers were shaking. That should have stopped him cold, set him back on his heels, made him think, but he wanted her too badly. Swearing, he tugged at her blouse, then her hands were there to help him, as impatient as his, and in seconds, she was bare and reaching for him.

She was beautiful. Another time, he could have spent hours just looking at her, touching her, delighting in her small, perfect breasts and slim hips and the impossible softness of her skin, but not now. Not when she pulled him into her arms, nipped at his ear and rasped softly, "Hurry."

As the day aged, the light shifted and mellowed and the shadows grew long. Outside, the sound of laughter from the apartment pool floated on the early evening air, but in the bedroom, the only sound was of Sabrina's soft, fractured moan as he slipped into her. Then her legs were closing around him, her wet, hot heat welcoming him, and his mind blurred. He moved, and she was there with him, catching his rhythm, taking him deeper. And as he took her like a man possessed, and she started to come apart in his arms, his name a keening cry on her lips, his only thought was that he had finally come home.

In the silence afterwards, their breathing was rough, the racing of their pounding hearts slowly easing. His face buried against her neck, feeling more satisfied than he'd ever felt in his life, Blake held her close and couldn't seem to make himself let her go. Not yet. Not when he could still feel the little aftershocks that rippled through her. He was crushing her, but even when he managed to roll to his side, he took her with him, his arms twin bands of steel around her. He couldn't stop touching her, caressing her, assuring himself she was real.

It had been a while for him, he told himself. It was just chemistry. And loneliness. Trina had been a part of his life for a long time, and he hadn't even looked at another woman until Sabrina had crossed his path and the sparks had flown between them. After such a long dry spell, it hadn't taken much to light a fire. But now that they'd made love, he could get her out of his head.

But even as he tried desperately to believe that, she stirred in his arms and dropped a kiss to his chest, and just that quickly, he wanted her again. More than before, in a hundred different ways. Shaken, he drew in the scent of her and knew he could have spent hours just exploring her, learning her secrets, loving her again and again and again, until they were both too tired to move.

Dear God, what had she done to him? he wondered as the light outside gradually darkened with twilight. When Trina ran off with that trucker the night before he'd planned to ask her to marry him, she'd ripped his heart out by the roots. Like a damn fool, he hadn't known that she was even seeing anyone else. And it had hurt, dammit!

Never again, he'd promised himself. He was never going to open himself up to that kind of pain again. Especially with a woman who had made it clear that she wasn't interested in anything that even hinted at long-term commitment. If he was going to get involved—and he still wasn't sure that he was—he wouldn't settle for anything less than the long haul.

Even as his hands trailed over her, loving the feel of her, he knew he had to get out of there. Now, while he still could. He had to think, figure out where he was going, where the hell *they* were going, if anywhere.

But leaving her wasn't nearly as easy as he would have liked. His arms didn't want to release her. His jaw clenched on an oath, he rubbed his cheek against the top of her head and said quietly, "I've got to go. I rushed over here like a madman when Kelly called, and Pop is probably worried sick by now thinking you've been murdered. You going to be okay by yourself?"

His hard, sinewy body pressed close from shoulder to thigh, Sabrina nodded, dazed. "Mm-hmm."

What in the world had just happened here? She'd been married, divorced; she'd made love more than enough times to know what to expect. But nothing and no one had ever swept the ground right out from under her the way Blake just had. For the first time in her life, she'd actually felt the earth move and she didn't know if she wanted to call AP with the news or run for cover.

Something of her inner agitation must have shown because Blake was suddenly pulling back to get a better look at her face, a frown worrying his brow as his eyes searched hers. "You're awfully quiet."

Heat burning her cheeks, she ducked away from that all-too-discerning gaze of his, afraid he could read her like a book. "Actually, I was just about to doze off," she said with forced lightness. "You make a nice pillow, Nickels."

His mouth quirked, but he didn't smile. "My pleasure," he said gruffly. "About what just happened—"

"We're both consenting adults," she said hurriedly, cutting him off. "There's nothing more to discuss."

She moved then before he could stop her, dragging the covers up to her breast as she turned to face him with half the width of the bed between them. Her smile breezy, she prayed that he couldn't see how fake it was in the gathering twilight. "Go on now, get out of here. It's getting late. Your grandfather will be worried."

He should have been pleased, she thought. After all, didn't most men worry about a woman getting the wrong idea after sex? He wanted out and she was making it easy for him, but instead of acting grateful, he was looking at her as if she'd just insulted him.

"All right, all right," he said stiffly. "I'm going."

Throwing off the covers, he rose naked from the bed and had no idea what the sight of him did to her. Her mouth dry, her heart skipping every other beat, she watched as he tugged on his clothes, the frown that wrinkled his brow growing darker with every article of clothing he pulled on. By the time he was completely dressed, he was positively scowling at her. "We're going to talk about this tomorrow," he warned, then stalked out.

The second the front door slammed behind his stiff back, Sabrina wilted like a week-old rose, the need to call him back almost more than she could bear. She wanted him to hold her, to reassure her that she wasn't the only one who'd been shattered by their loving. And that alone terrified her. What if he, too, had experienced the same free fall through space and he was just as thrown by it as she? What then? Where did they go from here?

The possible answers shook her to the core.

Her heart slamming against her ribs, she climbed out of bed and grabbed a robe, chiding herself not to lose her head. It was just lust. It had to be. Simple, basic desire. The kind that made fools of the women in her family and caused them to make all the wrong decisions about men and love and life. She wouldn't, couldn't get caught up in the wonder of it. Her mother and grandmother might love walking down the aisle so much that they were willing to risk the divorce that inevitably followed, but she couldn't handle it. Once was enough. Some people just weren't cut out for marriage, and she was one of them.

Not that Blake had asked her to marry him, or was even thinking about doing such an outrageous thing, she quickly assured herself. He wasn't the type of man to get caught up in the emotion of the moment and lose his head. But he also wasn't, she decided, the kind of philandering lowlife who jumped from woman to woman, bed to bed. According to his grandfather, his family had high expectations for him in politics and that meant nothing short of marriage to the right woman would ever be acceptable. She was not, and never would be, that woman.

Still, there was a part of her, deep in the heart of her, that remembered his loving and cried out for more. He'd touched something in her that no one else had, stirred something in her that she'd dreamed of without even realizing it until now. She didn't want to lose that. Didn't want to lose *him*. God, what was she going to do?

Torn, she spent the rest of the evening prowling around the apartment in search of a distraction from her own thoughts. But everywhere she turned, she was reminded of Blake. She tried reading, even television, but nothing seemed to help. She couldn't even look out the window without being reminded that there was a man out there, watching the apartment for Blake, keeping her safe. Her head told her that her safety wasn't his responsibility—her heart whispered that he cared.

Frustrated, exhausted, she finally went to bed, and though she slept, she didn't really rest. She couldn't. Not when her heart and mind spent the hours between midnight and dawn arguing like a couple of eight-year-olds. By the time the alarm went off at seven, she knew she had to go back home. Blake wouldn't be happy about it and neither, for that matter, would Sam Kelly, but she needed her own things around her—if only for a little while—to remind her of who and what she was.

She called in to work and asked for a couple of hours off, then headed to her place an hour later. Not surprisingly, Blake's hired gun followed her the whole way, never letting more than one car get between them during the drive, not even on the freeway. Scowling at him in her rearview mirror, Sabrina recognized him from Blake's description as Mitch Hawkins—a blond surfer-type who looked like he had more brawn than brain. He'd smiled and nodded at her when she'd first emerged from the apartment, but she hadn't made the mistake of thinking that he took his job lightly. Before coming to work for Adam, he'd been a border-patrol agent and could, according to Blake, track a scorpion across solid rock.

Not surprisingly, he didn't follow her into her driveway, but parked at the curb two houses down and across the street. By the time she stepped out of her car, he had already shut off his motor and slumped down in his seat. If she hadn't known he was there, she would have never seen him.

"Hey, gorgeous! Where you been hiding out? I ain't seen you in a while."

At Joe Gomez's sexily growled greeting, Sabrina turned to find him pushing a battered Harley toward her down the street, his brown eyes, as usual, sparkling with devilment. As far as Sabrina knew, he didn't own a motorcycle, and there was a good possibility he'd burrowed this one from a friend without asking, but he looked so refreshingly normal that she wanted to hug him. Restraining herself, she grinned fondly at him. "Hey, yourself," she said, striding down the driveway toward him. "What do you mean, hiding out? I've been around."

"Yeah, right. And I'm the Easter bunny." Hurt, he gave her a chiding look, his eyes, for once, dead serious. "Do I look like I'm stupid or what? In all the years I've known you, you've always come home at night. The word on the street is that dude killing all those women has got it in for you."

Alarmed, Sabrina stiffened. "Where'd you hear that?"

"I've got my sources, don't you worry about it. And they're right, aren't they? You're in deep—"

"Joe!"

At her sharp warning tone, he widened his eyes innocently. "What? All I was going to say was you were in deep trouble."

"Sure you were."

He grinned. "I don't know why everyone jumps to the conclusion that my mind is in the gutter...."

He would have said more, but before he could, a black Chevy pickup came roaring around the corner at the end of the street and slammed to a stop in front Sabrina's house. A split second later, Blake was striding toward where they stood talking, so angry steam was practically pouring from his ears. Sabrina took one look at him and felt her heart start to knock in her breast. She didn't have to ask how he'd found her—her watchdog had obviously called Adam Martin, who had reported to Blake.

"If you've come to chew me out, you can save your breath," she began quickly.

That was as far as she got. "There's been another murder," he said tersely. "Apparently the killer made good on his promise to you in his note. The body was found less than three blocks from here."

Chapter 9

The murder scene was a particularly gruesome one. The victim, Denise Green, a florist who had just opened her own shop and was still struggling to get the business off the ground, had been shot in the head and the heart in her own kitchen and had died immediately. Then the killer, going on a rampage, had ransacked her house with a viciousness that he'd made no attempt to hide. In his rage, he had paid particular attention to the bedroom, ripping the sheets and mattress with a kitchen knife, then shredding every piece of clothing in the room.

There was no note, but none was necessary. Denise Green's general description was the same as Sabrina's... she was slender and petite, with curly black hair and brown eyes. And the similarities didn't stop there. Not only did she live in the same neighborhood in a house that was almost identical in style to Sabrina's, she also, as a florist, loved flowers. Her yard and front porch, like Sabrina's, were overflowing with them. And though her body had only just been found, she had, apparently, been dead for several days. Her neighbors thought she had gone to a floral convention in Phoenix and only started to wonder if something was wrong when they noticed that her dog was still in the backyard instead of at the kennel.

The police wouldn't know for sure until they got the report from the medical examiner, but she appeared to have died the night Sabrina went with Blake to the awards ceremony at the convention center. The same night the killer had slipped into Sabrina's house and left that note on her kitchen table. He had, to put it mildly, had a busy evening.

Stricken, Sabrina stood in Denise Green's bedroom with Blake and Sam and stared at the bed, at the ruined clothes, and felt the rage that had been directed squarely at her. Chilled to the bone, she hugged herself, nausea backing up in her throat. It should have been her, she thought numbly. As much as she wanted to deny it, she couldn't miss what was right there in front of her eyes. She should have been the one lying stone-cold dead in her own kitchen with two bullets lodged in her head and her heart. She was the one the killer had been furious with, the one he'd struck out at, the one he would have killed if he could have gotten his hands on her. But she hadn't been available, so he'd gone out and murdered an innocent woman instead just because she'd had the misfortune to remind him of Sabrina.

Dear God, when would this end?

"We're still going through the house for prints," Sam said, breaking the shocked silence that had fallen over them at the sight of the bedroom. "The perp's been damn careful up to this point, but it looks like he lost it when he did this. If we're lucky, he slipped up and made a mistake."

And if they weren't, there would be more deaths, more of the same, before the killer was caught. "What about the neighbors?" Sabrina asked stiffly. "Did any of them see or hear anything? Whoever did this didn't do it quietly."

"Not that we've been able to discover so far, but the body wasn't found until after most people had already gone to work. We should know more later in the day."

Noting the condition of the bedroom in his notebook, Blake glanced up with a frown. "What about signs of forced entry? Whoever this bastard is, he can't have keys to all these women's houses."

"No, there was no key this time," the detective said flatly, leading them back to the kitchen. The body had already been removed and taken to the morgue, but there was still dried blood everywhere. Motioning toward a bouquet of wildflowers on the counter, he said, "We think that was how he got in."

"You mean the flowers?" Sabrina asked in surprise. "Like a delivery boy?"

He nodded. "The card was still on the flowers, unopened, and the body was found right by the counter. She was still clutching her open purse...."

"Digging for a tip while he shot her right between the eyes," Blake concluded, creating an image of the murder that they could all see with sickening clarity. "God, that's cold."

Sabrina shuddered. "If he had to use a delivery to get in the door, then he didn't know her."

"Probably not," Sam agreed. "Which means he's changed his M.O. slightly, and I don't like the sound of that. Up until now, he's taken out his rage with you on women he appears to have known who remind him of you—that makes it personal. Now he's killed a stranger, someone he knows nothing about and really can't pretend is you, and that can't give him nearly as much satisfaction. That's only going to increase his rage, which might be what he needs to finally work up the nerve to come after you. For your own safety, you really do need to get out of town for a while."

As the last of the blood drained from her cheeks, Sabrina had to give him credit. When he issued a warning, he shot straight from the hip and didn't pull any punches. "Believe me, Sam, nobody would like to do that any more than I would, but I just can't afford to walk away from my job and hide out somewhere until this weirdo is caught. Anyway, you said yourself it's me he wants. I'm the one he really wants to kill. If I just disappear, he might go underground until I show up again."

"If you're thinking of offering yourself up as a decoy, you can just forget it," Blake said harshly before the detective could so much as open his mouth. "It's not going to happen."

Just days ago, she would have bristled at his tone, but the loving they'd shared last night had changed her, and to her horror, she couldn't stop her heart from lurching at the possessive, protective glint in his eyes. What had he done to her? She should have been setting him straight on the fact that only one person was in control of her life and it wasn't him, but all she wanted to do at that moment was walk into his arms.

Instead, she said huskily, "Nobody said anything about being a decoy."

"Good. Just so we understand each other."

His eyes, as green as a high-mountain forest, snared hers and held them captive, setting the pulse at her throat jumping crazily. The rest of the world faded from her consciousness, and for a split second in time, it was just the two of them, alone and needy.

Clearing his throat, Sam said dryly, "Now that we've got that cleared up, we still have the problem of keeping Sabrina safe. Considering how reckless this bastard's getting, I think he's ready to snap. I wouldn't put it past him to go after her in broad daylight."

"That's not going to be a problem," Blake said, never taking his gaze from Sabrina. "From now on, I don't intend to let her out of my sight."

"What?" she exclaimed. "What are you talking about?"

"You heard me. You're not going anywhere from now on without me."

"But you've already hired a P.I.—"

"And he's doing a good job," he replied. "But he can't watch over you the way I can."

His lips twitching, Sam glanced from the grim resolve in Blake's eyes to the sudden flush stinging Sabrina's cheeks and had the good sense to cut and run. "Well, I can see you two need to discuss this. I'll just get out of your hair and let you at it."

Blake never spared him a glance. "There's nothing to discuss," he told Sabrina flatly once they were alone, "so don't even think about arguing with me."

"The hell I won't," she hissed, keeping her voice deliberately low so it wouldn't carry to the policemen in the other rooms of the house. "Dammit, Blake, have you lost your mind? You can't go with me everywhere I go!"

"I don't know why I can't. Who's going to stop me?"

"Well, my boss, for one," she snapped. "What are you going to do when I report to work in the morning? Go with me?"

Not the least daunted by the idea, he nodded. "Every morning until the creep who's after you is behind bars."

"But that could be weeks! Months! Do you honestly think Fitz is going to sit back meekly and let me bring someone from the *Times* into the city room when we're in the middle of the biggest subscription war ever? He'll have a fit!"

Grinning, he pushed away from the counter to sling a friendly arm around her shoulder. "Better watch it, Jones," he teased. "Anybody hearing you just might think you're worried about me." When she only sniffed at that, he chuckled and steered her out the door. "I can take care of myself and you, too, sweetheart. Are you through around here? Good. So am I. Let's get back to work."

He followed her back to his apartment, left her car there, then drove her downtown to the ninety-year-old building that housed the *Daily Record*. In spite of that and his claims at the murder scene, Sabrina still didn't expect him to go inside with her...until he got out of the truck and started to follow her toward the employee entrance, his hand riding protectively at the bow of her back.

Fighting the sudden need to melt back into his touch, she stopped in her tracks. "Blake, this is crazy! Even if you can somehow get Fitz to agree to this, what about when you need to report in at the *Times*? Your editor's not going to be exactly pleased to see me, you know."

"Don't worry about Tom. He's an old friend. I'll square it with him."

"But what if you can't?"

His green eyes twinkling with devilment, he teased, "In the words of a talented writer I happen to have the good fortune to know, 'We're in the middle of the biggest subscription war ever.' Do you really think your boss or mine is going to fire either one of us when we're the two best reporters they've got?"

"Well, no, but—"

"I rest my case." Reaching past her shoulder, he pulled open the heavy steel door for her and waited for her to precede him. "Let's go."

Stepping inside, she was sure that they'd be stopped any second for an explanation. But Blake's presence didn't raise so much as an eyebrow. The few reporters that they did encounter who recognized Blake only nodded and went on about their business, and those in the city room didn't even glance up from their computers. Relieved, Sabrina dropped into her desk chair and sighed like a woman who had just made it through an obstacle course.

Chuckling, Blake took the chair opposite her desk, out of sight of her monitor, and pulled his notebook out of his pocket. "Go ahead and work, honey," he said, shooting her a smile that would have made her grandmother's heart jump in her breast. "I'm going to organize my notes. Then when you're finished here, we'll go over to the *Times* so I can write my piece."

Sure she wouldn't be able to write a word with him sitting right there, Sabrina cast him a suspicious look, but he was frowning at his notes and never noticed. Turning her attention back to her computer screen, she didn't even have to close her eyes to find herself back in Denise Green's bedroom, the carnage there sickening her. Suddenly, her fingers were flying over her keyboard as the words just flowed.

Lost in her own thoughts, Sabrina never saw her boss walk into the city room, but suddenly he was standing three feet away from her desk and scowling from her to Blake and back again. "You want to tell me what the hell is going on here, Jones?" he growled.

She jumped, her heart in her throat, and sent a line of *S*s running across her computer screen. "Fitz! You scared the life out of me! This is Blake—"

"I know who it is," he said curtly. "What I want to know is what's he doing here?"

"He's with me—"

"I can see that. Any particular reason why? And this better be damn good."

He had that look on his weathered face, the one that warned Sabrina that he had already made up his mind not to like what he was about to hear, and it was all she could do not to shake him. "Now don't go getting your back up before you've even heard what's going on, Fitzy. I know this looks odd, but I can explain everything if you'll just give me a chance—"

"I didn't give her a choice in the matter," Blake cut in, pushing to his feet to tower over the elderly editor. Quickly and concisely, he filled the other man in on the latest developments. "The psycho's obviously after her and I'm not letting her out of my sight until he's caught. So you'd better get used to seeing me around, Fitz," he warned with a cocky grin. "You're going to be seeing a lot of me. From now on, Sabrina and I will be going everywhere together."

Known more for his bluster than his bite, the editor scowled. "Let me get this straight, Nickels. You're telling me you're going to waltz into my paper whenever you feel like it and I'm supposed to get used to it?"

Even to his own ears, it sounded damn arrogant, but Blake had no intention of backing down to Fitz or anyone else when it came to Sabrina and her safety. His jaw set like stone, he nodded. "You are if you expect Sabrina to come in personally to file her stories. Otherwise, she can call them in from my place. The choice is yours."

His cheeks flushing with temper, Fitz opened his mouth to tell him exactly what he could do with those choices, but something in the depths of Blake's eyes must have warned him he was making no idle threat. Closing his mouth with an audible snap, he expelled his breath in a huff. "You really think she's in that kind of danger?" he asked gruffly.

"Yes, sir, I do," Blake replied quietly. "Detective Kelly asked her to leave town but she refused because she knows how you need her right now."

Sabrina sniffed at that, frowning. "You don't have to make me sound like a martyr, Nickels. I had other reasons for staying besides that—like the fact that I happen to need this job. And no coward of a murderer is going to run me out of my town."

She might as well have saved her breath. Neither man spared her a glance. "I don't like the idea of anyone from the *Times* walking in and out of here like they own the place, but if I've got to put up with one of Edwards' crew, I guess I'd just as soon it be you. I can trust you not to use any insider information you pick up while you're here against us."

It wasn't a question, but Blake treated it as one anyway. Lifting his hand to his heart, he said solemnly, "On my word as a Boy Scout."

The old man nodded. "Good enough. Jones, don't take any more chances than you have to. That's an order."

Giving her one last stern look to make sure she got the message, he strode off, leaving Sabrina staring after him in amazement. He'd practically given Blake carte blanche to come and go as he pleased. She never would have believed it if she hadn't heard it with her own ears.

Shaking her head, she frowned up at Blake. "Were you really a Boy Scout?"

Shrugging, he grinned. "What do you think?"

Over the course of the day, they covered a robbery involving a tourist near the River Walk, a bank hold-up, investigated the rise of gang activity in one of the city's more affluent high schools and looked into a money laundering scheme among some businesses near Fort Sam Houston. Half expecting Blake to hover over her like an overprotective parent, Sabrina was pleasantly surprised at the first crime scene when he gave her plenty of space to do her job. Interviewing the investigating officers while she spoke to the victim, he kept an eye on her, but never got close enough to overhear her questions.

Walking back to his truck with him when they were both finished, she couldn't help but tease him as he opened the passenger door for her. "You know, Nickels, I think there really must be some truth to this Boy Scout stuff. I gotta tell you—I'm impressed. I didn't think you had it in you."

Playfully tugging on her hair, he grinned. "Don't let it go to your head, Jones. I still plan on winning our bet—this is just a temporary lull in competition. Once things are back to normal, you'd better watch out. I'm going to eat your lunch."

"Oh, yeah?" she tossed back, her own eyes starting to sparkle. "You and whose army? You're good, cowboy, I'll give you that. But I'm better and you know it. I guess it's a man thing."

Confused by the sudden shift in her reasoning, he frowned. "What?"

"Not being able to accept when you're beaten," she said sweetly. Flashing her dimples at him, she dared to reach out and pat him on the cheek. "Poor baby. Men have such fragile egos."

Lightning-quick, his fingers trapped hers against his face, and suddenly, neither one of them was smiling. His blood starting to warm in his veins, Blake deliberately reminded himself that he'd sworn not to touch her again. Not after he'd gone up in flames with her and come damn close to losing his soul to her. After he'd forced himself to leave her last night, he'd lain in his narrow bed at his grandfather's and spent what was left of the night convincing himself that he'd blown their lovemaking all out of proportion. It was just good sex, nothing more. His emotions weren't involved. They couldn't be. Then he'd heard about the fourth murder and called Adam to find out where Sabrina was. When he'd learned that she'd gone back home, his heart had stopped in his chest.

He'd broken all speed limits to get to her, and ever since then, he'd been fighting the need to snatch her close. Damn, she tied him in knots! He wanted her—she didn't want commitment. So where the hell did that leave them? Until he had the answer to that, he had no business touching her. But he couldn't seem to stop himself.

Holding her hand to his jaw, he said in a voice that was sandpaper rough, "My ego's just fine, thank you very much. And I wouldn't count my chickens before they hatch, honey. You just might end up with egg on your face."

Her eyes darkened, and becoming color stole into her cheeks. "I can handle whatever you dish out, Nickels," she promised huskily. "And don't you forget it."

Staring down at her, his heart beginning to knock against his ribs, Blake told himself they were talking about the bet, nothing more. But as he slammed her door and walked around the hood of his truck to slide in beside her, all he could think about was that she could handle him, all right. Anytime she damn well pleased, better than any woman ever had before. All she had to do was say where and when and he'd be there.

Awareness humming on the air between them, they both gave a start as Blake's police radio crackled to life and a disembodied voice called all available patrol cars within the vicinity of Loop 410 and Broadway to Texas State Bank for a hostage situation. With a muttered curse, Blake started the motor and pulled away from the curb with a squeal of tires. Seconds later, they were racing across town, each of them sending up silent prayers of thanks for the distraction of work.

When they ended up at the *Times* right before quitting time, Sabrina couldn't believe how well things had gone. After Sam Kelly's grim warning earlier that morning, she'd expected to spend the day looking over her shoulder, wondering when the killer was going to make his presence known. But it was usually Blake her eyes found whenever she looked around, and he didn't give her time to wonder about anything. When he wasn't discussing the stories they'd just investigated, he was distracting her with some tall tale that invariably made her laugh.

For a woman who valued her independence, she should have been more than a little exasperated with him—after all, he hadn't given her any choice when he'd designated himself her personal bodyguard, and she wasn't used to a man just taking over her life that way without so much as a by-your-leave. But he hadn't crowded or pushed or in any way interfered with the way she worked. He'd just been there, a protective shadow who worked alongside her as if he did it every day of the week. And as much as her head hated to admit it to her heart, she'd liked having him there. He was a man a woman could get used to having underfoot.

When they'd first walked into the *Times,* she'd expected his boss to demand an explanation once he discovered her identity, but Tom Edwards only lifted a brow in surprise, told her that something big had to be in the works if Blake was conspiring with the competition, then offered her a job if she ever decided to jump ship and come work for a real paper. She'd liked him on the spot.

Seated at the chair Blake had drawn up for her at his desk, she watched him pound out three stories in record time and couldn't help but be fascinated. He used two fingers—just two—and never looked at his computer screen until he was finished. And even then, he only made a few changes before he flipped to his notes for the next story.

Unabashedly reading over his shoulder, Sabrina had to admit the man was darn good at what he did. She could knock out a story in record time when she had to, but it always took her a few stops and starts before her writing really got going and she got out of the way of her own muse. Blake seemed to have no such problem. What came off the top of his head was pretty much what he turned in as his finished work, and there was a grittiness to it that reached out and grabbed her with the first word. She couldn't help but be impressed, and knew that long after he was out of her life, she would carry in her heart a picture of him sitting at his desk, his forehead wrinkled with concentration and his eyes intently focused on something she couldn't see, hammering out a story.

Then, as quickly as he had begun, he was finished. Turning to her with that wicked grin of his that never failed to jump-start her heart, he said, "Now that you've seen a master at work, what d'ya say we blow this joint and get out of here, Jones? I don't know about you, but I'm starving."

Feeling a little hungry herself, she started to agree with him, only to frown with mock indignation. "Hold it right there, Nickels. What was that crack about a master at work?"

His eyes crinkling with amusement, he rose to his feet and reached down to pull her from her chair. "The truth hurts sometimes, Jones. But hey, look at it this way—now that you've seen me in action, maybe some of my genius will rub off on you. Of course, some things you just have to be born with—"

Laughing, she playfully punched him in the gut. "Yeah. Like modesty and talent and true greatness. When I get my Pulitzer, you can say you knew me when."

Enjoying himself, he only snorted and hauled her after him toward the nearest exit. "I've been meaning to have a serious talk with you, honey, about these delusions of grandeur you've been having," he teased. "I know this good doctor—"

Glancing over his shoulder to laugh down into her eyes, he pushed open the outside door and never noticed that while they'd been inside, the sky had turned dark and threatening and the wind had picked up. The minute they stepped outside, the rain that had been forecast all day started to fall with just a scattering of drops.

Surprised, Blake glanced up as thunder rumbled threateningly overhead. "Uh-ho. Better hurry. We're in for it."

Well used to summer storms that could blow up out of

nowhere, Sabrina knew better than to linger. Practically running to keep up with Blake's long stride, she dodged raindrops like bullets and rushed across the parking lot. They were halfway to Blake's truck when the heavens opened up like a floodgate. By the time they threw themselves into the pickup's cab, they were both soaked to the skin.

Laughing, Sabrina shook her wet hair out of her face and turned to Blake, intending to make a crack about not having to wash her clothes when she got home, but the words died unspoken on her tongue. His shoulder almost rubbing hers, Blake sat as if turned to stone behind the steering wheel, totally oblivious of his wet clothes as he stared down at her, his green eyes hot and intense and devouring as they moved over her.

The thud of her heartbeat, along with the dancing of the rain on the roof of the truck, was suddenly loud in her ears. Sabrina automatically glanced down...and gasped. Drenched by the rain, her thin, white cotton blouse, normally sedate enough for church, was nearly transparent and molded her breasts like a wet T-shirt. Embarrassed color firing her cheeks, she hastily moved to cover herself.

Blake, however, was faster. Reaching behind the seat, he pulled out a lightweight cotton jacket. "Here. This'll help." His voice as rough as a gravel road, he draped it around her shoulders, then couldn't seem to stop touching her as he adjusted the collar and pulled it snugger around her. "Are you cold? I can turn on the heater."

Cold? Sabrina thought shakily, swallowing a moan of laughter. Even if it hadn't been a sticky ninety or more degrees, the brush of his hands would have warmed her if it'd been thirty below. Everywhere he innocently touched—and a few places he didn't—she burned.

"No," she choked. "I'm fine. Really. Just embarrassed to death."

"Don't be," he growled, lifting her chin so that she was forced to meet his gaze. "You're beautiful. And no one saw you but me."

And he had already seen all of her there was to see. The knowledge was there in his eyes, in the tension that curled between them like a lick of fire, in the breathlessness that suddenly seized them both. His hand slid from her chin to her throat in a slow glide, and just that quickly, they were back in his apartment, in his bed, and she was aching for another kiss.

His own need was just as fierce—she could see it in his eyes, feel it in his hands, which weren't quite steady as he moved to draw her closer, his head already lowering to hers. Then, on the street that ran in front of the *Times's* parking lot, they heard the blare of a horn and the sudden screech of tires as a BMW, going too fast on the wet streets, narrowly missed a van that pulled out right in front of it.

Stiffening, Blake drew back abruptly and swore, remembering nearly too late that they were sitting in a public parking lot in full view of anyone who cared to look. "Let's get out of here," he muttered. A muscle ticking along his clenched jaw, he started the motor with a sharp twist of his wrist.

They didn't speak all the way home.

There was no question that he was staying the night. Or that he was sleeping in his own bed...with her. Neither one of them said anything, but the knowledge was there in his eyes, in the accelerated thump of her heart, in the expectation that filled the air like a gathering storm.

Restless, all her senses attuned to his every move as he followed her into the apartment, Sabrina knew that making love with him again could be nothing but a mistake. He was coming to mean too much to her. He made her want things she knew she couldn't have. When he touched her, kissed her, took her into his arms, she felt that anything was possible, that together they could single-handedly defeat the curse that made it impossible for the women of her family to find lifelong happiness with one man. He made her ache to believe in fairy tales and happily-ever-after and the love of a good man.

Wrapped close to his heart, it was so easy to believe that anything could happen, that he would be with her forever and grow old with her. She hadn't realized until now how desperately she wanted that, ached for that. She knew, though, that was just her emotions crying out to her. With nothing more than a heart-stopping grin, he stirred the romance in her soul. In her family, romance didn't last. Deep down inside, she knew that. But still, she couldn't send him away.

"You need to get out of those wet things," he said gruffly from behind her, shattering the silence that engulfed them. "Why don't you climb into the shower, and I'll start supper?"

His jacket still around her shoulders, she nodded, hugging herself as a blast of air from the air conditioner hit her, raising goose bumps on her damp skin. "I think I will. With the rain and everything, I am kind of cold."

"Then I'll put on some soup. Take your time. It'll be ready when you are."

If he'd touched her—just once—she wouldn't have

needed soup or a shower to warm her, but he turned toward the kitchen and didn't see her need. So she headed for the bedroom to collect clean clothes, then stepped across the hall to the bathroom. She'd just started the shower and was adjusting the water temperature when there was a soft tap at the door. Her heart starting to knock like an out-of-balance washing machine, she called huskily, "Come in."

Without a sound, the door glided open to reveal Blake standing on the threshold, his expression solemn as his eyes met hers. "Sorry to interrupt, but I just remembered the city has a serious water shortage, what with the drought and everything."

Caught off guard, Sabrina almost smiled. The mayor had asked all citizens to practice voluntary conservation methods, just as he did every summer, but the water supply wasn't close to critical and they were hardly in a drought, especially considering the fact that it was currently pouring outside and showed no signs of letting up.

"A water shortage," she repeated in bemusement. "I hadn't realized the problem was that bad." Struggling to keep her expression as serious as his, she felt her heart shift into a heavy, primitive rhythm and could do nothing to quiet it. "What do you suggest we do about it?"

Without a word, he crossed the threshold and shut the door. A half step was all it took to leave only a few inches between them. Slowly, giving her time to object, he lifted his hands to the jacket she still wore and began to ease it from her shoulders. "We both need to take a shower," he said hoarsely. "If we took one together, think of the water we'd save."

Her eyes locked with his, she felt the jacket slide to the floor and found herself holding her breath, waiting for his eyes to drop to her wet blouse, but his gaze never left hers.

He didn't touch her again, but simply stood there, waiting as the bathroom filled with steam. The next move, if there was going to be another one, was clearly hers.

A wise woman would have taken a moment to step back and give herself time to think. A smart one would have insisted on it. But right from the beginning, she hadn't been wise or smart when it came to this man. He tempted her past all bearing, confused her, haunted her, made her long for the impossible. And in the end, he was going to hurt her. Oh, he wouldn't do it intentionally, but she knew him well enough now to know that there would come a time that he would want to talk of the future. And they didn't have one.

Still, she couldn't deny herself—deny them—these precious moments stolen out of a lifetime of being alone. Swallowing the lump that had risen to her throat, she lifted fingers that were far from steady to the top button of his shirt. "I suppose, then," she murmured, "that you could say it's our civic duty."

He nodded, a whisper of that wicked, wicked smile of his flirting with his mouth as his hands copied hers and reached for the top button of her blouse. Between one heartbeat and the next, he slid it free. "No question about it," he agreed huskily, turning his attention to the next button. "It's the only right thing to do. We save time…" His hands still busy with her buttons, he leaned down and nuzzled her ear. "And water. And—"

"Soap," she finished for him softly as her head fell weakly back and her eyes grew heavy with desire. "I could rub it on you. Then you could rub against me…."

She didn't finish the suggestion, but she didn't have to. He growled in approval, his hands fisting in her partially opened blouse as he pulled back to stare hungrily down into her eyes. "Is this one of your favorite blouses?"

Thrown by the sudden shift in conversation, she frowned. "Not particularly. Why?"

"I'll never forget it, but right now it's in the way." His fingers tightening in the material, he gave a quick jerk of his hands and sent the remaining buttons flying.

"Blake!"

He grinned. "There. That's much better. Do you mind?"

How could she mind when he was looking at her as if he'd just gotten three wishes for his birthday and all of them were her? His eyes scorched her, his hands worshiped her, and his mouth…she couldn't even think when he stripped her bra from her and kissed his way down to a nipple that pouted for his possession. Her cry of pleasure echoing above the drumming of the shower, she clutched his head to her breast and felt her bones melt one by one.

When he finally kissed his way back up to her mouth, she couldn't even remember her own name. Giving her a quick, hard kiss, he tore at his own clothes and what remained of hers until they were both naked. His green eyes dark and intense in the mist that shrouded them, he pulled her into the shower with him, laughing as the warm spray immediately soaked them both. Then he was pulling her in front of him, his back to the shower head, blocking the water from hitting her in the face. "Now what was that you were saying about soap?"

His eyes sparkled with a dare; his grin said she flat-out didn't have the nerve. He should have known better. With him, her heart was quickly discovering, she would dare just about anything. Happiness bubbling up in her like the clear, laughing water of a spring, she picked up the bar of soap from its holder on the side of the shower stall and slowly lathered it between her hands, her smile hot and sultry and wicked. "It seems to me," she murmured huskily, "that I mentioned something about rubbing…."

His grin broadening, he spread his hands wide, the outrageous man not the least bit self-conscious when it came to his body. "Start anywhere you like, honey. I'm all yours."

She could have started with his very obvious arousal and brought him to his knees, and she knew he wouldn't have offered a word of complaint. Instead, she reached for his hand—his left—and folded it between her palms.

"I like your hands," she said simply. Hugging his wrist to her bare breast, she gently transferred the soap on her hands to his, and all the while she talked. "Sometimes at night when I'm sleeping, I picture them touching me, undressing me, then slowly driving me out of my mind." Rubbing her fingers over the back of his hand in slow-moving circles, she looked up and asked in a sexy rasp, "Have you ever done that? Pushed a woman right over the edge with nothing but your hands? Stroking? Caressing? Everywhere?"

Staring down at her, her fingers lighting a slow burn deep in his gut, Blake could only nod. Did the little minx know what she was doing to him? She had to—he certainly had no way of hiding it from her—and all she was doing was soaping his hand! And seducing him with the kind of love talk that no man with any blood in his veins could resist. With infinite care she took his other hand, giving it the same attention to detail as she confided how she liked his hands on her breasts and sliding down her belly.

There was no doubt that she knew exactly what she was doing—her eyes were alight with naughtiness as she lathered her hands again, then carefully soaped each arm all the way to his shoulders, all the while telling him how safe she felt with his arms around her, how she knew nothing and no one could hurt her as long as he was holding her.

He'd thought he was a strong man, but with nothing more than that, she broke him. Groaning, he reached for her. "Come here, witch."

"Wait." She laughed as he hauled her against his chest where she belonged. "Don't you want me to wash your back?"

"Later," he rasped, kissing her senseless. "Much later."

On fire for her, he gave her no time to tease or argue or even catch her breath. Pushing her up against the shower wall, he tried to hang on to patience, tenderness, but he was beyond that. His hands were shaking—*shaking!*—his lungs straining. He could feel the fire in her, the need, and by God, he ached. Then her hands were on him, right where he'd wanted them, and something in him just seemed to snap. Sweeping her up, her urged her legs around his hips.

"Blake! What—"

"I've got you, sweetheart," he said thickly, surging into her before she could do anything but gasp. "I won't let anything happen to you."

He wanted to say more—that he hoped to God she hadn't been teasing when she'd said how safe she felt in his arms—but she moved, clutching him tighter, taking him deeper, and his entire universe shrank to the wet, hot heat of her surrounding him, her breasts slippery with soap as she slid against him, her name a chant, a promise, that called to him in his head. The world could have stopped and started turning the other way, but, lost in the wonder of her, he never would have noticed. There was nothing except Sabrina, pulling him toward paradise, taking him as he'd never been taken in his life.

Chapter 10

Too spent afterwards to do much more than clumsily drag a towel over both of them, Blake carried her to bed and crawled in beside her in the dark, dragging the sheet and bedspread up around them as the cool air from the air conditioner brushed over their still-damp bodies. Shivering slightly, Sabrina scooted back against him, her soft sigh a whisper in the night as he draped an arm around her waist and anchored her close. Outside, the rain drummed against the roof and dripped from the eaves, and occasionally, thunder rumbled far off to the east. Sated, content, they slept.

They turned to each other again in the night as naturally as if they'd been doing it for years, lazily exploring each other with slow hands and drugging kisses. The white-hot flash of heat that had driven them before was now a glowing ember that warmed instead of burned. This time, they had the patience to linger, to stroke, to pleasure each other until they were weak with the wonder of it. And when he swept her under him and she welcomed him with a soft moan, they looked into each other's eyes in the dark and couldn't seem to stop smiling. Whatever happened in the future, they had now, tonight, and nothing could ever take that away from them.

Still buried deep inside her, unable to let her go, Blake drifted back to sleep with her in his arms. Exhausted, replete, more relaxed than he'd ever been in his life, he never heard the rain stop or the nurse who lived next door come home after working the three-to-eleven shift. Not wanting anything to disturb this night with Sabrina, he'd remembered to shut off the phone on the nightstand after they'd made love in the shower, so he never heard the one in the kitchen ring around two in the morning. Ten rings later, it finally stopped, but his face was buried in Sabrina's hair, his dreams filled with her, and the rest of the world had long since ceased to exist.

When someone pounded on the front door at three, he frowned in his sleep, fighting wakefulness. It was thunder, he told himself groggily. Another storm had rolled in—it would blow itself out in a little while and be gone by morning. But the pounding continued, and he came awake with a start to realize that someone was hammering at his front door loud enough to wake the dead. Muttering a curse, he eased away from Sabrina, careful not to wake her, and reached for his jeans.

"Hold your horses," he grumbled as he quietly shut the bedroom door and hurried barefoot across the living room. "I'm coming, dammit! And this damn well better be good."

His jeans zipped but not buttoned, he glanced through the peephole and lifted a brow in surprise at the sight of the uniformed policeman standing there pounding on his door as if he intended to do so for the rest of the night if he had to, to wake him up. "What the hell!"

Turning the dead bolt, he jerked open the door and scowled at the fresh-faced cop who looked like he was hardly old enough to shave. "You want to tell me what the hell you're doing, Officer?" he growled. "Besides waking up everybody in the complex. Dammit, it's three o'clock in the morning!"

Flushing, the younger man said stiffly, "I know that, sir. I'm sorry to disturb you, but I'm just following orders. Are you Blake Nickels?"

"Yes, I am," he retorted, scowling. "Whose orders?"

"Detective Kelly's, sir. When he couldn't reach you on the telephone, he told me to hammer the door down if I had to to wake you up. There's been an arrest in the serial-killer murders, and he was sure you would want to know about it as soon as possible."

"An arrest!" Surprised, Blake cast a quick look over his shoulder to make sure the bedroom door was still shut, then stepped outside onto the open cement balcony that connected all of the second-floor apartments to the garden patio below. The gutters still dripped, splashing raindrops on his bare toes, but he never noticed. "I had no idea Kelly was that close to making an arrest. Who is the bastard?"

"His name's Jeff Harper. He was picked up a little over an hour ago at his home on the north side—"

"Jeff Harper!" Blake exclaimed, stiffening. "Are you sure about that?"

"Yes, sir," he said grimly. "He's downtown right now being booked, and he didn't come easily. From what I heard, he fought like the devil. It took four officers to bring him in."

Stunned, Blake couldn't believe it. Jeff Harper. Granted, he didn't like the son of a bitch or the thought of him coming anywhere near Sabrina, but she had trusted him once, loved him enough to risk marrying him in spite of her family history. She might not love him any longer—she couldn't, dammit!—but she didn't hate him, either. Harper had disillusioned her and hurt her, but finding out that he was the one who had stalked and terrorized her while she had defended him to the police was going to tear her apart.

God, how was he going to tell her?

She would have to know, of course. And then there was the story to write. They had to get downtown, find out what the hell had happened to break the case wide open tonight, and get some answers from Sam. "Thanks for the information, Officer Johnson," he said, noting his name tag. "Sabrina and I'll get downtown as soon as we can. Is Kelly at the station?"

"The last I saw him, he was at the suspect's house supervising the collection of evidence," the other man said. "But he expected to be back at the station within the hour. I can check if you like."

"That's okay," Blake said. "I'll find him. Thanks for your help."

His mind already jumping ahead to what he was going to tell Sabrina, he stepped back into the apartment and shut the door behind him and never saw her standing in the darkened living room until he started toward the bedroom and she switched on a light. She'd pulled on a robe and stood hugging herself as if it was the middle of winter, her brown eyes huge and haunted in her pale face, and he knew she knew.

"I woke up and you weren't there," she said huskily.

"When I couldn't find you, I noticed the front door was ajar...."

So she'd heard it all, every damning word. Watching the hurt darken her eyes, he would have given just about anything short of his first-born child to have five minutes alone with Jeff Harper in a dark alley. Stepping toward her, he reached for her and hauled her into his arms. "Honey, I'm sorry."

"I can't believe it," she said against his chest, clutching at him. "Not Jeff. There has to be a mistake."

He shouldn't have been surprised by her defense of the bastard—even when his car had been spotted near her house and her neighbor had given a description of a jogger that had sounded like the twin of her ex, she'd still refused to believe that Jeff could be involved—but it still twisted in his gut like a rusty knife. Stiffening, he said, "Why? Because you still care about him and you can't believe that someone you have feelings for would want you dead?"

"No, of course not," she began, only to suddenly become aware of his coolness. Drawing back, she looked up and gaped in amazement at the rigid set of his jaw. "You're jealous!"

"I am not! Don't be ridiculous."

He scowled, glaring at her, just daring her to repeat such nonsense, but she only laughed, not the least bit intimidated, and stood on tiptoe to loop her arms around his stiff neck. "If I weren't so surprised by the idea of you being jealous of anyone, I just might be insulted, Nickels. Do you really think I could have done what I did in that shower with you if I cared two cents about another man?"

His lips twitched, but he stood unbending before her, softening only when she melted against him, giving him an excuse to hold her again. "You were awful damn quick to defend him," he grumbled, stroking her hair as if he couldn't help himself.

"Only because I thought I knew him," she said quietly, sobering. Her heart suddenly aching, she laid her cheek against the hollow of his bare shoulder and fought the crazy need to cry. "Try to understand," she said softly. "It wasn't all that long ago that I was married to him, Blake. For two years, I slept with him, cooked for him, even washed his damn underwear. How could I have been so close to him and never sensed the violence in him? Was I that blind? Or just insensitive? What did I do to make him hate me so?"

"You didn't do anything," he said roughly, tightening his arms around her. "You aren't the one with the problem, honey. He is. The man's sick. He has to be. And you aren't the only one he fooled. He has friends, family, people that have known and worked with him a heck of a lot longer than you have. If none of them saw this coming, how could you?"

"But the Jeff Harper I knew couldn't even take a sick dog to the vet. How could someone like that kill four women and terrorize me?"

He shrugged. "People change."

"But not that much. There's been a lot of pressure on the police to make an arrest. Maybe someone made a mistake—"

He drew back, his hand cupping her chin to lift her gaze to his. "You know better than that. Kelly was the one who made the collar, and he never would have done that without a hell of a lot of evidence. You know how careful he is. Especially where this case is concerned. The whole state's watching, not to mention his superiors. He wants a conviction too badly to risk making a mistake."

He was right, but that didn't make it any easier to accept. Jeff. Dear God, how could it be Jeff? She hadn't lied when she'd told Blake that she didn't care two cents about him, but he was still the first man she'd ever loved, the first man she'd ever given her heart and body to. They hadn't parted friends, but she hadn't thought they were enemies, either. Obviously, she'd been wrong.

"I know," she said thickly, forcing a halfhearted smile that did nothing to conceal the pain squeezing her heart. "It just makes no sense. Why would he do such a thing now? If he was going to try to kill me, why didn't he do it when I divorced him?"

As short on answers as she, Blake shrugged. "I don't know, sweetheart. I wish I did. Who knows what pushes somebody over the edge? It might not have had anything to do with you at all—he could have just been looking for somebody to strike out at about something and your name came to mind. You know yourself that these types of crimes don't always make a lot of sense."

"Do you think Kelly will let me talk to him?"

Blake stiffened at that. No! Now that they knew Harper was responsible for terrorizing her, he didn't want her anywhere near the man. But she was the intended victim here, and he knew her well enough by now to know that this would eat at her like a cancer until she got some answers.

Still, his first inclination was to lock her up in the bedroom until Harper was tried and convicted and behind bars for a good, long stretch. She'd fight him on that, however, and he couldn't say he'd blame her. She had a right to know what was going on in Harper's head. But if she was hurting now, that could damn well rip her apart, and there wasn't anything he could do to protect her from that kind of pain. Except be there for her.

Slinging an arm around her shoulder, he turned her toward the bedroom. "Let's get dressed and go downtown and find out."

By the time they rushed into the central station downtown, it was going on four. Normally at that hour of the morning, the only ones about were cops and the lowlifes of society—drunks and brawlers and an occasional scumbag who got his kicks punching the woman in his life. But not tonight. Somehow, the word had already gotten out that there'd been an arrest in the serial killings, and the place was crawling with press. There were at least three field reporters from the local television stations, complete with camera crews, hassling the officer at the front desk for the story, not to mention radio and print reporters from every town within a fifty-mile radius. By dawn, there'd probably be some from Dallas and Houston as well.

Swearing at the sight of them, Blake shouldered his way through the crowd, pulling Sabrina after him. Finally reaching the front desk, he flashed his press badge at the scowling sergeant and said, "We need to see Detective Kelly."

"So does half the world," he drawled. "You're going to have to wait just like everybody else. He's called a press conference for seven. You can ask him anything you like then." Suddenly spying Sabrina where she was half-hidden behind Blake, his weathered face cracked into a smile. "Hey, Jones! What are you doing down here? The last time you covered the graveyard shift, you were still writing obits."

Sabrina grinned, affection lifting the heavy boulder that

seemed to be sitting on her heart. Stoney Griffen had been sitting at that desk the first time she walked into the police station as a nervous cub reporter. He could have made things hard for her, but he'd gruffly taught her the ropes and had been a friend ever since.

"There's not a whole lot of things I'd crawl out of bed for at this hour of the night, Stoney, but this is one of them."

Suddenly remembering who the suspect was they had in the lockup, his teasing smile faded. "Aw, jeez, Sabrina, I'm sorry." Snapping at the other reporters to back off, he waited until they'd stepped back a couple of paces before he confided quietly, "I don't know what I was thinking of. Of course you'd be here. Are you okay?"

"Well, I can't pretend it hasn't been a shock, but I'm dealing with it." Introducing Blake to him, she said, "We really need to talk to Sam, Stoney. Isn't there some way we could see him before the press conference?"

Sighing heavily, the older man shook his head. "Sorry, darlin'. He's not even here right now. He's still over at Harper's house with the evidence guys. And I wouldn't go over there if I was you, either—he won't have time to talk to you. The last I heard, they were taking the place apart brick by brick."

"Then when he gets back—"

"He's got a meeting lined up with the chief. There ain't no way in hell I'm interfering with that."

"He's meeting with Travelino at this hour of the morning?"

The older man nodded. "The chief's been keeping a close eye on this one. In fact, Kelly hasn't made a move without letting him know about it. The old man wants to go over the evidence the minute Kelly walks through the door."

Blake swore. "It looks like we're going to have to wait just like everyone else."

If it had been any other night, any other case, Sabrina would have been more than willing to do just that. But questions hammered at her, nagged at her, pulled at her like a persistent child who refused to be silenced. Given the least encouragement from Stoney, she would have been out of there like a shot and racing for Jeff's house. But she knew police procedure as well as he did, and even though Kelly had notified her about Jeff's arrest, there was no way he was going to give her special treatment at a crime scene of this importance. Not when Travelino was waiting for him back at the station.

Reluctantly accepting defeat, she sighed. "Great. So what are we supposed to do for the next three hours?"

"Eat," Blake growled as he steered her away from the front desk and headed for the nearest exit. "In case you've forgotten, we missed supper. I'm starving. Let's go over to Mi Tierra and grab a George's Special."

She hadn't forgotten anything, least of all *why* they hadn't eaten. And in the few minutes it took for them to walk down the street to the all-night Mexican restaurant that was the heart and soul of Market Square, find a booth, and order their food, all she could think of was those moments in the shower, then later in his bed. He was coming to mean too much to her. Even as her heart swelled with joy at the thought, her head insisted that she take steps to do something about it now that she was safe again and Jeff was behind bars—

Just that quickly, her thoughts were dragged back to the murders, the notes left for her, the deliberate attempt to terrorize her, the threats to kill her. What little appetite she had vanished.

Seated across from her, Blake knew the minute he'd lost her. One second, her eyes were all dreamy, a sexy little smile playing with her mouth, and the next, her cheeks didn't have any color and she'd withdrawn into herself. And it didn't take an Einstein to figure out that her mind was back at the police station with that murdering ex-husband of hers.

And he *was* jealous. He wasn't happy about it, but he couldn't avoid the truth when it slapped him right in the face. Somehow, without quite knowing how it had happened, he had come to think of her as his.

God, he had to get this caveman stuff under control, he told himself. But even as he lectured himself to get a grip, he pushed his iced tea and place setting across the table. When Sabrina blinked in surprise, he grinned crookedly and moved around to slide in next to her on her side of the booth. "You look a little lonely over here all by yourself, Jones. Mind if I join you?"

Since he already had, she could do nothing but laugh. "Don't mind me, Nickels. Make yourself at home."

"Thanks. I think I will." Slipping an arm around her shoulders, he drew her flush against his side, unmindful of who might be watching. It wasn't until then that he realized just how badly he'd needed to have her back in his arms. "You know, Jones," he confided huskily as he trailed his fingers up and down her arm, "I could get used to holding you. You're real...touchable."

Watching her, he caught a wisp of a smile, then he felt it, that softening that always seemed to steal his breath when she leaned against him, letting him take her weight. "We're supposed to be working, Nickels."

Her tone was gently reproving—but she didn't pull

away. Encouraged, Blake blatantly caressed her. "I am, sweetheart. I'm working real hard at controlling myself."

"Blake!"

"I just love it when you cry out my name that way," he growled outrageously. "Do it again."

She laughed, she couldn't help herself. "Stop that!" She giggled, casting a quick look around. "I swear, I just can't take you anywhere. We're in a public restaurant, for heaven's sake!"

Unrepentant, he leaned down to nuzzle her neck. "There's not another soul within twenty feet, and he's half-asleep. Which is what we would *not* be doing if we were back in my bed," he muttered roughly for her ears alone.

Telling her exactly what he would do to her if they were back in his apartment, he watched in growing satisfaction as the color flowed back into her pale cheeks, and her eyes lost that haunted look. And while she might have been chilled by her own thoughts only a few moments ago, the lady definitely wasn't cold now. Leaning more fully against him, she was warm and soft and responsive, and she never even flinched when the waiter brought their food, then quickly left them alone.

If he thought he was pulling a fast one on her, however, she quickly set him straight once the waiter was out of earshot. Capturing the hand that had dropped to her knee, she gave his fingers a warning squeeze. "You think you're pretty tricky, don't you, Nickels?"

"Who? Me? I don't know what you're talking about."

"You can cut the innocent act, cowboy. It's not working. The day you're innocent is the day the Alamo becomes the next Disneyland. You're not the type to seduce a woman in a public place. You're trying to take my mind off Jeff."

Amusement glinting in his eyes, he leaned down and brushed a kiss across her mouth. "So how am I doing?"

Surprised that he even had to ask, she grinned. "I'll let you know later—when we're alone." When he groaned, she only laughed and pulled his arm from around her shoulder. "Eat, Nickels, before your food gets cold."

For the next twenty minutes, by unspoken agreement, they avoided any mention of Jeff or the murders or the evidence that Sam Kelly was even now collecting against her former husband. Concentrating instead on their food, they enjoyed each other's company as if they didn't have a care in the world. They traded stories about their childhoods and colleges and every boss they'd ever had, then argued good-naturedly over their favorite movies. By the time they stopped to catch a breath, their plates were clean and they were both more relaxed than when they had walked in.

That couldn't last, however. As they headed back to the police station, Blake shifted the conversation to the weirdest stories they'd ever covered, but Sabrina couldn't concentrate. Tension crawled along her nerves, wiring her, and her steps unconsciously slowed as the station grew closer and closer. For the first time in her life, she actually dreaded a press conference.

"You start stiffening up again and I'm going to have to kiss you right here on the street in front of God and everyone," Blake warned as he laced his fingers with hers. "You'll get through this, Jones. Just don't beat yourself up over it. None of it was your fault."

She could have told him it was too late for that—somehow, she should have seen this coming—but they'd reached the front steps of the station by then and it was time to go back to work. Resisting the sudden childish need to cling to his hand, she gave his fingers a quick squeeze, then dropped them, squared her shoulders, and marched up the steps.

* * *

When Sam Kelly presented himself to the press at seven in the morning, he didn't look as though he'd been up all night. Clean-shaven and neatly dressed in a gray suit and white shirt that didn't show a single wrinkle, he walked into the media room with a confident step and took the podium like a man who was well used to taking control. All business, he greeted the crowd with a brisk good-morning and, without bothering to glance at his notes, began to relate the details of the arrest of Jeff Harper.

"Mr. Harper was taken into custody at 2:23 this morning at his home on O'Connor Road. He initially resisted arrest, but there were four uniformed officers on the scene and he was quickly subdued. Presently, he is being charged with the murders of Charlene McClintock, Tanya Bishop, and Elizabeth Reagan."

"Why not Denise Green?" Jason McQuire, a reporter for the local ABC affiliate, called out. "Are you saying that Harper didn't kill her?"

"No," he said carefully, "I'm saying that he's not currently being charged with that murder. The M.O. in Ms. Green's murder was slightly different, and we're not booking anyone until we've had a chance to sift through the evidence more thoroughly."

Seated next to Sabrina at the rear of the room, Blake spoke up. "When did Jeff Harper become a suspect?"

His expression grim, Sam said, "Right after Sabrina Jones got the first note about Tanya Bishop's murder. We knew the murderer was somehow linked to her—it was just a matter of finding out how. As most of you may or may not know, the suspect is Ms. Jones's ex-husband."

"Did you find physical evidence linking him to the

crimes?" a reporter from Austin asked. "Is that why you were at his house so long?"

Automatically taking notes, Sabrina listened as Sam described the extensive evidence found at Jeff's home. A gun—an unregistered .38 wiped clean of fingerprints—and a stash of bullets were found in the garage, wedged up in the rafters behind a box full of Christmas ornaments. They wouldn't know for sure until ballistics tests were done, but Sam and his men were pretty sure it was the same .38 used to kill the four women. The fact that it had been wrapped in various items of clothing that were believed to have belonged to the victims and were taken by the killer as trophies only added to the conviction that the gun was the murder weapon.

A radio reporter from the nearby town of Seguin said, "So the evidence you have presently is circumstantial?"

His mouth tightening, Sam nodded. "Obviously, we'd like an eyewitness or a confession, but given what we've got, we're sure we have the right man. The gun and clothes didn't just walk into Harper's garage by themselves and hide. And we have three witnesses who will testify to seeing a car matching the suspect's in the area at the time two of the murders were committed."

"What about an alibi?" Blake asked.

"Mr. Harper claims he was at home with his wife at the time of all four murders, but when we questioned the wife, she couldn't corroborate that because she was asleep each time and couldn't guarantee that he was in the house or not."

Stricken, her hand flying across her notebook as she jotted down notes, Sabrina wanted to cry out that this was all a terrible mistake. It had to be. But even as she tried to find an explanation for the facts that Kelly had so clearly laid out before them, her own professional objectivity forced her to admit that the evidence was damning. If it had pointed to the guilt of any other man but Jeff, she would have believed it in a heartbeat.

Sick at the thought, she had to force herself to concentrate on the task at hand. "What broke the case for you?" she asked Sam. "It couldn't have been the recovery of the murder weapon. You didn't find it until you went in to make the arrest, did you?"

"No, but we knew it was on the property some-where—"

"How?"

"We got an anonymous tip around seven-thirty last night," he admitted. "And before you all start throwing questions at me, there's not a lot I can tell you about that," he said quickly when most of the inhabitants of the room perked up in interest. "The call came in over a 911 line from a pay phone across the street from the Alamo. As you know, that area is usually crowded with tourists, especially in the middle of the summer, and no one noticed anything. We do know the caller was male, but that's about it. He claimed he preferred not to give his name because he's a neighbor of Harper's and has to live on the same block with him. If he was mistaken in what he had seen, he didn't want the suspect to know that he was the one who had turned him in. That's all I can tell you."

The roomful of reporters had no intention of letting the matter drop with that, and started firing questions at him. There was, however, little else he could add. If he had any other information, it wasn't for public consumption until the trial, which wouldn't be for months. Minutes later, the press conference broke up.

* * *

They rode back to the *Daily Record* in silence. His attention divided between his driving and Sabrina's withdrawn figure, Blake ground a curse between his teeth. He'd watched her all during the press conference, watched her agitation as she jerkily scribbled notes, watched her almost visibly flinch as Kelly gave an accounting of the evidence. She hurt, and it was all he could do to stop himself from reaching for her. She hurt, and he hated that.

For the life of him, he couldn't understand how she could have any kind of feelings for the bastard who'd had her looking over her shoulder every time she stepped outside. Harper had threatened to kill her, for God's sake! For no other reason than that, Blake would have liked to hang him up by his thumbs and leave him to twist in the wind. That, however, wasn't going to make Sabrina feel any better, and that was his only concern right now.

Braking to a stop at the curb in front of the *Daily Record,* he frowned. She was safe now. It was all right for him to let her out of his sight. The rational part of his brain knew that he could let her go back to her life and not worry about some sleazeball stalking her like a hunter after his next big kill. The nightmare was over, the danger past. He no longer had to feel responsible for her.

But even as he silently acknowledged that, he was reluctant to let her go. They needed to talk. But they couldn't do it now, not when they each had to get back to their papers and write their accounts of the night's events. Over the course of the next twelve hours, there would be recaps of each murder to do and interviews with Harper's friends and neighbors. And one with Harper himself if he could get it, he silently acknowledged.

Just the thought of that should have had him making his

excuses so he could get to the jail and convince the man to give him an exclusive. Instead, he said, "Do you want me to come in with you? I can wait while you write your story, then take you home so you can get your car."

Sabrina hesitated, wanting to jump at the offer, but she knew she couldn't. He had his own story to write, and she couldn't take advantage of him that way. But Lord, how she wanted to! For the first time in her career, she dreaded writing a breaking story. Just thinking about Jeff and the hatred he must feel for her made her want to jump into Blake's arms. But she was no longer in danger—she no longer needed his protection. Her heart ached at the thought of going back to an adversarial relationship with him, but she was the one who had insisted only a few weeks ago that there was no place in her future for him or any other man. She couldn't cling to him now.

Reluctantly, she shook her head. "Thanks, but that's not necessary. I don't know how long it's going to take me, and you've got your own work to do. I'll get a ride."

He wanted to argue—she could see the struggle going on his eyes—but she didn't give him the chance. Reaching for the door handle, she said huskily, "I've got to go."

He made no move to stop her, but just as she stepped out of his truck, he warned, "You haven't seen the last of me, Jones. When things calm down a little, we're going to talk."

His words carried the hint of a promise—and a threat. Her heart doing a flip-flop in her chest, Sabrina watched him drive away and bit her tongue to keep from calling him back.

Fitz told her later that her piece about Jeff's arrest was one of the best she had ever written, but Sabrina took little pleasure in the compliment. She'd tried to divorce herself both physically and emotionally from it and write it as she would any other story, but she just couldn't do it. By the time she finally finished, she was drained. Her head ached and her eyes burned, and all she wanted to do was go home and sleep around the clock.

But in spite of the fact that she had started work before four that morning, her day had hardly begun. She had a whole string of interviews she had to conduct, starting with the crime scene investigators who had uncovered the evidence at Jeff's house and continuing right down to the snow-cone seller at Alamo Plaza who might have caught a glimpse of whoever had made the anonymous phone call about Jeff to the police. But first, she had to have wheels.

When one of the sports reporters heard she was afoot, he volunteered to give her a ride home since he was headed in that direction. She jumped at the offer, and a few minutes later, had him drop her off at the corner half a block from her house. At barely ten in the morning, it was already hot, but she didn't care. She just wanted to walk down her own street without feeling that someone was watching her.

It was heaven.

Martha Anderson was, as usual, outside in her front yard gossiping over the hedge with Gwen Richards, the widow who lived on her west side. The two were fast friends who kept an eagle eye on the neighborhood—a leaf couldn't fall without them knowing about it. Reassured that some things remained consistent, Sabrina waved gaily at them, then hurried up the porch steps to her front door. Both women waved back and continued to talk to each other as if they didn't have a care in the world, but Sabrina wasn't fooled by their nonchalance. They weren't called "the Newspapers" by the rest of the neighbors for nothing. The minute Sabrina was safely inside her house, the two old ladies would call everyone on the block to let them know she was home.

Grinning at the thought, she let herself inside. Silence closed around her immediately, clammy and thick, intimidating. Unable to stop herself, she shivered, the pleasure she expected to feel when she walked through her front door just not there. She wanted to forget Jeff and the sick murders he had committed, but all too easily, she found herself remembering the night after the awards banquet when she'd come home with Blake to find her front door unlocked and the threatening note waiting for her on her kitchen table.

She shouldn't have come here, she thought. Not yet. She wasn't ready for the memories or the nagging silence of her own thoughts. She should have just grabbed her car keys and gotten the hell out of there. But it seemed like ages since she'd been home. Her plants needed watering, and there was mail to go through. She could take a few minutes to see to those things, then grab a quick shower. Maybe then she'd be able to get through the rest of the day without going quietly out of her mind.

She had just started to water the ivy in the kitchen when there was a knock at the front door. Not really surprised, Sabrina's lips twitched. If her calculations were right, it had taken Martha all of two minutes and twenty-five seconds to get away from Gwen and make her way over there to find out where she'd been for the last two nights. That had to be a record even for her.

Her eyes starting to twinkle, she turned back to the front door. But it wasn't Martha standing on her porch, or even Gwen. It was Louis, and he looked extremely upset.

Chapter 11

"My dear, I'd just heard about Jeff's arrest on the radio when I saw you walk up. I know you're divorced and all, but you must be devastated. Is there anything I can do?"

Sabrina appreciated his concern, but she couldn't take any sympathy right now, not when her emotions felt as though they'd just been put through a food processor. He was, however, only being kind. Her smile forced, she said, "Well, it was something of a shock, but I'm coming to grips with it. And I don't have to be afraid anymore."

"That's the important thing," he agreed gruffly. "He's behind bars now and he can't hurt you. You probably have a million things to do, but I just wanted you to know that if you needed to talk, I've been told I'm a good listener."

The throbbing of her head intensifying, Sabrina reminded herself that he'd been a good neighbor to her over the years, and she couldn't be rude just because the last six hours had been rough ones. "I've got to get back to work in about an hour, but I've got a little time now. Why don't you take a seat on the porch swing and I'll fix us something cold to drink," she suggested. "I'll be right back."

Leaving him on the porch, she hurried back to the kitchen, trying to remember what she had in the house to serve him. She knew he didn't like sodas, so that left iced tea or lemonade and she wasn't sure she had the makings for either. Of course, there was always water, but—

Lost in her thoughts and wishing she could have put this off until later, she was checking to see how much sugar she had when she heard a noise behind her. Startled, she whirled and nearly dropped the sugar canister when she spotted Louis standing in the kitchen doorway. "Oh!" she laughed shakily, her heart hammering against her ribs. "You scared me."

Contrite, he immediately apologized. "I should have said something, but I thought you heard me come in. Are you all right?"

"I guess I'm still a little jumpy." Replacing the sugar canister on the counter, she decided to brew tea and moved to the sink to fill the teakettle with water. "The last week has been pretty hairy," she admitted as she crossed to the stove. "Not knowing who was threatening me was the worst. I was constantly looking over my shoulder. Then to find out it was Jeff…" She shuddered. "I still can't believe it."

His expression suddenly hard and cold, Louis nodded. "I know. I'm sure he fooled a lot of people, but there's no question that the man is a first-class bastard, dear. I hope he gets the book thrown at him. It's no more than he deserves for hurting you."

His vehemence surprised her. She knew Louis was as

protective of her as an older uncle, but he'd always seemed to like Jeff, even after she divorced him. In fact, she'd never heard him say a harsh word against him. "I really think he has to be sick, Louis. Or he's on drugs or something. It's the only explanation. Four women are dead. The Jeff I was married to would have to be out of his mind to do something like that."

"I don't care if he's crazy as a loon. He hurt you, and he's going to pay for that."

Confused, she frowned. "He scared me, but he never touched me physically. It's those poor women who are the real victims—"

"They didn't suffer like you did," he said flatly, dismissing their deaths with a careless wave of his hand. "You were the one who constantly tried to please a man who couldn't be pleased. I stood by and watched you try to make that son of a bitch happy, and it made me sick to my stomach. He didn't deserve you."

Stunned, Sabrina could only stare at him. She'd never heard Louis talk like this, hadn't a clue, in fact, that he'd ever felt that way about Jeff. And how could he dismiss the death of those four women so easily, without an ounce of compassion? She'd always thought he was such a kind and gentle man, but there was a barely controlled rage in his eyes now that was more than a little scary.

Suddenly aware of the way he stood in the doorway, blocking it, she told herself to remain calm. There was no reason to get all paranoid. Obviously, something was going on here that she didn't understand. She would get him outside and they would talk about it.

The teakettle whistled then, and relief almost weakened her knees. "The tea will be ready in just a second," she said brightly. Her smile felt like it would crack her face, but it was the best she could manage under the circumstances. "Why don't you go on out to the front porch and I'll be right there?" she suggested. "I think I've got some cookies around here somewhere—"

"No."

She jumped at his sharp response, her smile slipping. "Okay, fine," she said carefully, watching him warily. "Then we'll just have the tea."

Never budging from the doorway, he only looked at her, his pale eyes suddenly coolly amused behind the lenses of his wire-rimmed glasses. "You just don't get it, do you, Sabrina? You're not going anywhere."

Her heart jumped into her throat, but she only laughed shakily. "Of course I am. I told you, I have to get back to work—"

"I've been watching you for a long time, you know. Years, in fact," he said casually, not even hearing her as he leaned against the doorjamb. "The first day the two of you moved in here, I knew Jeff was all wrong for you. Anybody with eyes could see that he was a selfish bastard who didn't deserve you, but you tried your damndest to make it work. Do you know how hard it was for me to stand back and watch you do that?"

Transfixed, she could do nothing but mutely shake her head.

"No, of course you didn't," he said bitterly. "You never even knew I was alive. And I couldn't blame you. You were married and you should have had eyes for no one but your husband, even if he didn't deserve you. But then you divorced him, and I thought I might finally have a chance. Surely you would see then how much I loved you. But you never looked twice at me."

Shocked, Sabrina couldn't believe what she was hearing.

He *loved* her? As a man loves a woman? Surely she must have misunderstood. But even as she tried to convince herself otherwise, she looked into his eyes and knew she hadn't made a mistake. He made no attempt to hide his pain—or resentment. Remorse stabbing her in the heart, Sabrina wanted to defend herself, but there was nothing she could say that wouldn't make him feel worse. He was right—she hadn't noticed, but he was over thirty years older than she was. He'd always been friendly when they spotted each other in the yard, but she'd never dreamed that he was romantically interested in her. Why would she? He was old enough to be her father!

"Louis, I'm sorry. I never realized."

"No, you didn't," he retorted, not making things easy for her. "You were young and pretty and you didn't have time for an old man. So I looked around and found myself someone else. She was a lot like you, a professional woman who knew what she wanted out of life. Unfortunately, she wasn't you."

Becoming more uncomfortable by the moment, Sabrina really didn't want to hear about his love life, but he hadn't budged from the doorway, and she knew he wasn't letting her out of there until he'd said everything he had to say. "That doesn't mean she wasn't right for you," she said earnestly, trying to reassure him. "Maybe you need to give her another chance."

"I can't. She's dead."

"Oh, I'm sorry!"

"I killed her."

He said it so easily, in the same casual tone he might use to mention that he'd mowed the grass, that, at first, the confession didn't register. Then her startled eyes met his and there was no question that he'd said exactly what she thought he'd said. Her heart starting to slam in her chest, she paled. "If this is some kind of a joke, I don't think it's very funny."

"Oh, it's no joke," he assured her seriously. "I tried to make her into you—the same perfume and hairstyle, but she kept fighting me. She said I was old-fashioned and domineering and no man was going to dictate to her what she could and couldn't wear. She didn't know her place, so I shot her."

Horrified, Sabrina realized she must have made a strangled sound of protest because he pushed away from the doorjamb, the smile that played about his mouth rueful and twisted and deranged. "Don't worry, she didn't suffer. None of them did."

A restless hand flew to Sabrina's suddenly tight throat. "None of them?"

"There were others," he said simply. "But they didn't work out, either."

"How many others?"

"Three more. I knew you would put two and two together, after the first two, and you did. Finally, you noticed me!" A pleased smile bloomed across his face. "It was wonderful. So I killed again. Then once more because I couldn't help myself. *You* made me mad." Suddenly noticing her ashen complexion, he frowned. "You should sit down. You're awfully pale all of a sudden."

Her blood roaring in her ears, Sabrina almost choked on a hysterical laugh. He'd just admitted to killing four women and he was concerned that she was a little pale?

It hit her then—*four* women. He'd claimed he'd killed four women, and the only murders she'd written about recently were those committed by the serial killer.

The logical part of her mind immediately rejected the

idea. The police had arrested Jeff; they were sure they had the right man. He had motive and opportunity, not to mention a garage full of incriminating evidence and no alibi. They couldn't have made a mistake. Could they?

Dread clutching her heart, she stepped around the table before he could help her into a chair. "I don't need to sit down, but I would like to hear more about these murders," she said quickly. "When did all of this happen? And who were these women? Did you know them personally or just pick them by chance?"

Amused that she even had to ask, he chided softly, "Surely you've guessed by now, Sabrina. I can't think of anyone in San Antonio who wouldn't know their names. Charlene McClintock, Tanya Bishop—"

"But Jeff was arrested for those murders. The police found evidence—"

"That I planted," he said quite proudly. "How do you think they even knew to look for it, dear? I called in the tip."

He was serious. Even though a smile still clung to his thin lips and he spoke in a tone that was warm with affection, there was a feral gleam in his eye that a blind woman couldn't have missed. "Why?" she choked out hoarsely. "Why are you telling me this?"

In the blink of an eye, his smile vanished. "Because I love you!" he raged. "I've loved you forever, but you couldn't see it. You couldn't see *me!*" he snarled, hitting himself hard in the chest with a clenched fist. "It was your work, always your work that got in my way. Then when I finally figured out a way to get your attention there, you couldn't see anybody but *him!*"

Agitated, his mouth twisting with contempt, he turned suddenly and swept all the canisters from the counter.

"Damn you, you're in love with Blake Nickels, aren't you? Don't try to deny it. Don't you dare! Do you think just because I'm an old man I can't see what's right in front of my eyes? *I saw you!*"

Startled, more frightened than she'd ever been in her life, Sabrina took a step back. "When? What are you talking about?"

"At that damn newspaper party when you couldn't keep your hands off each other. And then later on the porch when you kissed him like a slut. You left with him that night, after you found my note on the table. You left and went to his apartment, didn't you? You made love with him."

"No. Not then—"

"Don't lie to me!" he roared, jerking a very small, very ugly little revolver out of his pocket. "I won't stand for it. Do you hear me? I've killed for you, and by God, you'll love me or you'll love no one."

Trapped, caught between the locked back door and where he stood blocking the doorway to the rest of the house, Sabrina knew real fear for the first time in her life. He was going to kill her—there wasn't a doubt in her mind. If she didn't find a way to reason with him, he'd snuff her out as easily as he had Tanya Bishop and all the others. The police would know then that Jeff was innocent, but they wouldn't suspect Louis in a million years. They would look for someone with an obvious grudge, not an elderly neighbor who had never had a cross word with her.

Never taking her eyes from the gun, she slowly pulled out a chair at the table and sank down into it. Every instinct she had was screaming at her to run, but that was probably what he was hoping for, so he would have the pleasure of gunning her down. "Please," she pleaded shakily, "put the gun down and let's talk. Surely there's some way we can work this out...."

Staring at his computer screen, Blake quickly read over his story about Jeff Harper's arrest. It was good, he silently acknowledged. Damn good. The kind of thing that just might win him another award. And he didn't like it at all.

Scowling, ignoring the commotion of the *Times'* city room, he dropped his hands from the keyboard and sat back, wondering what the devil was wrong. He'd checked all his facts twice, arranged and rearranged them, and started over more times than he had on any other story in the last six months. And he still couldn't shake the niggling feeling that something wasn't quite right.

The facts just didn't add up, dammit!

Tapping a pencil against the edge of his desk, he told himself he was getting as bad as Sabrina. She'd tried every way she could to find an excuse for the incriminating evidence found in her ex's garage, and now he found himself doing the same thing. And not because he cared two cents about Jeff Harper. He didn't like the man. But if he was a serial killer, then Blake was Al Capone.

Oh, all the facts pointed to Harper's guilt; there was no doubt about that. *If* you just took them collectively and didn't ask any questions. Like who called in the anonymous tip. How had the caller known there was enough evidence in Harper's garage to choke a horse? And why would a man of Harper's obvious intelligence keep damning evidence on his property just days after he'd been questioned about the murders by the police? He had to know he was a suspect and the police could return at any time. And then there was the car. If Harper really was the killer and the same man who had left those notes for Sabrina, why would he use his own car in a neighborhood where it was known and he was sure to be recognized? Only an idiot would do that.

Or someone who was trying to frame Harper.

Instinctively, he tried to dismiss the idea. Kelly was an experienced detective—he would have smelled a setup like that in a heartbeat.

But he'd also been under a lot of pressure to make an arrest in the case, a voice in his head pointed out. *Harper made it easy for him by publicly confronting Sabrina and acting like an ass. With the evidence that was found in that damn garage, what else could Kelly do but arrest him? That doesn't necessarily mean Harper actually killed anyone.*

And if he didn't, then the real killer was still out there, still after Sabrina.

His blood running cold at the thought, Blake snatched up his phone and punched out the number for the *Daily Record.* "Let me speak to Sabrina Jones," he snapped the minute someone answered in the other paper's city room.

"Hold on a minute," a disembodied, bored feminine voice said. "I think she just stepped out for a second. Let me see if I can find her."

Blake winced as the receiver was thrown down on a desk, every instinct he possessed urging him to hurry. Too late, he realized he should have told the woman that it was an emergency, but he'd expected Sabrina to be right there. Dammit, where the hell was she?

Twenty seconds ticked by on the clock on the wall at the far end of the city room, then another thirty, before the phone was picked up again and the same feminine voice said, "Sorry, she's not here. She left about twenty minutes ago to go home and pick up her car. You want to leave a message?"

Blake felt his heart stop in his chest. Home? She'd gone *home?* Swearing, he growled, "Yeah. This is Blake Nickels. If she shows up there, tell her not to leave again without talking to me first. You got that? Don't let her leave!"

Slamming the phone down, he jerked it up immediately and called Sabrina's home number. But if she was there, she didn't answer, and with every ring, the muscles in his gut tightened. "Dammit!"

She hadn't gotten there yet, he told himself, and prayed it was true. If somebody at the *Record* gave her a ride, they could have had some errands to run before they could drop her off. If he hurried, he could beat her there. Hanging up, he ran for the door.

Her eyes locked in fascinated horror on the gun that Louis held on her with icy determination, Sabrina jumped when there was a sudden pounding on her front door. Before she could even think about screaming for help, Louis was around the table and pressing the revolver to her temple.

"One word," he snarled in a low voice, "and it'll be your last."

Her gasp quickly stifled, she nodded and felt the cold steel of the gun's barrel slide against her skin. Nausea churned in her stomach, backing up into her throat.

"Sabrina? Are you in there?"

At the first sound of Blake's voice, she bit her lip to keep from crying out, the need to call out to him almost more than she could bear. He'd come for her. Somehow she'd known deep inside that he would, even though he couldn't possibly have known that she was in trouble. He would take care of Louis. All she had to do was scream—

"I'll kill him," Louis grated, reading her mind. "I swear to God I'll kill him if he doesn't get away from that door."

"No!" Horror choking her, she ignored the revolver at her temple and turned to him with pleading eyes. "He must have called the *Record* and found out I got a ride home. Let me talk to him. I can convince him to leave."

"Yeah, right," he drawled sarcastically. "Before or after you tell him to call the police?"

"I won't. I swear!" she promised. "You can stand right there behind the door and listen the whole time. We had a fight yesterday," she lied in growing desperation. "I'll tell him I'm still mad at him and make him leave. Please. If you shoot him, the neighbors will hear and then what will you do?"

He hesitated, clearly not trusting her, the look in his eyes wild and panicky. Whatever was going on in that twisted head of his, he obviously hadn't anticipated this kind of kink in his plans. "All right," he muttered. "But you say one wrong word, you even look at him funny, and I'll shoot you both. Get up."

Jerking her to her feet, he jammed the gun in her back and pushed her through the kitchen door into the central hall that ran all the way to the front of the house. His breath hot against the back of her neck, he stopped her three feet from the front door simply by curling his fingers into her arm until she winced. "Remember what I said. One wrong move and you won't have time to regret it. I'll make sure of it."

Her knees quaking, her heart pounding so hard she could hardly catch her breath, she nodded stiffly and took two shaky steps toward the door just as Blake knocked again. Out of sight behind the door itself, Louis thrust the revolver into her ribs. "Put the chain on and keep it on," he said between his teeth in a nearly soundless whisper.

Her fingers far from steady, Sabrina did as ordered, then waited for his nod for her to open the door. When he grudgingly gave it, she braced herself. Her heart in her throat, the cold, hard barrel of the revolver pressing threateningly into her ribs, she opened the door as far as the chain would allow, all of four inches.

"Thank God!" Blake breathed. "I was beginning to think you weren't here."

"I was in the middle of something," she said coldly, and nearly snatched the words back when she saw his eyes narrow in surprise. Please, please, let him understand, she prayed, then demanded, "What do you want?"

He took a step toward her, only to stop, his dark brows snapping together when she didn't release the chain. "I need to talk to you. Can I come in?"

"No," she said curtly. "Everything we had to say to each other was said last night. I told you then to leave me alone and I meant it. Now, if you'll excuse me, I'm going to take a bath and go to bed. Alone." Without another word, she shut the door in his face and shot the dead bolt home. Stunned, Blake stared at the closed door in disbelief. She'd slammed it in his face. As if he was some kind of door-to-door salesman who didn't know when to take a hint, he thought in growing fury. So she wanted to be left alone, did she? Well, by God, she didn't have to tell him twice. He didn't push himself on any woman.

Fury and hurt clouding his judgment, he stalked down the porch steps to the curb and climbed into his pickup without once looking back. With a savage twist, he turned the key in the ignition and tore off down the street with an angry squeal of tires. What the hell did she mean, whatever they'd had to say to each other was said last night? He'd made love to her until they were both too weak to move and he hadn't heard a single word of complaint out of her. In fact, he would have sworn she was as caught up in their loving as he was. Dammit to hell, how could he have been so wrong about her?

Scowling, he was already turning the corner, intending to head back to the *Times,* when he realized that nothing she'd said had made sense. They hadn't exchanged cross words last night. In fact the only thing they'd come close to arguing about was Jeff, and that was only because she hadn't wanted to believe that he was capable of murder. She'd been upset, but not with him. So why was she acting now like she couldn't stand the sight of him? What the hell was going on?

Replaying the entire conversation in his head a second time, he still couldn't make any sense of it. She hadn't even taken the safety chain off! She'd stood there, pale and nervous, and stared up at him through that damn crack in the door as though he was some kind of rapist who was going to force his way in and drag her down to the floor. If he hadn't known better, he would have sworn she was scared to death. But why would she be scared of him? She had to know he wouldn't harm a hair on her head—

But the bastard who had killed four women and promised her she would be his next victim would.

His hands clenched on the wheel at the thought. No! He couldn't have gotten to her so quickly. He was just being paranoid. If she'd been in trouble, she would have said something, given him some kind of sign.

Everything we had to say to each other we said last night. I told you then to leave me alone and I meant it.

Her words echoed in his head, haunting him, chilling his blood. She'd never told him to leave her alone. Never! So why would she say that unless she was trying to relay some sort of message to him, a message she couldn't just spit out because someone else was there, listening? He hadn't seen him or heard so much as a whisper of movement from the other side of the door, but suddenly he knew in his gut that she hadn't been alone and she was terrified.

God, how could he have been so blind? Swearing, fear clutching him by the throat, he jammed down on the accelerator, uncaring that he was fairly flying down a residential street as he circled the block, his only thought to get to her before it was too late. He'd kill him, he raged. He didn't care who the son of a bitch was, if he so much as touched a hair on her head, he'd kill him with his bare hands.

Caught up in the fury burning like the fires of hell deep inside him, he turned back onto her street, just in time to see her step outside onto her front porch. With Louis Vanderbilt.

"What the hell!"

Stunned, he whipped over to the curb and jerked to a stop behind a parked car six houses from her place, unable to believe his eyes. Louis Vanderbilt was her stalker? The man who had shot four women in their own homes, then walked away and left them to bleed to death? *He* was the one who was in love with Sabrina and planned to kill her because she didn't know he existed?

Dazed, he shook his head. This case was driving him nuts and twisting his thinking. Louis Vanderbilt was an old man who wouldn't hurt a flea, let alone kill anyone.

Especially Sabrina. He was clearly fond of her and watched over her with an eagle eye. He would never do anything to harm her, he assured himself.

Then he saw the gun.

He only caught a flash of it, a glint of metal in the morning sun before Louis crowded close to her, concealing the small pistol between their two bodies as he urged her toward where her Honda was parked in the driveway. Then he was pushing her through the passenger door and making her scoot over the center console to the driver's seat. Seconds later, her face as pale as death, she backed out of the driveway and drove off in the opposite direction from where Blake was parked at the curb.

He swore and just barely stopped himself from racing after her. He couldn't do that, dammit, not without taking a chance that the old man would recognize his pickup behind them and shoot her on the spot. But, God, he couldn't just sit there! Snatching up his cellular phone, he quickly called Sam Kelly, his gaze never leaving Sabrina's red Honda as it moved slowly down the street.

The unfamiliar voice that came on the line, however, didn't belong to Sam. It was a secretary who informed him that the detective was currently out of the office but expected back at any moment. Swearing, Blake identified himself. "I can't wait for him to get back. Page him if you have to, but track him down. The wrong man was arrested for the serial killings." Rattling off his cellular number, he barked, "Have him call me the second you find him. And hurry, dammit! There's not much time."

At the end of the street, Sabrina turned right, and within seconds, her Honda disappeared from view around the corner. Muttering a curse, Blake pushed the end button, tossed the phone into the passenger seat and pulled away from the curb in one smooth, quick movement. It seemed to take forever just to reach the corner.

The cross street was a main thoroughfare that ran due north and was usually busy at that hour of the day. Several cars zoomed past before it was clear enough for him to turn right as Sabrina had, and he found himself holding his breath, afraid he'd lost her. But when he turned the corner, making sure to stay a healthy distance behind the car in front of him, Sabrina was nearly a half a mile down the road, but well within sight. Sending up a silent prayer of thanks, he started after her.

His cellular rang nearly ten minutes later, cutting like a fire alarm through the tense silence that filled the cab of his truck. Never taking his eyes from the red Honda in the distance, he snatched it up.

"What the hell's going on, Blake?" Kelly demanded in his ear. "I was in a meeting with the chief when I got your message, and it was kind of hard for me to explain to him how we could have arrested the wrong man when I don't know what the devil you're talking about. What—"

"Just listen," Blake cut in, swearing as Sabrina turned at the next light and headed west. Where the hell was she going? "Jeff Harper didn't have anything to do with killing those women—he was set up by Louis Vanderbilt."

"Louis Vanderbilt?" the other man repeated in confusion. "Sabrina's neighbor? C'mon, Blake, he's old enough to be her father!"

"I don't care if he's older than dirt," Blake snapped. "Right now, he's holding a gun on her in her car and forcing her to drive west on Hildebrand."

"*What?* Hell!" Throwing questions at him, the detective determined his location, then growled, "I've got three units on the way, Blake. As soon as they get there, I want you to back off and let them handle the situation. And don't give me a hard time about this," he added quickly, anticipating an argument. "You're unarmed and a civilian. Let my men do their job and Sabrina won't get hurt."

Silence his only answer, Blake wasn't making promises he had no intention of keeping. If the bastard hurt Sabrina, he was going to tear him limb from limb. "They're turning right on State Avenue," he retorted. "It looks like they're headed for Crocker Park. Get your men over there, Kelly. Now!"

"Dammit, Blake, don't you dare go rushing in there like John Wayne—"

For an answer, Blake pushed the button to end the call and tossed the phone back into the passenger seat. When it immediately rang again, he ignored it, his gut tightening as he, too, reached the intersection with State Avenue and turned right. Crocker Park lay less than a mile down the road. A popular recreation spot for families on the weekends, it wasn't nearly as savory a place during the middle of a workday. Occasionally, you might come across a mother with young children playing on the swings, but more often than not, the only occupants of the park were people who, for whatever reason, didn't want to be seen. They sat in isolated parts of the parking lot in cars with darkened windows, doing God knows what. Drivers using State Avenue to cut through the park seldom spared them a second glance, nobody but an occasional park ranger took an interest in what was going on, and no one seemed to care.

Wishing there were more than two cars between him and Sabrina, Blake followed cautiously, checking his rearview mirror every few seconds for the police, but there was no sign of them. Dammit to hell, where were they? Any second now, Sabrina was going to be in even deeper trouble than she was now, and the only thing he had that resembled a weapon was a tire iron. And while he'd like nothing better than to brain Vanderbilt with it, it wasn't going to do a whole hell of a lot of good against a gun.

Racking his brain for a plan, he abruptly ran out of time ten seconds later. Sabrina turned into the park entrance, and there was no way he could follow her. With so little traffic, Vanderbilt would spy him immediately. Swearing, he had no choice but to drive on past the entrance.

Daring to slow to a crawl, he cast a quick look through the park entrance as he passed and saw the red Honda disappear into some low-hanging bushes near the creek that marked the park's western boundary. When he was a teenager, it had been a popular necking spot for teenagers. Now it was deserted, with the nearest car nearly a hundred yards away. Vanderbilt could do anything he liked to Sabrina there, out of sight of prying eyes, and the few other occupants of the park wouldn't notice a thing.

God, he had to do something! The police were never going to get there in time if he didn't.

His heart slamming against his ribs, he waited until he reached the far end of the park and pulled into the parking lot of the church across the street. The need to hurry ate at him from the inside out, but this was no time to go rushing blindly in like a fool. He had to think! Grabbing the tire iron from behind his seat, he was just stepping from the truck when his cellular rang again. Muttering a curse, he almost ignored it. He had to get to Sabrina, dammit! But if it was Kelly, he needed to let him know exactly where Vanderbilt was holding her.

Answering it, he said, "Kelly? I'm at the church parking

lot at the end of the park. Do you know where the old lover's lane is?"

"At the south end of the park?" the other man asked. "Opposite the main entrance?"

"Yeah, that's the one. Vanderbilt's got Sabrina back there in the bushes. I'm going in."

"Dammit, Blake, I told you to sit tight!" Kelly snapped. "My men'll be there any second. You rush in there now, you just might get Sabrina killed."

"And if I don't, that just might get her killed, too. Don't ask me to sit on my hands on this, Sam. I can't. I'm going in, and there's not a damn thing you can do to stop me."

"The hell I can't. I'll arrest your ass—"

Without another word, Blake ended the call and shut off the phone's power. Stepping out of his truck, the tire iron clutched in his hand, he soundlessly eased the door shut. Across the street, the park was deserted except for the handful of cars parked in isolated spots under the trees. The freeway was on the far side of the creek and screened out by the thick stand of oaks there, and downtown was just over the hill to the south. Still, if you hadn't known better, you could have easily sworn you were miles from the hustle and bustle of the state's third largest city.

The quiet grating on his nerves and setting his heart thumping in his chest, Blake tightened his grip on the tire iron and jogged across the street and down into the creek bed that meandered all the way to the spot where Vanderbilt had Sabrina hidden among the trees. There, out of sight of the park's occupants and anyone else who might be watching, he began to run.

Chapter 12

"This is all your fault," Louis lashed out as he forced Sabrina out of the car and dragged her through the bushes to a small clearing that was totally cut off from the rest of the park. "*I loved you!* Do you know how many women I've said that to in my lifetime? Just you." His eyes tortured behind the lenses of his glasses, he glared at her accusingly. "You're the only one. The only one I ever wanted, the only one I ever dreamed about, the only one I wanted to share my life with. But you didn't even know I was alive."

Her gaze locked on the gun he was waving wildly about, fear churning like a storm in her stomach, Sabrina struggled not to panic. If she could just get him to drop his guard—and the gun—for a second, she might be able to escape into the bushes and lose him. It was a long shot, but the only one she had. No one knew she was here or in danger. If she was going to get out of this alive, she had to do it all by herself.

Facing him in the middle of the clearing, she fought to remain calm, but it wasn't easy, not when she could see the madness in his eyes. "That's not true," she said quietly. "I always knew you were just next door if I needed you—"

"But you never did," he cut in harshly. "The only thing you ever needed me for was to fix a leaky faucet or give your car a jump when your battery was low. You didn't need my arms about you or the security of knowing I was there beside you in the middle of the night. You didn't need anything but your job."

"I had to work, Louis. I have bills to pay just like everybody else."

"But you didn't have to love it!" Anger tightening every line of his body, he said bitterly, "You didn't have to drop everything and go running to it in the middle of the night just because some idiot beat up his girlfriend or a convenience store was held up. You shouldn't have been darting around town chasing stories at all hours of the day and night, putting yourself in danger and worrying me to death. You should have been home, with me, where you belong, talking about our future, planning children. I'm not too old to have children, you know. I used to dream about the babies I would give you...."

A loving smile playing about his thin mouth, he described the children he'd planned to have with her, the two boys and a girl that she would stay home with and take care of like a good, dutiful wife and mother, and Sabrina could do nothing but stare at him. How could she have lived next door to this man for years and not realized that he was totally and completely out of his mind? How could she have been so blind?

"Louis..."

He blinked, his expression changing from dreamy to

angry resentment in a split second. "But we're never going to have those babies, are we? We're never going to have anything. Not children. Not a home together. Not a future. Because of you."

Bitterness twisted his mouth. "God, what a fool I've been. You don't want me. You never did. You never will. All you want is Nickels."

She didn't have to justify herself to him, didn't owe him any explanation about her private life. But he was so close to snapping, she had to do something before he went completely ballistic. "Blake and I are friends—"

He snorted. "Is that why your face lights up like a Christmas tree every time he comes anywhere near you? Damn you, I'm not blind!" His thin face flushed with fury, he turned on her, brandishing the gun in her face, the haunted look in his eyes wilder than ever. "You love him," he snarled. "Oh, you might not think you do, but I know you. You don't give your heart lightly, and you've given it to Nickels. And that can't be tolerated. Not after all that I've done for you."

What had he done for her except kill four innocent women? she wondered in confusion. The coppery taste of fear thick in her throat, she said, "Please, Louis, you're twisting this all out of proportion—"

"So this is all my fault? Is that what you're saying?"

"No!" she said hastily as his silky tone slid over her, making her skin crawl. "I'm not saying anything of the kind. We're just both upset. Why don't we go somewhere and get a cup of coffee and discuss this rationally? I'm sure we could work it out if we could just—"

The sudden snapping of a branch in the bushes was as loud as a gunshot. For a second, neither of them moved, then quick as a striking snake, Louis whirled, his eyes crazed as he searched the surrounding brush for an intruder. "He's out there," he said, half to himself. "I can feel him. Go away, Nickels! Leave us alone!" And with no more warning than that, he fired into the bushes.

Sabrina screamed. "Louis, no!"

Hidden in the thick undergrowth, Blake threw himself behind a tree just as the bullet whizzed past his shoulder. Cursing himself for not watching where he was putting his feet, he leaned against the tree, waiting for his heart rate to slow. He didn't think for a second that Louis had seen him—the surrounding brush was too dense and he'd been careful to keep out of sight as he'd worked his way toward where he could hear them talking—but the old man was obviously paranoid where he was concerned. And not so crazy after all if he knew that he would eventually come after him for Sabrina.

Chancing a quick look around the oak, he spied Louis standing with his back to Sabrina, his face twisted with fury and madness as he studied the surrounding brush off to Blake's right. For the moment, at least, he was distracted and didn't even realize that Sabrina was slowly backing away from him. If Blake could keep the old man's attention away from her long enough, she just might have a chance to slip into the trees and hide.

Glancing around, he found the fallen branch he'd stepped on and picked it up. Barely two feet long and not quite as thick as his wrist, it was half-rotten but would still make a nice loud crash when it hit the ground. Silently praying that Sabrina was on her toes and ready for anything, he hefted it by one end and tossed it far to the right of him. As it came down through the trees, it sounded, at least for a few seconds, like the cavalry was breaking through the underbrush.

As jumpy as a first-time bank robber, Louis whirled, his eyes wild as he scanned the bushes for a threat he couldn't see. "Go away!" he cried, and fired wildly into the trees.

Blake didn't wait to see more. "Run, Sabrina!" he yelled, and dove into the thick stand of oaks off to his left in an effort to draw the old man's anger away from Sabrina to himself.

From the corner of his eye, Blake saw Sabrina take off at a dead run, but she'd barely reached the edge of the clearing when Vanderbilt realized that he was losing her. "No!" His scream echoing eerily through the trees, he spun on his heel to find her racing for the concealment of the bushes. Snarling, he lifted his pistol and fired just as she threw herself into the trees.

"You bastard!" Rage roaring in Blake's ears, fury blinding him to everything but the need to kill the old man with his own hands, he threw the tire iron and hit him right on his wrist. The gun went flying, and before he could do anything but cry out in pain, Blake was on him.

"You miserable piece of trash! If you hurt her, I'll make you wish you'd never been born."

Out of his head, his only thought to get the gun, Louis was stronger—and wilier—than he looked. Kicking and scratching and ranting like a wild man, he slipped out of Blake's hold and scrambled for the pistol, which had fallen under a bush at the edge of the clearing. His breathing ragged, sweat dripping down into his eyes, Blake launched himself at him, grabbing him just as the old man's hand closed around the barrel of the gun.

"Drop it!" he growled, jamming one hand under Louis's chin while the other locked around his wrist. "Drop it or I swear I'll put my fist through your face."

Past reason, Louis only grunted, his lips drawn back in

a snarl as he fought to hang on to the gun. Swearing, Blake rolled over the ground with him and finally came up on top as sirens wailed in the distance. With a vicious oath, he slammed the old man's hand down on a rock. Just that quickly, the fight was over. The pistol fell from his grasp, and in the next instant, Blake had it and was towering over him.

"Just give me an excuse to pull the trigger," he said coldly, pointing the gun right at his head. "Please…just one. That's all I need."

From behind him, there was a crashing through the underbrush, but Blake never took his eyes from Louis, who didn't even try to get up but lay in the dirt like a beaten old man. "Don't do it, Blake," Sam Kelly said as he and four uniformed officers pushed their way into the clearing. "He's not worth it. Let us take over from here."

"Only if you promise to damn well keep him away from Sabrina," he said coldly. "He's scared her for the last time."

"He won't be scaring her or any other woman for the next thirty or forty years by the time we get through with him," Sam assured him confidently as he stepped to his side and took the gun while two of the uniformed officers jerked Vanderbilt to his feet and slapped handcuffs on him. Glancing around while the old man was read his rights, he frowned. "Where's Sabrina?"

Blake started toward the thick stand of mountain laurels where he'd seen Sabrina dive for cover. "Hiding over here in the bushes unless she ran to get help. I distracted Vanderbilt long enough for her to get away, and that's the last I've seen of her."

Half expecting her to come bursting out of the undergrowth and throw herself into his arms any second, he pushed his way through the bushes. "Sabrina? Honey? It's okay, you can come out now," he called, but his only answer was the whisper of the wind through the leaves. Uneasiness curled into his stomach like a damp fog. "Sabrina?"

He heard it then, a soft moan that could have been his imagination…except that Kelly heard it, too. He saw the other man stiffen, then they were both fighting through the bushes, searching. Ten minutes later, Blake found her. Sitting on the ground, her back propped up against a tree, she was as pale as death and covered in her own blood. She'd been shot.

Later, Blake didn't remember Kelly calling for an ambulance. All he saw was Sabrina's bloodless face, the total lack of color in her cheeks, the pain that darkened her eyes. She stirred at his hoarse cry, a weak smile pushing up one corner of her mouth as he whipped off his shirt and dropped down beside her to press the cloth to the ugly exit wound in her left shoulder. "I-I'm all r-right," she whispered.

"Shut up." Rage tearing at him, his fingers shaking with fear, all he could think of was that the son of a bitch had shot her in the back. In the back, goddammit! And so close to her heart that if he'd hit her two inches lower, he would have killed her instantly. And she hadn't said a word. While he'd been fighting the bastard for the gun, she'd been quietly bleeding to death. Dammit to hell, hadn't anyone thought to call for an ambulance?

"Blake, the ambulance is here," Kelly said grimly, touching him on the shoulder. "You've got to let the paramedics take over from here."

Another voice, a woman's, said firmly, "You've done

all you can for her, sir. Let us do our jobs and she's got a good chance of pulling through this."

He didn't want to step back, to trust her care to anyone but himself, but suddenly, there were hands to take over for him and keep pressure on the wound, and he was in the way. He stumbled back, his eyes burning with emotion as he watched the paramedics work over her with sure, skilled hands. He couldn't lose her, he thought fiercely. But God, how could she lose so much blood and still live?

"Come on," Sam told him as Sabrina was loaded onto a stretcher and quickly transported to the waiting ambulance. "I'll give you a ride to the hospital. You're in no shape to drive."

He would have preferred to ride in the ambulance, but there was no room, and time was at a premium. Nodding, he said tersely, "Let's go."

With sirens blaring and lights flashing, they went through every light with the ambulance. His face haggard, his gaze locked on the window in the back door of the ambulance, where he could see the paramedics working fiercely over Sabrina, Blake never heard Sam speak to him or try to assure him that Sabrina was in good hands. Numb, fear gripping his heart and squeezing painfully, he prayed like he had never prayed in his life.

They reached the hospital in record time, but it seemed to take forever. Then Sabrina was whisked away from him, upstairs to surgery, and all he could do was wait. It wasn't something he was particularly good at. Kelly had to leave and get back to the station, but he promised to return when he could. Pacing restlessly, unable even to think about striking up a conversation with the three other occupants of the waiting area, he watched every tick of the clock and never felt so alone in his life. What was taking so long?

"Blake? Are you doing okay, son? I got here as soon as I heard."

Glancing up at the familiar sound of his grandfather's voice, he blinked as if coming out of a daze. "Pop! What are you doing here?"

"Detective Kelly called me," he said gruffly. "I figured you needed me."

He had, and he hadn't even known it. Emotion clogging his throat, he hugged the old man tight. "I can't lose her, Pop. I love her."

"Well, of course you do," his grandfather murmured affectionately, returning his hug. "You just now figuring that out?"

Blake gave a choked chuckle and blinked back the sting of unexpected tears as he drew back. "Yeah, I guess I am. I don't even know how it happened. I certainly wasn't looking to get involved with anyone so soon, especially after Trina."

With a click of his tongue and wave of his bony hand, the old man dismissed his ex-girlfriend as easily as if she'd been nothing more than a piece of fluff. "I never met the woman, but I could have told you she wasn't the gal for you. Not after you went with her for four years without even giving her a ring or anything. A man doesn't need that kind of time to decide if he's found the right woman—not if he really cares about her. Why, with your grandmother, I knew in the first week. For the next fifty-three years I never looked at another woman."

"Those were different times, Pop."

"Hogwash," he snorted. "Love was love, and it hasn't changed. Your grandmother didn't just fall into my lap, you know. She had plans and was all set to go to some fancy college in New York when we met. And let me tell you, it took some pretty fast talking on my part to convince her that she didn't want to go anywhere without me. But I knew as soon as I saw her that she was what I wanted when I hadn't even known I was looking. Anyone with eyes can see you feel the same way about Sabrina. When it's right, you just know."

Blake couldn't argue with that. He'd come to San Antonio with a bruised heart and ego, determined not to look twice at anything in a skirt. So much for his fine resolve, he thought ruefully. One look at Sabrina, and he'd gone down for the count like a boxer with a glass jaw. No one, not even Trina, had ever dominated his thoughts the way she had, distracting him at the damndest times.

And then when he'd seen her in Louis's clutches and realized that he could lose her before he ever had a chance to tell her what she meant to him, he'd wanted to kill Vanderbilt with his bare hands. The strength of his rage still stunned him. Because of his job, he saw violence and its aftermath every day of the week; he would have sworn he just wasn't capable of that kind of fury. He'd been wrong.

God, he loved her. So much that it scared him. He wanted to spend the rest of his life making her laugh, loving her, going to bed beside her and waking up with her in his arms. But even if she was able to pull through the surgery and make it, he might not get the chance.

Sinking into a nearby chair, he said, "Try telling Sabrina that. Even if I can get her to admit that she loves me, she's got this thing about marriage. Her mother and grandmother have walked down the aisle more times than Elizabeth Taylor, and she's convinced she just doesn't have what it takes to make a marriage work."

"So change her mind," his grandfather said simply. "If she loves you, she trusts you. And that's what marriage is all about, son. Love and trust. Not even the strongest attraction can work without that."

He made it sound so easy. But as an hour passed, then another, and people in the waiting room came and went and he and his grandfather still waited, he couldn't worry about the future when he didn't even know if Sabrina was going to make it through the rest of the day. What was taking so long? Unable to just sit there, he prowled around the Spartan room, watching minutes turn to hours, and had to fight the need to throw something.

Finally, three hours after Sabrina was rushed upstairs to surgery, her doctor, still in his green scrubs, stepped into the doorway of the waiting room. "Mr. Nickels?" he said as Blake turned toward him expectantly. "I'm Dr. Richardson. I understand you're Sabrina Jones's fiancé?"

Blake nodded, promising himself that the small lie would be the truth before too much longer. "How is she? What took so long? Is she conscious? When can I see her?"

He threw questions at the doctor like darts, not giving him time to answer one before he thought of another. Laughing, Richardson held up a hand in protest. "Hold it! Let me tell you what I know, then you can ask any questions you want." His twinkling eyes turning serious, he said, "Sabrina's a lucky young woman, though I doubt she'll feel like one for the next couple of days. That bullet came awfully close to her heart."

Blake paled. "But she's going to make it?"

"Oh, yes. She lost a lot of blood, and she's going to have to take it easy for a while, but she's young and strong. Barring any unexpected complications, I don't see any reason why she shouldn't live to see her great-grandchildren."

Deep inside, the knot that had tied itself around his

heart loosened. She was going to be okay. He felt his grandfather's hand on his shoulder and laughed shakily. "Did you hear that, Pop? She's going to make it."

"I never doubted it," the old man said, squeezing his shoulder reassuringly. "She may not be big as a minute, but she's tough. I knew it the second I laid eyes on her."

"When can I see her?" Blake asked the doctor. "I won't stay long," he assured him when the other man hesitated. "I just need to see her, touch her. Two minutes, tops. I promise."

"She's still in recovery. She won't even know you're there."

"That's okay. *I* will. C'mon, doctor. If she won't know I'm there, what harm can it do?"

"All right," he said reluctantly. "But only *one* minute, and not a second over. Ms. Jones might be tough, but a gunshot wound isn't something you bounce back from the next day. Once you've seen for yourself that she's really still breathing, I want you out of here for the rest of the day. Got it?"

Blake nodded. "One minute, no longer. Scout's honor."

He would have agreed to just about anything short of murder to get within touching distance of her, but once he was in the recovery room, standing at Sabrina's bedside, he didn't know how he was ever going to leave her. God, she was pale! And so still. The sheet covering her barely moved as she breathed. His throat tight, he reached out and closed his fingers around her limp ones. She never moved.

"Hang in there, sweetheart," he whispered roughly. "You hear me? You're going to be all right."

"You have to leave now, Mr. Nickels," the recovery-room

nurse said quietly from behind him. "Dr. Richardson said one minute."

"I know. I know. I'm going."

But he didn't. Not for another thirty seconds. Not until he took one last long look at her, committing every inch of her to memory. It was all he would have of her for the next fifteen or twenty hours. God, how was he going to stand it?

Turning away, he growled, "I'll be back," then walked out the door. It was the hardest thing he'd ever done.

Sabrina shifted slightly in her hospital bed, only to suck in a sharp breath as her shoulder seemed to burn. The doctor had given her something for the pain, but it only made it bearable as long as she was relatively still. Whenever she inadvertently moved the wrong way, she paid for it.

Sweat breaking out on her brow, she squeezed her eyes shut and waited for the throbbing to ease, silently cursing her own weakness. She didn't have time to be laid up, she told herself. Not now. Not when the biggest story of the decade was wrapping up and she had the inside scoop. She had to get out of here and over to the *Daily Record*. Nearly twenty-four hours had already passed since Louis had deliberately shot her in the back, and if she didn't get her version of the story out soon, it was going to be old news and worthless.

Fighting pain and exhaustion, she'd read both papers from front to back page, cursing what she was missing. After Louis's arrest, the police had searched his house, where a diary was found hidden under the mattress of his bed. In it, he'd described how he'd met his victims at the bookstore and grocery store, even the flower shop and a singles' club, then proceeded to make friends with each of them. And when they didn't fall in love with him, he killed them.

With her out of commission, Fitz had assigned someone to follow up the story—a cub who had done a decent enough job and who would, with time, develop his own style and ask all the right questions. But for now, he'd missed more than a few pertinent details, which made Sabrina itch to get out of bed and reclaim her rightful spot in the pecking order. He didn't do the job like she did and wasn't even in the same ballpark, let alone the same league, with Blake.

Her heart constricting just at the thought of him, she felt stupid tears well in her eyes and quickly blinked them away. She would not, she told herself fiercely, cry over the man. Just because he was too busy writing up the rest of the news about Louis to come and see her didn't mean she was going to get all watery-eyed. He'd get around to visiting her eventually. And when he did, she'd tell him what she thought of a man who took advantage of a woman with a bullet in her shoulder just to win a bet.

It wasn't as if she cared about him, she thought as a hurt ten times more powerful than the one in her shoulder lodged in her heart. Okay, so maybe she had let him get to her just a bit. She wasn't made of stone. The man was damn attractive and the kind of lover that most women would sell their soul for. If her heart wanted more from him than a few nights, a few weeks, in his bed, then no one would ever know that but her.

Staring blindly out the window as the day began to fade, she swallowed the lump in her throat. She wanted to go home. She knew it was too soon—she couldn't possibly take care of herself yet—but she needed some time to herself. She had a private room, but people still came and went at their own discretion, often without bothering to knock. If she could get home, at least she could cry in peace without anyone walking in on her.

As if on cue, the door opened behind her, but she didn't spare so much as a glance for her visitor. Meals were delivered like clockwork, and she'd heard the familiar squeaky wheels of the food cart as it was pushed down the hall ten minutes ago.

"You can just put it on the table," she said quietly. "I'm not very hungry. Maybe I'll eat it later."

"You sure?" a teasing male voice asked from the doorway. "I went all the way downtown to get you a George's special, and even had the nurse heat it up in the microwave in the staff break room. It'd be a shame to waste it."

"Blake!" Startled, she turned too quickly, only to groan as her wound clenched like a sprung trap. "Oh, God!"

Cursing himself, Blake swore and hurried to her side. "I'm sorry! Dammit, I should have said something, but I wanted to surprise you. I guess I did." Tossing the foam container of Mexican food on the bedside table, he leaned over her worriedly and gently brushed her hair back from her face. "Are you okay? Damn, you're as white as the sheets. Maybe I should call the nurse."

"No!" She didn't want the nurse. She didn't want anyone but him and it scared her silly. Her shoulder was on fire, the pain raw and biting, but all she could think about was leaning into his strong, sure hand and letting him make everything feel all better. But she couldn't do that. Her emotions were too volatile, her need for him too strong. And there would come a day in the not too distant future when he wouldn't be there for her. As much as she wanted to, she couldn't let herself depend on him.

Blinking back foolish tears, she had to force herself to pull back slightly. "I'm fine," she said thickly. "Really. Just a little sore. The doctor warned me I should move in slow motion for a while. I just forgot."

Not sure he believed her, Blake stared down at her searchingly. The last twenty or so hours had been the longest of his life. He'd lost track of the number of times he'd started for the hospital, his only thought to see her, when he'd suddenly remembered that she needed to rest, to recoup her strength. So he'd stayed away and filled the time haunting the police station and writing stories that only made sense by the grace of God, unable to concentrate on much of anything but Sabrina.

She was okay. He could see that now for himself, but it was going to be months, maybe years, before he'd be able to push the image from his mind of her lying in the bushes, covered in her own blood. Just barely resisting the urge to snatch her close, he had to content himself with taking her hand instead.

"You, slow down?" he teased. "Because of a bullet? I would have sworn that it would take nothing less than getting run over by a freight train to take the starch out of you, Jones. In fact, I expected to come in here and find you pounding out the story on a laptop."

"Don't think I haven't thought about it," she retorted sassily. "I saw your byline—it was good. But my version will be better, so don't go making the mistake of thinking I'm out of the running to win our bet, Nickels. This is just a temporary setback." Glancing down at their joined hands, she frowned in bemusement. "What are you doing?"

He grinned and tightened his fingers around hers. "Holding your hand. You got a problem with that, Jones?

Because if you do, you'd better speak up. From now on, I plan to touch you every chance I get."

Her eyes widened at that, but she quickly recovered. "I might have something to say about that, Nickels."

"You're damn right you've got something to say about it. I'm hoping it's 'yes.'" His smile fading, he said gruffly, "I thought I'd lost you, sweetheart. Dr. Richardson assured me after the operation that you were going to be fine, but you'd lost so much blood—"

"You were here?"

"Hell, yes, I was here!" he said, surprised. "Where else would I have been? Over at the *Times* writing up the story while you were fighting for your life?"

"I don't know. I didn't know—"

"Because you were still out cold when they let me in to see you," he said. "Richardson gave me one minute with you, then threw me out of here. Honey, I've talked to your nurses at least six times today. I couldn't come visit you until Richardson gave me the okay."

"Oh. I thought..." She swallowed, shaking her head as foolish tears stung her eyes. Obviously what she'd thought didn't need to be repeated. Of course he would check on her and make sure she was all right. He was a caring man— she'd seen the way he looked out for his grandfather and knew from firsthand experience just how gentle he could be. He wouldn't dump a wounded woman on the hospital steps, then head for work as if nothing had happened. "Forget I said anything. I guess I was just feeling sorry for myself."

"Considering what you've been through, I'd say you were entitled," he replied. "I guess you heard Vanderbilt confessed."

"No! When?"

"After his diary was found. He won't ever hurt you again, honey," he assured her quietly. "In fact, Kelly said the D.A. is going to make sure he spends the rest of his life behind bars."

Relief coursed through her, but the news brought her little joy. The women Louis killed weren't the only ones who lost their lives—he'd lost his, too, and she couldn't help but feel sorry for him.

"I'm just glad it's over." She sighed. "Maybe now life can get back to normal."

"Actually, I was thinking you should take a vacation when you get out of here and just forget all this for a while. It'll do you good to get away."

Surprised, she smiled faintly. "There's the small matter of my job, Nickels. If I left now, you'd steal all my readers while I was gone, then I wouldn't have a job to come back to."

"Then I guess I'll just have to go with you. Tell me where you want to go and I'll take care of the reservations."

Stunned, Sabrina just stared at him, sure he was teasing. But his eyes were dark with an emotion that set her heart tripping, and she'd never seen him more serious. Suddenly breathless, she said huskily, "You want to tell me what's going on here, Blake? I think I missed something."

For an answer, he drew her hand to his chest and pressed it to his heart. "You didn't miss anything, sweetheart. I just never asked a woman to marry me before and I'm not doing a very good job of it."

Sabrina couldn't have been more stunned if he'd asked her to do a striptease in front of the Alamo. He wanted to marry her. Her heart turned over at the thought, joy flooding her. Then she remembered, and the smile blooming on her face vanished.

"Blake, you know how I feel about marriage—"

He cut her off with a kiss, stealing her protests and her thoughts before she had a chance to put up her guard. Softly, sweetly wooing, his mouth played with hers, gentling her, seducing her until her head fell weakly back against her pillow and her blood hummed in her veins. And when he finally let her up for air, it was to discover that he'd stretched out with her on the bed on her good side, uncaring who might walk in.

"Blake, please…"

"Oh, I plan to, Jones," he groaned, nuzzling her ear. "Just as soon as you're strong enough, I plan to please you until neither one of us can move." Lifting his head, he gazed down into her eyes. "I love you, sweetheart. You've got to know that."

She did. Somewhere deep inside, she'd known it the first time they'd made love. She'd felt it in his touch, his kiss, seen it in the heat of his eyes and recognized the same feelings in herself.

The truth hit her from the blind side, shaking her to the core. No, she thought, swallowing a sob. She couldn't love him. She could care for him, want him, need him more than she needed her next breath, but she wouldn't, couldn't let herself love him. Pain squeezing her heart, she pressed trembling fingers to his mouth. "Please, don't say that," she whispered in a voice that had a tendency to crack. "It can't change anything."

"Honey, it changes everything if you love me, too," he argued earnestly. "If you don't, tell me now. I won't bother you anymore."

One word, a simple no, from her and he would walk out, just like that. He wouldn't pressure her, not if she didn't love him. He'd laid his heart on the line, and the next move was hers. If she couldn't return his feelings, he'd wish her a nice life and that would be it. They would be finished.

It would come to that eventually when he found out he couldn't change her mind about marriage, but she wasn't ready to say goodbye to him. Please, dear God, not yet. And what would it hurt to tell him, anyway? she reasoned. It wouldn't change anything, not in the long run.

"It isn't that I don't love you—"

"Then you do?"

"Yes, but—"

"I don't care about the buts," he said quickly, kissing her fiercely. His grin broad, he cupped her face in his hands and kissed her again. "You're not your mother or your grandmother. Just because they made mistakes doesn't mean you will."

"I already have," she reminded him. "Or have you forgotten Jeff?"

He dismissed that with a flick of his hand. "Harper's not even worth bringing up. You married a man you didn't have a damn thing in common with. The two of you together were doomed from the start, and I certainly don't blame you for having the good sense to quit beating a dead horse. I am not Harper."

She had to laugh at that. "No, you're certainly not." He was as different from Jeff as West Texas was from the Gulf Coast. "But there was a time I thought I loved Jeff, too."

"As much as you love me?"

Caught in the trap of his eyes, she couldn't deny him the truth. "No," she said huskily. "I never loved anyone as much as I love you."

"Then listen to your heart, honey. We were made for each other—you know we were. We think alike, work alike at the same jobs, we even like the same restaurants. We respect each other and love each other. With so much going for us, how can we fail?"

She wanted to believe him, God knew she did. And her heart was on his side—it had been for weeks now. She only had to look into his eyes and feel his hands on her to know that if there was one man on this earth she could spend the rest of her life with, it was Blake Nickels.

Knowing she was going down for the count, she grasped at one last feeble straw. "What about your family? Your parents are expecting you to eventually come to your senses and go into politics, and I just don't think I'm cut out for that kind of life. I would ask too many questions of the wrong people or say the wrong thing and embarrass the country—"

Stunned, he eased her back into his arms, chuckling softly. "Sweetheart, I've found my niche in life, and it's right here. My parents know and accept that. And my grandfather adores you. If he were twenty years younger and you were thirty years older, I'd have some real competition on my hands."

He'd shot down her last argument, and they both knew it. Dragging her hand to his heart, he asked solemnly, "Will you marry me, Sabrina Jones? I'm crazy about you and want to spend the rest of my life with you."

Tears spilling over her lashes, all her doubts swept away by a tide of love so strong that it seemed to steal her breath along with her heart, she grinned up at him. "I think I should warn you that I intend to keep working for the *Record*. Do you think you can handle competition from your wife?"

His eyes flaring with heat, he chuckled. "Jones, haven't you figured it out yet? I can handle anything you can dish out."

"We'll see about that, Nickels," she retorted. Sliding her arm around his neck, she pressed a teasing kiss to his mouth. "If I remember correctly, we still have a little matter of a bet to settle. Just because we're getting married doesn't mean I'm going to let you off the hook. I plan to beat you soundly."

He laughed, delighted with her, and pulled her close for a deeper, hotter kiss. He could see already that the next forty or fifty years were going to be very interesting. He could hardly wait.

* * * * *

DANGEROUS DECEPTION

Kylie Brant

For Jason, our budding lawyer. Good luck on the bar—we're so proud of you! Love always, Mom

ACKNOWLEDGMENTS

Because I have so little expertise of my own, I rely on experts to get the facts straight in my stories. Special thanks to Jim Harris, of Harris Technical Services, and to Michael Varat, KEVA Engineering, LLC, for your patience with my endless questions about accident reconstruction. Your assistance was impressive in its scope and ingenuity! And another thank-you is owed to Norman Koren, for sharing your wealth of experience in photography. Your kindness was appreciated more than you can know! Any mistakes in accuracy are the sole responsibility of the author.

Prologue

Voices from the grave swirled around him, haunting whispers of murder.

James Tremaine stared sightlessly at the scraps of paper laid across the desk before him and reflected that it was an appropriate enough night for ghosts. The wind shrieked through the sky, shaking the windows of the centuries-old estate with demented fists. The dark clouds shot needlelike shards of rain to stab the parched Louisiana ground, to machine-gun against the house. The single lit lamp in the room had flickered more than a few times in the last hour, but its uncertain illumination wasn't necessary. He didn't need the dim spill of light to read the words typed on the bits of paper on the desk. They'd been emblazoned on his mind.

You've got a target on your back.

This project will be your last.

The threats were easily dismissed. It wasn't unusual for

competition to rise to a dangerous level in his line of work. But it was the third one, the most recent, that commanded attention. *Your parents' deaths weren't accidents. Yours won't be either.*

The electricity finally gave up its struggle with the ferocious wind, and the room fell into darkness. James didn't notice. He was too busy fighting an internal battle of his own. He hadn't successfully grown a family business into a global security corporation by being easily manipulated. Not even his siblings, *especially* not his siblings, could realize the degree of treachery that lurked beneath every apparently civil contact in his world. As technology exploded daily with new advances, the race to stay ahead of his rivals was a careening, hair-raising ride.

He'd had far more creative schemes than this thrown his way by a competitor intent on beating him to a potential contract: he'd thwarted sabotage at his headquarters; he'd survived two attempts on his life to remove him from competition permanently; but nothing else had felt quite as personal as the words printed on the last note before him.

With cool logic he considered the possibilities, pushing aside for the moment the emotion churning and boiling inside him. The most likely explanation was business, of course. Dredging up his family's tragedy from two decades earlier would distract him from the deadlines imposed by the government contract currently occupying the majority of their manpower. Failure to deliver the newest encryption/decryption package for the Pentagon would remove his company from consideration for the next job, which promised to be even more challenging. Even more lucrative.

With his index finger he traced the edge of the message

in the center. Money was another possible motive, he supposed. His family was no stranger to the lengths others would go in order to reap profit by inflicting pain. What was the sender hoping for? To whet his interest for a payoff? But for what? To call off a potential assassin, or by promising decades old information in return?

The messages could just as easily come from a crackpot operating for reasons known only to himself. God knew, there were enough of them around these parts. He didn't need the police to tell him the futility of trying to trace the notes, and with the Pentagon contracts hanging in the balance, just now he could ill afford the resulting publicity.

Lightning lit up the sky outside his den, throwing the interior of the room into momentary relief. A moment later thunder boomed, close enough to shake the graceful antebellum home. But the storm outside paled in comparison to the storm within.

Because there was still a part of him, a part he was struggling to suppress, that wondered if it could be true.

Your parents' deaths weren't accidents.

He'd read the police reports. Made the identification. He could remember far too well what the battered, mangled bodies had looked like once extracted from the twisted wreckage of the automobile. A vicious memory of the wild, unchecked grief whipped through him, stunning in its power to inflict fresh pain. The twenty-year-old wound throbbed anew, stirring all the old questions that accompany the bitterness of loss. In the end, it was emotion that made the decision for him. Specters from the past tugged at strings of guilt, love and regret.

But it was stirrings of a far different feeling that had him opening the center desk drawer, smoothing the tip of his finger down the smooth barrel of the snub-nosed .38 inside.

A thirst for vengeance.

Chapter 1

One Month Later

James Tremaine had not yet grown so jaded that he failed to appreciate an opportunity when one presented itself. Especially when that opportunity was the most attractively packaged eye candy he'd run across in more time than he cared to consider. Shaking the rain from his face, he cocked his head for a better view while he peeled off his gloves and, with uncharacteristic carelessness, shoved them into the pockets of his Prada raincoat.

The form balanced precariously on the ladder inside the doorway was only half-visible, but what was observable was unmistakably feminine. Denim clung to shapely hips and snugged across a curvy bottom before slicking down mile-long legs. His gaze lingered on those legs now, and hormones, too long suppressed, flickered to life. It took conscious effort to drag his eyes upward, to where the woman's torso disappeared into the opening afforded by the missing panel in the suspended ceiling.

"You took your sweet time. I didn't know whether you were ever coming, so I got started without you."

Brows raising at the muffled words, James inquired, "Did you want some help?"

He wasn't certain, but he thought he heard a rather unladylike snort. "All that's left for you to do is to hold the ladder. I'm nearly finished here." He moved to obey, putting himself in even closer range to those long legs.

"I think the receptacle's shot, so you'll have to check that out. Probably needs to be replaced. You got the ladder?" Without waiting for a reply the woman started down it. "And you, my friend, can just put in some overtime fixing it. Serves you right for taking so long getting here."

James steadied the ladder with both arms, framing the slender form descending it. "Overtime can be expensive." Her well-formed rear swayed tantalizingly closer with each step she took. For a moment he forgot the grim errand that had brought him here and allowed his imagination free rein. It was doubtful the woman's face could match those incredible endless legs, but a man was entitled to hope. He was partial to blondes, so as long as this was his fantasy, he'd put his money on her being blond and blue-eyed. A rare smile crossed his lips. No, make it green eyes, and somehow he'd have to recover from the disappointment that was certain to accompany the reality.

He'd recovered from far worse disappointments in his time.

Her voice shook him from his reverie. "You can let go of the ladder. I don't have any intention of walking over you to get off it." When he didn't move away, she twisted around, practically in his arms. "So help me, Howie, you'd better not be enjoying this, or…"

Her words stopped abruptly, eyes widening as she realized her mistake. Eyes that weren't green at all, James noted. Instead they were a warm wash of colors that ranged from gray to brown, with flecks of gold in the irises to further defy description. And she wasn't a blonde, either. Her hair hovered somewhere between blond and brown, a poorly cut tangle that reached to her shoulder blades. Her nose was straight, her mouth wide and her jaw stubborn. Her chin had a decided dip in it, right in the center. It was an intriguing face, rather than a pretty one, and James felt a flicker of interest. It had been a long time since he'd been intrigued by a woman.

He watched her swallow and search for words. "Ah… you're not Howie." And then felt a flicker of amusement at her wince as the inanity slipped from her mouth.

He stepped back to allow her to finish her descent. "No. Sorry. I'm looking for Rob Landry. If you can tell him I'm here?"

There was a flash of pain in those changeable eyes, before they abruptly shuttered. "I…can't do that." She turned away, crossed to the lone desk in the room and sank into the seat behind it.

Impatience flickering, James eyed the door in the far corner of the room emblazoned with the man's name. "You mean he's not in? When will he be back?"

"He won't be." The woman's voice was stronger now, an obvious attempt to layer strength over grief. "He died three weeks ago."

James froze, the words seeming to come from a distance. He was too late. If he'd begun this quest a bit sooner, if he'd tracked Landry a little more quickly, he might have answers to the questions that had reared, spawning suspicion that would burn until he could put it to rest with answers.

Answers that wouldn't be forthcoming with Rob Landry dead.

Disappointment welled up, of a much different sort than he'd expected when he'd seen her perched on the ladder. With long practice, he pushed it aside. "I'm sorry," he said belatedly, recognizing both the woman's anguish and her attempt to mask it. "I understand he worked with a partner. I'd like to speak to him, if I may."

"That would be me. I'm Tori Corbett, his daughter." Emotion had been tucked away. The woman's tone was brisk now, her expression professional. "What can I help you with?"

He was beginning to doubt that she could help him at all, but he reached into the inside pocket of his suit jacket and withdrew a business card. "James Tremaine." He handed her it to her but knew from the look on her face that it was unnecessary. She recognized the name and that of his family's company on the card. He expected no less, since he'd worked for nearly two decades to promote both.

Rejecting the position of the chairs facing her desk, he dragged one around to sit beside her. "Your father did some work for mine a little over twenty years ago. After my parents' deaths, his services were again retained. You would have been just a child then, of course, but maybe he mentioned the investigations to you in the time since."

The shock on her face was its own answer, and the disappointment he felt this time had a bitter taste. "Perhaps he had another partner then? Someone who worked with him when he was running Landry Investigations at that time?"

Her gaze fell to her desktop. "No, Dad always believed in a one-man shop until me. I was the first partner he ever had." Her words sounded as though they'd been difficult for her to say. Certainly they were difficult for James to hear.

"He must have left records. I'd like to look through them, with your permission of course." He was a man accustomed to getting what he wanted, and equally adept at applying finesse to get it. But his fabled charm was difficult to summon. He was too close to discovering the answers he sought. Too damn anxious about what they might reveal.

"Our files are confidential." Tori—what kind of name was that for a woman?—swung her chair around to face him more fully. "If you tell me what you're after, though, I could…" Her sentence abruptly halted. "I'm sorry," she amended. "The files you'd want are what? Twenty years old?" James nodded. "I don't have anything that goes back that far."

He felt his blood cool, his stomach tighten. He withdrew his wallet and extracted several bills. Rising, he leaned forward and dropped them on her desk in front of her. "Why don't you check?" he urged evenly. "I'll wait."

She didn't even glance at the money. And her voice, when it came, had chilled by several degrees. "I don't have to look. My father's building was destroyed by a fire around that time. Shortly after, we moved to Minnesota. He didn't reopen an investigating business until we moved back here, three years later."

This line of questioning was a dead end. James hadn't gotten to his position without knowing when to cut his losses. There would be another way. There always was. It would require regrouping, a new strategy. This wouldn't be the first obstacle he'd encountered in his search for the truth. And it wasn't going to prevent him from finding it.

He rose. "Thank you for your time. And my condolences again for the loss of your father." She was staring at him, her varied-colored eyes wide, her mouth half-open in protest. And with a vague sense of regret, one that had nothing to do with the outcome of this meeting, he turned and walked out of her office.

Tori Corbett nosed her car up the long driveway leading to Tremaine Technologies and tried to ignore the nerves dancing along her spine. What she was about to do required bravado and guts, both of which her dad had always said she possessed in spades. But the plan that had seemed so logical three nights ago, hours after James Tremaine had left her office, suddenly seemed a little…well, ballsy. Not that she had anything against the quality normally.

But if she was going to continue to run the business she'd learned from her dad, she was going to have to actively pursue prospective clients. And the balance of her bank accounts were stark reminders that work meant continuing to eat. Though they never showed up on her lean frame, she'd always been fond of regular meals.

It wasn't as if Tremaine didn't need her. Although he'd been short on details when he'd visited, she was pretty good at piecing things together. They'd both benefit if he accepted her pitch.

The persuasive arguments she'd rehearsed had seemed perfectly rational on the drive over from New Orleans. And even most of the way through Tangipahoa Parish. It wasn't until she'd hit the first set of security gates surrounding these grounds that the first wave of anxiety had hit. It had grown progressively worse each time she'd been stopped by yet another guard and required to go through another clearance.

Okay, she admitted, as she slowly drove toward the sprawling complex of office buildings. So her idea of surprising Tremaine by showing up here had been a bit naive. She hadn't taken into account the level of security surrounding his business. Hadn't considered the fact that the only possible way she'd get through each of the successive security checks was by announcing her identity, having it called in to Tremaine himself.

She had ended up being the one surprised, though, because he had obviously cleared her through each of the stops. And maybe that was what had her stomach churning. She couldn't imagine why he'd agreed to see her, unannounced and refusing to state a purpose for being here. While she'd like to believe that it boded well for the proposition she'd come to offer, she couldn't shake the feeling that this meeting was going to end up far differently than she'd planned.

Her battered compact looked jarringly out of place among the sleek luxury vehicles in the parking lot next to the Tremaine Technologies offices. Grabbing her briefcase, she took a deep breath and got out of the car, not bothering to lock it. The class of the others made it highly doubtful anyone would lower themselves to bother with hers. Jogging up the walk, she worked on calming her nerves with a mental rehearsal for the upcoming meeting.

But thoughts of businesslike persuasion were erased when she stepped into the marbled halls of the headquarters for Tremaine Technologies. It took effort for Tori to state her name matter-of-factly for the man at the desk inside the door, and even more to keep quiet as he led her to an elevator and accompanied her upstairs. Obviously, uninvited guests couldn't be trusted to wander around inside on their own. Or maybe, she considered ruefully, glancing at her plain cotton shirt and khakis, her appearance didn't exactly inspire confidence. Even the man's dark-blue uniform looked as if it had cost more than her entire outfit, briefcase included.

The elevator doors opened, and the guard led her into

an office area roughly the size of her entire house. The floor was polished mahogany, the ceiling vaulted and the woman behind the desk reigning over the area appeared formidable enough to face down intruders with a single look.

"Ms. Corbett," the guard at her side said to announce her, and then backed away, leaving Tori alone with the female staring expressionlessly at her. Of an indeterminate age, the woman wore her brown hair smoothed back from her face like two soft wings, framing a face that was aging with grace and gentility. "Mr. Tremaine is expecting you. He has quite a busy schedule today, however, so if you could keep your meeting brief?" The way she said the words sounded more like a command than a suggestion, and Tori nodded mutely as the woman stabbed one long-nailed finger at a button on the intercom resting upon her desk. "Ms. Corbett has arrived."

A door on the other end of the room opened and James Tremaine filled it, his appearance too sudden for Tori to steel herself against reaction. As it was, she was ambushed by the exact same response she'd had when she'd turned to find herself practically in his arms three days ago.

Ohmygod, it's James Bond. The fanciful thought recurred, only to be firmly pushed away. Okay, there might be a passing resemblance, she conceded. His blue eyes were the color of the South Pacific and framed with a fringe of black lashes that matched his meticulously combed hair. Tall and lean, his body hinted at strength even clad as it was in impeccable Armani. But the sheen of danger lurking just beneath his polished surface must certainly be a product of her imagination. High-tech CEOs would hardly be likely to radiate an aura of menace, unless the afternoon golf games at the exclusive clubs he no doubt belonged to were a lot more savage than she'd realized.

"Tori." His use of her first name jolted her almost as much as the undisguised warmth in his voice. He opened his door wider in an unmistakable invitation. "I hadn't expected to see you again so soon."

So soon? She threw an uncertain look at his secretary, but the woman had returned to her computer, as if oblivious to the scene being played out between them. Turning back to Bond—*Tremaine*—she summoned a vivid smile and approached him. In her line of work, it paid to be a quick study. "I decided I couldn't wait to see you again." There was a flicker of amusement on his face as she played along with his opening gambit, adopting an openly flirtatious sway to her hips as she walked into his office, not stopping until she was standing square in its center.

She paused then to assess. His office was furnished in an eclectic style that mixed eighteenth century furniture with the functionality of the present. She had an impression of understated elegance with an edge of ruthless practicality. A bank of computers covered part of one wall, with the rest of the area utilized as a work space. His desk sat facing a huge row of windows overlooking massive oaks draped with Spanish moss encircling a small pond. There was a sitting area across the room, with wing chairs arranged in front of an ornate fireplace of polished walnut. Elegance, style and purpose. The room reflected all of that. She thought it was an equally accurate description of the man who occupied it.

The walls were covered in art that even her untrained eye recognized as genuine. During the short course of her marriage, she'd been dragged to enough museums and art showings to have acquired a modicum of knowledge. She recognized the small Degas hanging side by side with a painting of the French Quarter done by a local New Orleans artist. The next one, a surrealistic seascape was reminiscent of the Impressionist period. And hanging amidst them all, matted and framed with the same care, were three pictures obviously done by a child's hand, with the name Ana scrawled in the corner of each. The detail was the only unexpected note in the space, but she was given no time to dwell on it.

"To what do I owe the pleasure, Ms. Corbett?" With the door shut behind her, the warmth had vanished from his voice, to be replaced by polite interest. It didn't escape her notice that he didn't invite her to sit.

Reaching into her purse, she extracted an envelope. "I came to return something of yours." When he made no move toward her, she approached him, took his hand and pressed it into his palm. Her gaze fixed on his, she curled his fingers around the packet, and tried to ignore the warmth that transferred at the touch. "I don't keep money I haven't earned."

He glanced down, his expression blank for a moment. "Ah. I'd forgotten." He tucked the envelope in the inside pocket of his suit jacket.

"I can't remember ever being so careless with five hundred dollars, but I guess you had a lot on your mind."

"I did, yes," he replied.

Sensing that now-or-never time had arrived, Tori drew in a deep breath and barreled on. "Your visit got me a little curious." Okay, it had gotten her a *lot* curious, but it seemed wise to gloss over that fact. "I couldn't help wondering what could have been so important about a twenty-year-old case that would have had you looking up my dad again."

He lifted an elegantly clad shoulder, the casual gesture at odds with his aristocratic bearing. "Nothing to wonder about, really. Just tying up some loose ends."

He was, she decided studying him, lying through his perfectly even teeth. Running the tip of her tongue over the incisor she'd chipped slightly on Ralphie Lowell's head in sixth grade, she considered how to proceed. Although she was something of an expert in the art of bluff and parry, he didn't seem to be the type of man to appreciate such tactics. In the end she thought a straightforward approach would serve best.

"A man like you doesn't check on 'loose ends' himself unless it's a matter of some importance." She found it a bit disconcerting to meet his expressionless regard but kept her own gaze steady. "You could have called, or had any number of your employees dispatched to make the inquiry. That you came in person tells me the nature of your visit was personal. Two decades ago you would have been what? Eighteen?" Her words brought a frost to his eyes that dispelled any pretense of civility. He wouldn't appreciate that she'd researched him before coming here, although certainly he should have expected it.

She moved away from him, trailing her fingers over the back of a chair covered in midnight-blue leather with the texture of melted butter. "I've drawn some conclusions about what my dad might have been working on for your father. You never really said that day in the office."

"I didn't, did I? Most would consider that to mean I wasn't interested in discussing it with you."

His expression, she noted with a detached sort of amusement, had gone from frosty to glacial. She was certain she was supposed to be cowering before it. But she'd always had more courage than sense. "It occurred to me that you didn't get what you'd come for on your visit."

A sudden stillness came over him. "You mean you found the files after all?"

With no little regret, she shook her head. "The fire that destroyed Dad's office wiped out an entire city block. No,

I mean you came for answers but you didn't find them."
Circling the chair, she dropped into it, tilted her chin toward
him. "I'm offering to help you get them."

His smile was somehow more insulting than his earlier
dismissiveness. "An intriguing proposition from an equally
fascinating woman. However, I'm not in need of the services
you're offering."

"I think you are." She doubted he was used to being
disputed. A man didn't rise to the level he had in the
corporate world without encountering his share of yes-men.
"Whatever brought you to my office was something you
want to keep private, or you wouldn't have come yourself.
I can't get you the files you're seeking, but I think I could
reconstruct the information that was in them."

Reaching down for her battered briefcase, she placed
it on her lap and snapped the locks open. "You said
your father had hired mine. Given the time period you
mentioned, I figured this might have been what Dad was
investigating." She handed him the stack of newspaper
clippings, the headline of the one on top proclaiming,
Tremaine Tot Returned Safely. The others in the pile were
no less attention grabbing. Kidnapping Plot Foiled. Teenage
Boy Local Hero. It wouldn't do for Tori to admit to the
curiosity that had kicked in as she'd started researching
the Tremaine family. Growing up in Louisiana there was
no way she could have avoided hearing the occasional talk
about the tragedies that had dogged the prominent family
all those years ago.

But immersing herself in the stories, she'd soon grown
fascinated by the details. The passage of time didn't lessen
the horror felt at the thought of a three-year-old child being
snatched out of her bed in the middle of the night; hadn't
dimmed the tragedy of the girl's parents being killed in a
car accident less than six months after her safe return.

Tremaine made no move to take the stack of articles, and his voice when it came was more than a little disparaging. "If you were half as careful with your research as you'd like me to believe, you'd have discovered that I'm no fan of tabloidism."

Tori dropped the clippings back in the open briefcase. "And your family's no stranger to it. I got that. But a good investigator uses every tool at her disposal, and newspapers are a great place to start." Looking up again, she caught his gaze on her. "Do you have the name of the person who hired my dad after your parents' accident?"

He didn't respond. He didn't have to. She saw the answer on his face, in the deliberately blank mask that he'd drawn over his features. She sat back, a bit stunned. "It was you, wasn't it? But you were barely more than a kid yourself at the time."

"I've always felt that need dictates maturity more reliably than does age."

She could wholeheartedly agree with that sentiment. Even at twenty-eight her husband wouldn't have approached anyone's definition of mature. Which was only one of the many reasons he'd become her ex.

Thoughts of Kevin Stephen Corbett III were delegated to a particularly shadowy corner of her mind, where she preferred to keep them. "So you hired my dad to investigate your parents' accident?" She didn't need his answer to be certain she was on the right track. Which was fortunate, because he didn't appear disposed to give her one.

"Ms. Corbett…" It was clear Tremaine had reached the end of his patience.

"Earlier you called me Tori," she reminded him.

He drew in a breath, expelled it slowly. "Tori." She decided her name had sounded better on his lips when it wasn't uttered from a tightly clenched jaw. "The only help

I was interested in you cannot provide. You can't produce the files and, unfortunately for us both, your father can't answer my questions." He headed for the door, a not-so-subtle indication that the meeting was over. "Thank you for returning the money. I hadn't expected it."

"Then you must be used to dealing with a different caliber of people."

He turned, his lips curving just slightly. "I think we can both be assured of that."

"So if you're the one who hired my dad after your parents' accident, you'd have your own file on that investigation. He wouldn't have kept anything of interest in his that he hadn't shared with you." She ignored his stoic gaze, cocked her head, mind still racing furiously. "And why now? I mean, what would suddenly make you start looking for information that's more than twenty years old?"

There was a definite un-Bond-like muscle twitching in his cheek. "I just happen to have some spare time on my hands and thought I'd check into a few things I'd been wondering about."

Tori shook her head, slouched more comfortably in her chair. "Now you're not even trying. If you're going to lie, make it believable."

His eyes narrowed. Again she was given an impression of danger lurking just beneath his polished exterior. "Are you sitting in my office calling me a liar?" The lethal tone suggested that she backpedal, fast.

It was a suggestion she chose to ignore. "A not-very-good liar," she corrected. "I'd think it was lack of practice, but given your experience in the corporate world, you must have plenty of that. So I figure it's just me. You don't know me, so you don't respect me enough to expend the energy necessary for a really good story." She waved a hand, indicating she wasn't going to take offense. He appeared less than impressed with her forbearance. "I've given this some thought and I figure something had to have happened to torch your curiosity about those events."

"You have an overactive imagination."

She refused to take offense. "Uh-uh, just an ability to connect the dots. The FBI never did catch whoever kidnapped your sister when she was a toddler, but she was found safe and sound before your family paid a ransom. So it's doubtful that you're interested in that particular investigation. That leaves the one you hired my dad for. Since you've waited this long, something must have happened recently to convince you there was more to the story."

His face was impassive. "Are you finished?"

"Almost." Something about his still air had a chill skittering down her spine. She'd trailed unsavory characters through the back alleys of New Orleans and never experienced this level of unease. Shaking off the reaction, she went on with more confidence than she felt, "You may not have gotten what you came for when you stopped by my office, but I can get it for you." When he started to speak, she held up a hand to stop him. "I understand you've got a brother who has made a name for himself as a detective for the NOPD. He's probably capable of acquiring certain types of information, as well, but it occurred to me that had you wanted to involve him, he would have been the one to show up at Landry Investigations, instead of you."

She reached into her briefcase again, surprised to see her hands trembling, just a bit. Handing him a file folder, she said, "You came to me looking for answers of some kind, Mr. Tremaine. Whether you know it or not, you need me if you hope to find them."

Chapter 2

Chewing on the inside of her cheek was a nervous habit she'd outgrown when she was twelve, so Tori willed herself to stop doing it now. But that flinty-eyed stare Tremaine arrowed at her after glancing at the pictures in the file folder would have mowed down the firmest intentions. "Where did you get these?"

"From a scumbag photojournalist who's a great admirer of his own work." Kiki Corday wouldn't blink at the description, as long as he'd made a buck on the deal. He also never threw away a shot he'd taken as long as there was the remotest possibility he could still cash in this time. He'd certainly cashed in on it. "He assured me they wouldn't have been part of the police file."

"They weren't." Tremaine snapped the folder shut and thrust it toward her again. She felt twinges of sympathy and regret. Sympathy, because looking at old photos of the automobile wreckage that had killed his parents couldn't be pleasant. And regret that she'd been the one to make him do so. "They also don't prove a thing."

"I disagree. They prove that I have sources you don't." She lifted her shoulders, then let them fall. "They prove you need me, or someone like me, if you want information. Check out the other contents in the folder." With a visible show of reluctance, he did so. It took conscious effort for her to push aside a sneaky blade of guilt. James Tremaine was on a quest that was bound to stir up more than a few old wounds. She shouldn't, *wouldn't* feel responsible for his pain. She looked away from him, concentrating on the century-old oaks outside while he flipped through the reports and pictures in the file.

When he spoke, there was a strange note to his tone. "You have a copy of the sheriff's accident report in here. How'd you get your hands on that?"

Her brows skimmed upward. "It's what I do, ace. That's why my license says Investigator. I investigate stuff."

"I've always made it a point to avoid working with smart-asses," he said mildly, continuing to flip through the file. "Bad for the blood pressure, and who needs the aggravation."

It took a great deal of effort on Tori's part to avoid a delighted grin. Not over the smart-ass comment, although truth be told it wouldn't be the first time the description had been applied to her. But his comment could be interpreted, in a roundabout, insulting sort of way, that he might be considering working with her, couldn't it?

Adopting a more conciliatory attitude, she said, "If you hire me you'll have every bit of information that I come across. But I won't always be able to divulge my sources." That brought his gaze snapping up to hers, and she didn't flinch from it. "The sheriff's report was easy enough. All motor vehicle accident investigations are a matter of public record. But I'm thinking that the answers you're looking for won't be found by going through old records, will they?"

He stared hard at her, long enough to have her decide that those deep-blue eyes of his could be strangely hypnotic. Not that Tori was prone to instant mesmerization from a mere look, she thought uncomfortably, but she was a trained observer. She couldn't help but notice things like that.

Nodding toward the file he still held, she said, "My purpose in coming here was to show you what I can do. I put those contents together in a day and a half. But if you're looking for information other than what was included in my dad's original report to you, I'm going to have to tap completely different sources. And some of them have to remain confidential. It's a condition for their talking to me at all."

Tremaine flipped the file closed, tapped the edge against his open palm. "No offense, but I know countless individuals I can hire to look into this for me. Why would I need you?"

She'd been ready for this question, and her answer came smoothly. "I already know why you need a private investigator, which means one less person you have to share the information with. The fewer people who know, the easier it will be to keep quiet. And it was my father you wanted to talk to. I learned the business from him. I know who a lot of his contacts are…were," she corrected herself, ignoring the pang that accompanied the reminder. "With him gone, I work alone, except for some services that I contract out. You could go with a bigger company, one with more manpower, but that just means more people are going to know about your private affairs."

The last was a gamble. By the flicker in his eyes, she could assume it had paid off. James Tremaine was, by nature, a very private man. And his quest was an intensely personal one.

"You don't look old enough to have acquired all that much experience."

"I've had my license three years, but I'd worked for my dad on and off for years before that. My mother died when I was six. I was raised in and around his business." She stopped then, one of her dad's favorite sayings drifting through her mind. *Put your cards on the table and let the client decide if he wants to talk or walk.*

Dragging a matching chair to face hers, he sat, more elegantly than she had. Somehow she managed to suppress a sneer when she noted the care he took with the crease in his trousers.

"Decision-making time, Mr. Tremaine." Tori leaned back into her chair, the relaxed pose belying the nerves scampering along her spine. "That folder proves I'm capable of conducting the investigation you're interested in. I'm also tenacious and a good listener." Because that last had him raising his eyebrows, she shrugged modestly. "People tend to talk to me. That's a plus in my line of work. And it might be to your advantage to use a woman on this case, did you ever think of that?" At his arrested expression she knew she'd scored a direct hit. "I'm assuming you'll want this kept quiet."

"Discretion is imperative."

She nodded. She offered nothing less to her clients. "As a female I'm apt to rouse less suspicion in certain circles. I can go places, do things, that men can't."

He was silent long enough to have disappointment welling inside her, a slow steady surge. Until that moment she hadn't let herself think of failure, but it faced her now, stark and uncompromising. It was the first job she'd pitched since her dad had died. The first door, since then, to be shut in her face. His death had become a yardstick by which she measured a lot of firsts these days. And lasts.

Snapping the locks shut on the briefcase, she rose, ready to thank him for his time and determined to keep the emotion from her voice.

"I'll give you a week trial." Her mouth dropped. "A thousand a week plus expenses, within reason. At the end of that time, I'll evaluate what you've come up with. If I'm not satisfied, you'll hand over what information you've accumulated and we'll part ways."

"I..." She swallowed hard and tried to recover her power of speech. "All right. I usually give weekly updates, but under the circumstances..."

"I'll want daily reports."

His interruption had her gritting her teeth, but she managed to nod agreeably. She had, after all, gotten exactly what she'd come here for. "All right."

"I'll have my lawyer draft a contract tomorrow. You can wait until after you've signed it, or start work right away, whichever you're most comfortable with."

Now that his decision had been made, he'd changed slightly, she thought. She studied him as he strode to the desk. He'd reverted to type, she realized suddenly. It was the earlier indecision that had been foreign for him. James Tremaine would be a man very much in control of any situation. And now that he'd hired her, now that she'd become just another employee, he was firmly back in charge.

He approached her again with the money she'd returned to him. "You may as well keep this. Half now, and we'll settle the rest at the end of the week. Are those terms acceptable?"

Slowly, she reached out to take the money. "Sure." Taking the cash from him, she reopened the briefcase and dropped the money inside. "I'm assuming you kept the original file my father put together for you. I'd like a copy of it sent over with the contract." She didn't doubt that he still had it. He wouldn't be a man to leave anything to chance.

"I'll do that."

"So." Tori sat down and drummed her fingertips against the case in her lap. "Why don't you tell me what caused you to want to reexamine this? Why now?" She could wait for the file. She didn't expect to find any surprises in it. Her father apparently hadn't encountered any during his investigation all that time ago. Her curiosity was more focused on what had made Tremaine decide to dredge up painful ancient history. He wouldn't be the type to do anything without a reason.

As an answer, he unlocked the center drawer on his desk and withdrew a small white envelope. Crossing to her, he opened it and shook out three slips of paper atop her briefcase. Turning them over, Tori scanned each one, shock layering over adrenaline.

"When did you get these?"

"They began arriving four weeks ago. They were sent to my home, but I have all my personal mail routed to work. I'm here more, anyway."

"The envelopes?"

"I still have them, but a contact of mine in the postal department assures me they'll be of little use. They were postmarked in New Orleans, all by different offices."

Her gaze dropped to the notes again, her flesh prickling. "Have you thought of going to the police?"

"Please." His tone managed to be both derisive and amused. "If someone really means me harm, they aren't going to waste time warning me first. I'd be easier to take out if I wasn't on my guard."

At the certainty in his words, her eyes met his. "Is that the voice of experience I hear?"

He slipped his hands into his trousers pockets, rocked back on his heels slightly. The casual pose didn't fool her. She was beginning to doubt that this man ever truly relaxed.

"I don't consider these serious threats." It didn't escape her attention that he hadn't answered her question. "A private lab I occasionally use informed me there were no fingerprints on the notes other than my own. There were several on the envelopes, of course. But it's doubtful any of them belong to the sender, which means the police will likely come up with nothing. With their involvement, there's a higher probability of a leak to the press."

His tone became clipped, his expression closed. "My family dislikes publicity. With my sister's recent wedding, and my brothers' engagement announcements appearing in the papers, there's been a renewed interest in our history. My firm is on the verge of landing another sensitive contract with the Pentagon, and the last thing I need are new rumors about my family serving as news fodder to ratchet up slow ratings."

That was, she supposed, a reasonable enough explanation. Her brief foray into the Corbett family, the Dallas Corbetts—distinguished from the Houston Corbetts primarily by their bank accounts and penchant for social climbing—had taught her that wealthy people had an aversion to publicity. Unless, of course, it involved them handing over a very large check to a suitable charity.

"Let's talk about your brothers and sister for a minute. What do they think about this?" If she hadn't known better, she would have believed her question took him off guard. Which was ridiculous, of course. James Tremaine wouldn't be a man to entertain self-doubts.

"I'd rather not have to tell them," he said finally. "My sister and her new husband are just settling into married life. My brothers are both in the process of planning their weddings. Raking all this up again is bound to be painful, and in the long run will probably be for nothing. I'd like to spare them that if I can."

She wondered if they would thank him for that, and thought probably not. But his protectiveness of his family warmed something inside her. She could respect a man who looked out for his loved ones, even if his tactics weren't appreciated.

Glancing back down at the notes, she observed, "These could have just been sent by someone looking to hose you, you know."

"You're most likely correct. But if that's true, the sender will find that I'm not, as you put it so eloquently, easily hosed. I won't give in to blackmail."

She almost grinned. There may be a hint of humor beneath all that tailoring, after all. And she didn't doubt his words. He wouldn't be an easy mark, which meant that the sender had grossly underestimated him. Or else was holding something back that would yet prove truly compelling.

As if reading her thoughts, he said, "The only note that interests me is the one about my parents' accident. I'm not going to pay for any information that this person has, if it comes to that. That's what you're for. By reconstructing the investigation into their deaths, you should be able to answer any questions about what really happened."

During his speech, the temperature in the room seemed to have dropped ten degrees. She decided it was due to the chill in his voice. "And what if I find out there was more to their deaths than was ever reported? What then?"

His smile was as brilliant and lethal as a keen-edged blade. "Then...justice."

She stared at him while a shiver snaked over her skin. Something about the way he said the word leeched it of its nobility and instilled it with a sense of deadly purpose. "I won't do anything illegal." For the first time, it seemed prudent to point that out. "I'll use every avenue at my disposal and take advantage of every possible lead, sometimes utilizing unconventional methods. But I'll do it all within the boundaries of the law of Louisiana."

"Of course. I'd expect nothing less." His tone was normal, making her believe she might have misinterpreted it a moment ago. Except the gooseflesh on her arms was still raised, and her nape was still prickling. "With any luck you can have this thing wrapped up shortly, and we can both go about our lives. I'll contact you tomorrow." He approached her, pausing by her chair.

Slowly she rose, sliding the briefcase to the floor. "Tomorrow?"

"When I messenger over the contract and file that you requested."

"Ah. Yes." Her tongue suddenly thick, she resisted the urge to wipe her palms on her khakis. He was standing a little too close, as near as he'd been when she'd turned around on that ladder and found herself almost in his arms. Close enough to have her marveling at the deep blue of his eyes, but retaining enough of her scattered senses to wonder at the secrets behind them.

"To our partnership, Ms. Corbett, as brief as it may be."

Her hand raised of its own volition. "To our partnership." His hand engulfed hers. It suited her to blame the skip in her pulse on static electricity. But try as she might, she couldn't shake the feeling that she'd just made a pact with a very sophisticated, very charming devil.

* * *

The plaintive cornet of Bix Beiderbecke wailed from the portable CD Tori had carried into the attic. The blues music provided a perfect backdrop for the task at hand. With resignation layering the ache in her heart, she scanned the contents of the space and wondered where in the world to start.

Rob Landry had been an undisputed pack rat, and she didn't doubt that he'd saved more than he'd ever thrown out. Furniture was heaped and shoved into one corner, and overflowing boxes teetered in precarious towers, threatening imminent collapse. There were stacks of newspapers, neatly bundled and piled haphazardly almost to the ceiling beams. Why they'd been important enough to keep was beyond her, but then her dad had been the type to let junk mail accumulate, too, until she came in and tossed it. The man had been able to figure every angle of a case and work a source like a master, but hadn't been able to part with a single scrap of paper.

The memory made her lips curve and her eyes mist. The pain twisted just a bit, leaving a wound that she knew from experience would throb for some time. Cancer had stolen both of her parents now. First her mother, and now her beloved dad, who had seemed so indestructible. Right up until that day three months earlier when the pain he'd passed off as indigestion had been diagnosed as something a great deal deadlier.

Releasing the breath that had backed up in her lungs, she headed toward the furniture. She'd already been through the downstairs, putting aside the pieces she wanted to save and those that would be donated to the needy. She'd expected this to be easier somehow. The things that he had stored up here wouldn't hold the keen reminders of him, nor still smell of his aftershave. There wouldn't be memories of him here, as there were in every room below. He'd been a big man, but had filled a room more with his presence than his stature. It would be impossible to exorcise those memories from the house, and impossible to live with them. She'd placed it on the market earlier that week.

Tori worked her way through the chairs and tables that he'd deemed too good to throw out. It took an hour to decide there was nothing in the collection that she wanted to save, and she restacked the pieces. She'd use the corner to separate those things to be gotten rid of from the things she wanted to keep. Most of what she had decided to hang on to was downstairs, but there wouldn't be room for all of it in her small house. It would have to go into storage until she had a bigger place.

The newspapers could be tossed without going through them, she determined, passing by them in an effort to get at the boxes. But she must have brushed the stack as she went by, and the entire pile began a slow-motion sway. With a sense of futility, she leaped aside, just in time to avoid being nailed by the bundles as they tumbled to the floor.

The impact of their landing sent up a cloud of dust that sent her into a spasm of sneezing. When her eyes and lungs had cleared, she glared at the mess accusingly. Her dad had tended to keep any newspapers with articles that caught his imagination, talking vaguely about writing a book sometime when he retired. She'd never been able to imagine him in so sedentary a pastime, but had thought it a harmless enough intention until now.

Muttering a few choice words, she set to hauling the papers into yet another pile, this one designated for the trash heap. The headline leaped out at her from the top one of the bundle, and a quick flip through them showed a collection detailing the trial of the notorious New Orleans

Ripper, who'd been caught and tried a decade earlier after killing a dozen women.

With a grimace, she pushed them aside and started some smaller, steadier piles. He'd had varied interests. Some of the papers were articles on fishing, a passion of his, others on the history of the city. But it was the bottom bundle that caught her eye, with a headline very like the one she'd clipped and placed in the file she'd given to Tremaine.

Tremaine Heiress Returned Safely.

With a sense of déjà vu she had a sudden recollection of James Tremaine's face when he'd seen the similar headline in the file she'd given him. A grim mask had descended over his features, but not before she'd glimpsed the bitter resentment in his eyes. He'd made his feelings toward the press and public prying quite clear, but that didn't stop her from reaching out, tugging at the string that bound the papers together. Flipping through them, she found stories detailing the kidnapping and the car accident a few months later. She scanned the stories, but they elicited no information she hadn't found in her research earlier that week. Something clicked in the rereading, however, something she'd forgotten to ask Tremaine about. There had been a third passenger in the car. A third death.

To refresh her memory, she pulled the papers loose, looking for the articles detailing the accident and the follow-up investigation. The passenger's name was given, but she was identified only as a family friend. Tori made a mental note to look up more about the woman.

She set aside the bundle of papers on the Tremaines and finished stacking the rest to be destroyed. But during the task, her gaze strayed more than once to the papers she'd saved. Her earlier excitement at having landed her first job on her own had been tempered by her troubling reaction to Tremaine. She'd thought her interest in the opposite sex had been laid to rest permanently upon the ignoble end of her marriage. Or, to be truthful, months before the official ending. As her husband's criticism and dissatisfaction with her had grown, her hormones had gone dormant at approximately the same pace. Finding him in his parents' pool house on top of Miss Texas Rose 1998 had nearly shredded what was left of her confidence. She'd had enough sense, however, to leave him and their marriage behind. And enough self-respect to first send his canary-yellow Ferrari convertible crashing through the fence to sink to the bottom of the pool. It was the only memory of her marriage that still had the power to bring a smile to her face.

Given that, it was more than a little disturbing to experience that inexplicable...*awareness* when she was near Tremaine. A woman would have to be in the grave not to react to his looks, and so her response to him was only too natural, a cause for celebration, even. But as comfortable as it would be to believe that's all there was, Tori couldn't prevent feeling a sliver of unease. There was something about the man that heightened all her sensitivities, which really wouldn't do. Getting involved with a client was an ethically sticky situation.

A wry grin twisted her lips. Luckily, that was not likely to be a problem. She and Tremaine couldn't have less in common if they'd been born on different planets. Her brief foray into the monied class during her marriage had taught her only too painfully that the rich were, indeed, different.

Moving to the boxes, she hauled down the top one and opened it. A familiar sight inside it surprised a laugh from her. There, folded neatly, was a sweater her dad had worn for more years than she cared to count. She'd replaced it nearly three years ago with one enough like it to satisfy the man, but he must have rescued this one from the trash and hidden it away. Anything that was a favorite of his was always deemed too good to be thrown out, despite its missing buttons and worn-through elbows. What he'd intended to do with it was anybody's guess.

Nevertheless, she found herself folding it with care and setting it aside. Perhaps there was more of her father in her than she'd guessed, because she knew that she'd never be able to part with it now, either.

Beneath the sweater was a file folder stuffed with papers, which she shook out onto her lap. Her throat went abruptly dry as she recognized medical statements dating from the time her mother had grown sick. With hands that shook just slightly, she stuffed them back into the envelope. She could remember vividly when as a nine-year-old she'd packed away most of her mother's things to prepare for their move back to New Orleans. Her death had been the first and only time she'd ever seen her big, capable father helpless.

The envelope beneath was one she recognized. It was a packet of love letters exchanged between her parents when her mother was in the Mayo Clinic. For years they'd been in the bedside table of her father's room. When had he finally put them away? she wondered. Sometime after that instance when he'd come home unexpectedly and found her reading them. He'd been coldly furious, and she'd been ashamed of her snooping, unable to explain that the few letters she'd read had helped bring her mother within reach again, the words painting an almost real form for her that had previously only been viewed through a child's eyes.

A foreign sound had her catapulting back into the present. Looking around carefully, she eyed the piles of junk suspiciously. Any one of them could be a hiding place for some disgusting four-legged creature. Although

Tori was an animal lover, most were best enjoyed outside her home.

Rising to her feet she listened again, and her blood abruptly chilled. The noise that resounded didn't come from the attic. It came from the floor below.

Someone was in the house.

The open door and the music that still poured from the CD player left little doubt as to her whereabouts. Scanning the area, she moved silently to the corner with the furniture. She grabbed a small, particularly ugly lamp, removed the shade and light bulb, and wrapped the cord securely around it. Hefting it with one hand, she was satisfied that it would make a useful club.

She heard footsteps below, but no one called out, as she would expect if a curious neighbor or the Realtor had come looking for her. She'd left the front door unlocked, as it had been afternoon when she'd started her task. But a glance out the tiny window showed that it was early evening now. Dusk and shadows would have fallen over the street. Most of the elderly neighbors would have already finished up their dinner dishes and be seated in front of the TVs with their front doors carefully locked.

The footsteps paused, and the attic door squeaked a bit, as if the intruder had taken it in one hand and stuck a head inside the opening to listen. Tori could feel the blood pulsing through her veins. Her heart was beating a rapid tattoo in her chest, but her mind was cool as she flipped the lamp in her hand so the heavier base would be at the top. She'd feel more comfortable under a cloak of darkness, but the switch was at the base of the steps and out of reach.

The first step squeaked under the weight of the tread on it. Whoever was climbing the stairs now blocked her only exit out of the attic. There was another telltale sound.

Another step upward. Options limited, Tori melted back into the shadows afforded by the stacked furniture and waited, weapon in hand.

Chapter 3

"You know some people content themselves with a simple hello." James eyed the lamp clutched in Tori's fist, deciding she looked more than capable of wielding it.

"And most consider it rude to walk into people's homes without announcing themselves," she countered, setting the lamp on a nearby table. "How did you know I was here?"

"I went by your place. A rather unkempt individual by the name of Joe, informed me that you might be at your father's." When she didn't respond, he continued helpfully, "Ribbed undershirt? Uncertain hygiene? Pants riding low enough to show far more than most would care to see of his choice in undergarments?"

She made a face that was half recognition, have irritation. "My neighbor's son. He takes an annoying interest in my comings and goings. Must have heard me talking to his mother earlier today." She dusted her hands on her shorts as she approached, cocking a brow at him. "I have to say, when I heard someone moving around downstairs, I considered it might be the real estate agent or a neighbor. But I never thought of you."

Since she was heading toward the stairs, he turned and preceded her down. "Which one were you going to smack with that lamp, the agent or the neighbor?"

"There was an equally good chance it was a street punk looking for an easy score." The words, as much as the matter-of-fact way she uttered them, caused him to pause for just a moment. "It never hurts to be prepared."

"No, it doesn't." He turned, once he'd reached the open door, and studied her. She snapped off the light switch before following him into the upstairs hallway. He wondered how many women in his acquaintance would have dealt with the possibility of a stranger in her house with such cool calculation. There was no evidence of alarm in her demeanor, just a certain competency that was at odds with the unmistakable femininity of those long legs and lean curves. The observation was undeniably chauvinistic, so he wisely refrained from sharing it.

"I did telephone," he offered, surprising himself by making the explanation. "There was no answer at your house, and apparently you've had the phone here disconnected. I decided it wouldn't hurt to swing by and see if I could catch you. You didn't answer the doorbell, but I heard music from somewhere in the house and followed it."

She brushed by him, sending him a sidelong glance before she led him toward the steps to downstairs. "I didn't expect to hear from you until tomorrow."

"I had business in the city, so I decided to drop off the contract I had my lawyer draw up." He held up the hinged file he carried. "As well as a complete copy of the old investigative report."

If truth be told, his business in the city could have waited or could at least been delegated. But he'd found it strangely difficult to focus once she'd left his office that afternoon. They'd decided upon a course of action, and now he was anxious to see it through. Anxious to see what answers, if any, her investigation would supply.

"I thought if you had some time tonight, you could go over the contents of the file and decide where you want to start." He followed her into a small downstairs living room and, waiting until she'd seated herself on the sofa, sat in a nearby chair. He looked with interest around the room he'd merely glanced at his first time through. There was a battered recliner in one corner, facing a TV and stereo setup. It didn't take much imagination to figure that the chair had been well used by the man who had lived here. Above it hung a sampler, on which someone had painstakingly embroidered the words Integrity Above All Else.

He gestured to it. "Your work?"

"My one-and-only attempt. It was my dad's favorite saying. He had what some might consider an outdated code of honor."

James thought of the family crest that hung above the doorway in his family home. Honor. Duty. Devotion. It was the creed that his father had lived by. He and his brothers had grown up attempting to do the same. "Not everyone," he murmured.

When her gaze turned quizzical, he opened the file he carried, took out the contract inside. Withdrawing a gold pen from his suit jacket, he handed both to her. "I had my lawyer draw up this contract. The terms are outlined clearly in it, and they're not negotiable. We already discussed this, but you'll want to read the confidentiality clause near the bottom. If you or anyone in your employ violates it in the slightest, I'll direct my attorney to prosecute to the fullest extent of the law. Am I understood?"

"As you say, we discussed that earlier." Her voice was cool. She scanned the rest of the document, and he used the time to watch her. It was no hardship. She'd tamed that unruly tangle of hair by hauling it up in a knot and securing it somehow. The simple cotton shirt she wore was marred with dust, no doubt encountered upstairs, as were her shorts, which showed an intriguing length of slender thigh.

Not for the first time he noted that she didn't fit his notion of a private investigator. If he was lucky, she wouldn't fit anyone else's, either. Once she'd left his office, he'd been plagued by doubts about the wisdom of his choice. The feeling was too foreign to be borne comfortably. He could put an army of more experienced investigators on the matter, but she might be able to provide the one thing that no one else could—a direct line to her father's old contacts. It was possible that one of them knew something about the case he'd worked that hadn't been contained in the man's report. That, coupled with his reluctance to spread the word of these threats, had cemented his decision. He could spare a week. And if she failed to come up with anything new— He gave a mental shrug. Then there would be time enough to select another individual.

When she was finished, he took the contract, studying the signature with a sense of amusement. "Your full name is Victoria?"

He noted her barely concealed wince. "Use it at your peril. And be warned that the last guy to call me by it lost his right front bicuspid."

"I'll be sure to remember that. Do you have a cell?"

When she rattled off a number, he jotted it down on the top of the contract, before setting it aside and handing her the hinged portfolio he'd brought with him. "You'll find mine on the outside of the top file folder. Don't hesitate to call, regardless of the hour."

"Are you sure?" Her tone was light, but the expression in her eyes was speculative. "I don't want to be responsible for interrupting business. Or whatever."

"Business will take a back seat to your reports, and 'whatever' will have to wait until we get this—" he nodded toward the portfolio she'd set on the table beside her "—taken care of." Upon reflection, a personal life of any type hadn't been a priority for much too long. Few women tolerated being set aside once he became embroiled in a particularly challenging contract. He tried, and failed, to recall the last time he'd been involved in a halfway serious relationship. If he was actually spending time wondering if his P.I.'s legs were as silky as they looked, perhaps his sister, Ana, was right, and he *was* becoming too focused. Not that he'd ever admit as much to her.

"As long as you're here, I did think of a question earlier." She slid to a more comfortable position in her seat and crossed one long line of leg over the other. "Who was the third person in the car with your parents?"

It took a moment for him to switch mental gears. "Lucy Rappaport. She was the young wife of our production manager and a good friend of my mother's. They'd been on their way to New Orleans, where my father had business. The women were going to shop and have dinner there." The subject brought him back with a crude jolt to the business at hand. "She and her husband had an eighteen-month-old son."

The tragedy that day hadn't been limited to his family. Marcus Rappaport still worked for them, having risen high enough in the corporation to be his right-hand man. Although he was considered one of the most eligible men in the parish, he'd never remarried. Some losses, James knew, left a void that couldn't be filled.

"The time frame of this case will make it challenging," Tori stated. "Witnesses move away or die. Memories fade. But technology has grown more advanced, too." She gave a shrug. "Maybe that will prove to be to our advantage." She began pulling things from the file he'd brought and arranging them in piles around her on the sofa, in an order that made sense only to her. "At any rate, I intend to reinterview the people who processed the accident scene, at least those I can get hold of. Is the name of the salvage yard the car was sold to included in this file?"

"The remains of the car were destroyed long ago." And he knew that precisely because he'd already attempted to trace it. "There's nothing left to examine with new technology." James felt a surge of impatience, which he tempered. There ought to be ways to find the truth that he hadn't thought of…ought to be avenues to explore that he hadn't considered. Not for the first time he questioned whether he'd made the right choice pursuing this thing.

Then he thought again of the note that had arrived today. *Your parents were murdered. You're next.* And then it was really quite simple to recall just why he'd gone down this path. And just how badly he needed answers, one way or another.

He shifted in his chair, tamped down frustration. There was a sense of powerlessness in putting this into someone else's hands, however close he intended to supervise. He didn't much care for the sensation. "I received another message today."

Her gaze was sharp. "What did it say?"

Lifting a shoulder, he said, "More of the same. But it

did mention my parents again. If this was simply about extortion, I would have expected to receive the demand for cash already. Or at least some indication of what information the sender has to trade."

"He could just be whetting your appetite until you're anticipating just that, before striking with the promise of more for a price." Her head was still bent over the file, but her voice was certain.

"Sounds like you have a fair idea of how this guy would think."

"Well, I have met my share of dirt bags. And we don't know the sender is a guy." She did look up now, and caught his gaze on her. "Unsigned notes give a guarantee of anonymity, and they're nonconfrontational. They could just as easily be from a woman. But I tend to agree with you. I doubt the sender is after cash. The tone of the messages are a bit too personal. Have you made any enemies lately?"

He gave a grim laugh. "Honey, if we're going to list all my enemies, we'll be here all night." From the arrested expression on her face, he'd managed to surprise her.

"Let me guess. Your magnetic personality or boyish charm?"

He wondered if he should be offended. "Neither, although I can be quite charming, given the right circumstances. But Tremaine Technologies is considered to have made a pretty rapid rise in the global economy in the last twelve years. We're listed as one of the five premiere encryption/ decryption software corporations in the world. All modesty aside, there's only one other in this country even in our league, and that's Security Solutions. The biggest contracts in the past four years have gone to one or the other of us."

She cocked her head consideringly. "So if your company

was out of the running, they'd all go to this Software Solutions?"

"Probably, at least for a time. But sending anonymous notes hardly fits the profile of Simon Beal, its owner and CEO."

"Don't be so sure." Setting aside the paperwork she was sorting, she crossed to an overflowing desk tucked in one corner of the room and pulled a pen and a legal pad from the top drawer. "Didn't you tell me yesterday that you're being considered for an important new project?"

"Yes, and so are a handful of other companies. Beal is the only real competition, although Allen Tarkington of Creative Technology considers himself in the running." Rising, he slipped his hands into the pockets of his trousers, for once not mindful of the crease.

"So any one of those companies, Beal's especially, would have reason to want you distracted right now." She jotted a quick note down on her pad before looking up again. "I assume that this business is competitive, right? Companies willing to do what it takes to get an edge?"

His smile was as sharp as a blade. "That edge usually takes the form of corporate espionage. Arson. Sabotage. Even the odd bullet on occasion."

Tori gaped at him, her eyes wide. "Wow. Guess that's where the phrase *corporate warfare* comes from."

He inclined his head. It was an appropriate enough term. "If one of the other business leaders was trying to eliminate me from the competition, I think they'd engage in something more direct than anonymous notes."

Her expression had gone shrewd. "But a direct attack would have police scrutiny turned on them. Maybe this was deliberately planned to be more subtle, and you haven't reacted the way you were supposed to. The whole publicity angle is exactly why you didn't go to the police, but most people in your shoes would have. From there it would be an easy enough task to get the information leaked to the press. Fan the flames a bit, pay off a reporter or two and you have the Tremaine family history, past and present, in headlines and on TV for days, complete with hype and speculation about this newest development. Given the global prestige of your company, the story is sure to be picked up by the Associated Press, and lo and behold, all those Pentagon types are reading about you and your current problem over their morning coffee."

The accuracy of the picture she painted was startling. "You catch on fast. It would be a roundabout way to approach things, but it's conceivable."

"And even better, at least from the sender's standpoint, it's unexpected. So why don't you, for sake of argument, give me the names of the companies in the running for that contract, along with their locations and CEOs?"

James rattled off the information, only half thinking about it. The scenario she'd just described was possible. Entirely possible. And it would somehow be preferable to believe it than to discover that he'd been wrong all these years about his parents' accident. That he had failed them somehow by not suspecting the truth and bringing those responsible to justice.

He was very much afraid that, if true, his failure to act would haunt him for the rest of his life.

Belatedly he became aware that she was speaking again.

"...just a theory."

"I'm sorry, what?"

"I said, right now, with what we have to go on, this is a theory, one among many. I just don't want to overlook anything."

"Nor do I." He glanced at his watch, surprised to find

it was nearly nine. "I've taken enough of your time this evening. I should go."

She rose, in a fluid stream of motion that he couldn't help but appreciate. "You're going to drive all the way home tonight?"

He shook his head. "We have a place on Lake Pontchartrain. I'll stay there and drive to work in the morning." He headed for the door, leaving her to follow him. He felt an odd reluctance to leave. It was a sort of relief, he realized, to be able to talk this through with someone. To finally have a plan of action. He'd spent long hours considering sharing it with his brothers, but his first instinct had warned against it. When this was over, when he had the answers he needed, he'd tell them. He owed them that. But until he had something to report, the uncertainty could only cause them pain. He wasn't willing to inflict that unnecessarily, especially if this was just a ploy by one of his competitors.

As the eldest in the family, responsibility was ingrained in him. He wouldn't shirk it now.

Her voice had him hesitating with his hand on the doorknob.

"This thing between you and Beal...have you been keeping score?"

He looked over his shoulder at her. She had her thumbs hooked in the pockets of her shorts, her head tilted slightly. "Running a business the size of mine is hardly a game."

Her tone grew mocking. "So you haven't kept track of who has landed the hottest contracts. Come up with the most impressive technology."

She saw, he thought, entirely too much. "It's not something that can be reduced to win-loss columns."

Tori smiled knowingly. "You're ahead?"

"By three in this year alone." He shot her a feral grin before turning and going through the door. "And I intend to keep it that way."

There were worse ways to spend the afternoon than lolling on a grassy bank, fishing. Tori had an innate appreciation for life's little bonuses, and she was enjoying this one to the fullest. It wasn't often that she could work a case and indulge her love of fishing at the same time.

She cast her line and kept a watch on the man seated forty yards to her left, closer to the pond's edge. The former Tangipahoa Parish sheriff had been retired for almost six years, and from the size of his girth, his love for food at least matched what she'd heard about his fondness for his favorite pastime. It had taken surprisingly few phone calls to elicit the information she'd needed on the man. And the small group of elderly men playing cards in front of his hometown diner had been more than happy to share favorite local fishing spots and directions to them, once she'd provided some winsome smiles and small talk. Picking up their lunch tab hadn't hurt, either.

She'd spotted him on her third stop, on a secluded shady knoll on the banks of the Atchafalaya. For a while she was content to keep her distance. She didn't want him to feel crowded and leave.

Selecting a bright-green lure, she baited the hook and cast her line, settling into a comfortable position to wait. It wasn't for long. Within just a few minutes there was a tug on her line and she surged to her feet, reeling in slowly.

The yellowed speckled sunfish on the other end was a good size, at least sixteen inches, and she allowed it to thrash on the line just long enough to capture ex-Sheriff Halloway's attention. When she was sure she had it, she made a show of landing her prize, holding it up before her to admire it before deftly releasing it in the fish pail she'd brought along.

Thirty minutes later that fish had been joined by two others, and the man down river disgustedly reeled in his empty line, packed up his tackle box and began making his way to a new spot, one a great deal closer to hers.

"Looks like you found yourself a hot spot here."

"Caught three beauts and haven't even been here an hour," she said casually. "This is my first time fishing in this area. Is it always this good?"

Halloway wiped his brow, then adjusted the brim of the straw hat he wore. "Not for me. Not today, anyways."

"Well, you're welcome to try your luck here."

It was the only invitation he needed. Minutes later he had his equipment situated and was settled in a portable folding chair. He cast his line and it fell soundlessly into the river. "You're not from these parts."

"New Orleans." Tori leaned back in the grass, propped on her elbows and toed off her sandals. "Every day off I get I head to new fishing spots." She shot him a sideways glance, a bit concerned at his flushed expression. The sun was searing overhead, though it wasn't yet noon. For the first time she thought he might have been equally attracted by the shade nearby as he was by her fishing success. "Guess you must spend your free time same as me."

He grunted, reeled in his empty line and rummaged in his tackle box to choose a different lure. "I got nothing but days like these. I been retired now near 'bout seven years."

There was a tug on her line. Tori pretended not to notice, although the fact hadn't escaped Halloway. "I'm figuring you must live around here."

"How you figure that?"

"No lunch with you." She smiled easily and pointed to

the small basket she'd packed. "I came ready to make a day of it."

"Born and raised 'round these parts," he admitted. "Gal, you got something bitin' at your line, there."

"So I do." With a nonchalance that seemed to set the man's teeth on edge, she straightened, cocked her wrist back and reeled in her fourth and biggest catch of the day.

"Well, if you aren't having Sam's own luck," the man muttered, narrowed gaze envious. "What're you using there?"

She added the fish to her pail, and held the lure up for him to see. "Something my dad used to make himself. Sunfish go wild for it. What do you use?"

"Straight fly lure. Ain't seeing the kind of luck you're having, though."

Seizing the opportunity, Tori reached into her tackle box. "You're welcome to try one, if you'd like." She held out one of the neon lures and it took only a moment before Halloway pushed himself from his chair and came to get it. "I always put a bit of bacon on mine."

"Always use grubs for sunfish, myself." Nevertheless, he accepted the piece of bacon she offered and gave her a smile before lumbering back to his chair.

"So, what'd you retire from?"

"Used to be sheriff of this parish. Got myself elected unopposed every term but two, and neither of them elections was close. Don't know if that means most folks got more sense, or that I got the job done right, but put twenty years in office."

"People must have been satisfied," she said, with an obvious stroke to his ego. "I suppose things stay pretty quiet around these parts, though. Not like in the cities."

"You'd be surprised. Just a couple years ago, Cooter

Beecham shot his wife, Emma, stone cold after being married thirty years. That got the parish buzzing, I can tell you."

"I'll bet." Although Tori could care less about Cooter or his questionable ancestry, which Halloway described at some length, she let the man talk. And when he pulled in a sunfish a good foot long, he got even more expansive. "'Course no one was surprised overmuch," he concluded, his story winding down. "Got himself drunker 'n Bessy Bug most Saturdays. Went home after he'd tied one on and thought he saw a ghost standing in his doorway. Ran to get his shotgun from his truck and squeezed off three shots afore he figured out it was Emma in her nightdress."

She took advantage of his pause for breath to say, "I'll bet that created some excitement around here. Did it bring all the reporters in from the city to interview you?"

He looked a little crestfallen at that. "Well no, just the reporter for the local paper. But," his face brightened as he recast his line, "I was on WDSU once, you know the New Orleans channel? Near 'bout twenty years ago, it was. Everybody wanted to talk about that case, yes sirree. There was a mite more interest in the Tremaine family than in Cooter's."

"I think I remember that. It was a car accident, wasn't it?" Tori nodded, her nonchalant manner at odds with the jitter in her pulse. "I'll bet that did bring the reporters crawling."

"Reporters, photographers and more gawkers than a body could shake a stick at. Gruesome scene, it was," he said, shaking his head. "By the time I arrived there was nothing to be done for any of the passengers. Car ran off the road, over an embankment and landed fifteen feet below. Terrible sight." He looked, Tori thought, just a little green at the retelling. "The Tremaines have done a lot for folks 'round these parts. The tragedy was talked about for years. But an accident's all it was, just like I told 'em, and despite all the digging by journalists and P.I.s, that's all they came up with, too."

Since she'd spent the better part of the night reading the reports in the file, Tori was well aware of the conclusions drawn. "They didn't discover anything wrong with the car?" she asked.

"Not a thing, and I had Harris DuBlass look it over special. At that time there wasn't a finer hand with a car than his, and he said it was clean as a whistle. Not much left of it, of course, smashed up as it was. You'll still hear some folks 'round these parts talk about sabotage or some such thing, but I'm here to tell you, the steering and brakes looked just fine. Accident went in the books as plain, old DE."

It took a moment for Tori to follow his meaning. "Driver error."

"That's right. The road had just been reopened after road crews had worked on it for months. There was interest for a while to straighten out that curve, make the road into four lanes, but folks got upset about cutting down the big ol' trees along one side. In the end they just widened it. Most likely Joseph Tremaine took that curve too fast. Only idea I ever come up with. If it happened in these times, they'd probably all survive, what with the shoulder harnesses and air bags. But back then with just the lap belt." The older man shook his head. "Didn't none of 'em stand a chance of living through it."

"Didn't that surprise you, though?" Tori asked. "I mean, he must have been familiar with the area."

He let out a crow of delight as another tug on his line brought him to his feet. "I think I got me a big one here." He let the line play out a little before reeling it in slowly, watching the fish on the other end thrash. "Sure he knew the roads like the back of his hand," he continued his earlier thread seamlessly, "but like I said, that road had been changed some. And there's not a one among us that don't get behind the wheel when our mind isn't totally on driving. That's why they call them accidents."

"I guess there were no witnesses to help clear up any questions."

"Nope. Just a couple of Bernie Glasser's cows that musta got out and come downriver, and they weren't talking. Leastways, that's the story Glasser gave. Like nobody knew he brung them down regular every morning to avoid the cost of watering 'em. Used to tromp 'em across Cooter Beecham's property like clockwork, and didn't that make the old guy cuss a blue streak. Had a mouth on him, old Cooter did, and he didn't need to be liquored up to let loose, no sirree. Why I remember a time…"

Tori let the man ramble and her mind drift. Ex-Sheriff Halloway's retelling of the accident was different from his report only in the colorful details. Doubt about the cause of the accident hadn't lingered long in his mind, if at all.

If he was right, his conclusion would mirror her dad's. His report had been included in the file, as well, and she'd pored over it with particular attention. Just reading it, imagining him sitting at his battered desk painstakingly typing his findings, had summoned a lump to her throat that appeared only too easily these days.

For the first time she considered the fact that if she arrived at a different conclusion from his, it would mean he'd been wrong. That he'd overlooked something, or been too careless in his investigation. Neither of the possibilities seemed likely. Rob Landry had been meticulous about his work and his reputation. If there had been something to find twenty years earlier, something to support James's fear that the accident had been deliberate, he would have found it. Reported it. And remained on the case until the wrongdoer was brought to justice.

She let out a sigh, only half aware that Halloway had fallen silent. It was highly probable that there was nothing to the claims in those messages about Tremaine's parents. They'd likely been sent to distract him at a time when he most needed to focus his attention on his work.

But the conclusion didn't make her breathe any easier. She couldn't dismiss the threats in the notes as easily as James did. Even if the car wreck all those years ago had been an accident, he could still have a target on his back. Either way, this investigation could well prove dangerous to him. And if she was honest, the fear that followed that thought was more than just a professional one.

Chapter 4

James peered at the screen, tapping in commands rapidly. "I'm still not satisfied with the speed of the file-wiping function of the software. For optional utility, the task needs to be accomplished twice as quickly."

Marcus Rappaport, Vice President of Production and James's right hand in the company, shook his head. Bracing his hands on the table beside James, he leaned closer to the computer. "Figured you'd raise a breeze about it. But if you're bent on overwriting the data a dozen times in the wipe, it's going to take more time. We can speed it up by doing a sextuple overwrite, which still is twice as often as conventional methods, but…"

James lifted a brow. "Did you actually mention conventional methods in my presence?"

The man straightened, raising his hands in mock surrender. "What was I thinking? But it's getting pretty close to deadline to do more than fine-tune any aspect of the system. Maybe we should just…"

"Adjust the algorithm, compress the oppositional system and, if that doesn't work, see what our new supersonic chip would do to the speed."

Rappaport gaped at him. "Do you know how that would impact the cost?"

James pushed away from the computer table. He assumed the question was rhetorical. There was no one in his company as well versed as he in the profit/loss margin of every contract he undertook. "I have a general idea, yes. It's a last option, but if it comes to that, I'd rather shave our profit than put a product out there that doesn't perform exactly as I envisioned it."

Marcus stared at him a moment longer, then began jotting notes on a pad of paper. "This perfectionist trait of yours may be the death of this company yet."

James was too used to the man's pessimistic nature to take offense. He smiled and rose, clapping him on the shoulder. "I'm not a perfectionist, Marcus, just fussy. Give the job to Analiese and tell her none of us think it can be done. You know how she responds to a challenge."

The man visibly brightened. He'd always had a soft spot for James's little sister. "I'll do that, although your brother-in-law may not thank you if she starts putting in overtime to accomplish it."

"I'll let her manage Jones." Although his sister's husband was overprotective enough to meet with even her brothers' approval, Ana had a gift for wrapping the toughest man around her little finger. James daily counted himself lucky that the lion's share of responsibility for her could now be shared.

"What's the latest on the arrangements for the Technology Expo?"

"I've turned over the final details to Tucker." Tucker Rappaport, the man's son, interned with their company during summers and college vacations. He had one semester left before earning his M.A. When he was finished, James hoped to hire him for good. It wasn't only friendship and loyalty that had him making a place for the young man at his company. The kid was brilliant, with a mind for cryptography that was staggering in one his age.

"Have him coordinate with Jones. I've put him in charge of securing the physical grounds. Better yet, get a meeting set up for the three of us." Regardless of the questions that the anonymous notes elicited, nothing would distract him from business. Projects could be delegated, but his stamp would be all over them, down to the last detail. When he'd picked up the reins of his father's company, with the ink still fresh on his master's degree from M.I.T., he'd also donned a heavy mantle of responsibility, vowing to stay true to his father's vision for the business. In that way, at least, he hadn't failed him.

But now it was the failure of a far different kind that haunted. If there was any truth to the last couple notes, he'd allowed three people's deaths to go unchallenged. He'd let down his brothers. His sister. Not to mention the man standing next to him.

Truth wasn't often delivered anonymously, he reminded himself, jaw tightening. The messages were the mark of a coward, one who wished to inflict pain while staying in the shadows. No one had ever been allowed to strike at the Tremaines without certain reprisal. The sender would learn that all too soon.

James checked his watch, shifting his thoughts firmly back to business. "What about the Micro Secure? Everything set to showcase it at the expo?"

Rappaport nodded. "Corley and Soulieu have been

running it on mobile phones, PDAs and wireless equipment, and haven't hit a glitch yet. I think it's going to generate a lot of interest when we unveil it."

"It should do that." In fact, James was counting on it. The specially engineered tool kit they'd developed provided the strongest security available in constrained environments. The advanced safeguards it incorporated would bring a measure of privacy previously unrealized in the area. It would be debuted at the expo, then introduced to the market six months later. The time lag would give their PR department an opportunity to orchestrate the necessary media promotion to whet demand.

Marcus reached for the phone. "You'll want to check on the Micro Secure yourself. I'll tell Corley and Soulieu to wait for you."

As James nodded, his cell phone began to ring. Striding across the room, he took out his cell, checked the caller ID. Then, pulse quickening, he flipped it open and answered. "Tori. I've been waiting to hear from you." It was, he recognized, truer than he'd like to admit. Even as he'd tended to business throughout the day, thoughts of her, and the job he'd hired her for, refused to be banished from his mind.

"Hi. I talked to your ex-sheriff today, who's convinced the accident was just…" Static interrupted her next few words. It sounded as if she was in her car. "…pictures, and I'm on my way to a guy I know, an accident reconstruction engineer. I'll let you know what I find out."

"No. Wait." Aware that his sharp tone had aroused Marcus's interest, he deliberately softened it. "I don't want you to do that alone. I'll go with you."

Annoyance laced her voice, although it remained civil enough. "That's really not necessary. I'll call you as soon as I know something."

"It's no problem." He checked his watch. "Where should I meet you?"

There was a pause, as if she were reaching for patience. "I'm heading to a bar called Juicy's on the corner of France and LaSalle. But believe me, it's not your type of place."

"Are you calling me a snob?" he asked with genuine amusement. He could almost hear her mental gears grinding. Or maybe that was her teeth.

"Not at all. There's just no need for you to feel uncomfortable. And why come all this way when I can call you with the outcome?"

Since Marcus had ended his conversation, James hastened to do the same. "Because I want to be with you." His words, as well as the deliberately intimate tone of his voice would have his co-worker drawing his own conclusions about his call. "Does this establishment of yours serve food?"

There was an audible sigh, then the blare of horns. He hoped her frustration hadn't caused her to swerve into traffic. "I believe there's a loophole in the Department of Health guidelines that still allows them to refer to it as food, yes."

"Great. We can eat together while we wait."

"Suit yourself." From the abrupt end of her call it was obvious that his insistence hadn't set well with her.

"I told Corley and Soulieu to expect you. Should I reschedule?"

Belatedly, he looked up, saw Rappaport's quizzical look. With a glance at his watch, he mentally calculated the time it would take him to change and drive to New Orleans. "Set it for 7:00 a.m. tomorrow. I'll meet with Tucker and Jones immediately after."

Marcus nodded approvingly. "Won't hurt you a bit to

get out and socialize a little. Celia's always saying that you work too hard."

Celia had been his father's secretary before she'd become his. She regulated his office schedule with dragonlike ferocity, and lent the same zeal to her interest in his social life.

James strode toward the door. "Well, considering that I'm about to make Celia a very happy lady, I'll let you inform her about the changes to my schedule tomorrow." He turned his head just enough to catch the stark terror on the man's face, saw the protest forming on his lips. Marcus's reaction had him grinning, but it didn't account for the warm pool of anticipation pooling in his belly.

No, that was elicited by the upcoming meeting with Tori Corbett.

Tori took out her frustration with Tremaine on the pool hustlers at Juicy's. Although they'd seen her play often enough to know better, most of them had more ego than sense. She was up fifty bucks, and her mood had improved accordingly.

Circling the table, she studied the possible plays.

"She's gonna clear the table again."

"No, she ain't. Ain't possible."

"How easily they forget," Tori muttered under her breath. She bent, lined up her shot and banked the six ball off the opposite side to roll directly into the side pocket. Straightening, she observed, "One would think I didn't have your ten in my pocket by doing that very thing, Skeeter."

Skeeter shrugged his nearly seven-foot frame that was at least half as wide as a pool cue and muttered aggrievedly, "Just ain't right, letting a woman play, anyways. How's a man supposed to concentrate when you're all bent over like that?"

"By using your superior skills of concentration, just like I do." With a sure stroke, she used the cue ball to lightly kiss the three, sending it into the corner pocket. She looked up, threw Skeeter an innocent look. "How else do you explain me being able to keep my attention off your god-like physique and on the game?"

Guffaws broke out among the crowd around the table. Skeeter finally found the description too much to resist and cracked a smile, revealing a gold front tooth. "Shoot, if you could play as good as you talked, you'd be on the circuit."

"And if you played as good as you looked, there'd be statues erected in your name." She bent over, studying the lay of the remaining balls. She'd managed to leave herself with no clear shot, which was going to require some sleight of hand. After a few moments of consideration, she made her choice and shifted into position.

It was the quiet that alerted her first. The effect of a stranger walking into a neighborhood tavern was equivalent to a panther stalking through the wilds. The occupants went silent, sizing up the newcomer, assessing the danger, readying for action.

The identity of this particular stranger was never in doubt.

Without glancing his way, she sent the nine ball spinning toward the opposite pocket, bouncing it off the side, where it teetered precariously at the entrance and then, in slow motion, fell into place.

The crowd around the table thinned considerably. She could only imagine that they'd drifted toward Tremaine. Tori decided she'd let him sweat a bit before she called them off. If it gave him a few bad moments, well, maybe the next time he wouldn't be so pushy about inviting himself along.

"You musta wandered in the wrong place, mister." There was a pause, the unmistakable sound of Skeeter spitting on the floor. "I think you ought to wander back out again."

"Since it appears strenuous for you, perhaps you should give up thinking altogether." Tori winced as James's unmistakably cultured tone caused a low rumble to sound across the room. It was time to bring an end to things before he was sent flying back out in the street, with damage to his pretty jaw and two-thousand-dollar suit.

In an effort to distract them, she said, "Who wants to put another twenty on me clearing the rest of the table? Skeeter?"

There was a quick scuffling on the other side of the room followed by a loud thud. With a quick stab of guilt, Tori jerked around and pushed her way through the men encircling the body on the floor. "Dammit, Skeeter, you didn't have to…" And then stared dumbly, first at the body crumpled on the dirty wooden planks, then at the one standing over it, rubbing his knuckles.

James arched one elegant brow, stepped over Skeeter's prone body. The crowd separated for him like the parting of the Red Sea. "Tori. Didn't mean to interrupt your game."

Somehow she managed to close her mouth. Swallow. "No problem. I was just cleaning up."

His mouth quirked. "Me, too." He strolled to the table she'd vacated, surveyed it critically. She used the time to observe him. Far from the suit she'd expected, he was wearing well-worn denim that was faded to white at the most interesting stress points. With the blue polo shirt he had tucked into the waistband, he failed to resemble the Armani-clad executive she was used to seeing. But neither did he look like a regular at Juicy's with their undershirts or ripped tees. Especially with him wearing what looked like Gucci loafers.

Her gaze traveled upward again, lingered on the very respectably muscled wall of his chest. It was difficult to shift her attention once again to clearing the remaining pool balls from the table. It would have been too much to ask, she thought, with an odd jitter in her stomach, to discover that his shoulders owed their width to his well-cut suits. Using her thumb to balance her cue stick, she sent the cue ball smacking into the one, spinning it across the table and into a pocket. Or to find that his long hours at the company had turned his body soft and all too resistible.

She circled the table, noted that Skeeter was on his feet again, but swaying just a bit. Dispatching the five ball, she sent James a cautious look. With one hip propped against the table, arms folded across his chest, he projected a subtle aura of danger. With a jolt of shock, she realized that the power the suits merely hinted at was all too apparent in the more casual clothes. Skeeter had had the misfortune to discover that the hard way.

It was a relief to have something other than the man on the other side of the table to focus on. She sent the thirteen ball to the far pocket and then dispensed with the eleven. Straightening, she chalked her stick, giving the task more attention than was warranted. Why couldn't Tremaine have been like the majority of guys his age, and let himself go a little? she thought aggrievedly. With the demands of his job, it would be expected. Even her ex, jock that he'd been in college, had continued his exercise routine only halfheartedly once they'd gone back to his home in Texas.

"Eight in the left side pocket," she announced, to no one in particular. Those who had left the table earlier, in hopes of a good rousing brawl, were shying away from it now that the stranger had taken up residence there.

"You've got an easier shot to the right corner," James noted, observing the table critically.

"The best way isn't always the easiest," she replied lightly. Leaning over, she took her time lining up her shot, then banked the eight ball off one side to go spinning into the pocket she'd called. The game finished, she straightened, set her cue against the table, and, because she detested cowards, looked squarely at him.

A smile was playing about his mouth as he looked at the cleared table, then at her. "Showing off?"

She threw a meaningful glance at Skeeter, who was at the bar, sulking over a beer. "Weren't you?"

"There are times when diplomacy is overrated." Rounding the table, he took her elbow in his hand and led her to one of the booths that lined the walls. Once she'd seated herself, he slid in opposite her. Scanning the rooms, he raised a brow. "Menu?"

"On the wall."

Following the direction of her finger, he noted the choices scrawled with colored chalk on the rough plaster next to the bar. "Interesting display. How do they change it?"

"Changes wait until it's time to paint," she said blandly. In truth, she didn't recall any time in her memory when there had been a change or a paint job. Much of Juicy's dubious charm was owed to its constancy.

He scanned the short listing on the wall. "What's good?"

"Well, if you exchange *edible* for *good,* I can recommend the cajun crawdad platter." She gave him a bland look. Jeans or not, she couldn't see him cracking crawdads and sucking out their brains. Which was really the only way any self-respecting Louisianan would eat them.

"How's the gumbo?"

"Spicy enough to curl strips off your intestines."

He caught the eye of Stoner, the unambitious waiter, and gave him a short nod.

"You'll have to go up to the bar and order," she started, then trailed off as Stoner ambled toward them in what was, for him, a hurry.

"Two bowls of gumbo and the crawdad platter. What do you have on draft?"

Fumbling with the pad he was attempting to withdraw from his back pocket, Stoner reeled off the names of the beers. James ordered one, then cocked an eyebrow at Tori.

"I'll have another Michelob Lite."

Stoner bobbed his head, laboriously writing the order down on the pad. Since Tori had never seen him actually take an order before, it was a sight worth watching.

"Okay." He looked up, seemed to search for some waiterlike lines. "Ummm. I'll get you some silverware. Maybe napkins?" He sent James a hopeful look.

"Excellent." From the slight incline of James's head, Stoner seemed to realize he was dismissed, and moved away.

"That was worth paying tickets for." Tori's bemused gaze switched from the departing man to the one across from her. "Did you perfect that talent on snooty maître d's in the French Quarter?"

"Snooty maître d's rarely question the need for table linens, but they do respond to a certain attitude, yes." James folded his arms on the table and leaned toward her. "Why don't you tell me what you've been up to today? Besides fleecing unwary pool players?"

"Well, that was certainly the most lucrative part of my day so far." She gave him a brief account of her conversation with Halloway, ending with, "He's still convinced the accident was due to driver's error. But I went back to my contact, who provided me with the photos in the file I put together for you. I made him a very happy man and bought every picture he had of the accident scene."

Those sinfully blue eyes of his narrowed. "I take it he had quite a few of them?" At her nod, his mouth went flat. "When did he take them?"

Understanding the meaning hidden in the question, she hastened to reassure him. "It was hours afterward. The car was still there, though." She gave mental thanks that Kiki Corday hadn't been near enough to have gotten to the scene before the bodies had been taken away. He would have had no compunction about snapping whatever photos he thought he could make a buck from.

Stoner brought their drafts to them, setting them down with more care than usual on the table. Waiting until he'd left, she continued. "The owner of this fine establishment has a setup in the back. He specializes in accident scene reconstruction. I sent over the photos I bought today and a copy of the accident report. He's comparing them and will give us his impressions."

James looked skeptical. "He's the owner and engineer?"

"Don't let the ambiance fool you. Juicy has dabbled in this field for a long time. He finally went back to college a few years ago and got his engineering degree. All his money gets put into the latest equipment and gadgetry, and as you see, little of it goes to overhead. I could have gotten someone with a lot more glitz and polish, but Juicy's cheap and he's the best around."

James looked toward the back of the bar. "How long has he been at it?"

Because she recognized the impatience in his tone, she reached over, touched his arm lightly. "A while. But genius can't be hurried."

Touching him was a mistake. She realized it immediately. His heat transferred to her fingertips in a warm flood of sensation, before pulsing through her veins with quick jolts of awareness. The warmth was both an invitation to linger and a warning against the same. She didn't respond to men like this. Ever.

She jerked her hand away with a suddenness that sent her beer teetering. She steadied the glass, then brought it to her lips, sipped. It was more than a bit disconcerting to have her femininity return unheralded, especially summoned as it was by this man. The Tremaine family fortune made the Corbetts look like pikers. And two excruciating years living in that particular vipers' nest had taught her more than she ever wanted to know about high society. Give her the hidden perils of New Orleans's seamy side anyday. At least there she had a fighting chance of figuring out where the knife was coming from.

"You're jumpy tonight."

Although his observation was made mildly enough, it was issued in the same voice he'd used with her over the phone. Low and silky, like the stroke of a heated caress.

Giving him a bland stare, she set down her beer. "Not really. There was really no reason for you to come tonight. I'm just going to be sitting and waiting. It could be hours before he's ready to talk to me."

His eyes glinted. "I've decided, this time around, that

I'm going to take a more active role in the investigation. I want these questions laid to rest once and for all."

Inner alarms shrilled at the hidden promise in his words. No P.I. wanted a client looking over her shoulder every minute, but her reluctance to work that closely with him came from a far different source. "Leave the investigation to me. You've got other things that demand your attention."

Straightening, he lifted his glass to his lips. "Such as?"

"Well, there's the little matter that someone is threatening to kill you. Why don't we talk about the measures you've taken to ensure against it?"

Judging from the expression on his face, she'd managed to annoy him. "I told you…"

"I know, I know, you don't think a real killer would warn you before striking." With a wave of her hand, she dismissed that argument. "You've admitted to having enemies, past attempts on your life and a compelling reason for competitors to want you out of the way. You'd have to be stupid not to take precautions." She paused, one deliberate beat. "You're not stupid."

"You can't know how delighted I am by your conclusion."

He had, she decided, a rather irritating habit of responding without truly answering. He said nothing more, and Stoner arrived at that time with a steaming tray of crawdads, which he set between them. Then he presented two plates with something of a flourish, napkins and silverware.

She waited until he'd moved away, having obviously forgotten about the gumbo, before she fixed James with a steely stare. "Tell me you've taken measures to protect yourself."

He heaped a plate with crawdads, set it in front of her. "I'm not without resources or common sense."

"Tell me."

Seeming to recognize the steel in her tone, he halted in the process of piling his own plate. His eyes met hers. For the moment, she forgot to worry about what he might see in them. "I take precautions. I've always had to. Bomb sweeps, Kevlar vests, bodyguards... As the level of threat rises, so do my defenses. Does that answer your question?"

It did. It also shook her more than she thought possible. Once again she was reminded that his outwardly cultured world was filled with as many undercurrents of danger as one would expect to find in the toughest dark alley. She watched him as he snapped the head off the crawdad and brought it to his mouth, and her lips curved reluctantly. A man who knew the proper way to dispense with the disgusting-looking, succulent creatures had something in his favor. She reached for her own plate and went to work, discovering an appetite that had earlier seemed questionable.

"Actually, my firm recently has begun expanding into physical security," he surprised her by saying. Dropping some empty shells, legs still attached, to the plate, he scooped up another. "My brother-in-law has a certain level of expertise in that area, and it seemed a natural step for us to take. He'll head up that division when it's fully operational, specializing in antiterrorism tactics and personal safety."

Attacking the shellfish on the plate before her, she said, "Then you'll have a ready staff available to protect you. Sounds like a good plan."

"Plans are all we can make." Dropping an empty shell to the growing mound of them, he wiped his fingers on a napkin. "All the precautions in the world aren't going to be enough to stop someone intent on harm." When her gaze flew to his, he held it steadily. "I don't take unnecessary risks, but in my business I've gotten used to establishing realistic expectations. If someone wants me dead badly enough, sooner or later he's going to succeed. Unless I get to him first."

Chapter 5

The expression on Tori's face made James pause in the middle of attacking another crawdad. There was a flash of shock there, followed by what, if he hadn't known better, looked like concern. Both were equally intriguing. But before he could comment, she was shrugging, reaching for another crawdad.

"Yeah, you're right. Hey, I have an idea. Why don't you just have a big bull's-eye painted on the back of all those fancy suits of yours? Make it a mite easier all around."

Slowly, his eyes never leaving hers, he reached for his beer, tipped it to his lips. He drank, then lowered it to say, "I don't intend to make it easy for anyone."

"No, I got that." The caustic tone of her voice was matched by the glint in her eye. "You're just fatalistic, right? What's going to happen is going to happen." She snapped off the shell of the crawdad in her hand with just a little more force than necessary. "Seems a little odd for someone in the security business to be saying there's really no way for people to be completely secure. Just a tip—don't pass that line on to your marketing department. I doubt it'll do much for your sales."

It was on the tip of his tongue to agree with her. It was precisely because he was in the security business that he realized the limitations of the very products and services he sold. No matter how advanced the technology, there were always ways around them for the very, very talented. That was a reality of his field, which necessitated ever newer products, ever more sophisticated technology.

But he swallowed the words, recognizing that her remarks sprang from a far more personal level. He picked up his napkin, deliberately wiped his fingers, then reached out, caught her hand.

He waited for her gaze to meet his before leaning forward to say, "I like to believe that I'm not without skills in the area of personal safety." Her countenance remained stony. It shouldn't have warmed something inside him, something that had been untouched for far too long. His thumb caressed her knuckles, and her hand jerked a little in his. "I don't have a death wish—there's too much to live for." He paused deliberately before adding, "I've got season courtside tickets to the Hornets."

It took a moment, but her lips curved reluctantly, even as she slipped her hand away from his. Because her response pleased him, he allowed her to make her escape, and sat back satisfied.

"Courtside, huh?"

He resumed eating. "Mmm-hmm."

"Figures." The almost angry concern in her voice had changed to unmistakable envy. And then, grudgingly, she admitted, "So, I guess that would be enough to keep you careful. Those seats are tough to come by, even for people with more money than Midas."

He winked at her. "You just have to know the right people."

Tori reached for another crawdad, eyed him speculatively. "How many of those seats did you say you had?"

Enjoying himself hugely, he cracked the shell, dug out the seafood. "Two. Prime position, right across from the team."

"What do you do with them when you can't make it to a game?"

Crushing the tinge of hope in her tone, he wiped his hands and reached for his beer. "Then my brothers use them. Or sometimes my sister. Occasionally someone from work."

She folded her arms on the table and leaned forward. "Don't make me beg, Tremaine. Maybe you and I could reach an agreement. A…a…trade of some kind."

The suggestion summoned more than a casual flicker of interest. Not that he really thought she meant the offer in the way his mind was automatically interpreting it. But her words did elicit all types of fascinating scenarios. Fascinating, because she was as far from his type as it was possible to be. And he was intrigued in spite of it. Or perhaps because of it. "What did you have in mind?"

With excruciating timing Stoner arrived at the booth, carrying two precariously filled bowls. "Almost forgot the gumbo," he mumbled, setting the bowls down in front of them with a definite lack of grace.

Tori sat back, wisely, as it turned out, and narrowly avoided being scalded by the soup that slopped over the side of the bowl. James waited until the man had moved away before observing, "That guy missed his calling. With his light touch he ought to be a surgeon." His words elicited a smile, but the spell had been broken. The fragile link of intimacy between them was gone.

She spooned in some soup, tasted it cautiously. After swallowing, she drew a deep breath. "Oh, my. Hope you don't have ulcers."

He followed suit, took a taste and immediately found his eyes watering. "I didn't before now. That's...an interesting gumbo recipe."

"Yeah, I think they also use it to strip paint. As a matter of fact, I heard a rumor..." Something in the back corner of the bar seemed to distract her, and she stopped talking, laid down her spoon. "Juicy's come out of his lair. Looks like he's ready for us."

With little regret, James slid out of the booth and withdrew his money clip, leaving a bill on the table. Then with a drum roll of anticipation tightening his gut, he followed in Tori's wake, for once failing to give his full attention to the decided sway of her hips. He had no idea what, if anything, to expect from this meeting. But there was no denying that whatever the outcome, there'd be answers of some sort. And answers were something he was increasingly eager to discover.

"What have you got?" Tori didn't bother with introductions, and James was fairly certain it was by design. It suited him well enough. Closing the door behind him, he slipped the tips of his fingers into his jeans pockets and scanned the room she'd led them to. Surprisingly sophisticated computer equipment and peripherals lined the walls. Above the computers the walls were covered with cork board. Displayed there was a series of close-ups of a wrecked automobile. His gut took a quick, vicious twist. The car was instantly recognizable. It made frequent appearances in his nightmares.

He forced his gaze away from the photos to the man Tori was addressing. Juicy's name was the only colorful thing about him. Tall and gaunt, rather than merely thin, his manner of speech was as spare as his frame. The man wore his long, dark hair caught back into a queue that hit him midshoulder blade. From the pallor of his skin, James guessed he spent most of his free time hunched over one of his machines.

"Took me a while." Juicy walked over to a computer terminal and sat down. "You brought me a lot of data. Didn't have a chance to get through it all."

"I know how you like to be thorough." Tori took up a stance behind the man, and James moved to do the same.

"Thought I recognized most of the work." Juicy swiveled his head around to send her a quick look, which she returned calmly.

"I'm sure you did."

Somehow James was left with the feeling that a great deal more had been exchanged in the terse sentences than mere words. The photographer—what had Tori said his name was? Corday—was obviously known to this character.

With a grunt Juicy turned back to the computer. The man pointed the mouse at various spots on the screen and clicked, unfolding several pictures. "Here are the sheriff's pictures of the vehicle and the road. They reported that the car came around this curve—" he traced it with his finger on the screen "—too fast. Driver lost control, tried to compensate by braking." His finger stabbed at the picture of the skid marks on the road. "Car fishtailed, swinging around so the rear end hit the guardrail. The force of that spun the car 180 degrees, and this time it was the front smashing through the rail. Momentum carried it over the edge of the road, down to the riverbed beneath."

"We read the report," Tori said impatiently. "The question is, do you agree with it?"

"I can see how they came to that conclusion, yeah."

James released a breath he hadn't known he'd been holding. Was that relief he was feeling? He wasn't sure. There were too many emotions churning and bumping inside him to individually identify any one. Certainly it would put to rest a bit of the guilt that had haunted him since the notes started. Guilt that he hadn't done enough. Tried hard enough.

Guilt that wouldn't be assuaged easily.

"What about the other pictures?" he asked tersely. "The ones that weren't part of the report?"

"Like I said, I haven't gotten through everything yet. But I've seen enough to have a few questions."

"What kind of questions?" Tori crowded closer to Juicy, only to be elbowed away.

"Back off and I'll show you." With a few deft strokes he brought up a different set of pictures to the screen, clicking on one to enlarge it. "Here's the front left bumper of the car. Sheriff thought the damage to it came from smashing through the railing. And maybe it did. Might even have hit something fairly solid on the way down to the riverbed." He flexed his fingers on the keyboard. "But it also could have meant the car hit something else before it went off the road."

James stilled. "The report said the road was clear."

Never taking his eyes from the computer screen, Juicy nodded. "There's nothing in the pictures, anyway, but there was a mess load of machinery over on the west side. Why wouldn't the driver head that way? Better to hit a bulldozer than the guardrail."

"Driver error, the sheriff said," Tori murmured.

"Mebbe." Juicy clicked rapidly until he came to the

photo he was looking for. He dragged one of the corners, enlarging it on the screen. "I blew this one up a couple times. This boulder sat at the edge of the road."

"Still does." James never traveled that stretch of blacktop without a part of him wondering about that night twenty years ago. Recreating the scene over and over in his mind. Wishing for a different outcome.

"The ex-sheriff mentioned something about it, too. The parish engineers were working on that stretch of road, widening it. There was interest in turning it into a four-lane, but public outcry killed it. People didn't want the two-hundred-year-old oaks destroyed."

"Whatever." It was clear Juicy had no use for the history. "Looks like the engineers were just widening it up to within a couple feet of that tree there." He tapped a spot on the screen. "But beside it was this rock that probably had sat there since caveman days." With a shrug of his narrow shoulders, he indicated his lack of appreciation of that fact. "See how the dirt around it is disturbed? It had been moved recently."

"The road crew moved it." Tori's voice was flat. She looked at James. "It's in the engineer's report. It was moved back to sit even with the tree to make way for the work, but they left it there to pacify the public upset with the progress."

"You think the car hit the boulder?"

"You wouldn't think so." Juicy stood as he answered James's question and released some pictures that had been tacked to the cork board. "Can't figure a way for the car to swing that far around and still hit it with enough force to cause that kind of damage." His pause was full of meaning. "If that's where the boulder was sitting that night."

"Well of course it was." A bit of James's earlier

impatience sounded in Tori's voice. "We have the pictures to show the scene."

But James was rounding the man to peer at the pictures in his hand. Reaching out, he took them from him, flipping through the stack until he came to one that stopped him.

His gaze raised to meet Juicy's, who was bobbing his head. "Wouldn't have thought anything of it if I hadn't seen that picture. It made me stop and look at things a bit differently."

The pictures were close-ups of the boulder. The rock's position to the road. The flawless face it presented from that direction. But another shot taken from a different angle, intended, James guessed, to shoot the road from a different position, showed the back of the huge boulder. And the fresh scar marring it.

"Suppose that mark could have been made by the dozer that moved it," Juicy mused, going back to flipping through pictures he'd loaded on to his computer. "Not saying that it couldn't have been."

No, James mused grimly, he wasn't "saying" anything. But he'd already planted a seed of suspicion in their minds. "Are you suggesting the damage to the left bumper is consistent with it having hit the boulder?"

The man pursed his lips, skated a glance toward Tori. "Wasn't gonna say it that fancy, but yeah, it's a possibility. I'd need to run some tests to be sure. Only thing is there's no way in hell that it could have happened if the rock was sitting the way it is in this picture. Look at this." He scrolled down the screen, clicked on close-ups of the guardrail. "A car going at a pretty good clip hitting that railing isn't going to be stopped. It's gonna snap through it and go on down the embankment." He brought up another picture, shot through a night lens, and marked the path the car would have taken. "The damage done to the car's bumper looks more like it hit something solid." He brought one fist to hit his open hand in a loud whack. "Something with no give to it."

"Could it have hit something else as it went down the embankment?" Tori asked. "Another rock, or a tree, maybe?"

Juicy shrugged. "You didn't give me any pictures that showed something big enough in that area, but that don't mean there wasn't something."

"There wasn't." James's tone was final. He'd walked that scene in the days afterward, when thoughts of foul play had haunted him and overwhelming grief had whipped up fury. It had been easier to feel fury and suspicion than it had been to cope with sorrow. Simpler to want to blame a faceless nameless person, than to blame fate. He and his siblings had been orphaned. Another child left motherless. Until that moment he hadn't remembered how desperately he'd wanted to discover a human face to put on that evil.

He still didn't have a face. He didn't have facts. What he had was a *possibility*.

Realizing that Tori was looking at him quizzically, he tucked away the frustration that threatened to swamp him. "I checked the scene myself. There were no sizable trees, only brush. And the path was rocky, but nothing large enough to cause that kind of damage to the bumper."

"Unless impact from the car sent the rock rolling down the hill into the river below."

With an inclination of his head, he acknowledged the idea and addressed Juicy. "What could you do with this if we gave you more time?"

The man all but rubbed his hands together. "I want to go over the rest of the file you brought. Do some photogrammetic calculations. Examine the tire marks. Got the latest here in digital software and laser equipment. Give me a few days and I can run you a 3D reenactment of the accident itself."

"Do it."

Juicy slid a sideways glance to Tori. "The cost…"

"Will be covered. There's a bonus in it for you if you can get it to me sooner."

For the first time, a wide grin spread across the man's taciturn features. "I'll give it top priority."

"Call me the minute it's finished," Tori said, then turned to follow James out the door. He didn't shorten his strides; he couldn't. He had a sudden need for oxygen, to clear his head and fill his lungs.

A need to shake the insidious visions that were already forming, dark and sinister, in his mind.

He only half noted the occupants of the tavern, who eyed him sullenly but gave him wide berth as he made his way through the place. When he got outside, he headed to his car, not at all surprised that it was still there and seemingly in one piece, despite the neighborhood. Walking all the way around it, he did a quick, thorough scan, then nodded at the young hood sitting on the curb beside it. "Any problems?"

The other man shook his head, reaching out for the half of a hundred-dollar bill James offered. Fitting it together with the half in his hand, he stared at it for a moment, then gave a huge grin. "Anytime, mister. Anytime." He turned and headed down the street, a bounce to his step.

"Couldn't find anything more conspicuous?"

At Tori's droll comment, he looked over his shoulder at her. "My tank's in the shop."

She gave a rather inelegant snort, and circled the Dodge Viper. "I always wondered what inadequacy men were making up for with expensive…whoa." Tori stopped, narrowed her eyes. "Is this a V-10?"

"Yeah…505 cubic-inch engine," he affirmed. "And it makes up for my personal inadequacy of being unable to go from zero to sixty in fifteen seconds while on foot."

Further smart-ass comments apparently stifled, she ran an admiring hand over a front fender. "What's the torque in this baby? You don't mind popping the hood, do you?"

A jacked-up late eighties sedan rolled slowly by. Its windows were cranked down, with rap music and gangster wannabes spilling from them.

Noting their interest, James said, "Some other time, maybe. I don't think this is the right place for show and tell."

At his words, her attention followed his and she nodded. "Sorry. I know a little about cars, but I've never gotten under the hood of one of these. I used to pit crew for a friend, though. I know my way around an engine."

And it sounded very much like she was itching to get her hands on this one. Despite the darker thoughts summoned by their conversation with Juicy, his interest was piqued. Most women of his acquaintance could identify the car's ignition and little else. He had a sneaking suspicion that her expertise with car engines far surpassed his own, since his was limited to little more than pointing in its general direction.

He felt a flicker of amusement. No, Tori Corbett wasn't at all like the women he generally spent time with. And it was too damn bad for him that he found that so appealing. "So now I have two things you envy—Hornets tickets and this car. Good to know."

Her expression sobering, she came around the hood to stand next to him. Oddly hesitant, she said, "I didn't exactly envy what you must have been going through in there a while ago."

His lighthearted feeling fled, to be replaced with the

edge of anger that had been simmering since he'd seen the pictures. Heard the possibilities.

He reached into his pocket and withdrew his car keys. "Don't worry about me. I just wish he'd come up with something a little more substantial." Something that would have provided some answers, for once, instead of triggering even more questions. Something that would put to rest, once and for all, this nagging sense of failure that refused to die.

An image flashed through his mind, of the freshly scarred boulder, followed by another conjured up from his imagination. How easy would it have been, he wondered, to use one of those big Cats to move that rock one more time…into the middle of the dark night road? How quickly could it have been accomplished? In time to take the oncoming driver unaware? To cause an instantaneous decision…between a head-on crash and an unforgiving embankment?

His muscles tensed, and it took conscious effort to keep his fingers from curling into fists. Control had been his mantra for twenty long years, when he'd had to step, much too young, into his father's shoes. He wasn't a man given to rashness. With sheer force of will he pushed back the images that tormented. But he knew they'd return, unbeckoned, when sleep refused to come. Doubts always picked the midnight hours to creep in, when defenses were lowered and darkness dimmed logic.

Skirting the path his thoughts were heading, he used the automatic ignition to start the car. "Have you spoken to Sanderson's Towing and Recovery yet?"

Tori was still watching him with eyes that saw too much. "No, although I plan to. I doubt they'll be able to tell us any more than is contained in the report, but I want to be thorough."

"The original owner is still there." He'd checked out that much, at least, before he'd hired her. The company had been the one to tow the car after the bodies had been extracted, bagging the belongings and doing the necessary cleanup so the vehicle could be sold for parts. "I want to go with you when you talk to him."

"Maybe you should rethink that." Someone came staggering out of Juicy's, threw them a look, then hurried in the opposite direction. The distraction had her glancing away, even as she continued, her voice lowered. "You have a business to run. I'm sure there are things there that require your attention, and I don't expect the visit to come to much, at any rate."

He arched one eyebrow. "Why do I have the feeling I'm getting the brush-off?"

She raised her chin and crossed her arms over her chest. A warrior readying for battle. Gaze direct, she said, "I'm not trying to brush you off, I just don't see the need for you to put yourself through anything else…like you did tonight."

James went still. It was one thing to have the constant battle between reason and emotion waging war within him. It was quite another for her to sense it. To comment on it. Emotion equaled vulnerability, and he'd spent his life making sure he and his were never vulnerable. "If I didn't know better, I'd think you were trying to protect me."

She uncrossed her arms and let them hang at her sides, as if she was uncertain what to do next. Then one rose, as if of its own volition, to hover between them before resting, ever so lightly, on his chest. "It can't be easy, listening to people talk about that night. Why go through it when you don't have to?"

One of his hands came up to grasp hers, his fingers tightening when she attempted to pull away. He had the feeling that if he let her, she'd try to soothe away his imagined hurts, the way a mother did with a child. But her touch had just the opposite effect. It threatened to unleash the emotions crashing and churning inside him. "I don't need protecting, and I don't require stroking, Tori. At least not that kind."

He watched the storm gather in her eyes, and the sight called to something primitive inside him. He had two decades' worth of experience keeping that core carefully controlled. A man led by his emotions would be ruined by them. But right now, in this moment, temptation was beckoning and he couldn't summon up a single reason to avoid it.

Using his grip on her hand, he tugged her closer. The pulse was hammering at the base of her throat, and he dipped his head to taste it. Her scent lingered there, right there, where the blood beat madly under the skin, beneath his tongue.

Her reaction called to something inside him, a wild and reckless streak that was carefully harnessed but never completely locked away. Most who knew him would swear it didn't exist. But right now it had him, and he was relishing the freedom.

Pressing her lips open with his, he swallowed the protest she would have made. And she would have made one, he was certain of it. However much he demanded control, she strove for it, at least around him. There was a distance between them that she was usually careful to cultivate. Snaking an arm around her waist, he pulled her closer, denying her a physical distance even as he felt her trying to maintain an emotional one.

The taste of her was foreign, forbidden. It called to everything inside him that he sought to tame. This was a bad idea. The worst. The realization didn't make the sudden wanting lessen. Didn't slow the heavy tide of blood from coursing through his veins. And when her tongue met his for the first time, the intimate glide more sure than tentative, he dove headfirst into sensation.

Her response torched his hunger and ignited a need for more. Pulling her closer, he took the sensual battle a step deeper until they were sealed together, chests, hips, thighs. His mouth ravaged hers and was ravaged in turn. The flavor of her was heady, and he couldn't seem to get his fill. He jammed his fingers through her hair, cupped the back of her head and brought her nearer. A moment more, and the need that had risen so fast, burned so fiercely, would be quenched. Just one more instant to satiate himself with the twist of her lips beneath his, the exotic flavor of her that he couldn't have foreseen. Wouldn't forget.

There was a burst of sound in the street behind them, and she started in his arms. Her reaction keyed his own, and a belated awareness of their surroundings filtered through him. The blare of a car horn, the accompanying shouted suggestion, had logic returning.

Releasing her, he took a step away. And then, for good measure, another. The distance helped to keep him from taking her in his arms again as she stared at him, her eyes more green than brown, huge and deep.

"What the hell was that?"

The question, delivered in that faintly aghast tone, was almost enough to have him smiling. Easing a hip against the front fender of the car, he said, "If you have to ask, I must be out of practice." She shook her head furiously, one hand coming out in protest, almost as though she expected him to reach for her again. Which of course, he wouldn't. He folded his arms across his chest, just to make sure.

"Don't go getting all smooth and charming on me,

Tremaine. This—" the gesture she made with her hand was unmistakable "—can't happen."

"I couldn't agree more." And then, unable to resist, he added, "Why?"

She'd half turned away, but his question had her whirling back. "Why? Why? Because…" Words seemed to fail her for the moment. "Because it's a terrible idea, that's why. Mucking up business with personal stuff is the worst way to run an investigation."

"Very true. I usually frown on 'mucking up business,' as a general rule."

She peered at him suspiciously, but he was careful to keep his expression bland. "Well then, that's settled. This shouldn't happen again."

"It won't." The words were tinged with regret and filled him with a vague sense of surprise. Her reminder should have been unnecessary. Of course something so inappropriate couldn't be allowed to occur again. He didn't prey on his employees. He was normally quite adept at keeping his personal and business worlds from colliding.

"Okay." She didn't quite manage to keep the wariness from her voice. Backing away, she nearly tripped over the curb. He didn't trust himself to reach out and steady her. "If you're still intent on tagging along tomorrow…"

"I am."

"…how about if we just agree to meet there? I've got the address in the copy of the file you made for me. Is 10:00 a.m. all right with you?"

He thought of the meetings he'd already rescheduled. "Make it one." It would play hell with his calendar tomorrow, but he could go in early, get caught up. He didn't usually have to force the single-minded focus reserved for business.

But right now, watching Tori turn and walk back into the tavern, he had a feeling that focus was going to be more difficult to summon than usual.

Chapter 6

"You didn't hear a word I said."

The feminine words were uttered evenly enough. It was only experience that had James's sense of caution heightening. Raising his brows, he looked directly at his little sister and lied through his teeth. "Of course I did."

Analiese Tremaine Jones tossed her short blond curls and snorted. "Yeah, and pigs fly. I know you have a million things on your CEO mind, oh elder one, but maybe you could show a little interest in the way I'm going to save you about one point five million." After a pause she added, "And a smidgen of gratitude wouldn't be amiss, either."

Assuming what he hoped was a properly chastened expression, James folded his hands and recited the gist of her conversation. "You've figured a way to up the speed on the file-wiping software. Although it's only on paper right now, you're pretty sure you can accomplish the multiple overwrites at least twice as fast as it is currently, without using our new chip, which—you're right—will save us a nice bundle of change."

Her blue eyes, so like his own, narrowed at his glib summary. "And how did I say I was going to accomplish it?"

Neatly dodging that bullet, he gave a careless shrug. "Through genius, of course. I expected nothing less of you." To divert her from his lack of attention, he added, "You must have been here all night working on it. I can't imagine Jones is too happy about that."

Her smile was innocent. Too innocent. "Nice try, but we're still talking about you. It's not like you to be distracted when we've got this much going on. I mean, that's how a normal person would react." She delivered the dual compliment/insult with the smoothness of family. "Whereas you…you thrive on pressure and deadlines."

He reached out, yanked a curl before she could duck. "Brat. We're forty-eight hours from delivery of the Pentagon contract and within a week of the Technology Expo. I have just a few things on my mind."

"Mmm-hmm." Analiese twirled around in her chair, studied him speculatively. He reminded himself that this woman, despite her deceptively petite angelic looks, could put a bloodhound to shame if she caught wind of anything suspicious. "What about the bid on the newest Pentagon contract? They announce their selection soon, don't they?"

"They do, yes, but we'll be ready." Nothing, especially not some cryptic notes from an anonymous coward, was going to delay the bid. He made a mental note to speak to Jones about beefing up the security around their homes, and especially surrounding Ana. He wasn't willing to take a risk with her well-being.

She waited, but when he offered nothing more, she made

a face. "Secretive to the end, as usual." Giving a theatrical sigh, she switched topics. "What time did you come to work this morning? It was well before dawn, I know that."

"Early." He strolled past her, crouched down to look at her computer screen. Once he'd gotten home from Juicy's, there had been little chance of sleep. The information the man had given them triggered a seemingly endless stream of scenarios playing across his mind. Which just heightened his frustration, because he was no closer than before to finding definitive answers.

But that hadn't been what had had him bolting from his bed before the clock had struck three. Those hadn't been the only visions that had haunted him, keeping sleep at bay. Every time he'd shut his eyes, there'd been a sexy, sultry image of Tori drifting behind his eyelids. A memory of the faintly exotic taste of her. The way her body had fit perfectly against his. Followed, of course, by all the reasons she could never be in his arms again.

Since self-torture really wasn't his thing, it had seemed more productive to get up, dress and go to work. As Ana had pointed out, he certainly had enough going on here to keep him busy.

His fingers went to the keyboard, and he was immediately elbowed for his efforts. "No way, this is my baby." Slapping his hands away, she added, "You put me in charge, right?"

"Of course, but I was just…"

"…going to go back to your own office and leave me alone? Brilliant idea." Ana stood and gave him a small shove. "I'll let you know when I get this off paper and functioning. Should be before I leave this afternoon."

With real reluctance James tore his eyes from the keyboard. One of the most difficult lessons learned in running a company this size had been learning to delegate.

And it never got easier. "I'll check in later. I have a…an appointment. I'll be off property for a few hours."

Ana stopped shielding the keyboard with her body and surveyed him. "What kind of appointment?"

Back on familiar ground, he dropped a kiss on the top of her head. "One that's none of your business. I'll catch up with you tomorrow."

She fell back in her seat, folded her arms across her chest and stared at him, her suspicious little brain obviously clicking away. "What's wrong?"

Determining that discretion was definitely the better part of valor, he began moving to the door. "Nothing. Just a lot of irons in the fire."

"Which isn't out of the ordinary for you. So there's trouble or a woman. Which is it?"

"Save that imagination of yours for solving the overwipe problem. You're wasting it on me."

From the dejected look on her face, he'd managed to convince her. "Probably. I don't know what I was thinking… there hasn't been a woman born who could tear you away from work when you were busy. Not that we all wouldn't pay money to see you fall hard and fast, but…"

He closed the door with a quiet *snick,* effectively shutting her out. Unfortunately, he wasn't as successful at shutting out the thoughts conjured by her words.

It wasn't a woman dragging him away from work, he thought, striding back to his office. Ana was right, no female had ever had that kind of control over him. But there was a decades-old mystery to be solved, and damned if he was going to quit before he had all the answers.

The fact that Tori Corbett was all wrapped up in that mystery was just a detail he'd have to learn to ignore.

Tori leaned against the counter of Sanderson's Towing and Recovery and flipped through the papers the owner had obligingly dug out of the filing cabinet for her. He'd been obliging, at least, once she'd flashed a hundred-dollar bill in front of him. She didn't think Tremaine would worry overmuch about the cost of her cure for the man's reticence. He struck her as a man interested in results, and money had a nice way of eliciting cooperation.

Thoughts of what else had interested James Tremaine last night had the pages trembling in her hands and her focus on them blurring. She'd recovered, almost, from the rocketing response his touch had fired in her. But it would be a while longer before she was able to forgive herself for becoming a mass of stuttering hormones in his arms.

Her sudden scowl had the proprietor backing carefully away from the counter. Maybe she hadn't done herself any favors by steering clear of men since her divorce. Surely if she hadn't been abstinent for so long, she could have tempered her response a bit better. As it was, she was very much afraid that had it not been for the interruption, she'd have jumped the man's bones then and there.

And what an ignominious conquest that would have been, she silently jeered at herself. Ripping off James Tremaine's shirt in front on Juicy's, in one of the seediest neighborhoods that side of New Orleans. With her luck, some enterprising cameraman would have been around and the pictures could have been adorning this morning's tabloids. If mortification built character, they'd be erecting a freaking statue in her name right now.

Scanning the second paper in the file, she flipped it over to look at the next page. The only consolation she'd had in the long sleepless night that had followed their parting was that she'd been the one to step back. Eventually. And once she had, it hadn't taken long for sheer horror to replace the desire pumping through her veins. Getting involved with a client was inviting all sorts of seamy complications. Getting involved with James Tremaine in particular was about as bright as throwing herself in front of a fast-moving bus.

She'd lived, briefly and unhappily, in his monied sphere once. Or at least as close to it as she ever wanted to be. The people she'd met then, her ex and in-laws especially, had epitomized the term *shallow*. She'd encountered puddles deeper. She wasn't going to willingly dance the upper crust two-step ever again.

As the door opened behind her, her attention was captured by the sight of her dad's scrawled signature on the page. She slowed, read more carefully. It wasn't unexpected. In the file Tremaine had copied for her, there had been mention of this place, as well as the lack of any useful leads it had elicited. Still, there was an odd pang knowing she was following in his path, literally and figuratively.

Because her eyes wanted to mist, she blinked them rapidly before straightening to look at the man who'd joined her at the counter.

"Tori." The slightly intimate note to his voice jump-started her pulse, conjuring up a smoky image of their kiss last night. He must have come straight from the office, as he was fully decked out in corporate warrior mode. She recognized the Savile Row suit and Versace tie, but was forced to admit that in his case, the man definitely made the clothes, and not vice versa.

When she was certain her voice would be steady, she said, "Mr. Sanderson was kind enough to dig around for the records on the car's recovery." She nudged the pages toward James and waited as he thumbed through them, skimming quickly.

He looked up and flicked a glance at the apple-faced, narrow-shouldered man behind the counter. "You the owner?"

The man straightened, hitched up his pants. "That's right."

"You wouldn't have been at the time this car came in. Is your father still around?"

Sanderson pursed his lips. "Pa don't have much to do with the business anymore. He's semiretired."

"Is he around?"

"He's probably out back."

"Good. Get him." His words were repeated politely enough, but imbued with unmistakable command.

Tori watched the owner shuffle out the back door, into what was presumably a shop area. Irritation arrowed through her. Tremaine had managed to accomplish with two words what she knew intuitively would have cost her another fifty bucks. "Neat trick. Do you do magic, too?"

James slanted her a look as he spread the papers out to peruse. "I thought you were going to wait for me."

"Traffic wasn't too bad and I arrived sooner than expected." She inched away, just to give him room. Certainly not because she needed the physical distance between them. Nodding toward the papers, she added, "There's nothing of interest here. Just a record of the call and costs for towing and storing the car until it went to salvage. A notation made by the mechanic who conducted the physical examination. My dad collected the personal effects for you?"

"There wasn't much."

Sympathy stirred. The page hadn't detailed the contents of the box her father had picked up. The ladies would have had purses. Perhaps a shoe or two had jolted loose in the crash. She tried to suppress the mental image of James, barely more than a boy, receiving that box, symbolic of the responsibility that circumstances had thrust upon him.

The man that walked through the back door was

wiping his hands on a greasy cloth. Although his careful gait and the seams etched into his face bespoke at least eight decades, his gaze was alert enough as he surveyed them. "I'm Guy Sanderson. M'boy said you wanted to see me?"

"We wanted to ask you a few questions about a vehicle you recovered twenty years ago," Tori put in smoothly. She picked up the file folder and held it out so he could see the label on it.

Jamming the cloth into one hand, he reached the other deep into the pocket of his coveralls, drew out a pair of glasses. "Can't read a damn thing without my bifocals," he grumbled. "'Course at my age, I guess I'm lucky I still have my sight." He peered closely at the folder, moving his lips silently. Then he swung his head slowly from one side to the other. "Don't recall it exactly. Mebbe if I take a look at them papers…"

James pushed them together and handed them to him. But rather than taking them, the old man stared hard at him. "Seen you before," he said. "Take me a minute to recollect where…" He snapped his fingers. "I know. It was in them society pages my wife always has laying around. Fancy folk going to useless shindigs." He stared harder at James, and then studied the page lying on top of the papers.

"Tremaine." His gnarled fist thumped on the counter soundly. "Yep, I 'member now." He nodded sagely. "Nothing wrong with my memory, just takes longer to get it working at my age. Yer the one what runs that comp'ny nearby. We towed the wreckage from the accident what killed your folks. Terrible accident, that."

Tori sent James a quick look. If the older man's verbal meanderings had awakened bad memories, it didn't show in his expression. "That's what we wanted to talk to you about. The papers list every part you managed to sell off the car." The frame, two tires, axle rods, bumpers and windows had been a loss. Everything else imaginable had found a new home, down to the ash tray and cigarette lighter.

Sanderson nodded. "There's nothing left of it now, though. See?" With one bony index finger he stabbed at the faded imprint stamped across the top page. "It had been stripped down to its frame, and that was sprung so it was pretty worthless. When there's nothing useful left we sell it for scrap metal. This one has been gone for, oh…" He scratched his jaw, stared into space. "Seems like two, three years now."

Glancing at the date affixed below the stamp, Tori found he was correct. Maybe his memory would prove useful yet. "What about the front left fender? From the accident photos it appeared seriously damaged, yet you still managed to sell them."

"People look for something in better shape than what they got." The man shrugged. "It was pretty banged in but still had good to it."

"Do you remember the fender, specifically?" James crossed his arms, leaned against the counter. "Any idea what it had come in contact with?"

A shrug was his only answer. "Don't pay much attention to that kind of thing. I go over the vehicles once real good when we get them. Clean them up some." With a quick glance at James, he seemed to think better than to go into detail. "Make a note of what we can mebbe use and list it all down. That way when someone asks we can find the information real quick. Got us a computer 'bout ten years ago, and that makes the whole thing a lot easier, I can tell you."

"You don't remember seeing anything special about that

fender?" Tori probed further. "The accident report noted that it had slammed into a guardrail and then through it."

Raising his shoulders, Sanderson responded, "Don't recall any details about the car. Too long ago, and we handle nearly a hundred wrecked vehicles each year. Although seems like this was the one…" He started turning the pages, studying each of them intently. "Yep, I thought so." With a start, Tori realized he was pointing at her father's signature. "I 'member this fella. He's the one what collected the personal effects. Had him a signed release form. From you?" His gaze shifted to James.

At his nod, the man went on. "I remember it special 'cuz I ain't never seen one of them gadgets before. Never have since, tell ya the truth."

"What gadget might that be?"

She'd obviously spent too much time in Tremaine's company, Tori thought, because she was able to discern the sliver of impatience layered beneath the civility in his words.

"You know, that—what do you call it—tracking thing. Lets you follow whoever you plant it on. That was a first for me. Guess with your outfit into that high-tech security stuff, you're used to that sort of thing. If I could afford it," he mused, his gaze going faraway, "I'd get one of them things to plant on my braggin' dog. Tell ya, when it trees a coon it's all I can do to…"

"You're saying you found a tracking device in the car?" James's voice was precise, his expression still. But emotion emanated from him in waves. For some reason Tori was reminded of an explosive waiting to detonate. "How'd you know what it was?"

"I didn't, and that was a problem," Sanderson replied. "And I always did a detailed list of the effects I gathered from the car to return to the family, so's there's no confusion later about what was or wasn't in there. Had no idea what that thing was, so I had to ask."

"Who did you ask?" she questioned.

"The one who come and picked up the belongings. Made him sign for them." He stabbed a gnarled finger at the signature again. "Rob Landry was his name."

The room tilted and the floor seemed to shift beneath her feet. Tori tried to speak, found speech beyond her.

"You're sure?" James asked.

Sanderson nodded emphatically. "Dead sure. 'Member it clear as last week. When I fetched the box for him, I showed him that gadget, told him I'd been puzzling over it. He took a look at it and said right off the bat what it was. Guess he'd seen some before."

"That's impossible," Tori said flatly. She'd recovered her voice and with it came indignation. "You must be mistaken."

That drew a glare from the old man. "Missy, I might be old but my memory's in working order. How the heck would I have come up with the name for it when I'd never seen anything like it before?"

She opened her mouth to answer, but James beat her to it. "We want to thank you." He held out his hand, and after a moment the older man accepted it. "We've wasted enough of your time, but you've been very helpful."

Partially mollified, Sanderson gave a dismissive wave. "Not like I'm punching a clock these days. Y'all have a good trip back now."

Doing a slow burn, Tori waited until they were outside before pulling away from James's grasp on her elbow. "That's a load of bull. The man's obviously going senile." Her irritation made her strides long enough to keep up with James without problem.

"Maybe."

Certain she'd misheard him, she stopped in her tracks. "What? You can't believe that garbage. He even said he didn't know what it was that he'd found in the car."

The sun was brutal overhead, bringing an instant sheen of perspiration to her skin. With deliberate movements James slipped off his suit coat, folded it over his arm. "He also said your father identified it for him. Do you think he'd recognize a tracking device if he saw one?"

"He…" The question threw her off balance. "Yes, of course, but the fact that it wasn't included in Dad's report means that there's another explanation."

He inclined his head, slipped his free hand in his pants pocket. "I'm listening."

For some reason, his stance, his words, made her want to kick him. "Sanderson is probably mixed up. He must have been thinking of another vehicle, or this whole thing could be dementia induced. He's not exactly a spring chicken."

"True." The very reasonableness of his tone set her teeth on edge. "He seemed pretty sharp to me, though."

"If there was a tracking device in that car it would have been in Dad's report." Her tone was flat. "It's as simple as that. Who knows what happened? Maybe, and this is a big maybe, Dad thought that's what it was, but under further examination found he was wrong. There'd be no mention of it in the report if he'd mistakenly identified it."

The glare of the sun gilded his dark hair, streaking its inkiness with gold. "I think you're forgetting something. There was nothing in the box that even came close to fitting that description. I went through the whole thing. My mother's and Lucy's purses had opened and the contents were strewn across the inside of the car. I had to identify which belonged to my mother before bundling up Lucy's belongings for Marcus." He paused, as if ready for her protest, but she couldn't summon one. Not then. "There was nothing in that entire box that wasn't identifiable. That device, or whatever it was, wasn't included in it."

"You don't know that," she said stubbornly, "because you have no idea what it was Sanderson was referring to. Heck, who knows, maybe Dad was having fun with him. All I know is that I don't particularly care for what you're suggesting." She hadn't been aware that the volume of her voice had raised until he glanced around. Following his gaze, Tori saw they'd attracted the attention of a few people in the parking lot.

He took a step back. Voice clipped, he said, "There's no use having this discussion out in the sun when we can talk in air-conditioning." Without waiting to see whether she agreed, he turned, strode toward his car.

The air conditioner was already turned on when she yanked open the door, dropped into the passenger seat. And even churning out thick, warmish air, it was better than the temperature outside. It did nothing, however, to dispel the temper that was bubbling inside her.

"Let's look at this logically, shall we?" James released the steering column to move it out of his way and half turned in the seat to face her. "The messages, which may or may not be credible, suggested the accident might have been deliberate."

"One message," she muttered, his reasonable tone making her jaw clench. "The others didn't even mention it."

Ignoring her, he went on. "The expert that *you* lined up," his faint emphasis was unmistakable, "using pictures that *you* discovered also came up with some questions about the way the accident happened. Juicy came up with a pretty far-fetched possibility. But if he was anywhere close to the truth…"

He didn't go on. He didn't have to. A tracking device

could have alerted the killer to when the Tremaine car was coming, so the scene could be arranged in time.

The chill that broke out over her skin wasn't completely owed to the air-conditioning kicking in. "This whole thing is getting more far-fetched by the moment. Look, I know my dad. Integrity was his code. He would never have been involved in something shady, and he'd never double-cross a client. There has to be another explanation."

"There may be. But under the circumstances…" James took his wallet from his pocket, opened it and took out some bills. "Perhaps it would be best to part ways now."

His words acted as a sucker punch. Inwardly reeling, she stared dumbly, first at the bills, then at him. He spoke again, but it was hard to listen when the buzzing in her ears seemed to get louder by the moment.

"Ours was a trial relationship, remember? And upon reevaluation, I think it's best to terminate it. If nothing else, there's a possible conflict of interest here."

Fury, hot and ripe, clogged in her throat. And something else. Something that felt suspiciously like hurt. It took effort to nod, reach for a calm tone. "Because you think my dad might have sold you out twenty years ago. And me…I'd just do the same, is that it?"

Because she refused to reach for it, he dropped his hand, still holding the bills. "This isn't about you or me. You're reacting emotionally, but we have to consider the facts."

The knowledge that he was right did little to dissipate her anger. "Damn right I'm reacting emotionally. I tend to do that when someone calls my father a crook. Or worse, an accomplice to murder. But that's just me." She bared her teeth, fingers scrambling for the door handle. "You're right. It'd be better for both of us if we parted ways." She pushed the door open, swung out of the car. "And you can keep your money. I don't want it. I'll see this through on my own, and when I do find proof disputing your ridiculous scenario, I'm going to take great satisfaction in making you eat your words."

The heat scorched her the moment she stepped out of the car, shooting up from the soles of her feet to her brow. But it was nothing compared to the furnace that was stoked inside her. She needed to get away from this man, before she did something she'd regret. Like going for his throat.

She ran to her car nearby. But when she went to open the door James was already there, his palm pressed flat against the window. Gone was the cool reason he'd just treated her to as he'd dismissed her. Gone was any semblance at civility. Menace shimmered from him in waves. "You're off this case, Tori. All the way off. You no longer work for me in any capacity, and that means you won't be doing any investigating in this or related issues. It's over."

Jutting her chin out, she met his narrowed blue gaze. No doubt competitors quaked beneath it. But she wasn't so easily cowed. "Wrong, ace. I may no longer work for you, but I can investigate whatever I damn well please. And I will. The only difference is, I no longer have to keep you posted about my findings. Now get your hand off my door, unless you want to chance losing it."

His piercing regard didn't waver. His mouth was flat and grim. "You don't want to piss me off, Tori. I make a dangerous enemy."

She didn't need his words to know that. The man was dangerous, regardless of the nature of the relationship. It was just too damn bad that her defenses, usually so reliable, had turned to putty about the time he'd walked into her office.

Her smile brittle, she fumbled for sunglasses, jammed them on her nose. "Surprise, surprise. Here's a news flash for you. You make an even more dangerous employer. You strike me as the kind of man who knows when to cut his losses. This is a battle you can't win. I'm looking into my father's part of this investigation, and there's nothing you can do to stop me."

She shoved his hand off her car, and surprisingly he let her. Yanking open the door, she slid into its suffocating heat and turned the key in the ignition. "You have far better things to worry about than me, anyway. Like the person who wants you dead. You might want to concentrate your energies on that instead of wasting them defaming a dead man's reputation."

And with that she slammed the door and drove off.

Chapter 7

He'd handled her badly.

The knowledge ate at James, making the trip back to his company seem longer than it should have. He'd managed more tact when firing people, even while sending them away with a lukewarm reference and a dismissive severance package. Hell, he'd dispatched ex-lovers with more finesse.

And that, really, was what gnawed at his gut now. He'd wounded her with his words. She hadn't been able to disguise the hurt in her eyes. That sight, and knowing he'd been responsible for it, sent a sneaky blade of guilt through him.

Expertly he guided the car through the twisting parish back roads, for once taking no pleasure at the vehicle's smooth handling. The fact was that Tori Corbett drew a response from him that he wasn't always able to control. Which was another reason it made good sense to cut off all contact with her. The one thing he insisted upon in his life, both personal and business, was restraint.

Tori threw a wrench into that, and even worse, she represented far more complications than he wanted to contemplate. Of all the possible situations he'd envisioned when he'd decided to reopen this case, somehow he hadn't considered that the P.I. he'd hired twenty years earlier might not have been honest with him. That he might have discovered information suggesting the accident was anything but, and then covered it up.

The countryside zipped by with a blurring speed reflective of his thoughts. There were too few facts and far too many possibilities. But if Sanderson was right and there had been a tracking device found in the car, that would dovetail neatly with the spin Juicy had put on things yesterday. It would lend more credence to the prospect that the "accident" had been anything but. Landry knowing about the device and keeping it from James would be, at best, incompetent.

And at worst, criminal.

Jumping to conclusions wasn't a sport he usually engaged in. He reached for his sunglasses, flipped them open with one hand and settled them on his nose. Solutions were best arrived at after a careful analysis of all the data. Then options could be weighed and a specific course of action selected. But the one thing this case was short on was data. How the hell did he do an analysis when every day brought more questions than answers?

He'd made the decision to check into the warning messages based only upon the reference to his parents' accident. And although he hadn't yet discovered a smoking gun, enough troubling questions had arisen to warrant a continuation.

Without the help of Tori Corbett.

He pressed more firmly on the accelerator, unmindful for the moment of the posted speed limit. It was the best decision. The *only* decision. He couldn't blame her for defending her father's reputation. Hell, maybe she was even right. He could appreciate her loyalty to family, but he couldn't take the chance that it would blind her to discovering the truth. In her desire to clear her father's name, she might overlook something. Or worse, keep something from him that placed Landry in an even worse light.

This time, regardless of the outcome, he was determined that all doubts would be put to rest, for good. He had to ensure the integrity of the investigation. And the only way to do that would be to start over, with another investigative company.

It would mean bringing another P.I. up to speed but that shouldn't waste more than a day or so. He had plenty of contacts in the field. Finding someone to replace Tori wouldn't be a problem. In fact, it would eliminate more than a few. A man wouldn't present the distraction she had, and certainly wouldn't include a connection to Rob Landry that had so suddenly and completely complicated this case.

No, he could replace Tori easily enough.

But even as he had the thought, an unwanted memory flashed through his mind. Of the moments he'd had her in his arms, the surge of heat, the sudden, urgent punch of desire. He wasn't used to a simple kiss stirring up need quite so quickly. Wasn't used to fighting the temptation to ignore a lifetime of control for the promise he'd tasted in her.

He glanced down, vaguely surprised to see the speedometer had crept up past eighty. It was easy enough to speed in a car like this, but he was usually better at choosing the place and time to do so.

Deliberately he slowed to a more moderate pace, and set the cruise control. When this was over, he'd take some time, shed obligation for a while and indulge...various passions. Maybe take his sailboat down to the Gulf and spend a week battling wits with the tide and the wind. To enjoy the theater with an attractive, intelligent woman, and share Sunday brunch in bed with her the next morning. In short, to get back to a life that recently had become devoid of much besides business.

But before that could happen he had duties to perform. He was too accustomed to the mantle of responsibility to feel its burden overmuch. There were details to attend to at work, and his highly honed competitive edge wasn't going to accept anything less than the awarding of this latest contract he'd bid on. Once he'd hired a new investigator, he would have to rethink his other obligations, delegate where he could and begin planning for the next project.

The art of delegation had been one he'd learned under duress, but it was a necessary skill in his field. He was still reluctant to put the investigation of his parents' accident solely in the hands of another, however. What would have happened if Tori had been the one to go to Sanderson's alone? Would he have ever heard about the tracking device being found in the car?

Jaw tightening, he decided that there was no way to be certain. But surely with a different operative on the case, one with no personal stake in it one way or another...

A sudden thought hit him then, wiped his mind clean. There was no denying that Tori's stake was intensely personal. Intensely emotional. So he couldn't bring himself to believe that she wouldn't do exactly as she'd vowed, and continue investigating on her own.

His blood abruptly iced. She'd been maddeningly correct when she'd asserted he couldn't stop her.

The only difference is, now I don't have to keep you posted about my findings.

She was right, damn her. The realization hammered at him, taunting and persistent. There was really very little he could do to prevent her from poking about wherever she chose. He was neatly, irrevocably, trapped. The fact that he was constrained by his own decisions didn't make the matter easier to swallow. Firing Tori hadn't solved his problem, it had compounded it. Because with no way to keep her from continuing on her own, all he'd managed to do was to ensure he had no access to whatever she discovered.

He cursed, long and fluently, then set his mind to doing what he did best; figuring the angles, planning strategy. Hiring another investigator would guarantee the case was still being looked into, but it wouldn't gain him access to the progress she was making. Her connection to Rob Landry complicated this case all too hell.

And it also represented the closest link he'd find to the dead man himself. With a feeling of resignation mingled with anticipation, he reached for his cell phone.

James's intercom buzzed as he was sorting through the piles of mail Celia had efficiently bundled on his desk. "Mr. Jones to see you, sir."

His mouth quirked. There was very little his secretary didn't handle with equanimity, but it was obvious from the slight inflection in her voice that she still didn't know what to make of Ana's new husband. Big, tough and battle-scarred, the man's past was shrouded in mystery. What was known was that he'd been running a charter boat business in the tropics when Analiese had hired him for a secret caper that still had the power to make James's blood run cold. He'd managed to keep Ana safe while they dodged a corrupt country's military, and for that, James was willing to looking beyond the man's shadowy past and accept him as his brother-in-law.

It was an undeniable bonus that the man possessed skills gained in that unspoken past that came in handy at Tremaine Technologies, and that his wife had convinced him to sell his boat and utilize them.

"Send him in." Going to work on the pile of mail laid neatly on his desk, he reached for an envelope opener as his office door opened.

Jones entered the room, eyed the blade in his hand. "Going armed now?"

James held it up. "After making Ana work all night, I thought I might need a weapon when I saw you again."

Grunting, the other man dropped into a chair before his desk. "No one makes my wife do anything she doesn't want to, so I figure she couldn't tear herself away from the project. But from now on, I told her she was to call me for a ride. I don't like her on the roads after she's been up all night. She nearly got sideswiped by a truck on her way home this afternoon."

Everything inside James abruptly froze. "Did she get a look at the driver?"

His brother-in-law rubbed his jaw. "Hell, I doubt it. She probably wasn't at her best, running on no sleep. She just didn't see the guy coming until he was right on top of her. She was pretty shaken up when she called. Matter of fact, I was going to head home as soon as I talked to you."

It probably had nothing to do with the threats. James told himself that, and almost believed it. "Did she think it might be deliberate?"

Jones stared at him, his face going grim. "Any reason to believe it might have been?"

James set the envelope in his hand down on his desk. "Probably not, but I want everyone around here to be extra careful. There have been…threats. Nothing specific," he added, not quite honestly, when he saw the man's expression. "They're aimed at me, but I don't want to take any chances. Can you make sure she travels to and from work with you for a while?"

"Yeah, but she's gonna kick unless I tell her the truth."

Considering that, James nodded. "With everything we've got going on right now, we make a bigger target than usual. You can tell her there have been some anonymous messages. We're just being careful."

Jones's scrutiny was implacable. "The threats are directed at you?"

"It's not the first time." The words were no more than the truth. The only difference this time was the reference to his parents. And he definitely wasn't ready to make that known to his family. "Because Ana works here, she should be extra cautious. You, too."

"I'll tighten the security on the grounds," Jones said. "And you better start taking precautions, too. Use different cars each day. Take different routes."

"I know the drill." He'd walked this path before, in times where the threats were more certain, the intent more deadly. Compared to those situations, these messages were almost too nebulous to take seriously.

Except for the note about his parents. And now that it seemed as though there just might be something to the assertion in that note, perhaps he was going to have to treat all the messages with a bit more credulity.

"Wouldn't hurt to take the limo around for a while,"

Jones suggested laconically. "With the armored doors and reinforced glass, it's a bit safer. I'll make sure it's inspected each day."

James grimaced, ripped open another envelope. With only a glance at its contents, he placed it in a pile for Celia to deal with. One of the things he hadn't yet learned to delegate was letting someone else have first look at the mail. It seemed easier for him to do it, and then to pass the pieces on to whichever employee necessary.

Belatedly he realized Jones was waiting for a reply. "Let's wait a while longer on that." He preferred driving himself, and would continue to do so for as long as possible. "All our cars are protected by Safe-T, which reduces some of the risks." The Safe-T system, their own creation, sounded an alarm if anyone touched the vehicle.

"Okay." His brother-in-law stood and shot him a rare grin. "But once Ana finds out what's going on, you might have to change your mind about that. And a lot of other things." He sounded as though the prospect of his wife taking on her oldest brother gave him a great deal of pleasure. James didn't doubt his assertion. Though she was the youngest by several years, there wasn't a one of the Tremaine males who didn't tread warily to stay off Analiese's radar. She was as fiercely protective of them as they had always been of her. He refused to consider her frequent assertion that it was no more than they deserved.

He sliced into another piece of mail, slipped the letter out and perused it. "You could do me a favor and try and keep your wife in check." The suggestion sounded too much like a plea, even to his own ears. "Try to deflect her attention away from this news if you can." The letter was placed in a pile to be routed to Marcus later.

"Sorry, pal." Jones sounded anything but. "But I'd sooner get between a mama bear and her cub. No matter how I play it, when she hears about these threats, you're going to have to handle her." He walked through the door. "'Fraid you're on your own when it comes to dealing with the fallout."

He was entirely too old to experience this feeling of dismay at the possibility, James thought, sorting rapidly through the rest of the mail. But the response he was about to make went unuttered as his hand froze in the act of reaching for the next piece in the pile.

A plain white envelope labeled with his name, with no return address.

She should have told him to go to hell, Tori fumed, as she followed the guard silently up to James Tremaine's offices. The urge to do just that when he'd called had been overpowering. But he had a habit of overriding everything he didn't want to hear. It would be so much more satisfying to do it in person, she consoled herself. To listen to his "proposition" and then tell him, in succinct terms, just where he could stick it.

The elegance of the building's interior was lost on her this time. She was too busy thinking of all the ways she'd like to see Tremaine suffer. Like staking him out on a slug-infested anthill. Or, likely more painful for him, to take a well-honed knife to his closet of European suits. Preferably while he was wearing one of them.

"Ms. Corbett, sir."

Ignoring the guard, Tori walked into James's office carrying the sheaf of papers she'd brought with her. As she swung the door closed behind her, she fixed the man behind the desk with a disparaging glare.

"Tori. Thank you for coming. I wasn't certain that you would."

If the warm smile and civil tone were meant to soften her, they failed miserably. "Really?" Her voice was mocking.

"And here I was under the impression that you're quite used to getting exactly what you want, when you want it."

"You'd be surprised. Where you're concerned, I'm not certain of much. Come and look at this."

Her gaze dropped to his desktop and her stomach abruptly hollowed out. Without hesitation she rounded his desk, peered at the note with its typed message:

"Withdraw your bid or be the next in your family to die."

For the moment, her irritation with him was forgotten. "This came today?" At his nod, she said, "What bid do you think it refers to? The new one coming up with the Pentagon?"

"It has to be. It's the only one on the horizon that matters." He stared at the note for a moment. "I'm beginning to believe that was the purpose of these messages all along. To serve as a distraction from the business at hand."

"Except that it's looking as if the sender might have been right, and maybe your parents' accident was deliberate. Does that mean he made a lucky guess, or did he have actual knowledge of what happened twenty years ago?"

"That's exactly what we're going to find out."

She was transfixed by the transformation of his expression. The cool, savvy businessman wore a feral mask that was as chilling as it was startling. It took a moment for his words to register, but when they did, she straightened and took a step back. "We? Uh-uh, buddy, you fired me, remember? My only stake in this mess now is clearing my dad's name."

He swung the chair to face her, his hands clasped calmly across his chest. "You're here," he pointed out. "Perhaps only from an urge to take a swing at me, but you did come. That tells me you're at least willing to listen to what I have to say."

The sting of his words wasn't lessened by the fact that they were true. However satisfying it would have been to hang up on him earlier, his request had tugged at her curiosity. Because she couldn't refute his words, she stalked to a chair, sat and slid to a more comfortable position. "It's your party, ace."

"It occurred to me that our purposes aren't completely at odds." He'd slipped into CEO mode, all shrewd logic and reason. "There's no reason we can't continue to work together, keeping certain details in mind."

"It occurred to you that you couldn't stand not knowing what I was up to," she disputed. "You could afford to hire an army of P.I.s, if you weren't particularly concerned about discretion, any number of whom are capable of conducting this investigation. But they couldn't run the assignment and keep track of what I might be discovering."

There was the slightest smile on his face. She decided it didn't soften his expression at all. Especially not while his eyes remained speculative. "Yes. I think perhaps I was too hasty when I suggested we terminate our partnership."

"And now, knowing that you think the worst of my father, and of me, I'm supposed to forgive and forget and join up with you again, just because you're afraid I might discover something your new guy doesn't?" She pretended to consider the thought for a moment before suggesting, "Bite me."

"The invitation doesn't lack appeal. But our arrangement could be mutually advantageous. If it is discovered that my parents' deaths was murder, it will become a police matter. From there, it's inevitable that publicity will ensue. I can make sure your father's name is kept out of the resulting media frenzy." His regard was direct, the aim of his words on target. "I can tell you from experience that reputations are fragile things. And the taint of scandal is difficult to remove, especially for a man already dead."

The insinuation was impossible to miss. She let out a bitter laugh. "You son of a bitch. Are you threatening me? You'll put your own spin on things, implicating my father, if I don't agree to help you now? You're unbelievable."

"I didn't exactly say that."

"You implied it." She couldn't remember when she'd hated a man more. And it was strangely ironic that right now she was burning with far more righteous indignation than she had when she'd walked in on her ex playing mattress tag with the empty-headed beauty queen. There was just something about James Tremaine that inspired the most violent reactions.

"What do our reasons matter, really, as long as we both get what we want? You get the answers you're looking for, and I remain apprised of all your discoveries."

His voice was reasonable. Too reasonable. "To be sure I don't hide something, you mean." She tried to match his cool by shoving emotion aside and considering his offer. "I want your offer in writing."

"You'll have it."

Tori wasn't thrilled with the idea. She'd been free of him, for a few hours at least. But she hadn't been free of doubts—or of a niggling fear that she didn't even want to admit to. She was still convinced that Sanderson had made a mistake. But she wasn't willing to chance her father's reputation being smeared forever.

"All right." Trepidation knotted in her gut.

"Did you bring the information on insurance companies that I asked for?"

Without a word she got up, dropped the papers she'd brought on his desk. He picked them up, flipped through them quickly. "We've got work to do. Follow me."

He rose from his desk and strode to a door on the opposite side of the room. She remembered him using it one other time, the first time she'd come here, trying to land this assignment. With every fiber of her being, she wished she'd never made the decision to do so.

Trailing after him, she stopped short in the doorway, gaped. What she'd assumed was a file storeroom of some sort was, in fact, a smaller office space. It too was lined with computers and peripheral devices whose functions she could only guess at.

"Isn't this a little redundant?"

He'd already placed the papers she'd given him next to a computer and sat down in front of it. "The existence of this space is, of course, covered under the confidentiality clause you signed. Are we agreed?"

"Of course," she said stiffly. But her mind was racing. She knew just enough about technology to have a glimmer of what he was planning, without being completely sure it was even possible.

"This looks like a hacker's paradise. Please tell me that you're not planning on breaking into databases."

"It's not strictly 'breaking in' if they leave a way to infiltrate it." His smile was wicked and, if she wasn't mistaken, laced with anticipation.

He was gazing at the computer screen, fingers already dancing over the keyboard.

"But is it legal?" There was a tickle on the back of her nape, and she looked around uneasily.

"'Legal' is relative."

"Yeah, but jail isn't. What is it exactly you're looking for, anyway?"

This time he did stop, and looked up at her. "I'm going to shift my focus a bit. What if the accident really was murder? What would the motive be?"

On surer ground now, she got up to pace. "Motives for murder are pretty concrete. Greed—for power or money—jealousy. There are variations on those themes, of course, but that's pretty much what it boils down to."

"So we'll tackle those motives one at a time. Greed for power would point to one of my father's competitors. And we'll get to them later." There was a note that had entered his voice that sent a shiver skating down her arms. "But right now we're checking out money."

She stopped midstride, jerked to look at him. "You're checking to see who benefited from your parents' deaths twenty years ago?"

"It's a long shot," he concurred, switching his attention back to the screen. "But anyone can buy an insurance policy on anybody, and since the settlements aren't public information, the only way to be sure is to look for myself."

"What's the sentence for hacking these days?" she asked. In spite of herself, she went behind him and looked over his shoulder. With a shock she realized he was already in to the files of the first insurance company on the list. She checked her watch. It had taken him all of about three minutes. "Lucky for the world that you decided to turn your skills to good instead of evil."

"Companies like these don't even make it challenging." He sounded more than a little disappointed. "I'm going to print out the files and you can start checking through them for the names and dates we're looking for." The printer began to whir as it began the task.

"Aren't there ways for them to tell someone has been in their files? What if they trace this back to you?"

"This computer is totally secure. And all of my equipment is protected by a dandy little firewall I designed myself. Any attempt to probe this computer and there'll be a nasty little virus sent back along the path the hackers use, trashing a lot of expensive equipment at the other end."

Reaching for the first printed sheet, Tori took the highlighter James handed her and set to work. "Well, at least you trust me this much."

"I'll double-check it later."

She gave a bitter little smile. His focus on the screen before him was absolute, his tone offhand. But she knew exactly what he meant. They may be partners again, but nothing had really changed at all. He still didn't trust her.

And she certainly didn't trust him.

Chapter 8

Tori found it difficult to gauge the passage of time, holed up in the windowless room. She rubbed her eyes, which seemed to be on fire after hours of perusing the printouts. She slid a gaze at James, seated next to her. He'd finished his sneak computer attacks on the list of insurance companies an hour earlier. Some had merged, resulting in name changes, which had required some research to discover. Two had gone out of business altogether. But he'd successfully infiltrated the rest, with an ease that bordered on the criminal. She tried not to think about the jail sentence that would be leveled at an accomplice to the crime. Not to mention the threat to her license if his acts were ever discovered.

Integrity, above all else.

Her dad's voice sounded in her head, as clear as if he were standing next to her. And in that moment she knew she'd risk anything, everything, to prove to Tremaine that he hadn't sold him out all those years ago. She wasn't going to let the man beside her destroy her father's memory.

With renewed purpose she returned to the printouts. She'd run through them first and highlighted all the settlement dates that would be in the right time period. Now she was looking for names, but despite her brief respite, the words still insisted on blurring on the pages. She'd actually turned a page and started on the next before belated comprehension registered. Flipping back a sheet, she ran her finger down the list until she came to the one she was seeking.

Frowning, she asked, "Who's Dale Cartwright?"

James looked up. She noticed, with a touch of irritation, that other than heavier-than-normal eyelids, which somehow on him just managed to look sexy, he didn't show any effects of pulling an all-nighter. While she'd spent half the night running a hand through her hair, which was probably even now standing on end, his looked perfectly groomed. Tori was fairly certain her clothes looked as though they'd been worn for a week. He'd shed his suit jacket and rolled up his sleeves, but somehow managed to still look fresh. She decided in that moment that she could hate a man like that.

"He was my father's partner."

"What?" Surprise quickly turned to annoyance. "You never told me your father had a partner when he died."

"He didn't. Although they'd started the business together, my father had bought Dale out three or four years earlier. Why?"

As an answer, she shoved the paper at him, pointed halfway down the list. "His settlement upon your father's death was almost as large as that of your family's."

James studied the paper for a moment. "I remember that my father had one on him, as well. It's not uncommon for business partners to take out policies on each other. That way they can afford to buy out the estate's interest in the company after the death. They had a contract drawn up giving each other that right."

Tori made an attempt to smooth back her hair. "Is he still alive?"

Nodding, James added the man's name to the list he'd kept of those receiving settlements. "When they parted ways, he started a company of his own, on a much smaller scale. He focused on providing security officers to businesses and gated communities, and didn't do much with technology. He's been retired for about five years or more."

When she didn't say anything, merely looked at him, his voice grew testy. "He's my godfather, Tori, and a close family friend. I don't know how we would have coped after the accident if he hadn't been there for us."

Their relationship was an intensely personal one. She understood that. She also understood that it couldn't be allowed to blind them to the possibilities. With as much diplomacy as she could muster, she said, "Let's see what we've got so far."

After a moment he slid the list he'd made over to her. The largest settlement by far had gone to the surviving children. "Who was the trustee of your estate?"

"My grandmother. She moved in with us after the accident and still rules the house with a genteel iron fist." Obvious affection laced his tone. "It couldn't have been easy raising a second family, but with the help of the willow tree in the backyard she managed just fine."

"The willow tree?"

His expression was wicked. "The branches make pretty slick switches. My brothers were on the wrong end of more than their share of them. Since I was older and much better behaved, I escaped that particular brand of discipline."

"Humph." She wasn't buying it. "You were probably just sneakier." But he was several years older than any of his siblings. And the death of his parents had probably meant instant adulthood for him.

Since his grandmother made an unlikely suspect, she moved on to the next name on the list. "Marcus Rappaport, Lucy's husband, received a twenty-five-thousand-dollar settlement upon his wife's death."

"And he donated most of that to the library. There's a plaque bearing her name in the most recent addition." He shook his head. "Well, I knew it was a long shot. I think this lead was a bust."

"Maybe." Although she strove for a noncommittal tone, his expression grew instantly wary.

"What are you suggesting, Tori, that my grandmother had her own son and daughter-in-law bumped off so she could share the joy of raising four young heathens?"

She refused to rise to the bait. "I'm suggesting that enough money can make people do unforgivable things. And your godfather received a large sum of money after the accident. A policy the size of the one he had on your father would have had a pretty hefty monthly premium. Seems to me after they separated he had quite a few years to relieve himself of that expense. Why didn't he?"

"I don't know." And it was apparent from his expression that the uncertainty didn't sit well with him. "But if he was out to make a bundle of money, it's doubtful he'd wait for three or four years to do so."

He might be right. Or Cartwright might have wanted just to deflect any suspicion from him. "Did your father and he part amicably?"

James jerked a shoulder impatiently. "I was fourteen or

fifteen at the time. I barely remember hearing my parents talking about it. Dale was in California when the accident happened, though, I do recall that. He was one of the first people I called. He took a red-eye flight back and was at our place by dawn."

She didn't point out that being half a continent away made for a very solid alibi. Or that the alibi didn't mean he hadn't ordered someone else to do the dirty work for him. She straightened up the papers before her, bundling them with paper clips. "It's difficult to have suspicion cast on someone you love," she said simply. From his struck expression, she knew her words had found their target. It was a moment before he spoke again.

"You're right. And we can't allow emotion to cloud our judgment." With deliberate movements he tore the list he'd made off the legal pad and folded it, slipping it into his pocket. "I'll check around. See what I can find out about the details of Dale and my father's separation."

It was a peace offering of sorts, she supposed. He didn't relish the thought of it any better than she enjoyed him entertaining ideas about her father betraying him. His vow didn't make it any easier to swallow his distrust of her dad. But it did make her like him a bit better.

She rubbed her face and yawned hugely. "I'm beginning to believe that you run on batteries, but my energy wore out a couple hours ago. Since it looks like we're done here for now, I'm heading home to get some sleep."

A quick look of concern passed over his face. "You can't drive back to New Orleans now. You'll fall asleep at the wheel."

"I'll stop for a tall coffee and put Bruce Springsteen on full blast," she promised. But in truth she was dreading the drive. Right now she wanted nothing more than to fall face-first on the nearest horizontal piece of furniture and sleep for ten hours.

He stood and went to the door, pushed it open and waited for her to precede him into his outer office. She was shocked to see that it was later, or earlier, than she'd assumed. Dawn had come and gone, and the early-morning sun was shining through his office windows.

"I'll take you to my place."

She gave a startled laugh. "To the Tremaine estate? You've got to be kidding."

The expression on his face said he was dead serious. "Be reasonable. You haven't slept in twenty-four hours. You're swaying on your feet as it is."

The idea of sleeping down the hallway from James Tremaine, or even in the same building, made her blood heat and panic claw in her stomach.

"Thanks, anyway, but I don't think so. I'll pull over on the road if I get too tired and nap awhile." She would have promised to push the car back to New Orleans if that's what it would take to shake him from this idea.

"You're staying with me." His tone was final. "I'd never forgive myself if something happened—" His gaze went beyond her, toward the door, and his brows rose. "Don't you knock anymore?"

Tori turned to follow the direction of his gaze and saw a petite blonde standing in the doorway of the office, head cocked to one side, surveying them. Despite her bright head of hair and diminutive stature, Tori identified her instantly. This would be James's younger sister, Analiese. The woman's bright-blue gaze, so like her brother's, was a dead giveaway.

"Actually, I did knock. You must not have heard me." Despite her brother's unwelcoming tone, or perhaps because of it, she strolled into the room.

"Ana, I'm in the middle of something here. I'll get back to you in a half hour."

Ignoring the command in James's tone, the woman approached Tori, stuck out her hand. "He really has exquisite manners when he cares to use them. I'm Ana Jones, James's sister. And you are?"

"Tori Corbett." Ana's handshake was quick and firm. At five-ten, Tori was never more uncomfortable than when standing next to tiny women like this. She had a brief mental image of herself as a gangling giraffe, neck awkwardly bobbing above a sleek, petite feline. It took a conscious reminder not to slouch, in an effort to shave off a few inches. She was only marginally successful.

"So." Ana's bright smile didn't hide the speculation in her eyes. "You must have gotten here early. It's barely light out."

"Ah…" Tori sent a wild glance at James, but he only folded his arms across his chest, an enigmatic expression on his face. "We…ah…had business and, um, worked late."

Ana's sweeping gaze took in her wrinkled clothes and unkempt hair. "I see." It was apparent that she did see. Too much. And was drawing her own conclusions about it.

Tori had just opened her mouth to set her straight when James reached out, brushing her cheek as he pushed a strand of hair away from her face. The gesture was indulgent, unfamiliar and shockingly intimate. "I'm afraid I mussed your hair. I'll have to make that up to you. Later." The promise in his voice, in his eyes, fogged her brain and heated her blood. Both made it damn hard to think coherently. And maybe that was his intent, because it left her speechless.

He shifted his attention to Ana, casually draping his arm around Tori's shoulders. "Out, brat. I'll talk to you later."

"Oh, you will." Looking pointedly at his arm, she smirked, turned to leave. "You definitely will."

The door was closed behind her before Tori found her voice. "What the hell was that?" With a violent shrug, she dislodged his arm, took a step back. "She's going to think that we're…that we…"

"Yes." His face was coolly amused as he listened to her stutter. "She is. Ana has always displayed too much interest in my personal life. And she has an unfortunate habit of making her opinions on it known. She's also an incurable romantic. With very little effort we can have her thinking we're sleeping together."

Although she'd been mentally heading toward that conclusion herself, hearing him utter it was like taking a fast jab to the solar plexus. Needing a little distance, she turned, put a chair between them before facing him again, her hands clutching its back. "She may be a romantic, but she doesn't look stupid. I'm hardly your type."

He rolled his sleeves down his arms and fastened the cuffs, while watching her calmly. "And what type is that?"

"I don't know." She jerked a shoulder, reached for a sliver of coherence. "Tall, glamorous and empty-headed. The kind to fill her days doing good works and her nights doing you."

His mouth twitched, once, before he firmed it. "You're tall," he pointed out. "And from what I can tell, you do good work."

She looked at him suspiciously, but if that last was meant to be an innuendo, she couldn't tell from the bland expression on his face. "You know what I mean. There's no way she's going to buy that, and why would you want her to? What's the point?"

"Think about it. I'll admit I hadn't given it a great deal

of thought until she barged in here—another unfortunate habit of hers—and found us together. But this can suit our purposes exactly." He went to a low cabinet behind his desk and opened it, revealing a minifridge. Withdrawing two bottles of water, he returned, handed her one. "We're going to need a reason for us to be together all the time. Letting people think we're seeing each other fills that need admirably."

"No," she told him succinctly. "It doesn't. It makes me look like a sap. You can just tell her—tell everybody—that I'm a…consultant, or something. We're consulting on a new project."

James sat on the arm of the chair whose back she was still clutching with white-knuckled desperation. "Since people around here are very aware of all of our projects, that explanation won't wash. My idea, on the other hand, gets you in to every event I attend with no questions asked. The Technology Expo is in three days. Simon Beal will be there, as will every other major and minor player in the business. I assumed you'd want to attend, as well, but maybe I was wrong." He twisted off the cap of his bottle, took a drink.

His words stopped her, but only for a minute. "I can get a fake press pass. That'd give me a better motive for moving around and conversing with the participants, anyway."

He nodded, as if her idea made sense. Taking another long pull from his bottle, he lowered it to inquire, "And how will you explain that to my sister? Especially after telling her we were in here 'consulting' all night?"

Tori opened her mouth, snapped it shut. The man was never more annoying, she decided, than when he was right. "I'll think of something." Because there was no chance she was going to miss the opportunity to talk to Beal and several of James's other competitors. She wanted to make her own observations; draw her own conclusions. She didn't fool herself into thinking that James had given up suspecting her dad of betraying him. Whoever was behind these notes could probably point them to the truth of the matter, and in doing so, clear her dad's name. That had become almost as important to her as making sure the anonymous sender didn't make good on his threats against James's life.

"The expo's by invitation only," James informed her. There was a wicked glint in his eye that warned of a man accustomed to getting his own way. "Security's pretty tight."

A sudden suspicion occurred to her. "Just who puts on the expo anyway?"

"This particular one happens to be sponsored by Tremaine Technologies."

A sense of resignation filled her, but she wasn't about to give up so easily. "I'm going home to grab a few hours' sleep and I'll call you later, when I'm thinking more clearly."

He went to his desk, pressed a button and leaned closer to the intercom to say, "Tucker, grab someone and come to my office, will you please?" Straightening, he corrected, "I'll have someone drive you home since you refuse to stay. Sleep's a good idea. I'll pick you up at six."

Tori had the sensation of being on a rapidly sinking ship. "That won't be necessary." Surely it was sleep deprivation that wiped her mind completely clean of even one logical argument. "I'll call you when I've come up with a plan. There's a better way to work this out. You'll see."

A knock sounded on James's door and he nodded agreeably. "You're right. I think this is going to work out admirably." And then he was guiding her out the door, handing her over to the two polite young men standing outside it and giving orders to have them drive her back to New Orleans. But as she was being led away she was fully aware that he hadn't given up. And she needed to come up with one heck of a strategy to avoid playing along with the deception he had contrived.

Because even pretending to be involved with James Tremaine was too dangerous to her state of mind to consider.

"Funny, with your background in technology, that you should be so averse to using a device as simple as a telephone."

James grinned at Tori's caustic tone and held up the cartons he'd picked up from a nearby Chinese restaurant. "I brought a peace offering. Are you going to refuse to let me in?"

For a moment he thought she was going to do just that. Then her gaze lingered on the cartons for long enough to ease his mind. Unlatching the screen door, she swung it open. "Don't think you're going to get your own way by buying me Chinese, Tremaine. I have higher standards than that."

"I wouldn't dream of it. Not when I know that all it takes to buy you is Hornets tickets, courtside. But I thought our discussion would be more fruitful on full stomachs." Walking past her, he went to her kitchen and set the cartons on the table. Opening up her cupboards and drawers until he found plates and silverware, he set the table with swift movements. He looked up then, found her standing in the doorway contemplating him. James couldn't say exactly why he found her wary expression so appealing. He pulled out a chair, indicated for her to sit.

When she'd done so, albeit slowly, he began opening

cartons, deftly spooning food onto her plate. "Did you get some sleep?"

She grabbed his hand before he could make the mound on her plate any higher. "Yes. And I've been feeding myself for a few years now. I think I can manage."

Circling the table, he sat opposite her and reached for the cartons. "I'm sure that brain of yours has been clicking away all afternoon. Let's hear what you've come up with."

Picking up a fork, she began digging into the food on her plate with obvious appetite. "You'll have to put your male ego on hold for this idea, but give it a chance. I think we can introduce me as your personal bodyguard."

The food he was attempting to swallow abruptly threatened to choke him. It took several moments before he could manage. "I'm assuming you're skilled in that area."

"I am, yes. And you said your company was expanding in that field, so it seems a logical explanation."

He pretended to consider it, and to keep his mind firmly away from the more personal implications of the term. "Of course, Jones is in charge of that department, so my hiring you would be difficult to explain." A hint of amusement entered his voice. "Is it really more appealing to pretend to be employed to lay down your life for mine, rather than to date me?"

Her gaze firmly on her food, she said shortly, "Your idea has *complication* written all over it."

Although true enough, that wasn't precisely the term he'd use. Enticing came to mind. Tempting. And that, he thought, a slight frown forming, was exactly what made this sticky. "We need a pretense that would have you accompanying me to both social and family events. The week after the expo is my brother Sam's engagement party.

Family and friends will be in and out of our lake home for the entire weekend." He waited a moment, before adding meaningfully, "Including Dale Cartwright."

Judging from the sudden look of interest on her face, he'd gained her attention. "It doesn't matter whether I call you my personal assistant, a consultant or a bodyguard. Once we're seen together more than once everyone is going to assume the term is a euphemism for lover."

Now it was she who seemed to have trouble with choking. He rose and helpfully thumped her back. Waving him off, she said, her voice strangled, "Are you telling me that people assume you're sleeping with any woman you appear with?"

"I'm afraid so. And before you ask, I can assure you that if my personal life bore any resemblance to the rumors about it, I'd have died of exertion years ago."

"Good to know." There was a hunted expression on her face that almost made him feel sorry for her. Would have, if he hadn't sensed that success was imminent. "I've always found it's easiest to stay as close to the truth as possible. This way you don't have to manufacture a consulting firm that you supposedly work for, and I don't have to answer uncomfortable questions about why I would need a bodyguard."

Her gaze was direct, as were her words. "Allowing people to believe we're dating isn't staying close to the truth. We're not lovers."

Not yet. The words blazed across his mind, startling him with their clarity. For the first time he wondered at the wisdom of his idea. Tori was right about one thing—a personal relationship between them was out of the question. He had grave doubts about her father's integrity and concerns about her willingness to look at all the facts, especially if they implicated the man. She wasn't a woman he'd have considered getting close to in normal circumstances. If it hadn't been for this case, their paths would never have crossed at all. She was different in just about every way from any other woman he'd ever dated.

It was just too damn bad for him that he'd always been a man to appreciate the unique.

With effort he shook off those thoughts and looked at his watch. They had a full evening ahead of them. But first he had a few things to check out. Rising, he carried his plate to the sink, set it down. "Grab your purse. We need to leave in a few minutes."

"Where are we going?"

"However you want to explain it, the fact remains that we're going to be appearing in public together fairly often in the next several days. You'll want to look the part." He gave her dark khakis and plain blouse a bland glance.

Her brows lowered. "Whatever you're thinking, Tremaine, you can forget it. And just to be clear, there is no way you're getting me into a dress."

He headed for the stairs, figuring he'd find her bedroom—and closet—fairly easily. "Actually, it's the thought of getting you out of one that I find most intriguing, but I promise to keep your preferences in mind."

Chapter 9

"You are so dead, Tremaine," Tori muttered between gritted teeth.

The volume of the threat was muffled by the three hair dryers pointed in her direction. And it didn't lack conviction, despite repetition. It was at least the third time in the past hour and a half that she'd threatened him with grave bodily harm.

Sipping at a very decent complimentary Chardonnay, James realized with a faint start of surprise that he was actually enjoying himself. Oh, there had been a few pangs of guilt when he'd noted the look of sheer terror on her face after he'd delivered her to the tender mercies of Claude—no last name needed—and his associates. He'd much preferred the mutinous expression that had followed when he and New Orleans's leading and most temperamental hairstylist had discussed the styles that would suit her best. Or the lethal looks she'd shot at the women busily doing her manicure.

"Relax. Think of it as a disguise." Temper, he noted, turned her eyes nearly gold.

"And so much less conspicuous than a rubber nose and multicolored wig."

Being a cautious man, he carefully hid his grin behind his glass. The dryers shut off, and Claude wielded a styling brush with almost frightening competency. She would recognize the wisdom of the makeover once she got over her fit of pique. When one confronted the enemy, it paid to take him unaware, to don the mask that would be expected, and use it to disguise your real intent.

Certainly that was what his enemy appeared to be doing, and fairly successfully.

The truth of the thought burned, but it couldn't be denied. Whoever was behind the messages could easily be someone who knew him well. Perhaps someone he did business with. Even trusted. Whoever was threatening him was going to be destroyed. That wasn't a vow, it was a fact. It remained to be seen whether he'd be destroying friend or stranger.

"Monsieur?" Claude whirled Tori's chair toward him and whipped off her cape with a flourish. James surveyed her critically. The new length suited her, he thought, barely topping her shoulders in a sleek style that had required deft styling and straightening. He'd ordered the color to be left alone, and commended himself on the decision now.

"Well done."

Tori bolted from the chair and strode toward the door. "Wait." He followed her, used his automatic start to turn the car on and the alarm off, then handed her the keys. "I expect it to still be there when I get out."

"No problem." She bared her teeth. "You could save me

some trouble by lying down in front of it when you come out, though."

Wincing, he turned to write Claude a very generous check to compensate him for staying open late. The man looked at it, then beamed, followed him to the door. "Anytime, Mr. Tremaine. It is my pleasure to serve you. You have but to call."

Somehow James was certain that "pleasure" wasn't what he was going to have in store for him on the way back to Tori's house. He went to rejoin her at the car, and found it running, with the hood up and Tori bent, quite delectably over the engine. "It misses just a bit when it idles, do you hear that?" Although she didn't straighten to look at him, he cocked his head obediently and listened, heard nothing but a car engine running. "Your spark plugs don't look corroded but the points may need cleaning. I can take care of that when we get back to my place if you want."

"That's…ah…a very generous offer," he said bemusedly, watching her thrust her fingers into the unidentifiable tangle of machinery without a care to the ensuing damage to her one-hundred-dollar manicure. "But it's almost dark. Maybe we could put that off for now."

She didn't respond right away, which gave him time to appreciate the very feminine backside defined by her position. The casual clothing she favored did a masterful job of hiding the curves of her long, lean build. Crossing his arms, he angled his head for a better view. "Or, you could take your time, if you prefer. I'm in no hurry."

Reluctantly Tori backed out from beneath the hood and straightened. Taking the handkerchief he held toward her, she said, "Well, okay, but you aren't going to want to wait too long on something like this. Regular tune-ups really pay off in the long run." Absently she wiped her hands on the handkerchief and handed it back to him, a part of her mourning when he slammed down the hood. There was no telling when she'd get her hands on an engine like this one again.

"I'll keep that in mind." He waited to get in the car before continuing, "But if allowing you to tinker with my car is all it takes to distract you from your earlier death threats, I'll count it as an action well worth it."

"Hmph. Well." She yanked her seat belt on, snapped it securely. "High-handed seems to be your MO, but I can't say I'm surprised, all in all."

He waited several moments for a break to appear in the heavy traffic before pulling away from the curb. "People will be less apt to give your presence with me a second thought if you look the part." He allowed a meaningful pause to pass. "Whatever that part turns out to be."

She lifted a shoulder, slid down to a more comfortable position in the seat. "Your attitude doesn't surprise me."

"And that's supposed to mean…"

Tori lifted a shoulder, as if it didn't matter. She wished, more than was comfortable, that it didn't. "Let's just say, I'm familiar with your type. Appearances mean everything to guys like you. What people think. What they say about you. I was married to a guy a lot like that. I was expected to transform myself into someone that would suit his idea of a fitting wife."

"You've been married."

The way he said it wasn't a question, but still spoke of surprise. Slanting him a glance, she wondered at the cause for it. A person didn't have to be a P.I. to figure that out since she didn't share her dad's last name. "To a guy who thought he could change me into a simpering debutante in twelve easy steps."

"And you think that's what I'm doing here."

Pushing aside the edge of disappointment that threatened

to well, she said, "Hey, don't sweat it. You probably can't help being that way. It's the money or something, I don't know. But just for future reference, I've been through one major silk-purse-out-of-a-sow's-ear operation. Like the rest of my marriage, it was a miserable failure. You might want to consider that before you decide just what 'part' I'm to play in the next few days."

He was quiet for a few minutes, long enough to have her regretting her unusual openness. The last thing she wanted to do was to let James Tremaine into her head.

But when he spoke again, there was genuine puzzlement in his voice. "Why do people get married if they just want to change their spouse into someone or something else?"

She gave a startled laugh. That was, and had been, the million-dollar question for the twenty-eight excruciating months of her marriage. "He seemed satisfied while we were in college. We had a lot in common—we were both on scholarships, and we were only children. But when we went back to Dallas, back to his family, his friends, his social group…" She shrugged. "The contrast was too much for him. And I couldn't be what he wanted." That fact had hurt far more than his infidelity. Because she'd tried. The memory of her attempts to meet with his approval could still make her squirm. She'd lost a healthy dose of her self-respect along the way. Although time had eased the pain of her shattered marriage, it hadn't dimmed the resulting self doubts. It was difficult to trust her judgement again after she'd been so wrong about the man she'd married.

James pressed the gas pedal and turned the corner just as the light was turning yellow. "Your ex sounds like an ass."

She laid her head back, smiled slightly as she watched the scenery pass by. "He is." But thoughts of him didn't wield the same sort of hurtful power they once had. He'd long since ceased to matter.

"I know people like that. They define themselves by a certain style of living, the right clothes, cars and vacation spots, as if the surface appearance is all that matters."

Without lifting her head from the soft leather headrest, she turned to face him. "As far as surface appearance goes, yours is pretty polished," she observed dryly.

His teeth flashed. "Ah, that's the thing about polish. It reflects back what the viewer expects to see. A smart man, or woman, cultivates that trait. Exploits it. It's easier to take people unaware that way."

Her eyes narrowed, half-admiringly. "That's a very devious point of view." Once he'd voiced it, she didn't find his words surprising. She'd long suspected there was far more to the man than his meticulous tailoring. But what, exactly, remained a mystery.

He gave an elegant shrug. "You can't tell me that your profession doesn't call for the same thing. Fostering contacts, gaining their trust, requires donning a certain demeanor befitting the situation, or the people involved."

She couldn't dispute it. But the difference, which she didn't bother pointing out, was that her job didn't require her to live the pretense. Didn't have her believing that was all there was. Not for the first time, she was convinced that there was far, far more to James Tremaine than met the eye.

With a start she realized he was pulling up across the street from her address. The curb directly in front of her house was blocked by a large truck, it's side emblazoned with the name of a well-known boutique. Even window shopping outside the establishment made her billfold ache.

With a long-suffering sigh, she closed her eyes, wished

she could transport herself elsewhere. Anywhere else. "I am not…" she enunciated precisely, "…wearing anything sleazy."

James looked wounded. He parked, turned off the car and got out. "Would I dress you in something sleazy?"

"Yes," she said decidedly, pushing open her car door. "If it suited your purposes, you definitely would."

"Luckily for you, my purposes are better suited with you in styles of understated elegance."

Even knowing it was a lost cause didn't stop her from trying. "I've got my own style, Tremaine. I know what suits me."

"Really?" He took her elbow in his hand as they went toward the house. "You couldn't prove it with the flowered thing I found hanging in your closet. It was the only thing in there that might have been a dress, although it more closely resembled a shower curtain." At their approach the truck doors swung open and a burly man carrying a clipboard got out the driver's side.

Stopping in the middle of the street, she gazed at James menacingly. "You were in my closet?"

Exerting subtle pressure, he got her moving again. "I wanted to double-check sizes. You should be a perfect size six."

"I'm a size eight."

"Let's see, shall we?"

"We're looking for Tori Corbett." The driver's voice interrupted them. He took a pencil from behind his ear. "You her?"

Tori looked past him to where workmen were already wheeling racks and carrying boxes up the walk to her modest home. A shudder went down her spine. She detested shopping, and she absolutely loathed trying on clothes. She glanced longingly at her car, nestled snugly in the carport attached to the house. She could make it; she'd attended college on a track scholarship. Her keys were in her purse. In five minutes she could be a couple of miles away.

James stepped to her side then, effectively cutting off that means of escape. The image shattered, leaving her staring at a middle-aged man in a brown uniform, impatience stamped on his pudgy features. Gritting her teeth, she said, "Yes, I'm Tori Corbett."

Two hours later she looked at the shambles of what used to be her living room and wanted to scream. After a great deal of strategic planning and direction from James, the workers had crammed the racks and stacked the boxes so as to leave a narrow traffic pattern through the room. Of course, she couldn't get to the furniture or TV, but efforts to point out those details had been in vain.

The door closed behind the uniformed men, and she collapsed against a stack of boxes, knocking the lid of one loose to reveal very sheer, very exotic lingerie. With a look of horror, she dove to replace it, but not before James hooked his index finger in the strap of a daring lace teddy and drew it out to admire it.

"Nice."

When his glance went from it to her, as if picturing her wearing it, Tori snatched it from him and crammed it back into the box, jamming the lid in place. "Somehow I don't see how my choices in underwear can affect our investigation one way or another."

"The investigation? No. My imagination, however..." His grin was wicked, seductive, and caused a shiver to shimmy down her spine. She damned both the cause and the reaction. "They took me seriously when I placed an order for a complete wardrobe. Can't say that I can argue with their selections so far."

She really, really wasn't in the mood for exchanging

suggestive witty banter with James Tremaine. To be truthful, she'd never had much experience with it, and definitely didn't want to learn now. He'd shed his suit jacket and tie, and rolled up the sleeves of his white-on-white striped shirt. He'd pitched in and helped with the organization, and his hair wasn't as perfectly groomed as usual. There was a lock, directly over one eye, that had tumbled free and gave him a faintly disreputable look. He appeared entirely too human and outrageously sexy. Under normal circumstances she might have found the combination nearly irresistible.

As it was, all she had to do was force her gaze away and note the clutter in her home to feel her resolve stiffen. "There is no possible way for one person to wear all this in a month, much less in the next week or so. It was a waste of money. I could have just picked a couple of outfits up for whatever event we'll be attending. Now I'm just going to have to mess with sending most of this stuff back."

"Actually…"

He let the sentence dangle until she looked at him again. Propping one shoulder against the wall he went on, "Since the purchases are in my name, the returns will have to be, too. They won't accept any returns from you."

"Of course not."

Pretending not to notice the sarcasm in her voice, he suggested, "Why don't you wait until tomorrow to try on the rest of this?"

Horror must have shown on her face then, because he hurriedly added, "Or not. What you've tried on so far fits, so the rest probably will. But it can wait until tomorrow to be put away. Just leave the tags on. That way anything you don't use you wouldn't have to keep if you don't want to."

She didn't point out that just storing this amount of stuff was going to take up every ounce of closet space in the entire house. "Nice try, but I don't think so. I'm going to have to spend hours going through this junk and setting aside the stuff I absolutely can't wear." The thought of the time it would require to do just that made her want to weep. So she bared her teeth at him and added, "Don't worry, I'll bill you for the hours."

"I'd expect nothing less. But from what I've seen so far, there isn't anything inappropriate in the entire collection. Remember, your goal is going to be to blend in. Think of this—" he gave an elaborate sweep of his arm "—as disguise."

She went to one of the racks and pulled down a hanger with a very short, very low-cut cocktail dress in flaming-red sequins visible through the clear garment bag. "I'm guessing this will disguise very little, but maybe I'll have to use my imagination."

His smile was slow and wide and devastating. "Do. I'm certainly going to."

She shook her head, careful to hide an answering smile. The last thing the man needed was encouragement. "I've discovered a new and alarming part of your personality, Tremaine. Depravity."

His raised eyebrow didn't dispute her observation. "I'm a man. And so will be seventy percent of the attendees at the expo. Any guy who gets a look at you in a dress like that isn't going to be worrying about what you might be snooping into."

Oddly enough his words cheered her. "That's true. Maybe I'll happen on to some information that will clear this whole mess up."

"Maybe." Pushing away from the wall, he began to roll down his shirtsleeves. "In the meantime, have you heard from that friend of yours? Juicy?"

"I'll reach out and nag him tomorrow."

James went to the adjoining kitchen and retrieved the suit jacket and tie he'd hung over the back of one chair. She was too tired to even sneer at the care he'd taken with them. Shrugging into the jacket, he hung the tie around his neck and began moving toward the door. "You can call me after you contact him and let me know when we can see that reconstruction. I'll want to be there."

She followed him through the narrow pathway toward the door, a sudden thought occurring. "When was the last time you got some sleep?" Once she'd gotten home that day she'd hit the bed for a good six hours before stirring again. She was certain that he couldn't claim the same.

"I plan on getting some. I'll stay at the lake tonight."

She trailed him out onto the porch and down the front steps. The night was clear, with a half-moon surrounded by a night sky of diamond-studded velvet. But any thought of enjoyment of the evening was shattered by the sight of her next-door neighbor walking quickly from his garage to his house.

Suspicion surged. "Dammit, Junior, what have you been up to?" James stopped and turned, his gaze going to the man Tori was already closing in on.

Joe Jr., neighborhood lech, affected a surprised look. "Hey, Tor, what's up? You just get home?"

Rapidly closing the distance between them, she said between her teeth, "What were you doing in that garage?"

He hitched up his low-riding jeans with his free hand. "Hey, it's my ma's garage. Guess I have a right to be in there."

"Don't make me kick your ass again, Junior." Reaching out, she grabbed a handful of his ribbed undershirt and yanked him closer. "So help me, if I go in there and find out you've set up your telescope again, you won't be walking upright for a week."

He must have heard the promise in her voice, because he covered himself with one hand. "Calm down, Tor, that was a big misunderstanding, just like I told ya back then. I didn't even know how to work that thing. I didn't aim it at your bedroom window on purpose."

She hadn't bought it back then, and she wasn't buying it now. "Uh-huh. And the window of your garage doesn't give you a perfect view into my living room." A discovery that had had her searching for the thickest curtains she could find.

"Honest, Tor." The fury in her voice must have made him nervous. A whine crept into his tone. "I was out there trying to fix Ma's radio. See?" He waved the tool he held as if for proof. "That's all. But I couldn't fix it. Maybe you'll take a look at it later, huh?"

She gave the tool a pointed look. "Fixing a radio with a wrench? Either you're dumber than I thought or you think I am."

"Do you require some assistance?"

For a moment she'd forgotten James. But he was beside her now, a lethal undertone to his otherwise innocent words that Junior obviously recognized. He backed up several feet, babbling the whole time.

"Hey, buddy, there's no problem here. Just a little neighborly chat, you know? I gotta go in now, gotta check on my ma. She doesn't like me to leave her alone too long." He was backpedaling rapidly, putting as much distance as possible between him and the man at her side, who was fairly radiating menace.

She glanced at James, put a hand on his arm. It was tight with bunched muscles. She had the impression of a big jungle cat, ready to pounce. There was a feral expression in his eyes, like a hunter who had scented prey. "There's nothing going on here that I can't handle. C'mon." It was several long seconds before he allowed her to turn him, and fell into step with her as they crossed the yard.

"How long has that been going on?" His voice was clipped.

Tori thought it wiser to pretend to misunderstand. "Joe Jr.? Oh, he moved in with his mom about a year after I bought the house." And had been a royal pain in her side ever since. "He's annoying but harmless."

From the tone of his voice, he wasn't buying it. "A polite description of a lowlife Peeping Tom. Have you reported him to the police?"

"I took care of it myself, okay?" He stopped, just looked at her. Finally she blew out a breath. "Look, he's a slimeball, but his mother, Pauline, is the sweetest woman I've ever met. As long as I can keep things strictly between him and me, she won't have to be upset." She had to exert more force to get him to turn, accompany her across the yard. "You, of all people, should appreciate the sentiment."

"I don't like it," he said flatly. "Sure he's a loser, but even guys like him get a little braver with some booze or their drug of choice in their system. How can you be sure…" His gaze returned to the street before them and he stopped dead in his tracks. He threw out an arm to halt her, as well. "Do you recognize that car?"

Puzzled at his abrupt change of subject, she followed his gaze to his vehicle, and the one parked in back of it, close enough for the bumpers to almost touch. "No, why?"

He grabbed her sleeve, spun her around and pushed her toward the house. "It doesn't belong to your neighbor? One of his friends maybe?"

Bewildered, she looked over her shoulder, difficult to

do as she was stumbling over the lawn with his hand at the small of her back. "No, I've never…"

The night erupted into an inferno that shook the ground and singed the air around them. Heat enveloped them, brutally intense. Time fragmented, split into short stills. There was the sight of Joe Jr. standing on his porch, his jaw agape. Then the hard ground rushing up to meet her, the oxygen streaming out her lungs when a heavy weight landed on her. She had a single last image of the street, James's car and the one behind it engulfed in flames. Then something flew through the air, and her head exploded in agony. After that, there was nothing at all.

"Someone sure went to a hell of a lot of trouble to plan a bonfire in your honor." Detective Cade Tremaine looked up from his notebook, his green gaze sweeping between James and Tori. "If you have any ideas who, you'd better be letting me in on it, and quick."

Broodingly, James looked toward the scene half a block down the street, where the bomb squad had cordoned off the entire area. The fire was under control now, showing the skeletal remains of the two cars. "If I was the target, and that's a big if, there are any number of people who might have reason to want me out of the way."

"Yeah," Cade deadpanned, "but do any specific names spring to mind? I mean, outside of family?" When Tori's attention jerked to him, his mouth quirked up and he shrugged. "Hey, I'm joking. But you haven't pissed Ana off lately, have you?"

That remark pulled a smile from James. "No more than usual." He blew out a breath. "But she's going to be hard to contain once she hears about this. Unless…"

Cade was already shaking his head. "Not a chance,

buddy. I'm not going to try to keep this from her. And I couldn't if I wanted to. The press is all over this already."

As if on cue, a white news helicopter flew low across the scene, a cameraman leaning out the door, filming the scene. That sight, and the chaos on the street, had James choosing his words carefully. "I'd appreciate you being as vague on the details as possible. I don't need this kind of publicity right now."

He felt the shudders working through Tori next to him, and without a thought he shrugged out of his jacket to hang it over her shoulders. That was the first time he noticed that it was completely missing one sleeve. Anchoring it in place with his arm around her waist, he ignored his brother's interested stare and went on. "I'm delivering on a big contract tomorrow. I hope to be awarded the bid on another very soon. This sort of publicity I can do without."

Jotting down a few notes, Cade inquired, "Is that what tonight was about? These projects of yours?"

"Hard to say. We don't even know that I was the target." Tori stirred beside him, but James tightened his arm warningly. "If I were you I'd check out the guy that lives right there." He gestured with his free hand at Joe Jr.'s house. "He's a dirt ball, and there's no telling what he's mixed up in."

"I told you before, he's harmless. Joe's got nothing to do with this." Tori finally roused from her shell-shocked state and entered the conversation. "Can I get into my house now? I want to get an idea of the damage."

Cade half turned, and motioned to a uniformed cop standing nearby. "The homeowner would like to get into that house. Has it been cleared?"

The cop approached them and nodded. "The windows are blown in on the street side, but no structural damage has been observed. I can take her in."

James frowned. "Why don't you wait a few minutes. I'll go with you."

"Hey, I handled your idea of a fun evening, Tremaine." Tori's attempt at a smile wobbled at the edges, but she seemed steady enough. "I can handle this." She moved away, fell into step with the uniform and headed to her house.

"So…" Cade let the word dangle. "She's the reason you were in the neighborhood, huh?"

Bringing his attention back to his brother, James said shortly, "She's an…associate of mine."

"Yeah, got that." Cade rocked back on his heels. Damned if it didn't look like he was enjoying himself. "And you were in her house…associating…for how long before the bomb went off?"

"We'd only been home about two hours," he started, and then another thought had his blood running cold. Using abandoned cars full of explosives was typically a terrorist stunt, designed to take out an entire block of buildings and create the greatest damage possible. But someone had gone to a great deal of trouble to limit the destruction. The only person meant to die in the blast had most likely been him.

"Well, if it was meant for you, the guy took some risk. Most would have hooked it to the ignition or accelerator to detonate when the vehicle was turned on, or pressure applied to the gas pedal. It's chancier to hang around the vicinity waiting for the chance to blow it."

Looking back at Cade, James said, "All the vehicles used by me or by the company are protected by Safe-T, an antiterrorist alarm system. If anyone had gotten close enough to try, to wire the engine or the body of the car, I would have been alerted."

Cade tapped his pen against his pad. "So someone either

made an incredibly lucky choice, or they knew about that protection." His somber stare met James's. "Who's that narrow it down to?"

"Hell, anyone who'd done their homework." He jammed his hand into his hair, frustration riding him. Any of his rivals would know, since his system, minus some perfections for his own private use, was on the market. Anyone who worked for him would know, as well.

After that thought, a brief mental image flashed across his mind. His curse had his brother's brows raising.

"What?"

"Tori had the hood up and her hands in the engine less than three hours ago." The blood in his veins seemed to ice up. If he'd brought a car that hadn't been protected and someone had tampered with it, it might have blown the moment she'd unlatched the hood.

The ice in his blood dissipated, melted by the fury that began to simmer. He'd brought the danger to her doorstep, literally. Through their association, she was at risk, too. And he wasn't quite sure how he was going to cope with that.

In succinct sentences he told Cade as much as he'd shared with Jones about the threats, purposefully staying as vague as he could. "It wouldn't hurt for you to stay on guard," he concluded. "And alert Sam, too. I don't know if the purpose is to distract me or get rid of me, but going after anyone in my family would be just as sure a distraction as something like this." They exchanged a sober look. "Be careful."

Cade's notebook shut with a snap. "Sounds like good advice for you to be taking yourself. Why the hell didn't you come to me when those notes started arriving? Do you still have them?"

Carefully he skirted the last question. "It's not the first

time something like this has happened. It won't be the last. I had the notes analyzed by a lab I use, and no fingerprints were found, except for the outside of the envelopes. I didn't think you could guarantee they wouldn't leak to the press, and as I've said, that could really scuttle things for the company right now."

Cade's response to that was unprintable. "You're unbelievable, you know that? You're actually more worried about *business* than being straight with your family?"

James drew back, watched his brother more warily. The man was obviously furious. There was a nerve twitching in his jaw that always indicated temper kept tightly leashed. "I didn't want to worry you all unnecessarily. This kind of thing…" He hesitated, finally deciding that half a truth was better than none at all. "There's danger in all of our jobs. Sam's—despite the fact we're all supposed to believe he's an international attorney—and yours. You're the one who had three bullets dug out of his chest just months ago, remember? I'm already taking precautions. I'm asking that you do, too."

Jaw still tight, Cade looked away, slapping his closed notebook in a rapid tattoo against his leg. "You have a point. But there's another you're refusing to consider here. When someone targets one Tremaine, he takes on all of us. And if you think the rest of the family is going to sit back and let you handle this alone…well, you're even denser than I thought."

The brotherly insult was mild, given some he'd endured in the past, and when Cade brushed by him, he let him go. The memory of his own stunned grief when Cade was in the operating room for hours, his life hanging in the balance, was still fresh. Recalling it, remembering the helpless rage that had filled him at the time, gave him some insight into his brother's feelings now.

Scrubbing his face with his hands, he removed them to see Tori approaching him again. He watched carefully, but there was nothing showing in her expression but resignation.

"Well, the damage doesn't look too bad, although I'm told everyone on this block will have to have structural assessments done. But glass is everywhere. I'll probably have to replace the furniture and the carpet." Irony was rife in her voice. "The clothes you bought seem to be fine. Everything was still boxed or covered."

"I'll take care of your house." He raised a hand to stem the protest he sensed on her lips. "There's little doubt that if I hadn't been here, you'd be sleeping peacefully right now. The police will be in the area for hours yet. I'll have workmen here first thing in the morning." He waited a moment before adding nonchalantly, "We'll have to get those deliveries out of there so they can work, though. I'll have the collection sent to our place on the lake. That's where I'm taking you."

The medics on the scene had pronounced them both fine, but for a few bruises and lacerations. He wasn't so sure. He was still worried that she might have a possible concussion. She'd been out a couple of minutes when a piece of debris had hit her. There was a good-size lump on her head, a dark smudge across one cheek and a rapidly spreading bruise along her jaw. Yet she showed no signs of crumpling. What she did show signs of was temper. Ridiculous, really, to be reassured by the sight.

"What makes you think I'm going to let you call the shots? And I'm not staying with you. That's out of the question."

Pulling his cell phone out of his pocket, he called for a cab. There was no way she'd be able to get her car out and maneuver around the emergency vehicles blocking the street. Not for a few more hours at least. As an aside he said, "I suppose you could always bunk in with Joe Jr. over there." She followed the direction of his glance, where Joe and his mother stood on their porch, watching the goings-on avidly. This was more excitement than their quiet neighborhood had seen in decades.

"I could go to a motel."

"You could." Having ordered the taxi, he flipped the cell phone shut and slipped it back in his pocket. "You're not going to."

Hands still clutching his jacket around her shoulders, she narrowed her gaze at him. "You know, you really irritate me, Tremaine."

The words, the tone in which they were delivered, lightened something inside him. Wrapping an arm around her, he rested his chin on her hair, for just a moment. "And you fascinate me, Corbett. I guess we're both going to have to learn to deal with it."

Dawn was still hours away when a cell number was dialed for the third time that night. This time it was answered by a familiar voice, sounding groggy. "H'lo?"

"You failed tonight. Miserably."

There was silence for a few moments, as if the man on the other end of the line was mounting his argument. "Look, it was a clean attempt. How was I to know he'd spot the car and get wise before he got close enough to—"

"It's your job to *know*. I pay you to *know*. You failed, and now Tremaine will be on his guard. The police have been alerted. It will be more difficult next time." Thoughts of there having to be a next time made fury surge. Incompetence was intolerable. And time was growing short. "Had you done your job correctly, he would have been eliminated standing within a half block of that car."

"Hey, that was your idea. You said you wanted as little collateral damage as possible. I put enough C-4 in the vehicle to blow Tremaine to hell and back if he'd gotten closer. You want me to take out an entire city block, I can do that."

Calm was never more difficult to summon. Deep cleansing breaths were hauled into lungs, attempting to push aside the haze of fury. "You can't try the same thing again, you idiot. I'll have to think of something else. Did they get near enough to see you tonight?"

"Hell, I was long gone before the cops arrived. And there's no way they can trace the vehicle or the explosives back to me. Relax. You've got nothing to worry about."

Nothing. If only he knew. "I'll be in touch." The caller abruptly ended the conversation, set the cell phone down on the desk with more care than the act called for. Shimmering waves of rage mixed with panic. It had been a mistake to trust another party to do the job correctly. Tremaine's elimination was going to require a personal touch, and, thanks to the bungling idiot that had been hired, it had just grown more complicated.

Things had come together so much more neatly twenty years ago. Using outsiders was risky.

But the calendar on the desk was a taunting reminder that time was growing precious. Another plan would have to be devised. But first the man who'd made a mess of things would have to be taken care of.

Leaving loose ends was sloppy work.

Chapter 10

Despite the comfort of the surroundings, there was always something disorienting about waking up in a strange place. Tori rolled over in the huge four-poster bed, opened her eyes and blinked several times. Then she sat bolt upright and reassessed the space around her, trying to summon memory into her exhausted brain.

The lake house. Tremaine's. The explosion.

She fell back on the bed, burying her face in a pillow. Before James Tremaine had walked into her office, she'd been spared this type of excitement. Oh sure, there was the occasional knife fight. And she'd once chased down a would-be mugger and subdued him until the police arrived, but most of her work was pretty mundane.

There was nothing mundane about her current client or the feelings he elicited in her.

Discomfited by the thought, she flopped over in bed, opened her eyes again. She would have been as concerned about any client of hers who had barely avoided getting blown up in front of her place, she assured herself. Would have felt the same fears for anyone she knew who was being stalked by someone who might very well have killed before. Who was intent on killing again.

The reassurances were rational and should have soothed her. Unfortunately, Tori wasn't one to lie to herself about anything. And she couldn't pretend, even to herself, that James Tremaine was just a client. Couldn't pretend that she didn't have deeper feelings that went far beyond the client-P.I. relationship.

Recognition of that fact was anything but calming. Throwing back the covers, she noted that the clothes she'd shed the night before were lying in a heap on the floor beside the bed. She snagged her shirt and surveyed it resignedly. There were streaks of dirt down the front, and one sleeve was hanging by threads. Her pants weren't in much better shape, sporting two ripped knees and covered with grime. It was difficult to say how much of the damage had been sustained when James had knocked her to the ground and covered her body with his and how much had come from the debris that had showered upon them.

That memory sparked another, and her fingers went to her head, probing tenderly. There was a sizable lump there, but she thought her hair should cover it well enough. The biggest problem right now was getting cleaned up and out of Tremaine's house wearing little but the rags that her clothes had become.

Reaching for her purse, she dug out her phone and rang his cell number. From the look of the sun pouring in the windows, it was nearly noon. She knew him well enough to be certain that he wasn't still in the house, enjoying some well-deserved sleep.

He answered on the second ring. "Tremaine."

"Where are you?"

"Good morning." His voice warmed several degrees, and so did her blood. "Did you just wake up? How are you feeling?"

"Taking inventory. I think I'll live and if goose eggs and rags are in style, I'll be the height of fashion."

"If I remember correctly, the clothes need to be destroyed. Your new ones should have been delivered by now. Use the house phone to check with the maid."

House phone. Maid. She definitely wasn't in Kansas anymore. "I'll do that. You never told me where you are."

"Approaching D.C. in the corporate jet. I decided to deliver the project personally." A touch of dark humor laced his tone. "Call me paranoid, but I didn't want to leave anything to chance."

"You had the jet thoroughly checked out?" She wasn't able to keep the worry from her voice. She didn't even try.

"Don't worry, it's secure. And I'm not alone, Jones is accompanying me. We'll be back by the middle of the afternoon. You may as well take it easy. There's a hot tub in your bathroom. Use it. You must be sore."

"Thanks." She tried and failed to remember the last time she'd sat naked in bed and talked to a man on the phone. Come to that, she tried to remember the last time she'd been naked with a man, period. And on the trail of that thought came a mental image of James in bed with her, his body as bare as her own, his skin against hers, limbs tangled, mouths melded…

The uncustomary thought had her throat closing. Where had *that* come from? She didn't engage in fantasies about men she barely knew. Well, okay, Russell Crowe, maybe, but that didn't count. She didn't actually *know* him, so he

was safe enough to star in the occasional X-rated daydream.
Far, far safer than the man on the other end of the line, who
would be all too available, all too tempting and maybe, just
maybe, willing, as well. Her intuition about such things
could be rusty, and God knows, it had never been too
keenly edged.

"...today?"

Belatedly she realized James was talking again.
"What?"

"Do you have anything planned that can't wait until I
get back today?"

"I'm going home." She hadn't realized just how badly
she needed to until the words left her mouth. "I want to get
a look at the house in the daylight, and see about repairing
the windows and stuff."

"Let me know if there's anything you need." There was
a burst of static, before she heard him say, "...approaching
Dulles now. I'll call you later."

"Later," she echoed, but the line was already dead. It
wasn't until she'd lowered the phone to stare blindly at
it that she managed to shake herself out of her funk and
get out of bed. It definitely had to be related to the blow
on the head she'd received last night, she excused herself.
Because she'd never mooned over a man in her life. And
she wasn't about to start with one as totally unsuitable as
James Tremaine.

Resolution filling her, she reached for the house phone,
pressed the red button. "This is Tori Corbett, in—" she had
no idea what room she was in "—the guest room? James
ordered some deliveries..."

"Oh, yes, Ms. Corbett, they've arrived. Would you like
them delivered to your room?"

No, definitely not. She didn't think she could face that
again. "Would you mind going through them and bringing

me the most casual outfit you can find?" It shouldn't be so hard talking to a maid, she decided, if she just pretended she was speaking to a clerk in a clothing store.

Come to think of it, that was one of the reasons she never went shopping. "Jeans, if you can find a pair."

"Yes, Ms. Corbett."

Hanging up the phone, she headed to the bathroom, becoming aware of a chorus of aches and pains from various parts of her body. She gritted her teeth and started thinking seriously of that hot tub James had mentioned. She may as well take advantage of it, before she called a cab and headed home. She had no intention of coming back here tonight, regardless of what James had to say about it.

Money worked magic, she mused a couple hours later, standing in front of her home. Workmen streamed in and out of the place. The windows had all been replaced, and the carpet ripped out. She wondered wryly whether James had intended to allow her to pick out new carpeting and furniture or if that would have been decided for her, too.

But when she saw one man wearing a home security logo on his uniform passing her to go back to his truck, she snagged him and asked what he was doing there.

"Orders from Mr. Tremaine, ma'am." The worker, a tousled blonde just shy of thirty, gave her figure an approving glance before going on. "Putting in a state-of-the-art alarm system, and installing new dead bolts. The work will be finished by the end of the day, as promised."

Clenching her jaw tightly, she nodded curtly and marched away. High-handed didn't even begin to describe James Tremaine. He'd never know just how lucky he was to be a thousand miles away right now.

There was nothing she could do here, besides trip over

the men he'd hired, so she went next door and knocked on Pauline's door. Joe Jr. opened the door, peeked out and then made as if to shut it again.

"Wait a minute." Tori pressed the heel of her palm against the door. "Where's your mom?"

"Ma ain't here. I put her on a bus to stay with her sister in Shreveport until I get things fixed up."

Given Junior's work ethic, Tori thought, the work could take years. "Have you called the insurance company?" Worry filled her at the financial hardship this might mean for the elderly woman. "Are they sending out an adjuster?"

"I dunno. That guy is taking care of it. At least that's what he said." Her expression must have been as blank as she felt because he added sullenly, "That guy you were with last night? Came by here this morning and said how he'd be sending workers over here once they're done with your place. But then he started making threats and stuff. That is one mean dude." A familiar whine entered his voice. "I don't know what you've been telling him, but he's got some wrong ideas about me. Dead wrong. He might dress all uptown but he's got a vicious streak a mile wide." The door closed a bit more. "And I'm not supposed to be within ten yards of you, he said, or else he's coming back. I don't need that kind of trouble."

James had threatened Joe Jr.? Over her? It was possible to feel an undeniable warmth at his concern, she decided, while still wanting to throttle him.

"Wait." It may have been the authoritative tone to her voice, but Joe stopped in the act of closing the door the rest of the way. "I wanted to ask you some questions about last night."

"I don't know nothing." His voice was sulky, but he pulled the door open a bit more. "I told that to the cops.

But if you asked me, that guy that was with you pissed someone off, big-time. And I can see how that would happen, because like I was saying, he's…"

"…a mean dude. I remember." She stared at the younger man, long enough to have him shifting from one bare foot to the other. "What were you doing in the garage last night, Joe?" she asked slowly, a thought beginning to form in her mind.

"Nothing." The word was vehement. "It's just like I told you last night, I was working on the car and I…"

"You told me last night you were fixing your mom's radio." She spun on her heel, jogged down the steps and toward the garage.

"No, wait!" Joe Jr. raced after her, stumbling over the hems of his low-riding jeans and nearly falling on his face. "The thing is, what you won't understand is…"

She pushed open the door of the garage, unsurprised to see the telescope on its tripod once again. She looked from it to the slimeball standing in the doorway. "I'm really, really going to hurt you this time, Joe."

"Don't tell that friend of yours, he'll kill me," he babbled. "C'mon, I'm beggin' ya. It's not like I could see anything, anyway. You got curtains on all the windows. Thick ones, too."

It took effort not to kick him in the teeth. "Why should I do you any favors?"

"Who'd take care of my ma if I wasn't around? Huh? You gotta think of that."

Pauline had seemed to do very well for herself until her bum of a son had shown up, but Tori left the thought unuttered. "How long were you at the telescope?"

"I wasn't, I swear!" He hitched up the back of his pants and tried a sickly smile. "Really I was just trying to fix it and…"

"How long, Joe?"

"Oh, hmm, well just since you got home with the guy. And that truck came and I was just wondering what they were carrying in."

"And you didn't leave the garage until we left the house so you must have seen the guy who left the car there." Having painted him neatly in a corner, she pounced. "What did you see, Joe? Who did you see?"

He was swinging his head wildly from side to side. "I didn't see nothing, I swear. That big-ass truck was in the way about the whole time and I never saw the car until the truck pulled away."

"And its driver?" she pressed. She was on to something and she knew it. She could tell by the way he began to sweat.

"I don't know. I never saw anyone get out of the car."

"But you saw someone, didn't you, Joe? Something kept you in here until we left the house, and since you couldn't see in my windows you had to be looking at something."

The fight seemed to stream out of him them, and his shoulders slumped. At the moment he looked rather pathetic. "I was just checking out the sports car, the one that belonged to the dude, you know? And I saw a guy, but I don't know who he was. He was just walking away, real fast like, when the truck pulled away."

"Describe him." Excitement began to pulse inside her. Maybe, just maybe, this would be the break they were looking for.

"A little guy. Shorter than me, about one-fifty. Bald, but not old. Had on jeans and a dark shirt." He shrugged. "That's all I noticed. I was looking at the car, you know?"

"And did you tell the detective this?" She already knew the answer to that question, even before seeing the hunted look on Joe Jr.'s face.

"I can't do that. I'd have to explain how I seen him, you know? And then they'd start getting bad ideas about me, like that friend of yours."

"You're going to call the NOPD," she ordered, "and ask for Detective Cade Tremaine. Then you're going to tell him everything you just told me. Yes," she retorted, when he began to shake his head again, "you are. I don't care how you explain it. Tell him you're a junior astronomer, if you want to. But you are going to talk to the detective right away. And if you don't, the dude," she mimicked him, "is going to come back. And he's not going to be happy with you."

He wasn't eager, but he obviously feared James more than the police. After gaining his agreement to make the call and to look at some photos she promised to drop off later, she got into her car and drove to the office. It wouldn't hurt to have him examine any pictures she could find of Cartwright and the CEOs of the other companies competing with Tremaine Technologies for this next contract. And she'd call Cade herself to suggest he have Junior take a look at the mug shots they had on file. Maybe something would pop that way.

And after she did all that, she had another stop to make. The sun was shining brightly, so she found her sunglasses and slid them on. This seemed to be her day for sleazeballs. Because she had every intention of paying another visit to Kiki Corday.

If Joe Jr. looked like an oily, wannabe Lothario, Kiki Corday reminded her of a man who'd long since traded away pride, and hadn't missed the quality overmuch. His gut hung over his waistband, and the button-down shirt he was wearing was grease-stained. The few strands of hair that he still had were combed over his pink scalp and sprinkled heavily with dandruff. There was white powder all over his hands and dribbled down his chin. She'd obviously interrupted his brunch of Irish coffee and beignets.

The house he lived in seemed to have given up hope years ago. Even in this questionable neighborhood, his seemed to slump a bit more on its foundation. The siding seemed older. The roof sagged. She'd heard rumors that the man actually had a heck of a stash put aside. Tori thought it might be true. He sure didn't spend anything on himself or his surroundings. The only top-of-the-line products he was interested in were cameras and photographic equipment.

Kiki pushed open the door minus a screen and greeted her with a grunt. "Yeah? You need more pictures? 'Cuz I got to thinking, I shoulda charged ya more. Those were high quality shots, every one of them."

"Actually, I came to see if you were interested in a job." She hadn't run this by James, but after the decisions he'd been making for her recently, she dared him to disagree with this one. "Have you heard about the Technology Expo starting tomorrow?"

He licked the powdered sugar from his fingers. "Yeah, so? You need a press pass to get in. I already checked." His expression went sly. "Not that I can't get my hands on one, you understand, but there's not likely to be anything of interest going on there, anyway."

Meaning, he didn't think he'd be able to sell any of the photos to a news rag. "Maybe it'd be more interesting to you if I can arrange for your admission, and pay you to take pictures."

That piqued his interest. He held open the door. "C'mon in." She did, gingerly. She'd been inside before, and each time the place seemed to get dingier. She could see the clutter in his kitchen from here. He'd been eating on a tray in front of the TV, she saw now. Filing cabinets lined one wall. She already knew there were more in the spare bedroom that served as his office. He never threw away a picture. That room would also be the only part of his house that he kept in halfway respectable shape.

"Here are some shots of people who'll be there, that I'm especially interested in." She handed him a manila envelope with duplicates of the pictures she'd shown to Joe Jr., who hadn't seemed to recognize any of them. "I want you to mingle, seem to take pictures of everything, but the actions of these men are of particular interest. I want a shot of whoever they talk to." She couldn't be certain if Cartwright would be at the expo, but she'd included his photo just to be safe.

He grunted again, shook the pictures out and studied them. "How much?"

She quoted a price that had his eyes going beadier than normal. She knew it was too much when he smiled, revealing stained crooked teeth. "Sweetheart, for cash like that, I'd take pictures of myself getting up close and personal with a donkey."

Tori didn't have to feign the shudder that ran down her spine. "Consider this an advance against that, as well. I'll arrange to have a pass delivered for you, and get you cleared at the door." She edged toward the exit, anxious to be gone. After dealing with Joe Jr. and Kiki in the same day, she felt the need for another shower.

Once safely on the porch, however, another thought occurred. Speaking through the windowless door, she said, "Oh, and Kiki? Search your closet for something that might have been in style in the last decade, all right? And laundered in the last year or so."

"You've been busy."

The words seemed innocuous, but Tori was getting to

know James well enough to know when he was displeased. She also knew him well enough not to care.

When she'd called Juicy earlier and prodded him about the project, he'd promised to have it done that evening. She'd relayed the information to James when he'd called, and they were on their way there now after he'd insisted on picking her up at her house, in a limo complete with driver, no less. She spent the trip filling him in on her day while trying to ignore her surroundings.

"I'll make you a deal. You don't rag at me for making decisions without you, and I won't even start on what I found at my place this morning."

He opened his mouth, then, with a quick glance at her, seemed to reconsider. "Well," he finally said, "when you put it so charmingly... Was there something wrong with the arrangements I made? From the quick look I had, it appeared as though the workmanship was topnotch."

For a man who'd risen to the position he had, he could be singularly dense. "It is. And though I would have preferred to be consulted before installing a new alarm and dead bolts, they seem top of the line, as well. Trouble is, I'm used to taking care of myself. And I don't like people making decisions for me without consulting me first."

"I'm sorry."

The apology had her swinging her head around, gaping at him. There was a slight frown on his face, and his gorgeous profile was serious. "It's a habit of mine, and one that regularly ticks my family off. I'm used to making judgments in my business and don't always remember the need to consult others in—" he hesitated. "—my personal life."

Tori very nearly squirmed in the plush leather seat. He'd managed to make her feel churlish. If she thought that had been his intent, she would have made a sarcastic retort, but he looked so genuinely puzzled, so nearly *abashed,* that something inside her softened. "Oh, well…no harm done, I guess."

There was a part of her deep inside that actually gave a derisive hoot at that. The man had hijacked her hair, showered her with clothes she wouldn't normally be caught dead wearing and then commandeered her house, and no harm was done? That voice, along with a measure of spine, forced her to add, "But it has to stop. You can't go around arranging things to suit yourself and expect people to forgive you. Most of us feel pretty capable of running our own lives."

"So I'm told. Frequently." From the curve of his lips, she figured he was thinking of his family again. Maybe his sister. Ana didn't seem the type to take an older brother's interference quietly.

"In any case, I contacted your brother to double-check that Joe Jr. actually called and gave him the information he told me about. He had, and they were pairing the description with the details from the bomber's MO to see if something shows up in the database."

"I'm annoyed as hell with you for approaching your sleazy neighbor on your own." He sent her a quick admiring glance. "But very impressed with your detective work. How did you know he had information that he hadn't given the cops last night?"

"It never really occurred to me until I spoke to him again today. But the more I thought about him in that garage, the more certain I was that he had to have seen something." She made a rueful face. "Something other than what he was hoping for, obviously."

"At the risk of being accused of being pushy, again, I'd like to point out that having you live next to a pervert doesn't do much for my peace of mind."

There was an odd jitter in her pulse, and she took care not to look at him. A woman could read all sorts of things into words like that. Like thinking that he cared, on a deeper level. That he'd forgotten the distrust between them—his belief that her father had betrayed him…and his fear that she would do the same.

All of a sudden a vast distance seemed to yawn between them that couldn't be bridged. Despite all that had happened in the last twenty-four hours, nothing had really changed. She was still intent on proving her father's innocence as she solved this case.

And she was just as intent on making sure James stayed alive while she did it.

"Did Joe happen to mention our conversation this morning?"

She sent him a droll look. "Yes, he did babble incoherently about the 'mean dude' who was going to do unspeakable things to him if he got within ten yards of me."

There was a definite note of satisfaction in his voice. "Good. Then he's smarter than he looks. I did wonder." He leaned forward and fiddled with the back controls of the CD player until some mournful jazz filled the interior. "I don't like him living next door to you." The simple words were anything but, when delivered in that tone. With that intense light in his eye. It fired an answering warmth in her system, suffusing her with heat.

And because she could hear the genuine concern in his voice, she kept her words even. "It's not like I haven't taken precautions. Unless he's got an X-ray lens on that scope of his, he isn't going to see anything at my house. Peeping Toms rarely escalate into more violent crimes." And she knew this precisely because she'd researched it. She gave him a slight smile. "However, if your brother was to be tipped off and the telescope got seized and not returned, I wouldn't be upset."

James nodded grimly. "Consider it done." At the risk of offending her sensibilities yet again, he was planning on telling his brother far more than that. If the NOPD could put a little pressure on Joe Jr., he just might be convinced to move to a climate better suited to his health. Because James certainly couldn't guarantee the man's continued well-being as long as he was within speaking distance of Tori.

"So." In an obvious effort to lighten the mood, she looked around the limo. "Some ride. Bet you hate not being at the wheel, though, huh?"

He shouldn't have been surprised at the accuracy of her observation. "More than you can imagine." The words, the feeling behind it, were heartfelt. "But having a driver gives me another pair of eyes." The limo also had the added safeguard of armored doors and bulletproof glass, but he knew better than to put too much stock in that. There were myriad ways to kill someone. It was impossible to protect against all of them.

The driver and car was a concession to the concerns of his family. Cade hadn't been the only one who'd given him hell last night, or, rather, early this morning. Ana had ripped into him, as well, and he didn't totally blame either of them. He owed it to his family's peace of mind to take precautions. And he owed it to them to stay alive to solve the mystery of their parents' deaths, once and for all. To bring the person responsible to justice.

The car glided to a halt, and James looked up to see a familiar, flickering neon sign. Anticipation mixed with trepidation was snaking through his chest, squeezing. The trouble with finding answers, he thought, was dealing with the emotions that came along with them.

In the next moment a slim soft hand slipped into one of his and gripped hard. Startled, he looked down at the woman beside him, saw the understanding in her warm hazel gaze. She didn't speak; she didn't need to. For better or worse, he wasn't by himself in this. It was a disconcerting feeling for a man who was used to dealing with whatever life threw at him decisively and alone. But not an unpleasant one.

For just a moment he squeezed, returning the pressure. And when they got out of the car and walked up to the tavern door, they did so hand in hand.

"Sorry this took so long. I got another job for a defense attorney." Juicy looked exactly as he had the last time they'd seen him. In fact, James was certain even the patrons outside in the bar were the same. It was as if the place had been caught in a time warp since they'd last been there. "There's this guy up on vehicular manslaughter, see, and his lawyer wants to show…"

"We're glad you could fit this into your schedule," Tori put in, with a sidelong glance at James. Unable to remain still, he roamed the small area, studying the prints hanging on the bulletin board. One set obviously belonged to the new case the man was working on. But the set next to the computer were from the file they'd left with him. He didn't recognize the three photos hanging above it.

The vise in his chest eased, infinitesimally, as impatience edged out other, darker, emotions. "What are these?" He gestured to the three.

Juicy ambled over, pointed to each in turn. "Those aren't from your accident scene, I just got them as examples to refer to when I explained something. Most people see skid marks on a road and think they're all the same. But they're actually very different. Here," he pointed to the first photo, "is a picture of an acceleration skid. Laying rubber, we used to call it in my day. This next one," he moved his finger to the second photo, "well, that's what laymen think of when they hear the term *skid mark*. It's left by a tire that's locked, not rotating, while the car continues moving forward. That's what you see on the road when the driver slams on the brakes for whatever reason. And this—" he moved to the third and final picture "—is a yaw mark, left by a vehicle when a wheel is rotating and sliding sideways."

James peered intently at the last picture. "So if my father took the curve too fast, lost control on it, this is the mark we'd expect to see on the road."

Juicy was bobbing his head enthusiastically, a teacher pleased with a particularly bright student. "Exactly. Problem is, that's not the kind of mark shown in the accident photos." He pulled several from the envelope and tacked them up beside the ones already hanging on the wall.

"What?" Tori crowded closer to them, peering at the photos. "You mean the investigating officer misidentified them? How is that possible? Accident investigation has been included in police science for decades."

"Since the fifties, for sure," Juicy said cheerfully. He bent his thin frame into the seat before the computer and punched up a program. "Problem is, it's still the most common police investigative error. Sometimes what we think we see is warped by what we expect to see, ya know? The officer probably figured since there was nothing in the road, those marks were left by a car going too fast on the curve. But the rear end would break loose, see, and swing to the side if in that were the case."

He tapped the screen, where a close-up of one of the photos appeared, with the tire marks evident. "Person screws up the kind of skid mark, it's going to affect the projection of how fast the vehicle was traveling, too."

James felt as though each of his organs was encased in ice. Frigid waves radiated throughout his body, numbing his system. His mind, though, remained dangerously clear. "So you can be certain that these marks are braking skids."

Juicy nodded. "The accident driver was trying to avoid hitting something."

"The left front fender was smashed."

Juicy nodded at James's flat statement. "Whatever was on the road, the driver didn't completely miss it. I performed some photogrammetric calculations to determine just where the object was. If you hadn't brought me those other pictures, I'd have figured maybe an oncoming car veered into the lane. But look at this." His fingers danced over the keyboard, and yet another scene appeared. This one was obviously a 3-D simulation.

The man stabbed a finger at a spot on the screen. "Now, a second car, if there was one, would have needed to be at this angle here in order for your driver to start braking where he did. But there are no corresponding skid marks to indicate another car was involved. Which means the driver hit something else."

He quickly typed a command and a close-up of the road appeared on the screen. "See that gouge there?" He pointed to the asphalt. "The road crew had just blacktopped that section a week earlier."

James bent lower and stared at the dirty gouge visible on the road's surface. "Something a lot heavier than a car rested right there."

With another quick press of the keys, he had a picture of the boulder, with the fresh scar marring its surface, sitting in the precise spot the gouge had been. "Long story short, I did some calibrations from past photos. If that boulder was sitting right there, it could have caused the damage to the left front fender, and the braking skids would match up exactly."

"It was gone when the police got there, so whoever moved it must have been waiting," Tori put in softly. "He would have had to act quickly to move it back."

"Yeah." James couldn't look away from the photo of the boulder. "Which means there was a witness to the accident after all. The killer himself."

James was grateful for the silence in the car. His mind was a chaotic jumble of anger, despair and a wild, unchecked grief. It was almost like reliving that night all over again. The shocked disbelief. The curious numbness that propelled one to go through the necessary motions. The overpowering sorrow.

And layered over it all, a shattering sense of failure.

He laid his head against the back of the seat, exhaustion punching through him. For twenty years he'd lived with a delusion. One far more comfortable, if he was honest, than the truth he was faced with now. For twenty years a murderer had gone free. Free to enjoy what life had to offer. Free to plan James's own destruction when the timeline was right.

The razored fury would come later, slashing all other emotions until it pushed to the surface, all cutting edges and white-hot heat. But for now there was only a deep, abiding sense of sadness, and an almost unbearable sense of guilt.

He knew, deep in the darkest corner of his mind, that it was an emotion he would never dislodge.

"You couldn't have changed anything, you know."

Tori's voice, any voice, was unwelcome. Her words particularly so. But she was unrelenting, speaking in the dark confines of the car like a persistent echo in the shadows. "No matter what you'd done. Who you consulted. If you'd found the killer back then, the only thing that would be different now is you wouldn't be targeted yourself by the same person. But the result back then would have been the same."

He shoved aside the logic of her words. Of course it would have been different. Someone would have paid. There would have been a sense of justice, revenge. And *that* at least would have counted for something. He and his brothers and sister wouldn't have lived a lie for two decades. Wouldn't have accepted a shattering act of violence for truth.

"Your actions after the accident wouldn't have changed the results. You couldn't bring them back, James, regardless of the outcome. So don't sit there beating yourself up now because of it. It's pointless, and distracts you from the real issue facing you."

Her words were annoying, only partially because they might be correct. He opened his eyes, turned his head to look at her. She was shrouded in shadows, but he could make out the reflection of lights in her eyes, the shape of her mouth. "Do you know what's more irritating than a woman who's right?" He could barely make out the shake of her head. "Nothing."

Her low laugh filled the car, and something shifted inside him. He went quiet for a time, too many thoughts and emotions crashing inside him to identify any one. Finally he spoke again. "Knowing that, understanding it, doesn't make it better."

"No." Her voice was soft.

There was understanding in the single word; in the touch of her hand when she reached over to take his. He laced his fingers with hers, amazed to find a measure of peace in the simple touch.

The intercom beeped. "Where to, sir?"

He looked at Tori, an unfamiliar need battling with a lifetime of solitary competence. "Come home with me tonight?"

She was still for a moment, before her fingers curled more tightly in his. "Absolutely."

Chapter 11

The ride home was accomplished mostly in silence, wrapping them in a shroud of intimacy. James had opened up the overhead panel so the stars glittered above like diamonds sprinkled across an inky sea. And then he'd wrapped his arm around her, pulled her close. She spent the remainder of the ride with his heartbeat sounding in her ear and emotion filling her heart.

It was easy to resist a man who seemed invincible; a well-trained warrior who needed no one and nothing. It was a far different matter, she was finding, to turn away from one who was reaching out. Especially when she knew how rare that was for him.

Still, she would have tried. Could have succeeded if her own heart didn't ache for the emotion she knew was twisting through his. If she couldn't imagine the way he was blaming himself. Wrongly. And if she didn't care, all too much, that he was hurting.

There was no heat in his touch as it smoothed over her shoulder and down her arm, back again. It was more of a promise, a gilded kiss of sensation that whispered of things to come. The certainty of it calmed anticipation until it was just a quiver in her belly. For now, this quiet embrace was enough.

She undid a button on his shirt and slid her hand inside, resting it quietly upon his chest. The warmth of his body transferred to her fingertips, danced along those sensitive nerve endings.

When he tipped her chin up with one finger, she expected his kiss to be light, languorous, like his touch. And for the first few moments it was just that. His lips brushed hers, gossamer soft, as if relearning their shape. She gave a little sigh and sank into it, hazily wishing to capture this moment in time; to freeze-frame it for replay later, when reason returned and doubts resurfaced.

But then he caught her bottom lip in his teeth, applying just enough pressure to have the muscles in her stomach clenching. The angle of the kiss changed, and the world abruptly shifted. Her lips parted and she met his tongue with his in one long, heated stroke.

The stars above were more seductive than candlelight. The mournful tune of lost love more sensual than harp song. But she didn't fool herself into thinking that atmosphere played a part in the sensation crashing through her system. Her response was due to the man beside her.

With one smooth move he tugged her onto his lap, settled her there with her head against his shoulder. She had a moment to marvel at the fit before his mouth went to her throat and a shudder of pleasure worked down her spine. She'd known he'd be good at this, but hadn't counted on her own reaction to his touch. His teeth scraping the cord on her neck sent off electrical currents that flickered to life beneath her skin. And when her eyelids fluttered shut, she firmly closed the door on the last bastion of reason. Whatever happened, she'd deal with. What came next, she'd handle. Now was a burning pulsing need that wouldn't be quieted. Whatever the outcome, she wasn't going to deny this, or him.

What had begun as a languid slide into pleasure quickly became more. The moment James felt her shiver in his arms, a silent savage hunger leaped to life. Desire, too long suppressed, took him unawares, made a mockery of control.

It wasn't supposed to be like this. He had the dim thought even as he pressed his mouth to the pulse beating wildly at the base of her throat. Sex, in all its varied faces, was meant to be a natural, pleasurable release. He didn't treat it casually, because intimacy made the act fuller somehow. More complete. He didn't know this woman in any of the usual ways. Hadn't spent quiet times sailing or at the theater; hadn't done the usual courtship dance over expensive meals and fine wines.

And yet she understood him, and he her, in a way he never could have foreseen. Circumstances had thrown them together and stripped them of their usual guard. With defenses lowered, vulnerabilities peeked through. And every moment with her had him more intrigued.

He caught the cord of her neck in his teeth and drew a gasp from her. The sound called to something primitive buried deep inside him. Caution reared, distant but insistent. There was danger here. Feeling too much too fast wasn't his normal way.

But the unexpected could be damn inviting. The foreign an almost overwhelming temptation.

She twisted against him, and he pulled her closer, inhaling the scent found below her ear, at her temple. Her skin was silky there, baby soft. And he was suddenly eager to explore the rest of her, to discover all the textures of her body. Find out what made her sigh and moan and gasp.

Need rose in him, edgy and fierce. He tugged the blouse from her waistband and slipped his hand inside, finding sleek skin molded over fascinating curves. He covered her breast with his palm, felt the warmth of her radiating through the lace. Her heart was hammering against his hand, and he knew its pace matched his own.

He took her mouth again and felt her hand slide to his hair, fisting there. Her flavor was heady, and it was difficult to get his fill. Especially when her tongue was flicking the roof of his mouth, sliding along his teeth, darting daringly against his own. He was certain in that instant that whatever the outcome of the night, he wouldn't regret this. Or her.

Tori didn't know how long it was before she became aware that the car had stopped. James barely lifted his mouth from hers to murmur against her lips. "I want to take you somewhere. Show you something."

His low voice was raspy with desire. The same emotion was reflected in his hooded eyes. He caught her hand when she smoothed it over his hard jaw; pressed a kiss in its center. Closing her fingers, she trapped the warmth that lingered there. "Show me," she said.

He helped her from the car and then laced their fingers. Tugging her along with him, they started off across the drive at a leisurely pace. But when the limo moved away toward the garage, James shot her a grin of pure wicked sin. "This will be easier barefoot."

A delighted smile crossed her lips at the playful challenge. It was unexpected. And, like many other experiences tonight, showed a side to him she wouldn't have guessed at. Once he'd shrugged out of his jacket and tie, and they'd both shed their shoes and socks, he grabbed her hand again and they ran flat-out across the dew-kissed grass.

The yard was long, lush and rolled softly toward the shore of the lake. They dodged the shadowy gardens and ornate walks and raced across the lawn.

Tori reached her stride easily, lungs expanding with air that seemed unbelievably fresh, amazingly sweet. And when a glance at James showed that he was matching her stride for stride, an innate competitive streak kicked in.

She could hear his low husky laugh behind her as she pulled ahead, could imagine his long legs stretching to keep pace. And felt a flash of pure enjoyment as sensation layered over sensation. The damp grass beneath her feet and the studded velvet sky overhead.

And most provocative was the presence of the man beside her. A man who, until now, she never would have pictured doing anything so carefree.

A small building loomed on their left, several yards away. His arm snaked around her waist, spun her to meet him, and then they were both tumbling to the grass, rolling across it. By the time they came to a stop she was dizzy and laughing helplessly, pushing at his chest. "Get off me, you fool."

James propped himself up on his elbows and grinned down at her. "Is that any way to show your appreciation of my seduction technique?"

"You've finally convinced me that your reputation in that area has been overstated."

"I told you." His easy agreement was in contrast to the kisses he strewed along her jawline, leaving fire in their wake. "It's always a mistake for people to believe their own press."

Her hands linked around his neck even as a sneaky sliver

of doubt stabbed her. "I've made my share of mistakes. I don't want to regret this. I don't want you to."

James paused. Her words, the shadow of uncertainty in them, unleashed a bolt of tenderness that was as unfamiliar as it was undeniable. "No. No regrets." To convince her, his kiss was slow, rife with promise. Her flavor was still sweetly unique. It still fired his hormones to instant readiness. But beneath the desire was an understanding that this wasn't going to be easily dismissed, or easily forgotten. And any regrets he experienced would be most likely to come at their parting.

The moonlight dappled the lawn, painting it with threads of silver. He wanted, quite desperately, to see her skin streaked with its pearly glow. To taste the areas bathed in light and explore those left in shadow.

To drive them both mad, he unbuttoned her blouse slowly, starting at the bottom, distracting each of them from his actions by pressing light, nibbling kisses to her lips. Two buttons open. The warm, smooth stretch of skin beneath his palm. He didn't look, but his imagination supplied him with an image that was temptation personified. Pressing her lips open with his, he found her tongue, sucked lightly.

Two more buttons undone. He heard the slight hitch of her breath when the night air met her bared skin. He kept his eyes closed and his touch restrained. Light brushes, fingertips on satin. Anticipation thrummed through him. Muscles grew tight with tension. And her mouth opened more eagerly for his, her hands clutching at his shoulders.

When the last two buttons were released, he gave a slight tug and the fabric parted. And only then did he raise his head, open his eyes and send up a fervent prayer.

Her long lean form was a delight to the eyes, a treat to the senses. Spreading his hand over her rib cage, he kneaded lightly, watching the shadows meld into glistening ivory and back again. The lace covering her breasts was rough in comparison to her skin. He wanted to see her wearing nothing but moonglow. He unsnapped her bra and tossed both it and her blouse aside.

Her breasts were high firm mounds that begged for a man's hands, for his mouth. He took a nipple between his lips and sucked, filling his palm with her other breast. He was aware of her hands in his hair, pulling him closer, but even more aware of the taste of her, unspeakably erotic; the exquisite softness of her curves; the bite of need in her nails digging into his shoulders.

Tori fumbled with the buttons on his shirt, lacking his finesse or restraint. She wanted to feel their skin pressed together; chest to chest; hips to hips. When she had the garment unfastened, her hands streaked inside, in a hurry to chart every inch of flesh she'd bared.

He had the long, spare build of a runner, lightly padded with muscle. She wasn't surprised to find strength lurking beneath the polish, but she was tempted by it. Incredibly so. Hands greedy, she slid them over his torso. There were surprising hollows beneath angles, sleek skin stretched over bone and sinew. The ribbon of hair trailing below his navel was silky where she traced it, the muscles quivering beneath her touch a stark testament to a need that mirrored her own.

She dragged her eyes open, tried to focus. He was leaning half-over her, part of him in light, the other in shadow. He still cupped her breast, the thumb rubbing over her nipple, drawing it to a tauter point. Odd, with the distrust that lay unspoken between them, that at this time, in this place, she trusted him as no other. Hunger painted his face nearly savage, but it wasn't fear that quickened inside her at the sight.

Leaning forward, she ran the tip of her tongue over his collarbone, tested it lightly with her teeth. Then lost her breath when, with one quick move, he had her in his arms and was rising, like a statue of a Roman god come to life.

She stretched, muscles tight with anticipation, and hooked an arm around his neck to anchor herself. The other was free to roam across his hair-roughened chest, finding the flat nipple hiding there and flicking it teasingly.

He nipped her throat for her efforts, then laved the spot with his tongue. With a sense of disorientation, she realized he'd brought them to the building she'd seen earlier.

"Look out there. See that view?"

Obeying his low, raspy voice, she turned her gaze on the lake and caught her breath. The half-moon hung low in the sky, painting the ripples in the water with a pearly stripe of ivory. The sky was an endless glittering spread of midnight, deep and unpenetrable.

"I've been all over the world, and nothing can match this spot for beauty." His eyes looked dark in the night, fathomless. "I'll never look at it again without remembering you here. Remembering this moment."

Her heart did a slow roll in her chest. An aching thread of tenderness, far more dangerous than passion, filled her. Words failed her, but words weren't needed. His mouth found hers, gentleness quickly turning to something sharper. More urgent.

Once inside the screened gazebo, James reluctantly set her on her feet. His mouth traced the curve of her shoulder as he swept his hand over the surprisingly delicate line of her spine, found the intriguing hollow at its base. Her slacks impeded his exploration, and patience proved elusive. He managed the zipper but wasn't as careful with the scrap of silk beneath. There was a sound of shredding fabric, before he filled his hands with her silky bottom.

There was more, far more than he'd imagined to stroke, to knead, to explore. The curve of her waist, the underside of her breast, the sleek line of thigh, the slick softness of her femininity. He tolerated, for as long as he was able, her hands at his waist, unfastening his pants. But when she inched the zipper of his trousers down one excruciating inch at a time, he was certain he was being punished for forgotten sins. Breath hissing between his teeth, he stepped away, stripped off the remainder of his clothes and drew her close again, marvelously close.

Bending his head, he took her nipple between his lips and filled his mouth with her. Her broken cries torched the fever of his desire. Stoked it higher. He could feel the hunger rise in him and strove to check it. Not yet. There were too many discoveries he'd yet to make. And far too much of the night remained to rush through this now.

And then those intentions fragmented when she found him, wrapping knowing fingers around pulsing heat and stroking him to madness. His eyes went blind. His lungs strained for oxygen. And the sharp and vicious edge of need grew keener.

His hands became increasingly urgent, just shy of desperate. He caressed her thighs, found her damp cleft and pressed rhythmically. When she softened against him he cupped her femininity and slid a finger inside her damp center.

The cry that escaped her scraped over nerve endings already taut and straining. She was exquisitely soft, tight and warm. Even days ago he would have sworn that lovemaking could hold no surprises for him. And yet here he was, sensation raining over him, a storm in his system.

And the indisputable cause of that was the woman going wild in his arms.

Her response shredded the veneer of civility he was usually careful to maintain. It called forth an untamed element that he'd always been aware of, had always hidden. It drew from him a determination to take all she had to give and then push her higher. Further. Until the image of what had passed between them was etched forever in her memory, as it would be in his.

He felt the precise moment when she stiffened against him, surprise and pleasure drawing her up into a tight fist of need. One more stroke, one deep touch would send her crashing over the edge, leaving her gasping and limp.

He withdrew his fingers, muffled the low whimper she made with his lips. When she went over the first time, it would be with him buried deep inside her, with every inch of their bodies touching, straining toward release. And it would have to be soon. Sweat slicked his forehead, and he couldn't see through the haze of his own desire.

Moving more from memory than sight, he tumbled them both to the futon. Ragged breaths mingled. Greed took over, on both their parts. Damp skin pressed against damp skin. Hands raced over tense muscles. Mouths met while teeth clashed and tongues battled.

Control shredded.

He had a moment of clarity, as the hunger sliced through him with a single savage stroke. Blindly he reached for his pants, dug out the foil-wrapped package in the pocket. And then what was left of his tattered control was tested as Tori took the condom from him and sheathed him with it, fingers staying to caress.

His brain misted, reason receded. Moving her hands away, he slid over her body, positioned himself between her thighs. His intent was to go slow. He entered her by excruciating inches, his throat clogging at the tight perfection of her, his muscles quivering with restraint. And then intent was shattered when her hips rose wildly, forcing him deeper, faster.

He needed to see her face. He dragged his eyelids open, fought for focus. Her eyes were open, dazed and huge, fixed on his. And in that moment he was certain that what they shared was a first of sorts for both of them.

She clutched him closer, the tiny sting of her nails on his back whipping his hunger to fever pitch. His hips lunged against hers, each frantic movement edging them closer to a brilliant culmination. He felt her body buck beneath his, swallowed the helpless cry on her lips. He tried to fight against his own climax, but she was liquid fire around him, her inner muscles clenching and releasing, milking his own response. With his gaze still locked on her face, her name on his lips, he felt the sensations slam into him. He surged against her one last time before following her headlong into pleasure.

Time and distance were qualities necessary to steady the pulse and resettle sanity. Tori hadn't seen James all day, which, she considered, was for the best. Perspective, she decided, was something she very much needed to restore.

The night they'd spent together defied description. Melting tenderness, primitive hunger and, laced through it all, a burning desire that had been quenched, over and over, only to quicken again. She had expected the lovemaking to be hot and, given her response to him, satisfying. She hadn't known that it could be meltingly touching at the same time. That it would wipe out every previous experience she'd ever had and stamp her indelibly with his touch.

A frisson of worry shot through her at the thought,

and her spine straightened. Obviously lack of sleep had affected her brain, as well. She wasn't *stamped*. She didn't do *stamped*. Okay, it had been good between them, she told herself, struggling to pour herself into the dress he'd had the maid bring to her room. Great even. He'd needed someone last night, and she'd happened to be handy and available.

Maybe a little too available—where was the zipper in this thing? Contorting herself into an impossible position, she yanked at one of the myriad straps that crossed what she fervently hoped was the back and inched the dress up a fraction. But she wasn't going to waste time second-guessing herself. They'd both said last night they weren't going to do regrets. And despite how this thing ended, and it would end soon she was certain, she couldn't be sorry for something that had been…almost magical.

Once she finally got the garment on, she strode to the mirror, gaped in horror. Where was the rest of the material? In vain, she tugged at the hem in an attempt to lengthen it a few inches. And the back—she half turned to peek and gave a groan—was completely bare, save for the criss-crossing of stretchy straps that didn't seem to be much more than decoration. Certainly they meant she'd have to lose the bra.

She scowled at her reflection, considered her options. She could track down the maid and ask her to select something else. But she had no idea where to find the woman, and she was running short of time as it was. She was very much afraid that anything else in the collection would be as bad as or worse than this one.

Finally giving up that idea, she shifted so she wouldn't be faced with her reflection and dragged a brush through her hair. She started to strap on her watch, then noticed that the functional style would hardly go with the dress. Muttering beneath her breath, she laid it back on the dresser and snatched up the shoes that went with the dress. Resignation filled her when she noted the heels. They added a good three inches to her already over-average height. In the bright-red dress, which she had a sneaky suspicion James had selected on purpose, she now looked like a flaming Amazon.

A knock sounded as she attempted to jam her cell phone into the tiny matching purse. Starting for the door, she didn't get two steps before she darn near twisted her ankle. Cursing the uncustomary heels, she hobbled the rest of the way and threw the door open, glowering at the man standing there holding a flat case in his hand.

"Why don't you just take a gun and shoot me? It'd be less painful."

Brows raised, James strolled in, his gaze traveling over her form and lingering on the shoes. "Is it the dress or the heels? Both, by the way, are very becoming. I knew they'd suit you."

She shut the door behind him, with a little more force than necessary. "The dress is about four inches too short to wear in public, and the heels should qualify as lethal weapons. I'm not sure I could chase down a suspect in them, but if I happened to trip one I could always use a shoe to beat him to death."

Tori saw the smile quivering on his lips and the admirable effort he took to firm it. Neither endeared him to her. "Easy to be amused when you're not the one attending this thing half-naked wearing stilts."

"I don't suppose it will improve your mood to add some glitter to the mix. You're not the type to go gooey-eyed over jewels." He flipped open the jeweler's box to reveal a gold necklace dripping rubies and diamonds. Taking it out, he said, "Turn around and I'll fasten it for you."

She didn't move. Couldn't. She was very much afraid her mouth was agape, as well. "Is that real?"

"A hundred grand worth of 'real.'" Since she still hadn't moved, he stepped behind her and fitted the necklace beneath her hair. Latching the clasp he turned her in his arms, studying her critically. "Perfect."

"Are you crazy?" Each jewel seemed to burn like a brand. "I can't wear this." She slapped a hand over it, as if to keep it in place. "What if I lose it?"

"Then the insurance company used by Hansen, Hansen and Smith are going to be very upset with the store manager. I've borrowed this for the night. I'll messenger it back in the morning."

That made her feel only a modicum better. "So all I have to do is manage not to lose it for a few hours. Great." Another thought occurred, and she frowned. "They actually lend this stuff out? Are they crazy?"

"I'm a very good customer." He cocked his head, appreciation obvious in his expression. "And at the risk of having you use one of those heels on me, I have to say you're a gorgeous advertisement for their jewels. And you're breathtaking in that dress."

"I look like a stork," she said shortly. "All legs." She couldn't begin to count all the times in her life that she'd wished to saw about four inches off them.

He moved behind her again, shifted her so that the mirror reflected both of them. In the heels, she was only a couple of inches shorter than he was. "You look like every man's fantasy," he murmured in her ear. "We're a pretty primitive lot, darling. When we see endless legs like yours we tend to think only of how they'd feel wrapped around our waist."

His words robbed her of speech. The stinging kiss he placed on the side of her neck stole her breath. Raising his head again, his eyes met hers in the mirror, an unmistakable sheen of desire in them. "And having had that exquisite experience recently, I'm going to have the devil's own time tonight keeping my mind on business."

Because her throat seemed clogged, she cleared it. "Well, I wish I'd known that before I invested in all those self-defense courses I took. Next time I get in a jam, I'll just flash some leg."

He reached past her, picked up the red-sequined purse. The sight of the frivolous accessory dangling from his arm relaxed her in a way nothing else could have. He nudged her toward the door. "And if you get in a jam tonight, remember I've got your back." As if to accentuate his words, his hand slid to her butt and squeezed.

A well-placed elbow dislodged his hand and brought a satisfying wince to his face. "Don't you think we're a bit overdressed for a…what exactly is a Technology Expo, anyway?" He was dressed in a dark suit that looked every bit as formal as a tux. They headed down the staircase and out the door, where the driver had the limo running.

"The expo actually starts tomorrow and runs for three days. Tonight is a more formal cocktail gathering for the participants and press." Reaching into his breast pocket, he withdrew an ID for her, slipped it inside her purse and handed the purse to her.

The sight of it reminded her of something. "Did you remember to have an ID sent over to Corday?"

"I did. I also…" His cell phone rang then, and he answered it, even as he helped her into the car. It was a struggle to swing her legs inside while maintaining her modesty. Catching the look of sheer male appreciation in his expression at the sight, she lost no time reaching over to slam the door.

Once he was inside, she listened unabashedly to his

side of the conversation. It wasn't difficult to discern that he was talking to Cade. She waited impatiently until they were down the drive and on the road before he ended the conversation.

"NOPD got a lead on the bomber," he said without preamble. "Nothing popped in the database, but the detectives worked some snitches. With Joe's description and the MO, one name kept surfacing. Dennis Francis."

Hope leaped to her throat. "Did they catch up with him?" He nodded, face grim. "But not before someone else caught up with him first. He's dead. Shot three times in the front seat of his car, close range."

As quickly as hope had surged, disappointment replaced it. "But we can look into his history. See if he might have been acquainted with your father…"

James was already shaking his head. "He was only thirty-three. He would have been too young to have anything to do with the accident. More than likely he was hired for the bombing and was killed when he failed."

Mind working furiously, Tori said, "Well, this still might shake loose a lead. What about his phone lines? Have they done a dump on them?"

James gave her a look that was half admiring, half amused. "You're right on track. He didn't have a landline, and no cell was found on him. But they did find cell phone bills when they tossed his apartment. Cade said they put a rush on the order, but it will still take a couple days."

"Something tells me we may not have that long." She looked at him consideringly, knowing he wasn't going to like what she had to say next. "I heard back on some feelers I put out a few days ago on Dale Cartwright."

He stiffened, very slightly. Voice cool, he said, "That wasn't necessary. I told you I'd take care of it."

Silence stretched, the tension in it palpable. Then, with obvious reluctance, he asked, "What did you find?"

Discreetly, Tori tried, and failed, to tug the hem of her dress farther down her thighs. "He and your father didn't part especially amicably. Word I heard was your father forced him out. Apparently he had an alcohol problem and it cost them too many contracts."

"And where'd you get these details?" There was a light in his eye, a dangerous burn. She refused to quail beneath it.

"From information brokers I use from time to time. I got the same story from two of them, so I tend to think it's credible." And because she saw through the anger to the hurt beneath, she said, "I'm sorry, James. I know it's not what you wanted to hear."

He took a deep breath. "No. But then, there's been damn little I've wanted to hear in the last few days. But a lot that I needed to know. So." He seemed to draw himself in, a warrior preparing to rejoin the battle. "He could have harbored a grudge over that, I agree. I tend to think if he had, however, he wouldn't have waited three years to get revenge."

Tori wasn't so sure. There were plenty of people who believed that the best revenge was served cold.

"I don't want it to be Dale. I admit that." She knew the admission didn't come easily for him. "It'd be easier, less personal, if it turns out to be one of the CEOs of one of the other companies."

"Tarkington's and Beal's were the only two of the other competitive companies you cited who were even around at the time. Your parents' accident and the threats on your life are linked. So the suspect almost has to be someone from that time period." She thought for a moment before inquiring, "If I were the sender, I'd have followed up the bombing with another message."

"Another came today," he admitted. "Said next time I'd be dead and to withdraw my bid from the upcoming Pentagon contract."

The chill that broke out over her skin had nothing to do with her scanty dress. "And when do they award the contract?"

"Next week."

Time was running out, and the sender's desperation was sure to escalate. The concern she felt wasn't new. The stark fear was. "So what are you going to do?"

"The only thing I can do." His voice was even, full of promise. "I'm going to find this bastard and nail him to the wall. And if I find out that the same person threatening me killed my parents…" His tone sharpened, a sword whetted on stone. "The law will be much more merciful than I will be."

Chapter 12

It resembled theater opening night rather than Tori's idea of a technology expo. The hotel conference rooms were overflowing with people, and more of them were wearing press passes than she'd expected. She saw Kiki in the distance, camera flashing away, and winced. He hadn't taken her fashion advice. With his loud, plaid polyester suit coat and striped pants, he looked more like a seventies used-car salesman than a photographer. But he appeared to be doing the job she'd hired him for, so she would have to be content with that.

James kept her close to his side, introduced her to a dizzying array of people, but none were the ones she most wanted to meet. If Beal, Cartwright or Tarkington were somewhere in the crowd she was busily scanning, she'd yet to see them.

"Tori." She pasted a smile on her face and turned to

greet the woman James was greeting. She looked vaguely familiar.

"You remember Celia, don't you? My assistant?"

The name didn't ring a bell, but the job description did. The woman who vetted all of James's visitors at the company. "Of course. Nice to see you again." Rather than the colorless suits she'd seen the woman wearing at work, tonight she was dressed in a tasteful navy dress and pearls. Tori felt positively bare beside her.

"Miss Corbett." There was a puzzled note in the woman's voice, as she looked from Tori to James. "I didn't expect to see you here."

"Well, actually, I'm Mr. Tremaine's…"

"Companion." James slipped an arm around Tori's waist, ignoring the way she stiffened. "She was kind enough to accompany me here tonight. Looks like we've got a good crowd."

"Yes, I knew you'd be pleased." Celia turned to scan the mob. "I arrived with Marcus a little bit ago. I believe he's searching for you."

"I'll look him up. Why don't you see if Tucker and Jones need any help? And if Corley and Soulieu have the Micro Secure set up and ready for the demonstration."

Celia took a pad from her purse and began scribbling his orders, the picture of competence. "I'll do that. Do you have your cell with you?" At James's nod, she promised, "I'll let you know what I find out."

Once the woman had departed, Tori slipped away from his arm. "Can we at least go with 'associate' rather than companion? You make me sound like the faithful family dog."

He snagged two flutes of champagne from a passing waiter's tray and handed her one. "'Associate' works for me. Of course, when I introduced you that way to my brother the other night he immediately assumed we were 'associating.' The word dripped innuendo."

Throat suddenly dry, Tori sipped. It was rather hypocritical, she supposed, to object to having people thinking they were sleeping together, now that they were, in fact, doing just that. Wisely, she kept the rest of her protests to herself. So far she'd managed to avoid any discussion about last night, and she would like to keep it that way. They'd moved from the gazebo sometime before dawn to her bedroom. And when she'd awakened, he was gone. The only signs he'd been there at all was the indentation on the pillow next to her, and her clothes, neatly folded on a chair.

She took a bigger drink. Yes, any discussion regarding their relationship, real or pretended, was something she'd rather evade.

"What's on the agenda tonight?"

James checked his watch. "Happy hour will continue for another forty-five minutes, and then the participating companies will begin the exhibition. Each will highlight one of the products they'll be showcasing for the next few days." His voice was laced with certainty. "Of course, we feel that Tremaine Technologies will garner the lion's share of attention with our product."

"All modesty aside, I'm compelled to agree."

Tori immediately identified the tiny blonde in the black cocktail dress who'd joined them. Ana ignored her brother for the moment and said, "Tori, isn't it? How are you? Cade said the bomb went off in front of your house." She swept her figure with her gaze. "I'm glad to see that you don't look any the worse for wear."

"I've got a bump on the head and makeup took care of the worst bruises." Tori shrugged. "We were lucky."

Ana sent a meaningful glance to her brother. "His luck

is about to run out. He's been avoiding me all day, but I want to know what kind of precautions he's been taking. This psycho who almost killed the two of you isn't going to stop. Did he tell you the family wanted him to delay the expo?"

Tori shook her head. She wasn't surprised, however, that James had refused. He wasn't the type to back down in the face of danger.

"We've got security all over this area," James informed them quietly. "And I'm using a driver and an armored car."

Ana smiled, but the worry was still evident in her expression. "I know exactly how much you hate that, too. When I'm tempted to brain you for being bullheaded, thinking of that fact cheers me right up."

Looking slightly hunted, James said, "I thought you'd be getting in position to see how the Micro Secure performs."

"I already know how it will perform," she replied sweetly. "Magnificently. Tell me you're wearing Kevlar tonight."

He looked down at his suit. "No, Armani."

"Don't be cute, James. This would be a perfect spot for someone to take a shot at you." At the real concern threading Ana's voice, Tori looked around uneasily, wondering if she was right. Certainly the mob of people would make discovering a sniper more difficult.

"You can talk over the security details with your husband. He arranged them. We tightened up the registration ID process, and the metal detectors make smuggling in a weapon unlikely." He reached out, gave her a hug. "I know you're worried, but you shouldn't be. This is probably the safest place I can be."

Ana didn't look satisfied, but she hugged him back,

hard. To Tori she said confidingly, "He tends to think he's indestructible, which has the rest of us a bit worried. Add to that his irritating quality of thinking he knows best, and he can be a bit of a trial."

"I'm familiar with the trait," Tori said meaningfully. "Maybe we could double-team him."

Ana laughed delightedly. "I like her, James. She's not a fawner." To Tori she said, "Most of his women drip all over him. It's absolutely nauseating."

Tori was beginning to enjoy herself. Certainly she was enjoying the pained expression on James's face. "I'm standing right here," he reminded them. "And I thought you wanted to quiz your husband on the security details." He turned his sister firmly around. "He's over there by the windows. When you're finished with him go make sure Corley and Soulieu are ready to start."

"Okay." She began moving away. "I can take a hint."

"Not well," he muttered. Grasping Tori's elbow, he began leading her away. "Don't believe anything she says."

"I don't know." She pretended to consider. "Seems to me she had you dead to rights."

His cell phone rang again then and while he answered it she did another scan of the crowd. It had grown considerably in the past few minutes. Taking advantage of his distraction, she tugged on his sleeve. "I'm going to mingle." His answer, if he made one, was lost as she moved away.

James had just finished his phone conversation with Celia when he felt a clap on the shoulder. "Hell of a shindig you got going on here, son. Can't say I'm surprised."

The familiar voice elicited twin feelings of happiness and dismay. Turning around, he exchanged a handshake with Dale Cartwright and wished he'd had more time to prepare for this meeting.

"I didn't expect you until the engagement party later this week."

Dale beamed at him. "Got to thinking a few extra days in town wouldn't hurt a bit. Give me a chance to catch your expo and a little extra time to flirt with Ana. She here tonight?" He sent a searching gaze across the room. "Might steal her away from that new husband of hers to catch up. Shirley sent along pictures of the grandkids, and Ana always gets a kick out of those."

The man never seemed to change. Big, bluff, hearty, with hair that had been gray for as long as James could remember. Shirley, his wife of forty years, matched him in looks and in personality. The two had been a mainstay in his life since he'd been able to walk. Try as he might, he couldn't imagine the man capable of anything as nefarious as the plot they'd uncovered.

He imagined Tori felt the same way about her own father.

"Ana's here." His next words, as distasteful as they were, had to be spoken. "I'm glad you came tonight, though. I've been wanting to talk to you."

"Well, shoot, son, why didn't you say so? Let's head out to a balcony." James set his empty glass down on a nearby tray and didn't pick up another. For as long as he remembered, Dale had been a nondrinker.

Once outside, he had difficulty summoning the necessary words. So he listened as Dale rambled about his wife, their travels and their grandchildren. It was several minutes before the man wound down, saying, "Well, listen to me go on. You had something you needed to talk to me about, and I haven't stopped rattling on for a minute. What'd you need? Business advice?"

James responded to Dale's hearty laugh with a faint smile. "I need you to help me understand some history.

Specifically how you and my father parted ways after years of partnership."

Dale's laughter abruptly halted. Eyes narrowed, he said, "That's old news, and better left alone. Why would you be asking about that after all these years?"

"Indulge me."

The man studied him a moment, a serious expression settled over his face. Finally he gave a slow nod. "All right. We wanted different things for the company, your father and me. We each had our own ideas for how to make it grow. Heck, you can imagine how that would be if you had a partner. You're a fella who thinks he knows how things should be done. Take a couple strong-willed guys like your dad and me, and we didn't always agree, I can tell you that."

James looked away. It was hard to have this conversation with a man he respected. One he loved. Harder yet to deal with the uncertainty of what had transpired all those years ago. "You had an alcohol problem, I heard. It affected your work. Affected the business."

Dale took a step back, leaned heavily on the balcony railing. "Yep. I sure did." He waited for James's gaze to meet his again. "It's not something I'm proud of, but it's something I deal with every day of my life. I'm an alcoholic, son. Been on the wagon more than eighteen years, but it doesn't change what I am. They say everyone of us has to hit rock bottom before we admit we have a problem. Well, your dad shoving me out of the business was the beginning of my bottom. It took me three years to forgive him. Another three to get sober."

"But you did forgive him," James probed. He wanted, badly, to believe him. He wanted it to be the truth.

Now it was Dale who looked away. "I loved that man like a brother. Loved you kids like my own. That didn't change, but I'd be lying if I said I wasn't angry with him at the time. I had my problems, God knows, I'm not denying it. But shoot, son, we were all young upstarts back then, wild in our own way. With me it was drinking. Marcus liked to gamble more than he should have, and Celia… well, your father nearly fired her when we found out she'd been consorting with one of our rivals."

James felt like the recipient of one too many right jabs. "I never heard that about Marcus. And Celia…who was she involved with?"

"Simon Beal." The man shook his head sadly. "Whoa, that was a long time ago. He took advantage of her, of course. Wooed her and then tried to use her position to get information on the company. Once she found out what he'd been up to, she came right to your father and me and told us the whole story. Took us a couple days to wrestle with it, but eventually we decided to keep her on. Don't think she ever got over it," he mused. "She never did get married, did she?"

"No." James swallowed. "She never did."

The man seemed to shake himself from his reverie. "Well, like I said, it's ancient history. Old hurts, old scars. But you know what they say, time heals all wounds. And I gotta say, most of them are better left covered." Clapping him on the shoulder again, he moved away, back into the crowded conference room.

Broodingly James considered the street below without really seeing it. Old wounds, he knew intimately, didn't ever really heal. Sometimes they could still throb viciously two decades later.

He didn't catch up with Tori until people had begun drifting out of the area. Then he spotted her standing across the room wearing an expression that could only be described as dangerous. The sight lightened something inside him. There was something about the contrast she presented, he supposed. In the feminine dress and foolish purse, she'd appear at home on a fashion runway. But the look on her face spelled trouble for whoever had been foolish enough to raise her ire. He started toward her, half expecting her to take off one of her heels and start swinging at the poor sap.

He saw her shift, a deliberate movement designed to dislodge a hand from her rear. Then the crowd parted around them, and James identified the man at her side.

Allen Tarkington.

There was a single savage leap inside him, something primal. It took a moment to tuck away that flame of visceral possessiveness before he started toward them again. It wasn't an emotion that Tori would welcome. He didn't welcome it himself. Since he didn't get possessive over women, not ever, he chalked up the emotion to the dislike he had for Tarkington.

He'd never been able to link the man to the fire at his corporate headquarters nine years ago, but that didn't mean he didn't still suspect him as the arsonist. There was little the man wouldn't do to get ahead in their field. His tactics hadn't won him many friends in the business and his personality even less.

"Allen." His voice pleasant, he stopped next to Tori, nodding at the man. "Caught your presentation on that new password decryptor. Interesting."

Tarkington straightened his jacket. "We're thinking it'll start a buzz. Who knows? Might even give us a leg up on that contract next week. That'd be ironic, wouldn't it? If the exposure from your expo sent some attention my way from the Pentagon bigwigs?"

James thought of the arson once more, and smiled.

"Funny, I've always thought exposure would do you good, too. Will you excuse us?" Tori moved away with him, leaving Tarkington to stare after them.

"I didn't catch your company's presentation," she said. "How'd it go?"

"The Micro Secure performed well. Sometimes there are glitches in the preliminary programs, but Ana did a great job working them out. I have high hopes for it."

They strolled back toward the entrance. The rooms were quickly emptying of people. "I had occasion to talk to several of your competitors," she murmured.

"Form any conclusions?" He raised a hand to acknowledge Tucker, Corley and Soulieu, who were heading for the door.

"Well, Tarkington's a grab-ass who'll chase anything in a dress. The man's lucky I didn't drive my heel through his jugular."

The mental picture brought a smile. "There are more people than you know who'd pay good money to see that."

"I also had a few minutes to speak to Beal." She stopped them, turned to look at him, concern apparent in her gaze. "He's the one that scares me, James. He's cold all the way through. And he'd take any advantage, use anyone, to get a jump on you. He must have known I was with you, because within thirty seconds of my getting near him he was pumping me for information. He was smooth. He disguised it as small talk, but the minute I convinced him I had nothing to do with Tremaine Technologies, his interest in me dried up fast."

"He's an opportunist." A fact that, according to Dale, Celia had learned the hard way. "But that doesn't necessarily mean he's our man."

Tori looked around. "How much longer do you have to stay at this thing?"

Checking his watch, he said, "Maybe a half hour. Since we sponsored the expo we're assisting the hotel staff with security for the setups. Why?"

She slipped her arm in his and began walking again. "Let's make it fast. I'm betting Kiki went right home and started developing those photos. He can be very industrious when there's cash on the line."

Interest piqued, he glanced at her. "You're planning a trip over there at this hour?"

"I think I can safely guarantee that where money is involved, Kiki's visiting hours can be very flexible."

But when they pulled up in front of the man's home an hour later, James wasn't so sure. There wasn't a light on in the house Tori directed him to, although the man's car was in the drive.

"It's barely midnight," she said impatiently when he pointed that out to her. "I know him. The first thing he would have done is come home and load the pictures on to his computer. Where money is involved, Kiki is meticulous."

He'd have to take her word for it. The slovenly man he'd briefly seen at the expo certainly hadn't seemed meticulous about much else.

"If he's awake, he'll still be at the computer. It won't hurt to check."

Giving a shrug, he followed her up the cracked front walk to climb the steps. "That's weird," she muttered. The front door was open, as it had been the day she'd come to hire him. The screen was still missing from the storm door.

"Kiki," she called, banging on the door. "It's Tori. I've got your money." Her greeting failed to get a response.

"Maybe if we call," James suggested.

"The heck with it. He's one guy you don't have to stand on ceremony with." She pulled open the storm door, stepped inside. "And he's never been unhappy to see anyone with money in hand."

Warily James glanced around before following her inside. This wasn't exactly the kind of neighborhood that inspired faith in humanity. But there was no one in sight. Not a sound could be heard, other than Tori still calling out the man's name. Her voice echoed in the too-silent house. "Exactly where is this office of his?"

"Right back here." She continued through the house, pushing open the office door. "Talk about engrossed in your work, Kiki, you really take the—" She stopped so abruptly that James nearly ran into her. A moment later he saw the cause for her reaction.

It was instinct rather than comprehension that had him reacting. He pushed her behind him and searched for the light switch, flipping it on for a clearer look, but that first glance had been enough.

Kiki Corday lay crumpled on the cracked linoleum floor. And from the amount of blood pooling around him, there was little doubt that he was dead.

"Ohmygod." James heard Tori's low moan, turned to see her staring horrified at the figure on the floor. "Is he…"

"Yes." From this angle he could see the man's sightless eyes aimed at the ceiling. "Use your cell to call my brother." He recited the number as he gingerly stepped over the body and went to the computer. Taking off his tie, he wrapped it around his hand before touching the mouse, bringing the screen to life.

"It looks like he was loading the pictures, all right," he said grimly. The compact flash reader was hooked to the USB port, but there was no sign of the memory card itself.

The CD carousel was standing open and empty. Muttering a vicious curse, James used his covered hand to type in commands, but it was quickly clear that the images had been erased. A quick check proved that the recycle bin had been emptied, as well. "Damn."

"He's on his way." There was a slight shake to Tori's voice. He looked at her sharply, noted that she was keeping her eyes firmly away from the body on the floor. "He said not to touch anything." Despite the words, she moved closer. "Everything's gone?"

"Looks like it." Frustration rose, keen as a blade. "It could be retrieved. The only way to really get rid of them is to format the hard drive, and he sure didn't have time to do that. If I could have a half hour and an undelete program…"

"Somehow I doubt your brother will hold off on the crime-scene investigation until you get that done. They have a tech department for that, though, right? So eventually we'll get a look at them once they're recovered."

"Eventually being the operative word." He rose, frowned down at her. "You said he was meticulous."

"He is…was." Her voice stumbled over the past tense of the word. "He wouldn't have made just one CD, he'd have made several. He'd give me one and then keep the rest in case he could sell them to someone else later. I suppose the killer took them all." She stopped, looked toward the door. "Unless…"

"Unless what?"

When she didn't answer, just nearly ran from the room, he followed her. Flipping on a light in the living room, she went unerringly to a filing cabinet, reached for a drawer.

"Here." He handed her his tie, and she wrapped it around her hand before pulling the drawer open. Looking over her shoulder, he observed, "He'd have filed it under Tremaine wouldn't he?"

"Nope. I hired him, you didn't." She stopped when she found a file folder marked "Corbett." Taking a deep breath, she pressed it open.

And revealed two disks inside, marked with tonight's event and date.

"Thank God," she breathed. "This should speed things up for the police."

A siren sounded in the distance. James blew out a breath. "We should wait for Cade outside." At his suggestion, she straightened shut the drawer. He slipped an arm around her shoulders, and they walked out together.

Cade Tremaine held his flashlight in one gloved hand and shone it at the figure on the floor for a few seconds. Then he looked up at his brother. "Okay, here's the deal. This isn't my territory, but if this guy's murder is connected to the bombing, that will give us jurisdiction. And judging by your presence here, I'm guessing there's a pretty strong link."

"He was hired to take pictures at the expo," Tori said. "James tightened security, but we thought there was still a chance someone attending might have had something to do with the bombing. So he was taking photos to give us an idea of who talked to whom, maybe pick out some faces that shouldn't have been there." She stopped, swallowed hard. "It was my idea to hire him."

James heard the guilt beneath the words. He was familiar with the feeling. "Don't. He took the job because we were paying him handsomely." Tightening the arm he had around her waist, he looked at his brother. "He dumped the images, but a good tech should be able to recover at least some of them. If you need a good undelete program, we manufacture the best. And there's a disk filed under Tori's name in the file cabinet in the living room. Hopefully it's a copy of what he loaded tonight."

Cade rose and took out his cell phone. "I'm calling this in. Do you remember what you touched before you phoned me?"

Tori drew in a shaky breath. "The front door. The light switch in here. The doorjamb and knob to this room. For everything else James wrapped his hand. We didn't touch the disks."

From his narrowed gaze, it was obvious that Cade was less than impressed with his brother's forethought. "Made yourselves at home, didn't you?" He pressed a button on his cell, held it to his ear. "It'd probably be best if you two waited outside. I don't want you contaminating the scene." Tori turned, seemingly anxious to reach fresh air. As James followed her, his brother's voice trailed after them. "Oh, and stick around for a while. You're going to need to give a statement."

Disaster had been narrowly averted. A deep breath was taken. And then another. It was easy now to remember how distasteful it was to involve oneself personally. There was no thrill in taking a life. Just relief that a crisis had been averted.

The CD was snapped in two, and then each half broken again. The pieces could be disposed of easily, as could the CF card. It wasn't so much what the man had photographed that could have caused complications; it was what he may have heard in doing so. There could be no real regret in ridding the world of yet another bottom-feeding paparazzo, snooping and prying into matters that didn't concern him.

One had to create one's own opportunities. Tremaine

couldn't be awarded that new Pentagon contract. His death would be the most certain method to ensure that. But he'd be on his guard now, more difficult to take by surprise.

The woman, however, was a different story. Corbett, that was her name. Tremaine seemed taken with her. And as single-minded as the man could be, it was unlikely that he could complete any new project if she suffered an unfortunate accident.

Lips were pursed and the idea given consideration. There was usually more than one way to reach an objective. Whether Tremaine died or the woman, if the end result was the same, the choice really made very little difference.

Chapter 13

"I don't want to go back to the lake," Tori objected, after James gave the order to the driver. They'd just left Cade and it was nearly three in the morning. "I just want to go home." Sneaky fingers of regret tugged at her conscience. Kiki would still be alive if she hadn't hired him. That fact was indisputable.

"I can take you home," he said agreeably. Then his hand went to his suit jacket, withdrew a flat object. "But I thought you'd want to see these."

She stared at him, aghast. "Tell me you didn't steal evidence from the crime scene."

"*Steal* is such a negative word. Since I have every intention of returning it, I prefer the word *borrow*."

"When did you get that? We were together the whole time." Tori was beginning to believe that the man had more than a hint of the criminal in him.

"Not every minute, obviously."

Her initial shock had been replaced by temper. "I doubt very much whether your brother is going to share your fine distinction between stealing evidence and borrowing it. You just may end up in a jail cell before the killer does."

"Let me worry about my brother. The killer went to some pretty shocking lengths to get those pictures. Given the investigation we've done so far, if there's a clue to the killer's identity in those photos, you and I are far more likely to pick up on it than the police will. And much more quickly."

The fact that he was right didn't excuse his actions. Interest stirred, but she wasn't about to admit it aloud. "I hope," she said huffily, folding her arms across her chest, "that you still feel that way when you're introduced to your toothless bunk mate named Bubba."

"Darling." Amusement threaded his voice. "Your concern overwhelms me. And here I was counting on you to bake me a cake with a saw inside."

"You'd better pin your hopes on a good lawyer. I'm not much for baking." But despite her sarcasm, hope was unfurling inside her. Hope that the images would finally elicit a clue that would bring the killer to justice.

And hope that they could do so before another attempt was made on James's life.

Since she couldn't tolerate the thought of him looking at the disk without her, her objections subsided. Besides a few more pointed remarks about his light-fingered ways, the trip to the lake was made in silence. He was grateful he didn't have to argue with her about going home.

He wanted, more than was comfortable, to keep her near him. To keep her safe. And the logic of that particular emotion eluded him. He was accused, on a regular basis, of being fiercely protective of his family. This was the first time he'd felt the same emotion for a woman.

It was the situation, he told himself, discomfited. He was a man accustomed to taking responsibility for others. But it wasn't solely a sense of responsibility that made him remember, far too often, what she felt like in his arms. It wasn't responsibility that made him anxious to have her there again.

When they reached the house he led her to the den where he kept a secure computer. He put the CD in the drive, clicked on its icon when it appeared on the screen. She seemed to be holding her breath until the first image opened and showed a scene that had unmistakably been taken that night.

"Meticulous to the end," she murmured. As one, they leaned closer to the screen while he clicked first on one image, then the next. "If you get me copies of the registration photo IDs, I can cross-reference the people in the images to identify them," Tori suggested.

"We'll work on it together so we can eliminate the people I know by sight. The preliminary count was close to five hundred."

He clicked through the images fairly quickly. Even with his powerful computer, it took several seconds for each to open. After a few minutes Tori leaned closer to get a look at an image he'd just opened. It had been taken from a distance, and depicted Dale and him on the balcony. "I didn't know Cartwright was going to be there tonight."

"Neither did I." Nor had he considered the emotional impact of the conversation they would have. Briefly, he filled her in on the information the man had imparted.

"Sounds like there were hard feelings, at least at the beginning," she said. "And plenty going on with several of the employees at the company at the time."

He clicked out of that image and opened another. "Ancient history, that's what he called it." There was, he supposed, skeletons buried in every decade. It was damn impossible to tell which ones, if any, were relevant.

Several pictures later she said, "This one's interesting." It showed Tarkington and Beal in a corner of the conference room, in what appeared to be deep discussion.

"Not necessarily nefarious," he commented. "I spoke to both of them tonight myself." A few minutes later, though, he paused on a different one, a frown forming on his face. There was an image of Marcus and Tucker talking just inside the entrance of the building. From the expression on their faces they appeared to be arguing.

"I know him." Tori pointed at Tucker. "He's one of the young men you had drive me home that day. Who's he with?"

"His father, Marcus Rappaport, my vice president of production."

Obviously recognizing the name, Tori peered more closely at the shot. James took a moment to study it, as well. Marcus doted on his son; James had rarely heard a cross word spoken between them. The man could, however, be something of a perfectionist. He made a mental note to ask if there had been any complications in the expo setup that would have had Marcus more stressed than usual.

Tori took control of the mouse and was clicking more rapidly through the images. Apparently, he hadn't been moving fast enough to suit her. Pausing on one, she observed, "Here's your assistant." Celia was shown clearly, but her companion was only half-visible. James gave it a cursory glance but Tori was peering at it more closely. "That almost looks like…" She tilted her head. "It is. See that tie? What's showing, anyway. I recognize the suit, too." She looked up at him, expression sober. "She's talking to Beal." Sitting back in her seat, she drew a deep breath. "Think they're discussing ancient history?"

* * *

By the time they'd been completely through the images twice, exhaustion was taking its toll on both of them. At least, Tori assumed that James felt it, as well. For the first time since she'd met him, there were signs of weariness on his face. "When was the last time you got some sleep?" she asked abruptly. If she'd rested as little as he must have in the past few days, she'd be walking into walls by now.

He sat back, stretched. "A full night? It's been a while. And something tells me it will be a while longer."

She looked out the window, where the pearly dawn was beginning to lighten the sky. "Then let's wrap this up for now. Tomorrow will be soon enough to figure out our next step." She was half-surprised when he complied, ejecting the CD and locking it in the desk drawer. She was even more shocked when he rose, caught her hand and pulled her up to bury his face in her hair, holding her tightly to him.

"I know you feel guilty about Corday," he murmured, rubbing her spine soothingly. "But I have it on good authority that blaming yourself doesn't change anything. Leave the guilt to the person responsible. Your hiring him didn't get him killed—the person who shot him did."

A long breath shuddered out of her. Despite his words, despite hearing her own advice parroted back to her, she knew it would be a long time before she would forget the inadvertent part she'd played in the man's death. "Do you know what's more annoying than a man who's right?"

His low chuckle was response enough. He loosened his embrace, leaving his arm around her waist. "Let's go to bed. I think I could sleep, eventually, with you in my arms."

The invitation summoned a smoky wisp of need. She could feel her pulse beating, strong and slow. After tonight she was even less sure than ever that this thing between them was right. But she was also less prepared than before to turn away from it. Life, as the past few hours had shown, was a fragile thing. And surely at its end, it would be the chances not seized that would elicit the greatest regrets, rather than the risks taken.

And so she allowed him to lead her up the stairs. Walked with him hand in hand into her bedroom and, at his urging, into the bath. While he turned on the jets, she stepped out of her heels, and her feet sobbed in gratitude. He straightened and shrugged out of his jacket. But when her hands went to her dress, he stopped her. "Let me."

Slowly she swayed toward him. Hooking an arm around her waist, her brought her closer. "I've been wondering all night what keeps that darn thing up." His hands ran down her back, over her bottom and back up again. "No zipper? How'd you get it on?"

Her limbs were taking on the consistency of melted wax. "Ingenuity…" She paused, and nipped at his chin, "and dexterity."

"Well…" His fingers stroked her back, where it was bared by the straps. "Never let it be said that I lack ingenuity." With a quick twist of his hand, he had two straps separated from the material. The bodice sagged, revealing the tops of her breasts. Another tug, and the rest snapped free. The dress slid to her hips.

"Most would consider that a terrible waste of money," she informed him.

"Honey, for this view, there's no price I wouldn't pay." He was looking entirely too pleased with himself, so she took her time working the dress over her hips, down her thighs, one excruciatingly slow inch at a time, until at last it was puddled around her feet, leaving her clad only in a scrap of silk panties. The look on his face more than made up for the fact that she was practically naked, while he was fully clothed.

When he would have reached for her, she stepped out of reach. "One of us is overdressed." Hooking her thumbs in the sides of her panties, she whisked them down her legs. "And I don't think it's me. *Honey*."

His low groan drew a smile to her lips, and she stepped into the water, sank low in it. He dug in his pocket, withdrew a foil-wrapped package and set it on the edge of the tub. Then it was her turn to watch as he stripped off his clothes, with considerably less finesse than she'd exhibited. His body was, she decided dreamily, rather magnificent. She would have liked a chance to study it, a visual journey to map each plane and sinew. But in the next moment he was joining her, drawing her to kneel with him in the center of the tub. The bubbling water lapped at their chests while their lips met with scorching intensity.

The world careened, receded. There was only the taste of him, the unchecked urgency of his mouth, his teeth, his tongue. The hint of wildness in his kiss should have alarmed her. Instead it excited, igniting heat and desire that had only seemed to simmer until bursting forth again, summoned by his touch.

He had quick, clever hands, and had already committed to memory which places made her go weak and boneless. She slicked her hands over his torso, enjoying the feel of sleek wet masculine skin beneath her fingers. Her touch faltered when he took the lobe of her ear between his teeth, and her body jerked helplessly against his. It didn't seem quite fair the way her body betrayed her so easily, passion fogging intent.

His mouth was as heated as the water, and avid as it followed the line of her throat, skimmed over her shoulders. Wanting, needing to give the same pleasure, she leaned forward, used the tip of her tongue to scoop up the tiny rivulets of water that ran down his chest. Her hands glided down his back, settled on his hard masculine buns and kneaded.

Her breath hissed out and her head lolled as he bent his head, and took a nipple between his lips. With each tiny tug of his mouth, the ache in the pit of her belly intensified. It didn't seem possible that the passion between them could burn this hot, return this quickly. She was helpless to deny a response; helpless to temper it. Recognition of that fact made her doubly determined to elicit the same from him.

She found the hard length of him, slid her fingers up and down in a slippery dance that had his jaw clenching, his muscles tensing.

His arm banded across her back while the pressure of his mouth grew more hungry. The evidence of his desire only stoked her own, sending the blood sizzling under her skin. Sensation slapped against sensation. Wet flesh twisted against wet flesh, the friction a delight, a torment.

He reached blindly for the condom, swore viciously as he struggled with it. Then, hands beneath her hips, he pressed her against the smooth back of the tub, the water splashing precariously high, as he urged her legs around his waist. The position left her open to him, vulnerable. With a movement that hinted at desperation, he seated himself deep inside her.

His possession was sudden, complete, and drove the breath from her lungs. She tried to regain a measure of control, but he was driving into her now, each thrust deeper than the other, and thoughts of restraint went spinning away. They were as close as they could be, and yet still not close enough. Her hands streaked over his skin, trying to draw him nearer. Her teeth scraped ungently on his shoulder a.

one of his hands reached between their bodies, fondled her, applying pressure that drove her higher, wilder.

And when the dual assault had her back arching, the climax ripping through her, she was distantly aware that it had taken him, too. They tumbled together headlong into the rush of pleasure.

It had a been a singularly satisfying experience for Tori to wake up in James's arms that morning. Even more so when she'd managed to sneak from the bed and leave him sleeping. He'd put up a fierce battle, but sheer fatigue eventually overcame even the strongest will. She'd left him a note detailing her plans for the day and slipped from the room, fervently hoping he would sleep another few hours before his internal clock would wake him up.

She'd summoned a cab to take her home, and once there she determined that the workmen must be finished with her house. There wasn't a soul in sight. Of course, the front room was stripped bare of carpet, sofa and chairs, but once this was over, the first thing she'd do would be to get them replaced.

Once this was over. The phrase replayed in her head all the way to her office, making it difficult to concentrate on the work she needed to accomplish there. She had a bad feeling about this, a niggling blade of foreboding that warned of future catastrophe. It was worry for James, she told herself. But if she was honest, there was worry there for herself, as well.

A wiser woman, one with a faster learning curve, wouldn't have fallen for a man like James Tremaine. The admission was there, unvarnished and terrifying. She was in love with the wrong man. Again. The recollection of her failed marriage no longer stung, but the memory remained of how glaringly out of place she'd been in her ex's world.

The one bright spot in the whole mess was that James wasn't aware of her feelings. When it ended, she'd be able to slip from his life as easily as she had his bed, with a modicum of pride intact. She was certain that pride was going to be less than satisfying, compared to what she was leaving behind.

But first she had to keep James Tremaine alive. And the only way to do that was to hunt down the killer and see that he paid. For everything.

To that end she worked feverishly all afternoon. She'd directed one of her information brokers to dig up more information on Celia. James hadn't seemed overly concerned, but the digital picture they'd seen last night of her with Beal, after hearing of their past relationship, made Tori wary. She spent several hours combing any databases she could access for more details on Beal and Tarkington. The most interesting tidbit she'd gleaned was that thirty years ago, for a brief time before he'd started his own company, Beal had worked for the other man.

Tori was still leaning back in her chair, chewing on that piece of information when her phone rang. A quick glance at the caller ID showed that it was the real estate agent for her father's house.

His news brought mingled emotions. He'd found a buyer, but they wanted to move quickly. And he wouldn't end the conversation until he'd gotten her promise to empty the house within the next week.

Giving a resigned sigh, she shut down her computer. If the information broker came through with anything today, he'd contact her cell, she consoled herself as she locked the office and headed to her car. It was about time to take a little personal time for a task she'd been avoiding for too long.

Heart growing abruptly heavy in her chest, she headed out the door.

James never slept until noon. And he rarely put in only six hours at the office before heading back home again. Albeit six very productive hours.

It hadn't hurt that several employees had been busy at the expo, and he had been relatively undisturbed while he was in his office.

The sight of a familiar car in the drive gave him pause. But it was the scene that awaited him when he opened the door into his den that made him immediately wary. Cade, Sam and Ana were gathered there, and from the tension in the room, their conversation hadn't been pleasant.

Cautiously, like an animal testing the air, he stepped inside. "Sam. I didn't know you were back."

His younger brother came up to him, and the two slapped backs, a gesture of genuine affection. But the stoic expressions on his siblings' faces were starting to worry him. Looking from one to the other, he observed, "What's wrong? I know Jones is at the expo." He frowned, looking from Cade to Sam. "Are Juliette and Shae all right?"

"They're both fine," Sam said, dropping his long frame into an easy chair by the desk. "It's you we're worried about."

The tension in his chest eased, just a fraction. "Don't be. It won't be long before this guy is caught. Then we'll all rest easier." Easier, when he'd unmasked his parents' murderer. When the person responsible for all their suffering was dead or behind bars.

"I'll tell you what would have me resting easier," Cade said evenly, strolling across the room toward him. "If you gave anyone in your family credit for having a brain. If you treated us with an ounce of the respect we give to you."

A quick glance from one sibling to the other told him that they were all in agreement. It was time to tread carefully. "Why don't you tell me what has all of you upset. We can talk about it."

Cade stopped before him, rocking back on his heels, his jade eyes snapping with temper. "I suppose we could talk. Or I could just haul out some cuffs and throw your ass in jail for tampering with evidence."

James took a deep breath, released it. "Ah."

"Ah," Cade mimicked. "I thought it was odd that Tori referred to the disks as plural, while you made it sound as if there was only one. Our tech squad was able to recover part of the images today. They also determined that three copies had been made. Now if I can trust you enough—' his voice dripped sarcasm "—to believe what you said about the killer taking one, that still leaves us one short."

Through James's wariness filtered real admiration. "That's some pretty fast police work, son. We may make a techie out of you yet."

Cade's fists balled. Years of experience had James certain he was aching to take a swing at him.

Sam must have thought so, too, because he said warningly, "Let's tone it down, shall we?"

Cade's smile was lethal. "Shoot, if that tech work impresses you, you'll really like the investigating I did into your relationship with Tori Corbett."

James's amusement immediately faded, to be replaced by a simmering anger. "What the hell are you talking about?"

"You came to me, remember? A few weeks back you came to headquarters and asked me to look into finding one Rob Landry." He let the words settle. "You never did tell me why you were looking for a P.I., and hell, I never asked. Until it became clear to all of us that you were up to your neck in trouble that you wouldn't admit."

Suddenly weary, James rubbed the back of his neck. He walked away from his brother, moved to the desk and leaned his hips against it.

"I should have known it was too good to be true," Ana muttered, her eyes flashing at him. "I just knew you couldn't have suddenly gotten the sense to start dating a real woman, instead of one of those empty-headed bimbos you usually favor. I just don't know how you got her to go along with letting you pass her off as your girlfriend."

"It wasn't easy," he said feelingly, remembering how Tori had balked at the prospect.

"It didn't take long for Cade to start wondering why you were looking for Landry," Sam put in. "But if it hadn't been for Ana, I doubt we'd ever have known."

James went still. The silence in the room stretched. "Known...what?"

"That you hired him twenty years ago to investigate our parents' accident."

The floor seemed to shift beneath his feet. Then it righted itself, and he sent a killing look at his baby sister. "You were in my files?" The defiant angle of her chin was his answer.

"Hell, why should *your* files be safe from her," Sam asked feelingly. "Serves you right. You taught her everything she knows. She didn't discover anything that you shouldn't have told us yourself."

"Such as..."

"We figure there's a relationship between the threats you've been getting and the investigation Tori's dad ran for you two decades ago," Cade said flatly. "But we're through with the guesswork. It's time for you to level with us. For once in your life, have a little trust in your family."

Genuinely bewildered, James looked from one of them to the next, saw the agreement on their faces. "I was just trying to clear this up without letting it hurt you all. If I had turned out to be wrong, there'd be no reason you'd ever have had to know about it." God knew, there had been many times he'd wished he could be free of the doubts. The worry. The guilt.

"You'll always be the oldest, but we've been adults for a long time, James." Sam's voice was sober, his gaze direct. "It's about time you realized it. If you have reason to believe that accident was something else, you should have told us at the beginning. But barring that, you'll tell us now."

In an unspoken gesture of unity, the three had drifted to stand facing him together, a united front. And it was hard, much harder than he'd imagined, to start at the beginning. To watch their shock and despair when he starkly told them what he'd suspected twenty years earlier. The entire story about the threats. And about what Tori and he had discovered so far.

When he was finished, there wasn't a sound in the room, but the emotion was thick. And the sight of the tears in his sister's eyes made him regret he'd been forced into divulging the information at all.

It was second nature to push away from the desk, to pull her resisting form into his arms and to soothe. He'd been trying, to the best of his ability, to take care of her all of his life. He couldn't stop now if he tried.

"Don't," she sniffed, the word muffled against his shirt. "I have a right to grieve, James. We all do. You can't spare us that, and you shouldn't have tried. We won't let you again."

There was a murmur of accord from her brothers.

"As of right now," Sam said, resolve evident in his voice, "we're all in this together."

Cade nodded, and Ana stepped away, wiped her eyes. "The first thing for you to do is catch us up on the ground you've covered so far. We may think of an angle that you haven't. With all of us working on it, we're bound to come up with something."

Cade's cell rang then, and he stepped to the other side of the room to answer it.

"You need to be prepared for the fact that this might be motivated purely by business," James said. "And it might involve someone we trust."

"My money's on Tarkington," Ana said darkly. "A man that smarmy is capable of anything."

Cade rejoined them, gaze trained on James. "Francis's cell phone dump came back. We've got six calls to his phone within twenty-four hours. Three have been identified as coming from his girlfriend. Two came from different phone booths and the last came from this number." He handed him a slip of paper with a number scrawled on it. "Recognize it?"

James glanced down and froze. There was a moment of incomprehension, of utter denial. Swallowing hard, he nodded. "Yeah. I recognize it." It took a moment for the tight band in his chest to ease, for his lungs to work properly again. Thinking rapidly, he turned, headed for the computer.

"What are you doing?"

He didn't look up at Ana's question. "Checking out something that should have occurred to me a long time ago."

Tori looked around the attic of her dad's house with a sense of quiet satisfaction. She'd made some headway up

here, at least. Everything was organized in neat sections
to be thrown away, put in storage or sold. She'd arranged
for a Dumpster to be delivered tomorrow, to get started on
the project. Once she sorted through the downstairs, she
would place an order for a small moving trailer and rent a
storage unit.

But for now she was content to sit awhile, in the light
afforded by the single overhead bulb and steep herself in
memories of him once again.

Raised without a mother, she supposed it was normal
that she'd be close to her dad all her life. Normal to want
to keep his memory untarnished. She reached out, dragged
the ragged sweater off the top of one of the boxes, and sat
on the floor cross-legged, holding it on her lap. Of all of the
things he'd left her, she thought the ones she would value
most were this tattered garment and the box of love letters
he'd kept, from all those years ago, when her mother lay
dying. With these things she could keep them both close,
while getting to know a mother she barely remembered.

She reached out, drew a letter from the box, opened it.
Her eyes swam at the obvious love poured out on the page.
Her father hadn't been an especially sentimental man. To
read the raw emotion in the words had her throat going
full.

One letter led to another. Soon she had a pile around her
feet, and she was bent over the papers in her hand to make
out the words in the dim light. She decided to organize
them chronologically. Then when she had the time, she
could read them in order and…

Her gaze scanned the letter in her hand, froze, then
swept back up again, to read her mother's writing more
carefully.

"You have to learn to forgive yourself. You were faced

with an awful choice, and I understand why you had to do it."

Tori dropped the paper as if scalded. There was a roiling in her stomach, an internal realization that arrived ahead of true comprehension. Then, frantically, she rose to her knees, started pulling handfuls of letters out, discarding all but the ones with dates close to the one she'd just read. One of them would hold an explanation. It had to.

And the next one did. But it wasn't the explanation she'd been hoping for.

My dearest Lisa,
Not a night goes by that I don't reach for the phone, wanting to call that boy back and tell him the truth about his parents…

There was a roaring in her ears. Her stomach lurched, and she thought for a moment she'd be ill. Her hands were operating independently of her mind. The letters were raining like brittle confetti as she dug frantically through them, skimming, tossing them aside to pull out another, phrase after damning phrase leaping off the page to sear her eyes.

I had to protect you and Tori…
It was too late to help those people, but I could save my own little family…
God forgive me. I'll never forgive myself.

She dropped the last letter and this time she didn't reach for another. Rising awkwardly, she backed away from the box, pressing both fists against her mouth to stifle the cry that she could feel trembling on her lips. She closed her eyes, wanting to shut out the damning evidence, but she could still see the words, could hear her dad's voice sounding in her head.

Integrity, above all else.

...tell him the truth about his parents...
Integrity, above all else.

God forgive me...

Unconsciously she wrapped her arms around her middle and began to rock, her mind frantically supplying, then eliminating, possible explanations for what she'd read. One would come, she assured herself. When her mind cleared and her thought settled, an alternate answer would present itself.

But deep inside she knew the heartrending truth, and the pain of it threatened to shred her soul.

Her father had betrayed James and his family twenty years ago. Because of it, a killer had gone free.

Chapter 14

"You've checked her house?" James asked tersely.

Cade nodded. "It's empty. I've got officers stationed there, though, and an APB out. It's just a matter of time."

Pacing the length of the room, James took out his cell phone, tried Tori's cell again. There was still no answer. He tried her house next, with the same result. He had no more luck with her office number.

Making a decision, he headed for the door.

"Whoa." Sam leaped from the chair he was sitting in, he and Cade closing in on James. "Where do you think you're going?"

"I can't reach Tori. I'm going to find her."

His brothers exchanged a glance. "There's no way we're letting you out that door, especially now. Have you forgotten there's someone out there who'd like to see you dead?"

"Then prepare to offer some police protection," James

said, shoving between them and through the den door. "Because I'm going, and there's not a damn thing either of you can do to stop me."

The two men looked at each other, shrugged. "Oh, hell." Cade grabbed his shoulder holster. "Wait for us."

Feeling raw and battered, Tori drove back to her home in a fog. Her cell phone had rung for the third time. The caller ID identified James's number. She didn't answer it. Couldn't. She couldn't summon the words for him. Wouldn't have been able to utter them if they occurred.

There would come a time, probably much sooner than she would prefer, when she'd have to face him. And when she told him the truth, she'd watch the distrust bloom in his expression again, and know this time it was deserved.

Her body shook, a great racking shudder. But God help her, she wasn't ready now. She felt as if she'd been cast adrift. Everything she'd always believed was a lie. What she'd been certain of only days ago had turned to quicksand, shifting beneath her feet. How could she explain to him what she couldn't comprehend herself?

By the time she had pulled into her carport, her temples were throbbing, a vicious headache jackhammering in her brain. She was distantly aware that Pauline's house was dark. Maybe James had frightened Joe Jr. enough that he'd joined his mother in Shreveport.

James. Just the thought of him made the pounding in her head intensify. Hands shaky, vision blurry, she let herself into the house, locked it and, without switching on the lights, made her way upstairs. Sleep, if it would come, would offer a blessed relief both from the headache and the situation that had caused it.

She stopped in the bathroom long enough to find the bottle of pain relievers and shake three out. Swallowed them dry. She stumbled to her bedroom. She was halfway to the bed before instinct filtered through the pain, and she realized she wasn't alone.

Before she could turn around, the figure stepped out of the shadows and brought something crashing down on her head. There was a bright burst of pain before unconsciousness rushed up and sucked her under.

"Her car's here." Relief surged through James until he noticed another vehicle parked in front of the house.

Cade saw it and identified it at the same time. "So is Tucker."

James was out of the car and running before it came to a complete stop. "Cover the back," he shouted at his brothers. He leaped to the porch, tried the door. It was locked.

Without wasting the breath for a curse, he jumped to the ground, started around the side of the house, as his brothers headed around it in the opposite direction. He hadn't gotten more than a few steps before he saw the figure running in his direction.

Obeying instinct, he sped up, tackled the intruder, rolling over and over until he subdued him with a single blow to the jaw. "Mr. Tremaine, wait." Tucker shielded himself from another blow. "You have to listen to me."

"Where's Tori?" he demanded. Nasty fingers of panic were licking up his spine. There was a feeling of urging in his gut that he couldn't shake.

"I…I don't know," the young man stammered.

Sam ran up to them, stopped to pick up some containers the boy had dropped. Unscrewing the caps, he sniffed first one, then the other. "Gasoline."

James got to his feet, yanking the boy up with him. Grabbing him by the collar he growled between clenched teeth, "Is she in the house?"

But the kid was wild-eyed with fear now and babbling. "I don't know, maybe, he must have thought so. The gasoline isn't mine, though, it isn't! I found it in the back. I thought if I got rid of it, he couldn't, he wouldn't..."

"Who?" James gave him a vicious shake.

"My dad!" Tucker seemed to crumple then, started to weep. "I think my dad's going to try to kill her."

"Look!" Sam yelled.

James followed the direction of Sam's pointed finger, saw the smoke curling from the upstairs windows.

"Call 911!"

James shoved the boy toward Sam and raced to the back of the house. With one quick look he identified the window that had been broken out. Without a second thought he heaved himself up and over the sill into the kitchen. The downstairs was already filled with smoke, burning his eyes. He identified Cade, several feet away from him, gun drawn and finger to his lips.

Easing his way toward him, he heard his brother whisper soundlessly, "He's still in the house."

James nodded and took his handkerchief from his pocket, quickly tying it around his face. He pointed to the gun, then to himself and then toward the upstairs. Cade gestured for him to go ahead, and he dashed for the stairs, knowing his brother would cover him. The smoke was rolling down the steps. Dropping to his knees, he stayed as low as he could, crawling rapidly. He had to get to Tori on time. He wouldn't even consider another possibility.

There was no smell of accelerants in the house. James wondered if Marcus had been saving it to torch the outside. But the flames were spreading rapidly upstairs. In another few minutes there'd be no path to take to the bedroom.

Crouching down, James pressed himself as flat as he could against the undamaged wall, and inched toward her room. The heat was intense. Straining his ears, he could hear fitful coughing. His hopes soaring, he broke free, skirted the flames near his foot and ran into her room.

He nearly tripped over Tori. Dropping to one knee, he scooped her up and turned, preparing to exit the way he'd come. But once he'd got back to the door he saw that would be impossible. The stairway was engulfed in flames. There would be no escape that way.

Keeping her face pressed to his chest, he made his way back to her bedroom. Both of them broke out in a spasm of coughing, and for the first time, Tori's eyelids fluttered open. He laid her on the floor beside the bed, whipped the handkerchief from his face and tied it around hers. Then he tugged the sheets off the bed, rolled them into coils and tied them together. Tori tried to help, but her movements were feeble. Her voice, when she spoke, was more so. "Someone…was waiting…hit me…"

"I know, baby." He paused a moment to drop a quick kiss on her forehead, sending up a silent prayer of thanks that he'd found her alive. There would be time later to deal with the sick fear he'd felt before he'd discovered her.

And plenty of time to indulge in his primal need to make Marcus pay. For everything.

Shoving the bed as close as he could to the window, he secured one end of the makeshift ladder to the leg of the bed frame and then looked over at her. "Can you climb on my back and hold on?"

She nodded determinedly, but he wasn't so sure. She looked barely conscious. When he bent down for her, though, her grip was stronger than he expected. With a deep breath, he opened the window, picked up one end of the sheet ladder and threw his leg over the sill.

Every time another fit of coughing shook her, James was fearful it would loosen her grip. But she managed, somehow, to hang on. They were still several feet from the ground when he shouted, "We'll have to jump the rest of the way. Ready?"

Without waiting for an answer, he let go. Although it was probably less than six feet, the ground seemed to rush up unmercifully hard. He twisted his body, landing with Tori half on top of him, the impact driving the breath from him.

It was a moment before he could draw in air. Another before he heard the distant wail of sirens. "Are you all right?" He turned to Tori, pulling down the handkerchief to search her features frantically.

"I think so."

Helping her up, they both limped to the curb, where a small crowd had gathered. He looked around for Sam. He was standing watch over a huddled Tucker near the cars.

"Where's Cade?"

The question had Sam turning toward him. "He hasn't come out yet." The two men exchanged a grim look before they both charged toward the back of the house.

The smoke was thicker inside now. The fire had made its way downstairs. There was no sign of Cade in the kitchen where James had left him. Inching carefully into the interior of the house, they both spotted their brother's crumpled figure in the middle of the living room. There was a man standing over him, holding Cade's gun.

"Drop it, Marcus."

Marcus Rappaport let loose a wild laugh, the sound as foreign as his appearance. Usually meticulously groomed, his clothes were in disarray, and there was a bruise blooming on his cheek. He looked like a crazed stranger. "Damn you, Tremaine, it should have been easier than this. I never wanted to hurt the rest of the family." He seemed to be weeping and laughing at the same time, a sign of hysteria, or worse.

With a meaningful look at Sam, the two men split up, Sam heading toward Cade and James toward Marcus.

"Tucker's outside, Marcus," James said conversationally. "He's been injured. You should go to him."

The man jerked, seemed strangely uncertain. "Tucker's hurt?"

"Badly," James lied. "The ambulance was called for him."

"He didn't understand," the man mumbled, his gun hand shaking. "No one will understand." The ceiling overhead was showing signs of stress. Casting a look at it, James figured it was the spot where the fire had been started. They wouldn't have much more time.

"Tucker told me he understood, Marcus." It was hard to keep the pretense going. More cracks appeared in the ceiling directly above Cade. "All you have to do is go out and talk to him."

The man glanced dazedly toward the window and that was the chance James was waiting for. Leaping for him, he knocked him to the floor, grappling for the gun. Sam took the opportunity to dive for Cade, and drag him to safety.

Marcus screamed and nearly broke away. James caught his gun hand and slammed it against the wall. Again and again. Until it dropped from the man's nerveless fingers. Balling his fist, James punched the other man in the jaw, jerking his head back, sending him staggering farther into the room. There was a giant *crack,* and James jumped backward as the ceiling fell in raining pieces of fiery two-by-sixes into the room. One struck the man across the shoulders and pinned him to the floor.

"Get the hell out of the house!" Sam's voice was in his ear, his grip on his arms, but it was a moment before James could obey. A moment before he could see from the odd angle of Marcus's neck that he realized the man he'd known all his life was beyond saving.

"You come to my hospital, you follow my orders, James." Shae O'Reilly pushed into the hospital room with a scowl on her face to match his own. "I told you that I was keeping you overnight for observation and that's final. In your own room."

"You can observe me in here." James had no intention of leaving Tori's bedside. He didn't worry about annoying his future sister-in-law. She had her hands full right now with Cade. The concussion he'd suffered had given all of them a few bad moments. "Besides," he pointed out, "your fiancé isn't in his room, either." He reached over, took Tori's hand in his good one.

Tori gave him a disgruntled look. It hadn't escaped her attention that of all the so-called patients in this room, she was the only one being kept in bed.

And being kept there.

"He will be." Shae turned her stern glance on her future husband and stalked toward him threateningly. "If he knows what's good for him."

"I know exactly what's good for me," Cade said. "A night in my own bed with my favorite doctor applying a little TLC."

"Give it up," Sam advised Cade. "Even Juliette and I know enough not to cross Shae when she's in doctor mode."

"That would be more insightful if we didn't all know what a horrid patient you make yourself," Juliette, his fiancée, remarked. "I'm beginning to believe there isn't one Tremaine man who has the sense to take care of himself."

Ana nodded, while Jones wisely remained silent.

Shae pointed to each of the patients in turn. "Concussion," she snapped, gesturing to Cade. "Broken wrist," she indicated James. "And smoke inhalation," she ended with Tori. "We don't keep people in hospitals because we like their company. You're all exhausted and need rest."

Recognizing that her temper was dangerously close to the boiling point, James looked at Cade. Before Shae bullied them back to their rooms, he needed some answers. "What was Tucker able to tell you?"

"He was the one sending the notes." Cade's voice and his facial expression were somber. Tucker had been more like a cousin than a family friend. "You know what a brain he's got for encryption/decryption. He got the brilliant idea to take on his dad's files this summer. He saw it as a challenge, I'm sure. He cracked the security on Marcus's computer and discovered far more than he'd bargained for. Marcus had everything detailed in one of his files."

"Rappaport arranged for the accident that killed his own wife?" Tori sounded horrified. "So it wasn't really your parents he was trying to kill?"

"You and I were on the right track when we hacked into those databases for the insurance companies," James told her. "I just didn't look far enough. Didn't even consider it seriously until Cade learned that one of the calls to the bomber's cell phone had come from Tremaine Technologies." He shook his head. "I don't know. I had a flash of that image of Marcus and Tucker arguing, and decided to give the database another go. Lucy Rappaport wasn't from Louisiana originally. She was from Mississippi. Her elderly ailing parents had fully paid for a million-dollar policy on her when she was a teenager. Since they were dead, that money went to Marcus upon her death."

"First, though, he'd tried to get money by arranging my

kidnapping," Ana put in. "When that was foiled before the ransom was paid, he came up with another idea."

Tori shook her head uncomprehendingly. "But why? Just for the money? Was he really that cold?"

"Dale hit on it when I talked to him yesterday." James sent a thumb skating over her knuckles and focused on the relief of having her safe. "Marcus had gambling problems and apparently still does. At least that's what the Nevada Gaming Commission says. He'd been banned from Nevada nearly ten years ago. Apparently he began going to Europe after that." Certainly he'd have had plenty of opportunity. Tremaine Technologies competed for projects all over the world.

"Well, going after you wasn't about the money," Tori said to James shrewdly. "Unless a third party was in the mix."

He grinned. She really did have the most fascinating mind. "You're quick. We don't have it nailed down yet but we think Beal was willing to pay him a fortune to make sure I wasn't awarded the next Pentagon contract. Of course, we can't prove it yet."

"That's only a matter of time," Cade put in. "We'll pore over his phone records, trace financial transactions… doubt it's the first time he's teamed up with Beal. Hell, for all we know, they could have planned our parents' accident together. Whatever connection they had, though, we'll trace it."

"Two people, at least, would be alive today if Tucker had just come forward with what he'd discovered," Tori said softly.

James squeezed her fingers lightly. He knew she was still haunted by Corday's homicide. "Tucker thought he could scare me into backing off the contract, which, to his mind at least, would keep me safe until he could figure out what to do about his father. He should have gone to the police. But regardless of what you discover about your parent, it's hard to turn your back on them. No matter what they've done."

Tori turned her face away, the words like sharp little arrows, nicking her heart. All the trauma of the last several hours paled in comparison to the discovery she'd made about her father.

"Okay, everybody out," ordered Shae. "Tori needs to rest. And most of you have your own rooms to go to."

One by one the family filed out, amid much goodnatured bickering over whose room they were going to take up residence in next. When James closed the door behind the last of them, Tori drew in a deep breath, struggled to find the words. "You were right about my dad." They came in a rush, amidst a jumble of pain. "I found some letters he and my mother wrote to each other before she died. I think... I'm almost certain, they refer to you and your parents' accident."

"I know." Her gaze flew to his, incredulous. "It was in the files Tucker found."

The pain seized her heart again, gripped hard. "I don't know how to reconcile the man I knew with the one who betrayed you." Her eyes burned. She had no tears to shed, but her heart still wept. "I can't imagine what might have been different, if he'd told you the truth about the tracking device."

James lifted her chin with his finger, turned it toward him. "Honey, Marcus was following that investigation every step of the way. He managed the accident pretty much as we figured, and he knew about the P.I. I'd hired. He'd planted the tracking device in Lucy's purse, figuring he'd receive it back as her personal effects. But when it wasn't there, he knew immediately your dad must have discovered it. That

fire that destroyed his offices twenty years ago? Marcu
set it. And then he threatened yours and your mother'
lives. Your father did what he thought he had to in orde
to protect the two of you."

You were faced with an awful choice... The line fror
the letter came back to her, and she released a shaky breatl
"I don't know what to think. I'd like to think there was
better way."

"Maybe there was." His bright-blue gaze was intense
"But it doesn't affect us, either way, Tori. Some of th
answers we found were painful as hell, but at least we hav
answers. It's time to move on."

The words seemed curiously significant. She tried t
slide her fingers from his grasp, only to have them grippe
tighter. "You're right. About moving on, I mean. Neithe
of us expected this...what happened between us. We can
let it change anything."

He reached out to smooth a strand of hair back from he
face. "Sometimes the unexpected can be the most satisfyin;
There's more here, Tori, than either of us looked for. I can
walk away from it. I don't think you can, either."

There was a wild leaping in her chest, but she quelle
it sternly. Experience had etched a bitter brand, and sh
couldn't forget its burn. "I've tried living in your worl
before. I didn't fit there. We can't change who we are, eve
if we wanted to."

Her efforts at logic were rewarded with a bruising kis
When he lifted his head, he muttered, "The hell wit
that. We'll make our own world, where we both fit. An
changing isn't an option. Are you going to keep hidin
behind excuses, or are you finally going to admit that yo
love me?" He seemed to enjoy the way her mouth droppe
open at the words. Taking the opportunity, he pressed
soft, nibbling kiss to it. "That you can't live without me.

Her arms linked around his neck of their own accord. There was a glint in his eye, a smoky heat. But it was the softness in his expression that shattered defenses she had once thought stouter. Stronger. "I do. Love you, I mean. And the thought of living without you makes me miserable."

"You'll never have to worry about that." He brushed his lips over her brow, her eye, her jaw. "I started falling for you the moment I saw you with your head stuck in the ceiling tile. I have every intention of living with you, loving you, for the next sixty years or so."

She smiled, her heart full. Sixty years was a lifetime. And that sounded about right to her.

* * * * *

REQUEST YOUR FREE BOOKS!

2 FREE NOVELS PLUS 2 FREE GIFTS!

HARLEQUIN®

INTRIGUE®

Breathtaking Romantic Suspense

YES! Please send me 2 FREE Harlequin Intrigue® novels and my 2 FREE gifts (gifts are worth about $10). After receiving them, if I don't wish to receive any more books, I can return the shipping statement marked "cancel." If I don't cancel, I will receive 6 brand-new novels every month and be billed just $4.24 per book in the U.S. or $4.99 per book in Canada. That's a saving of at least 15% off the cover price! It's quite a bargain! Shipping and handling is just 50¢ per book.* I understand that accepting the 2 free books and gifts places me under no obligation to buy anything. I can always return a shipment and cancel at any time. Even if I never buy another book from Harlequin, the two free books and gifts are mine to keep forever.

182/382 HDN E5MG

Name _____ (PLEASE PRINT)

Address _____ Apt. #

City _____ State/Prov. _____ Zip/Postal Code

Signature (if under 18, a parent or guardian must sign)

Mail to the **Harlequin Reader Service:**
IN U.S.A.: P.O. Box 1867, Buffalo, NY 14240-1867
IN CANADA: P.O. Box 609, Fort Erie, Ontario L2A 5X3

Not valid for current subscribers to Harlequin Intrigue books.

Are you a subscriber to Harlequin Intrigue books and want to receive the larger-print edition? Call 1-800-873-8635 today!

* Terms and prices subject to change without notice. Prices do not include applicable taxes. N.Y. residents add applicable sales tax. Canadian residents will be charged applicable provincial taxes and GST. Offer not valid in Quebec. This offer is limited to one order per household. All orders subject to approval. Credit or debit balances in a customer's account(s) may be offset by any other outstanding balance owed by or to the customer. Please allow 4 to 6 weeks for delivery. Offer available while quantities last.

Your Privacy: Harlequin is committed to protecting your privacy. Our Privacy Policy is available online at www.eHarlequin.com or upon request from the Reader Service. From time to time we make our lists of customers available to reputable third parties who may have a product or service of interest to you. If you would prefer we not share your name and address, please check here. ☐

Help us get it right—We strive for accurate, respectful and relevant communications. To clarify or modify your communication preferences, visit us at www.ReaderService.com/consumerchoice.

HI10R

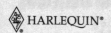

Try these Healthy and Delicious Spring Rolls!

INGREDIENTS

2 packages rice-paper spring roll wrappers (20 wrappers)

1 cup grated carrot

¼ cup bean sprouts

1 cucumber, julienned

1 red bell pepper, without stem and seeds, julienned

4 green onions finely chopped— use only the green part

DIRECTIONS

1. Soak one rice-paper wrapper in a large bowl of hot water until softened.

2. Place a pinch each of carrots, sprouts, cucumber, bell pepper and green onion on the wrapper toward the bottom third of the rice paper.

3. Fold ends in and roll tightly to enclose filling.

4. Repeat with remaining wrappers. Chill before serving.

Find this and many more delectable recipes
including the perfect dipping sauce in

HARLEQUIN Presents

USA TODAY bestselling author

Sharon Kendrick

introduces

HIS MAJESTY'S CHILD

The king's baby of shame!

King Casimiro harbors a secret—no one in the kingdom
of Zaffirinthos knows that a devastating accident has left
his memory clouded in darkness. And Casimiro himself
cannot answer why Melissa Maguire, an enigmatic English
rose, stirs such feelings in him…. Questioning his ability
to rule, Casimiro decides he will renounce the throne.
But Melissa has news she knows will rock the palace
to its core—*Casimiro has an heir!*

Law dictates Casimiro cannot abdicate, so he must find a
way to reacquaint himself with Melissa—his new queen!

Available from Harlequin Presents
February 2011

www.eHarlequin.com

HP12972

SPECIAL EDITION

FROM *USA TODAY* BESTSELLING AUTHOR

CHRISTINE RIMMER

COMES AN ALL-NEW BRAVO FAMILY TIES STORY.

Donovan McRae has experienced
the greatest loss a man can face, and
while he can't forgive himself, life—
and Abilene Bravo's love—are still
waiting for him. Can he find it in himself
to reach out and claim them?

Look for

DONOVAN'S CHILD

available February 2011

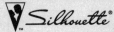

ROMANTIC
SUSPENSE

Sparked by Danger, Fueled by Passion.

NEW YORK TIMES BESTSELLING AUTHOR

RACHEL LEE

No Ordinary Hero

Strange noises...a woman's mysterious disappearance
and a killer on the loose who's too close for comfort.

With no where else to turn, Delia Carmody looks
to her aloof neighbour to help, only to discover
that Mike Windwalker is no ordinary hero.

Conard
County *THE NEXT GENERATION*

Available in February.
Wherever books are sold.

Visit Silhouette Books at www.eHarlequin.com

SRS27709R2